THE INFINITUS SAGA BOOK 1

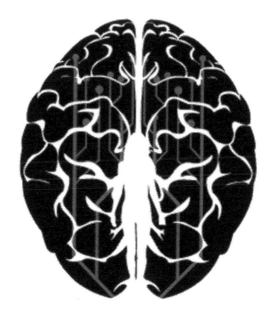

CHRISTIANE JOY ALLISON

Allison Publishing

Wasilla, AK

Allison Publishing

www.AllisonPublishing.com

Edited by Joy Anne Vaughn
Cover Art by Brandon Moore
Map Design by Christiane Joy Allison

Allison Publishing
PO Box 877945
Wasilla, AK 99687
AllisonPublishing.AK@gmail.com

Library of Congress Control Number: 2020906094

Names: Allison, Christiane Joy, author.
Title: Infinitus / Christiane Joy Allison.
Description: Wasilla, AK : Allison Publishing, [2020] | Series: The infinitus saga ; book 1
Identifiers: ISBN 9781733844642 (hardback) | ISBN 9781733844659 (paperback) | ISBN 9781733844666 (mobi/Kindle) | ISBN 9781733844673 (ePub) | ISBN 9781733844680 (PDF)
Subjects: LCSH: Young adults with disabilities--Fiction. | Imaginary societies—Fiction. | Computational grids (Computer systems)--Social aspects--Fiction. | Transgenic organisms--Fiction. | Survival--Fiction. | LCGFT: Science fiction. | Cyberpunk fiction.
Classification: LCC PS3601.L4477 I54 2020 (print) | LCC PS3601.L4477 (ebook) | DDC 813/.6--dc23

To my own Crazy Rob—
who has never stopped fighting for me.

PROLOGUE

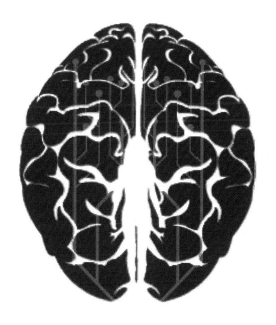

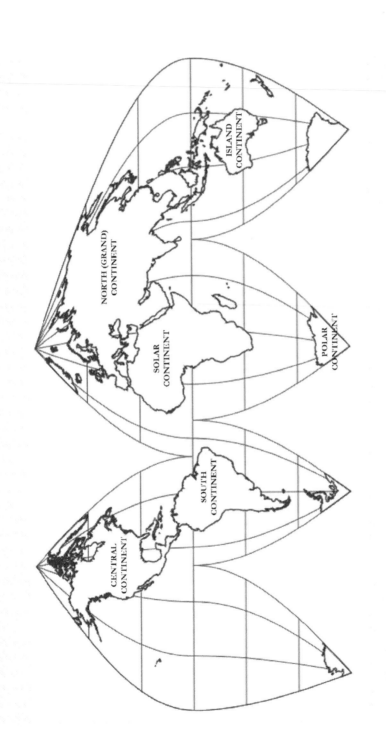

NORTH (GRAND) CONTINENT

ISLAND CONTINENT

SOLAR CONTINENT

POLAR CONTINENT

CENTRAL CONTINENT

SOUTH CONTINENT

1

September 24
North Continent, Region 130, Sector 26, District M

Fifty-six tables is a massive showing. The defiant statement a meet this size makes to the Global Fellowship has me uneasy, even this many stories underground. Every year that passes, the black market traders lose some of their fear that shields will step in and shut them down. It would help if the Community didn't need the markets as much as the dealers do.

"Hey, Jared!" Kegan shouts from two tables over. "Nice to see you in sector, man. Come over here!"

I nod and saunter through the crowd. "What's up?" I ask. "You have something worth seeing?"

Kegan is a little guy, only about five-foot-six, and chronically wired on caffeine and amphetamines. One of these days, his heart will explode, and he'll drop dead. I hope I'm not there for that. "I'm telling you," he says, rubbing his hands together, "I've got a great systems update for your med pods."

"What kind of update?"

He launches into his sales pitch. Within a couple of lines, I can tell I got it months ago. He's got nothing I need.

Normally, I'm here to offload tech the Community doesn't want to take a loss on while using my front as a tech dealer to gather intel from these underworld powerhouses. This time, I have another assignment. It's not every day I'm given someone to purchase. I look for that myself.

Word on the street spread quickly that there's a chimera up for sale. One whose animal traits will be deadly in the wrong hands. I'm bringing them in for a memory reset, which would be a lot easier to do if my handler gave me any information at all about the chimera they're looking for. The lazy ass just expects me to sniff them out.

Faking continued interest for Kegan's benefit, I pull a rolled-up flex out of my pocket and scroll through the items I have for trade. The smart glass is starting to crease. I'll have to replace it soon. Looking around, the expansive room is filled to the brim with dealers and their goods, walls gleaming with silver Faraday paint. I'm not sure where to start, but after drawing the scent of the market in, a subtle, unpleasant musk catches my attention. I turn my head to search for the source. It's reptilian. The scent is four tables down, drifting from a shipping crate you'd use for a large dog.

"What's with the crate?" I ask.

Kegan usually sticks his nose, and anything else he can, into his neighbors' business. "Man, I'd steer clear of that shit," he says with a low whistle. "I don't see why people don't just get their poison from snakes. It's gotta be diluted with the human genetics, you know?"

"Huh," I say, keeping my shoulders from tensing. "I'm gonna check it out."

Ignoring Kegan's continued protests, I approach the booth. My hands are secured in my pockets to resist strangling the booth's dealer if there really is a person shoved in that tiny aluminum box. When the dealer finally wanders back over, I recognize her—blond, short, curvy, and always wearing six-inch stilettos she could kill with. She's a titanium arms dealer, newly upgraded from stainless.

"Hey Juanita," I call with a smile. "What's with the crate? You selling exotic pets now?"

"Oh, this is no pet." She cranes her neck to look up at me. "Have we met before?"

"Jared." Extending my hand, I combat the urge to crush her smaller, softer one. "Just a platinum dealer, but I'm always looking for a way up."

"Well honey, this is your formula, right here."

The stench that hits me as she pulls back the crate's window curtain makes me nauseous. The person inside is definitely a chimera. In fact, he has genetics I understand extremely well. He's got ebony skin with cream-colored scales above his eyebrows, beneath his mouth, and peeking out under his shirt along his collar bones. He's not a man. He's a kid. I'm not around kids much, so I'm not sure, but I'd size him as over ten and under thirteen years.

So, this is the big, bad, venomous chimera everyone is so freaked out about? This kid wouldn't even be out of training yet if he'd been raised like me. He was probably abandoned by his birth mother. Well ... unless he bit her.

The kid's eyes are hollow in a way I'm all too familiar with. Now focusing on my face, his head cocks sideways slightly as he draws a deep breath. Keep it cool, kid. I wink at him. No giving away my secrets with that nose of yours. He shrinks back into the shadows of the crate.

"How much you asking?" I cover the crate back up.

"Three million coin."

Hawking's Ghost! She can't be serious. Kegan spews some colorful language behind me. If his heart doesn't explode, one of these dealers is going to shoot him for listening in on the wrong deal.

"Come on. Be real, Juanita," I say. "How many people have the connections to use an opportunity like this? I do and I'm standing here. I'll give you two million."

Kegan walks up, leaving his partner at his table. "What in the Universe are you going to do with a chimera?"

"Sell him to an elite." I shrug. "What else?" I wish that elite wasn't Alex.

Juanita runs her tongue over her teeth and glances around the market, taking in who else may come to the table. "Two and a half."

"Two and a quarter, or I won't even make a profit on him. No one else will either. Don't push your luck." I make a subtle show that I've caught sight of another interesting prospect. "I'll come by later."

"You've got a deal." Juanita gives a half-hearted shrug, but her eyes are pleased. Finally, she passes over her flex.

2

Same Day
Central Continent, Region 84, Sector 10, District T

"Gina." Tommy's rich, deep voice calls me out of my tortured thoughts. "Sweetheart, you haven't moved in over an hour. I'd be hard-pressed to catch you blinkin'."

Tommy leans down on his elbows, bringing his concerned black eyes level with mine. His armbands, tattooed on his enormous biceps in bright white, black light ink, stand out starkly against his ebony skin and black t-shirt. I hate making him worry.

"Sorry." Lifting my moonshine daiquiri—What the heck? I'm out?—I scoot the glass toward Tommy and tap the rim, glancing away.

"You can't mean that." His eyebrows wrinkle together with concern. "Girl, that's already your third. Is your pain really that bad?"

The question brings a knife-like sensation to my chest and I struggle to breathe. In seconds, traitorous tears spill down my cheeks. Dammit. I don't want to make a spectacle of myself.

"Shit." Tommy heads for his backroom.

I shouldn't even be here. I knew I couldn't sing my normal gig today—not tomorrow either. Stress amplifies my chronic pain—a lovely little symptom called fibromyalgia that sets my nervous system on fire. As bad as it is, though, it's nothing compared to the pain in my heart.

One year ago today, my parents died in a horrific autocab accident.

God help me. Another assault of bloody images arises from my memory as a shudder runs through me. Rob warned me. I shouldn't have looked, but I couldn't stop myself.

Five days later, my nineteen-year-old little brother disappeared. He was too weak and fragile to have made it alone. He was always so much sicker than me, and the shock of Mom and Dad's death made both of us so much worse. He wouldn't have been able to carry anything or walk far. He never could leave home for more than an hour or two, and he had zero experience with how to stay safe.

My mind starts to spin with all the ways he could have been killed or hurt along the way ... No! No. He wouldn't have attempted it unless he knew he could get to Drustan, our missing older brother. Which means, Drustan must have heard about the accident.

But why didn't they wait for me?

The problem is, I have no idea how to find them. My parents were our only link to Drustan, and they took that information with them in death. So here I sit, using moonshine to dull my sorrow, still hoping that someday Drustan and Arthur will come for me.

"Here ya go," Tommy says.

He sets a new daiquiri down on the bar and I take a deep drink, ignoring the combination of chill and burn.

"If ya drink much more of that"—Tommy frowns—"I'm gonna have to call you an autocab. I'll pay for it."

I choke on the drink, recoiling from the suggestion so severely I nearly topple from the barstool. Tommy reaches over the bar, grabbing my shoulders to steady me.

"Sweet baby Einstein! What on Earth was that about, girl?"

"I don't ... want a c-cab."

"Do you really think you're gonna walk all the way back down to the Dregs like this? I could just ..." Understanding dawns in his eyes before he closes them momentarily. He probably pulled up his calendar interface. "Aw shit Doll, I'm sorry. I didn't even think when you asked for the day off. I should've realized then."

"It doesn't matter." A wave of dizziness catches me by surprise so I lay my head on the bar.

"Does it still hurt after all this time?" He gently strokes my hair.

"It will—every year."

"Then come on to the back."

Tommy comes to my side of the bar, sliding his strong, dark arm around my waist to pull me from my seat. "What ... doing? I can't sing."

"Girl, that's obvious." He laughs and I appreciate the rich sound. My father used to laugh like that. "But ya drink much more and you're not gonna be sitting in that chair either. Ya gonna be lying on the floor."

Tommy helps me into the tiny dressing room in back and sets me down on the futon. I lie down, battling a new wave of dizziness as he brushes my hair back from my face. The weight of a thin blanket settles across my body. "I'm sorry," he whispers. "I didn't know your OAS was so bad. I don't know how to help ya without a doc."

OAS—Obsessive Attachment Syndrome. Glancing at Tommy's face, my heart sinks further as I acknowledge his belief that my condition is a mental illness, the most feared mental illness in the Community. "I'm not sick."

"Girl." He sighs. "How can ya look at yourself right now and say that? You've worked for me for six years now and I haven't ever seen ya in pain like this—except a year ago."

Tommy is like most people in the world. He didn't know his parents—or siblings, if he had any. After he left University, his birth mother did track him down, but only to pass along the moonshiner tradition—their little rebellion in a world where alcohol is illegal. She didn't stick around. He lives the typical life: unattached, unobsessed, and perfectly healthy according to everyone else.

"You don't know what you're missing. If I could have them all back today, I'd take 'em."

"You still believe those brothers are coming for ya?"

"No." The truth slips past my lips. Weak. Traitor. Fraud.

"Well, then they a couple of fools." Tommy brushes my hair back again. "If ya gonna break the rules, ya might as well break it for something pretty and smart. With those green-brown eyes and that heart that holds ya tight."

Careful, Tommy. You're going to develop OAS yourself. We can't have that.

"Where is that man of yours anyway? He should be loving ya and taking your mind off all those attachments that been hurting so hacking bad."

Ah yes. My ever-present imaginary boyfriend and primary excuse. No one understands a desire for monogamous love, and they understand chastity even less. I may as well declare that I dance around altars and sacrifice fluffy bunny rabbits to a herd of unicorns. "Delivery. Out of town."

"Bad timing if ya ask me. I tell ya what, Doll. You just stay back here and sleep for the night. You can start that long walk home in the morning. After all, we don't want our moonshine secret found passed out on the street now."

"Fine—I mean … thanks." The nerve pain is starting to flare back to life in my legs. I won't be able to work tomorrow anyway.

3

HAWK

September 25
North Continent, Region 109, Sector 4, District A

The hotel room is freezing, so I close my eyes and mentally pull up GRID access. Instantly, I'm standing by the pond in the nicest park mid-sector—a standard hotel menu theme.

"Good evening, Jared," Manuela says as she walks up beside me in the mental landscape. "What are your needs?" She always appears exactly the same with highlighted black hair, brown eyes, and bronzed skin. I could change her up if I want, but never interact with her long enough to deal with it.

"Just help me with the room. It's like a bogon fridge in here." I reopen my eyes, abandoning the mental menu since Manuela can do it for me. She projects herself into the room through my mind. I need to seal up for security and prepare the environment for the chimera's unique needs. "Raise the temperature to 72 degrees. Lights on full."

"Adjusting settings now. How was your trip?"

"It was normal." I begin a full security sweep of the room.

There's nothing under the queen bed or nightstand.

"Are you upset?"

"No." Even though I only use this identity sporadically, Manuela should have learned by now that I don't make small talk with AI. The hall closet and bathroom are empty. "I'm fine."

"My sensors indicate there are no additional people inside this room."

"Yeah." And your sensors can be tricked. "I just …"

"I know you like to check," she says with a smile. "Would you like me to order entertainment for you?"

There's no left-behind tech beneath the small table in the corner or the two wooden chairs. "No. I want to sleep and not be disturbed in any way."

"I do not have the ability to override emergency alerts."

Glancing out the balcony door, my exact drone delivery instructions were followed. Thank Science for quality control protocols. The crate is on the balcony beneath a heat-shield, to keep the boy cool and hamper both curious eyes and Manuela's body heat sensors. The kid came with samples of the venom he produces, and I received confirmation during hyperloop travel that the antivenoms I carry for Cobra should be effective against the brunt of it. Not that I'm going to let him bite me.

"Manuela, tint the windows to 100 percent. I need to sleep."

"Tinting now. Would you like a hot bath?"

"Not tonight. Leave only emergency protocols active. Activate Do Not Disturb."

"Very well, Jared. Have a good night. I will be here when you need me."

I glance at the entry panel to confirm her disconnect, then activate my signal jammer, sealing the room. The balcony door opens with a slight hiss as I approach.

"Instructions?" the crate's cheap voice says, sensing my movement.

A thorough scan of the surrounding area doesn't turn up any problems. There are two people on a balcony on the building across from this one, but they're in some kind of heated discussion. Neither of them have bulges in their clothing that would indicate weapons. None of the street cams have direct angles on this room. At street level the autocabs and pedestrians are moving steadily except for a young mother struggling with her flailing infant, who has spotted the stray cat around the corner. I don't see any nosy people or drones. "Enter."

"Authorization?" the crate asks.

"Jared Altrax, confirm CID. Security code 9-2-4-Bravo-Delta-Tango-6-2-Charlie. Confirmation Azure-Epsilon-Granite."

"Authorization confirmed." Wheels emerge from the crate's bottom before it steers itself inside. After the door shuts, I flip the switch to disconnect its power supply.

I've got incredible hearing, but the kid inside isn't making any sound aside from breathing. "Hey, kid." I tap on the crate's aluminum top. "You still alive in there?"

He doesn't respond so I pull the heat-shield off and drop down, looking through the thin front bars. Two wide, terrified eyes gaze back at me. Hawking's ghost, he smells awful. "Do you speak English?"

He nods.

"Did the food and water I put in there last?"

He nods again.

"Look, kid." I sigh, sitting down to face the crate. "I'm sorry you've been stuck in that shit hole this whole time, but it was the best way to get you here. I'd like to let you out, but you've got to convince me that you're not gonna bite me the second I open this door."

He blinks a few times but otherwise doesn't move.

"You got a name?"

I'm surprised when he shakes his head. I didn't expect that answer.

"What about one you like? Something you want to be called?"

He's quiet for a long time, tilting his head this way and that. Finally he whispers, "Human."

"Sorry, kid. No one's gonna mistake you for that, but I can help you live a life outside this box if you want."

"You can?" The boy leans forward to grab the bars. "You look like them, but smell like me. You are like me."

Hack, this kid's nose is one in a trillion. I need to know just how sensitive it is. "What do I smell like?"

"Snake. Cat. Bird." He tips his head. "There's more, but it's too mixed up."

"Good nose. What about you? What's in your genes?"

He shrugs. "Snake. Spider. Something from the sea. Everything bad."

"Why don't you have a name?"

"I don't know."

"Do you remember your birth mother?"

"They said she was dead—said I did it."

Shit. Humans can be cruel. "Well, no pressure. You pick a name when you want. Till then, I'll stick with kid. Is that alright?"

He nods, then his eyes settle where his hands grip the bars. "Why don't they put you in a box?"

"They decided I'm more useful outside of one. I do a ton of important work, including buying kids that shouldn't be in boxes."

I wish I could look this kid in the eye and tell him life is great on this side of the bars, that he has amazing things to look forward to. Reality sucks. We're all confined by the roles we fit, but at least we're not aimless or exploited.

The retirement ad I saw last week made me wish I had options like everyone else. I could make an appointment, walk in, tell them I don't want to keep going, and they'd put me to sleep for good. It's painless and your body's recycled.

The Community would never let that happen though. They've already freaked out enough to put me on pills, which I can't take and do my job. I'm a well-trained, highly-skilled asset. They need me to do this kind of work because there aren't enough of us to do it. "Can I trust you not to bite me, if I let you out?"

"Yeah." He tucks his chin down to his chest. "I didn't mean to hurt anybody."

When I open the crate, the kid takes his time unfolding. I can tell it causes him pain. An hour later, I'm able to coax him up to the table by eating in front of him with a second bowl out, acting as casual about the food as I can. He starts asking questions about my work, so I explain my role in the Community to him while he eats.

If he works extra hard, he might be able to catch up to the other chimera kids his age, or pass them. Then he can get into work like mine. It's not the best future, but it's a lot better than life in a box.

The chime from the door startles us both. For Tesla's sake, how long have we been talking? The kid dives back inside the crate before my eyes have even closed to pull up the feed from the external cam. It's who I expect. I wish I could avoid seeing him, but I walk over and manually open the door.

Alex steps through wearing an ivory silk shirt and brown dress slacks that I'm sure conceal thin body armor beneath. I hate how much of his face looks back at me in the mirror every morning— the sharp jaw and strong nose of western North Continent look more natural with his paler skin and brown hair.

Despite contributing half my DNA, Alex is a Community elite, a respected scientist. Instead of being ashamed of my genetics, he revels in what I am. He chose to be the lead researcher for all global chimera units. If only he had a human soul. "This is the boy?" Alex asks after the door closes. "Why in Tesla's name is he still in that crate?"

"Because you startled us."

"Startled you?" Alex scoffs. "Keep your mind on your work. The child's needs aren't something for you to deal with."

I decide not to argue and scare the kid more. "He doesn't have a name. I told him I would just call him kid for now."

"Thus, you don't work with children."

"Whatever, Alex." He hates it when I call him that. "Are you going to help him or not?"

"Obviously. Young man, come out here so we can get moving." Shitty thing is, Alex is the one who should never be trusted with children. The man is a sociopath, but he's my only option.

"Come on, kid." I sit on the floor by the crate to get back on his level. "You've got to go with Alex now."

The kid pokes his head out past the door, and he has tears on his face.

"He's not gonna hurt you." I hope that's the truth.

"I want to stay with you," the kid says, wiping his tears. "I can help you. I know I can."

"I'm sorry. That's not an option. They're going to give you a new life. Let you start over. You'd like a new life, right? You'd like to be like me?"

"But I don't want to forget you!" The kid suddenly sobs.

Alex jerks his head back and raises an eyebrow. "You told him about the memory wipe?"

"Of course I did. He's had enough people lie to him. It's not going to hurt him to know what to expect. He'll forget the pain when he forgets the rest of it."

"No please!" The kid bursts out of the shipping container and nearly knocks me over when he jumps in my lap. "Please, Jared! I want to stay with you!"

"Hey, hey, whoa." I wish I had the right words to calm him. "It's not going to be what you imagine, kid." I run my fingers lightly through his hair, feeling oddly peaceful from this sense of connection to someone I barely know.

I saw a birth mother do this at a commissary once for a much smaller child, and I remember wishing I'd had a mother who'd done that for me. My mother couldn't wait to turn me over. She put me into Alex's questionable care on the day I was born. I have no memories of being held.

"What do you mean?" The kid continues crying.

"Right now, you remember being stuck in that sick box," I say. "You remember all the people who've been cruel to you. Maybe I seem like something special, but it's only because you've spent your whole life being treated like shit. Sure, after the memory wipe you won't remember me." The thought makes my throat tight, but I cough it away. "But you won't remember the shitheads either. You'll be able to start over. Clean slate. You'll get the respect you earn, and you'll meet new people who'll treat you with the respect an operative deserves."

"You promise?"

I glance up at Alex and, of course, he has no reassurance to offer. "Yeah, kid," I say. "I promise."

The next time I think about retirement, I'll just remember what happens to these kids without me. Better than pills any day.

Obsessive Attachment Syndrome (OAS)

A common mood and behavioral disorder that leads to serious social impairments, emotional distress, and violence. OAS leads citizens to develop extreme interdependency with the object of obsession (OO) and an unhealthy mental framework for their place within society.

The following criteria are required to make a diagnosis of OAS. The citizen must be experiencing three or more symptoms for a minimum one-week period and at least one of the symptoms must be (1) or (2) below.

1. Treating the OO with preference over other citizens who could meet the same needs.
2. Placing the needs and desires of the OO above the Community of citizens and self.
3. Emotional vulnerability and dependency upon the OO.
4. Constant and obsessive communication with the OO.
5. Worry or concern over the OO's opinions and with pleasing them.
6. Keeping pictures, drawings, or representations of the OO to look at when the OO is not present.
7. Realigning duty schedules and leisure activities to mirror those of the OO.
8. Desire to bestow constant gifts upon the OO.
9. Need to touch or hold the OO in a way that is not exclusive to sexual intercourse.
10. Decreasing sexual variety leading to sexual exclusivity.
11. Creating future plans or daydreaming that involves the presence of the OO in order to be happy.
12. Profound emptiness, loss, or anxiety when separated from the OO.
13. Possessiveness and jealousy over the OO.
14. Inability to feel safe or secure without the presence of the OO.
15. Enduring hardship or suffering in order to be near, to please, or provide assistance to the OO.
16. Residing with the OO.

Community members are advised to watch for the manifestation of these unhealthy signs and symptoms in themselves and others, and to report them to their doctors as soon as possible in order to receive appropriate separation and treatment.

— *Excerpt from GF Diagnostic Criteria Guidelines (DCG-13)*

PART 1

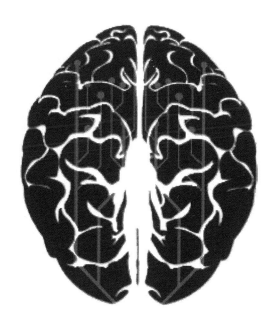

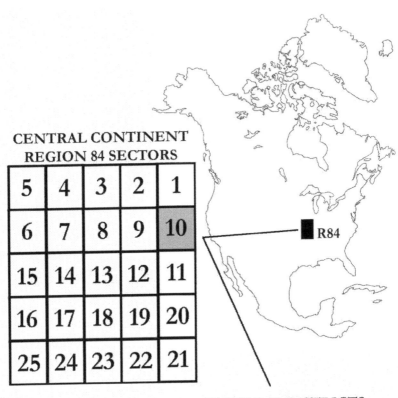

CENTRAL CONTINENT REGION 84 SECTORS

5	4	3	2	1
6	7	8	9	10
15	14	13	12	11
16	17	18	19	20
25	24	23	22	21

R84

SECTOR 10 DISTRICTS

E	D	C	B	A
F	G	H	I	J
P	N	M	L	K
Q	R	S	T	U
Z	Y	X	W	V

THE DREGS

1

GINA

Nine Months Later
Central Continent, Region 84, Sector 10, The Dregs

"Come on, Stella ..." I groan, weary from the long walk. "I know they look delicious, but Momma needs to go lie down."

I can feel the flutter of Stella Luna's excitement tumble through my mind as clearly as if her own little bat wings were trapped inside my skull. She's flipping and twirling—tossing bugs into her mouth with her nimble wings and tail. My mind-link with her is incredibly strong, but I can choose to be less aware of it; especially when I have a bit of a buzz going like I do now. She's narrowing in on an enormous moth and swooping in for the kill. I chuckle as she relishes her meal off to my right.

I hate the cracks and holes in these old, empty, textured glass streets. It's hard to get around without spraining something even when I'm completely sober. But, I remind myself again, lack of attention is a blessing in this little hole in the world.

Stella flutters over and settles close to my face, hanging by the epaulet of my green, flannel vest. She's a puff of fur no bigger than the palm of my hand, with a tiny, pointed face and round, mouse-like ears. Her brown, leathery wings are folded up to protect the delicate skin. I can see and feel her delight as I gently stroke her silky, tan back. These twilight hours are her favorite time of day.

As we approach the condemned high-rise office building we call home, my back is aching and exhaustion is settling into my bones. I wish I had access to a shower when it's this muggy. At least there's not much farther to walk. The fires are burning in their barrels out front, welcoming beacons for a weary soul.

Crazy Rob ambles up beside me as I walk into the building's crumbling concrete entrance. By appearance, he's in his late 50's or early 60's with gray hair and beard, both long and ill-groomed. Sometimes, when he talks, he sounds like he's from the Old World.

His skin is pale, weathered and permanently reddened in places from extensive time outside. He must have been more than six feet tall in his youth but is now stooped from age and rough living.

His clothes are what you would expect from a shirker—a patchwork of random pieces with numerous repairs and re-purposes. His black silk trousers are reinforced in the knees with green camouflage material. His yellow wool sweater has large holes, which display the stained, white cotton t-shirt beneath. The red flannel blanket around his shoulders is new, but the two halves of the green and orange winter caps which have been sewn together around his head are not. I'm always surprised and grateful that, like myself, he at least manages to keep himself smelling fairly clean.

"How's your little sweetie tonight?" Rob asks in his rough baritone voice, leaning over to peer at Stella as she stretches her wings.

"At least she has a full stomach." I yawn, trudging toward the stairs.

"Gina … you uh … you eating alright? I've got extra MRE's if—"

"No, no." I wave him off with an attempt at a smile. "I'm fine, Rob. I've just been too busy." That, and I decided to bargain with Tommy for another drink instead. I've got enough meals-ready-to-eat and canned goods back in my burrow.

"Alright, well …" He shifts his eyes back and forth down the corridor, watching for spies no doubt. "You be careful. I know you're stayin' strong off the GRID like you should, but don't let yourself get too worn down either. If you ever need some to get by … just … don't tell anyone."

His sudden concern is as heartwarming as it is comical. I have a much better quality of life than most folks here in the Dregs, as Crazy Rob and all the other occupants of this supposedly abandoned building are well aware.

"Thanks, Rob," I say with a genuine smile this time. "You'll be the first to know if I'm ever in a bind."

"Good, good." He nods, then turns away and hurries back down the corridor we came through.

I scold myself as I climb the stairs. Why, in God's name, did I make my burrow three stories up? It's genuinely moronic for someone with my condition. Surely the ground floor could have been just as safe, maybe more in some ways. I knew no one was left to help me carry my crap.

I punch in the entry code on my padlock. It spins open and chimes a short pattern confirming no one has tried to hack it since I've been gone.

As soon as the door swings open, Stella Luna wings her way to her favorite spot, some cotton mesh above the small aloe plant I keep in the far corner of the room. I secure the series of chains, bolts, and locks I've installed inside the door.

Seeing her hanging comfortably from her perch, I remove the small mind-link disk from behind my ear and feel sudden relief as her staccato voice vanishes from my mind. Well, it's not really her voice. It's more like a flood of rapid-fire observations from a being living in a world moving a thousand times faster than mine. I have learned to understand her patterns, patterns that correspond to navigating through tight spaces, closing in on prey, or maneuvering to alight under a perch. To her, I must seem a lumbering sloth-like creature with a mind bereft of useful sounds, scents, and images.

Stripping off my Faraday vest and t-shirt, I swap into my favorite jade tank top. It makes my auburn hair and pale skin shine. No one is ever here to see me, but I like to feel prettier when I'm home.

The coil on my grill sparks as I turn it on, and Stella stirs restlessly on her perch. I'm going to have to find a damn replacement coil pretty soon, or these cans of soup are going to get too difficult to swallow.

Come on, God. Is it too much to ask for? Just an extra coil. They're not too antique yet.

As I flop down with my food into the royal blue chair that Dad found for Mom years ago, I feel blessed relief from the pressure and pain in my back. Air rushes in and out of the chair's sections as it adjusts to eliminate the remaining spots of pressure. Just before my eyes close, they settle on a holographic image of my family rotating through the frame on the small end table beside me. With my enormous stockpile of images, I don't see this one often. I pick up the frame to pause the march of my past.

My chest hurts at how happy Mom and Dad were back then. I glance at their urn, tucked safely behind where the holoframe lives. The Community is opposed to family ties, of course, but my brother's friend Joe, from Southside Brothel, was able to get their ashes. I'll never understand how he did it, but I know better than to ask too many questions—and I'll always be grateful.

I can hear Mom lecturing me that I need to move on from the Dregs, and Dad gently reminding me that God has a plan for my life. They wanted me to see more of the world. I can't though. I need to stay close to where my brothers will search for me when they come back. If they come back ...

Suddenly, I'm startled by a rapid knock on my painted glass wall. Jumping up, I head for the door, stumbling over my autodrive backpack along the way, and spinning to carefully set the small picture frame down by the door. I hear Stella flit into one of the bat houses I've mounted on the wall for her to hide in. Whoever is knocking moves over and begins pounding frantically on the door instead.

"Who is it?" I shout through the closed metal door.

"Gina! It's me," Crazy Rob says. "Open up! Quick!" I glance through the peephole to see him—hair sticking up in all directions—struggling to hold onto a man who is slumped over his shoulder. Oh Jesus, what now? I race through unlocking my complicated series of locks and swing the door open.

Rob plows right past me, straight toward my bed. "He's bleeding." He wheezes as he heaves the torso of the limp man onto it, leaving his legs dangling half off. "I can't get it to stop."

"Who is he?" I demand as I begin digging through my trauma supplies.

"Right now, someone who needs your help."

Back when I moved in here, I found my antique hospital bed in the Sector 10 recycling center and managed to convince some other shirkers to help me haul it back in exchange for three months of wound care and first aid. I wired it to a solar battery system I rigged up on one of the exterior windows of this building.

I make an effort to always have medical supplies on-hand.

Everyone who lives here knows that if they're ever injured, they can come see if I can help. If I can't, they'll have to beg at the Community hospital.

Grabbing a pair of trauma shears, I cut away the man's left pant leg in a hurry. God, there's so much blood! Please help me handle this one right.

He's bleeding profusely from his lower calf. As I hold a clotting bandage over the wound, I examine the rest of him as quickly as I can with my free hand.

The mystery man is short and very stocky with a flat, dark face, a wide nose, and almond-shaped eyes. He doesn't look like a shirker. His clothes are too nice and his skin's too clean. He appears more like me, so if he's a shirker, he must deal in tech or have other connections. His breathing is labored and he's dazed, so I begin checking for a head injury.

As my fingers graze the back of his neck, I feel the tiny tell-tale scarring of a GRID inoculation. "Rob!" I jerk my hand back with a hiss. "This guy is wired! He's broadcasting, and you brought him right to my—"

"No! Look!" Rob pulls at one of the stainless barbell hoops in the man's ears.

I take my sweeper off the small shelf above my bed, and a quick pass confirms that they are frequency jammers designed as jewelry. I deal in more elegant pairs myself. "How did you know he was wearing jammers? Who the hell is he, Rob?"

"I found him in the alley. He was bleeding all over the place. Told me about the jammers when I said I couldn't help him. He just needs a patch. His people should come get him in less than an hour."

"His people? Who the hell are his ... oh no. No! He's a squid, isn't he? Dammit! You know better than to help those nut cases!" You brought a terrorist into my home!

"He's a kid, and he's hurt!"

"He's not a kid! He's at least my age."

Crazy Rob concentrates on his shoes for a moment, then looks up with a sheepish, "How old are you?"

"I'm twenty-four." I breathe deeply, trying to calm down. "And that isn't the point, Rob. If the shields come here looking for him, I'll lose this burrow."

"The shields only track CIDs," he says, "and he's got jammers on."

"And do you know when he put them on? Or whether the cams or drones were tracking him here?"

"He was with me."

"Oh ..." Relief washes over me. I wish I had skipped that last drink for a clearer mind and steadier hands.

Crazy Rob got his nickname through no small amount of paranoia; however, not everything he raves about is craziness. Unlike me, he attempted to join the Community and grow the mental wetware to access the GRID. Normally, the inoculation process is completed in infancy, unless the mother opts out and sentences her child to life as a shirker. Rob had his done when he was much older. However, when he tried to connect, the GRID went haywire somehow and Rob was sent home without pay.

Since then, he has done some experimenting and discovered the Citizens ID he broadcasts somehow shuts down all GRIDtech in his vicinity. He's like a walking, talking electromagnetic pulse that crashes anything GRID-based. Anyone with him wouldn't be able to be tracked by CID either if he has his hat off.

"I told you," Rob says, gearing up for one of his rants. "Those Fellowship bastards don't wanna give me my coin. They did this to me on purpose, so they could track me and still not pay me. They just want to keep an eye on Ol' Rob all the time. Backfired on their asses, I say. I should—"

"Rob!" I interrupt his standard tirade. "You brought him here, so help me with his leg."

"Right," Rob says, looking back at the injured man with obvious concern.

I pull back the trauma bandage cautiously. The bleeding has slowed. There is a gaping wound in his calf, but no major arteries are damaged. Shields use high-energy weapons that cauterize on impact, so this isn't from one of those. It could easily be from some kind of fragmentation weapon, but those haven't been authorized by the Global Fellowship in my lifetime.

Of course, a squid could get hit with their own weapons.

I instruct Rob to keep holding pressure on the wound while I mix up a quick poultice and retrieve a tincture. "Can you get him to swallow this?" I hand Rob the tincture in a dropper.

"Down the hatch kid." He squirts it in the dazed man's mouth. The man gags in response.

I apply the poultice to his wound and wrap it in several layers of gauze. "Now take him back out to the street." Looking back at the weariness on Rob's face, I sigh. "I'll help."

We drag the wounded man to the stairs and down in stages. Taking a rest at the second floor landing, I close my eyes and steady myself against the wall to concentrate on turning the pain roaring in my joints into white noise. My God, how am I going to make it back up?

When I open my eyes, Rob is brushing back the man's hair and examining his face with concern. Who is he, really? I know better than to pry further. As much as he rants, Rob is very careful with his secrets, and I admit, it's probably better not to know too much.

Finally out in front of our building, we prop the stranger up against a wooden crate. It should be easy for *his people* to spot him here by the barrel fire. My arms feel strangely light after I let his weight settle on the street, and I glance down with frustration at the blood decorating my ruined tank top.

Oh well, you know better than to get attached to things.

"I'll watch him until he gets picked up." Rob sighs, taking a seat beside him on a small aluminum shipping box.

I nod, too exhausted to speak.

"Hey …" the man slurs, grabbing my arm as I turn to leave. "What's your name?"

"No names," I say, shaking my head. "Just get yourself to a better doctor. Quick."

"Thanks, lady," he mumbles, struggling to focus on my face.

I turn away and head inside to clean up the blood and collapse for the night.

2

GINA

No matter how hard I scrubbed, all night my burrow smelled like blood. The ventilation in here has never been great. It's not the first night I've spent that way, due to my agreement with the other shirkers.

The wound was much worse than I'm used to. Someone was coming to get him, so I didn't do as much to help the guy as I could have. I think I stopped him from bleeding to death.

It's stupid to lie here worried that my suspicions about him made me too uncaring. Medical supplies are a precious commodity in the Dregs, and a shortage could cost someone else's life later, if I'm not able to replace them.

I guess I'll know soon enough if I was right to worry. If any shields show up, snooping around my little makeshift home, I'll have to relocate. That would suck.

This building used to be part of an old office complex of some kind, in an era the Community now chooses to forget. Other folks use it for shelter, but most of the population is transient. Crazy Rob, Hosni and his kids, old Yeon-Jae, and I are the only ones who've remained for more than a few months. Crazy Rob was the first to tag along with me when I moved from my family's old burrow a few blocks away. He was really worried about me after Arthur disappeared.

Transforming these small inner offices into a burrow was simple enough. There were two of them joined together in the center of a much larger, completely open area. They join through a single doorway, and must have belonged to someone important because they have their own tiny, non-functional bathroom attached on the west side. The east-facing wall of each office was made of glass, even though they only faced the building's interior.

After cleaning the spaces out, I placed a small Faraday bomb in the center of each room and detonated it, coating them with a composite paint filled with conductive hair-like needles that dry in a tightly woven micromesh. It's more reliable than metal fencing at keeping out radio and other communication frequencies, and much more practical than hauling sheet metal around to install. A Faraday shield means privacy and peace-of-mind in a world run by the GRID.

I reach down and massage the aching tissue around my kneecaps. The condition I was born with flares up in response to stress. My family was diagnosed centuries ago with a genetic condition called Ehlers-Danlos Syndrome or EDS. Our form is autosomal dominant, meaning it has a very high probability of being passed along to our children. Not everyone who carries the genes is disabled by it, or even necessarily symptomatic. It affects each of us in our own unique way. Mostly, it makes our joints and tissues overly stretchy, easy to injure, and slow to heal. Many of us learn to cope with nearly constant pain.

I can't quite tell whether my pain this morning is fibromyalgia or if all the walking I did yesterday irritated my legs. It makes little difference when I have limited options for pain management anyway.

Carrying the probable squid down the stairs certainly didn't help. I'm usually careful how I move and what I do to keep from stressing my fragile joints. If I get hurt, I could end up down for weeks which I can't afford. But Rob looked bad when he brought him in. Sure he's old, but he's still tough, and strong too. Yesterday he seemed really stressed—over-tired or something. It reminded me of how he looked when Mom and Dad died.

Anyway, the more pressing problem now is getting myself out of bed. Unlike most people, unless I get far more than eight hours of sleep, I wake up nauseous and exhausted. I usually try to sleep ten hours, but last night that proved difficult. The stench of blood and unanswered questions still gnaw at me.

Who was that guy and what was he doing in the Dregs? How had he been injured? Will the shields trace him back to me? Can you get in official trouble for healing a wounded man you don't know?

My body feels unnaturally heavy so I use the side rails on my bed to pull myself up to sit. I feel slightly faint for a moment as I wait for the blood to return to my head. Then I get up to decide on the best outfit for the day.

It's nearly noon, and if I don't hurry, I could be late for my delivery. I'm heading into one of the elite districts, so looking my best is paramount. I grab one of the bathing wipes out of the small resealable packet by my bed, head into the small bathroom to stand in front of the mirror, and set to work freshening up.

My face is narrow with closely spaced eyes, a slightly upturned nose, small but full lips, and a strong jaw that helps me appear determined when I want to. I hate that my teeth are crowded, but at least my smile is almost symmetrical. My unusual hazel eyes look like they are made of two concentric rings—green surrounded by brown—with a starburst pattern in the middle. They are so striking that I find I can get away without much makeup even among the elites—despite my ultra-pale skin. When I look this close, I'm reminded that strangely, I have a small patch of freckles on only my right cheek.

Digging out the sample bottle of perfume I negotiated in a deal months ago, I dab a little under one ear. I pack my autodrive backpack with a complete disguise and then dress in my standard clothes: black cargo pants, a black t-shirt, a Faraday vest disguised in jade green flannel, and a pair of well-worn, waterproof hiking boots.

I'm five-foot-ten inches tall, last I checked. My body is curved like a woman, not a girl, which comes in handy from time to time and helps me appear older than I am. It can be a handicap when trying to go unnoticed, however, so these clothes add the illusion of bulk and straighten some of my curves.

The reflective wall in my home warps my image and makes me appear rounder, but I'm actually rather thin for my height. I've got thick auburn hair that ends just past my shoulders, legs as long as a man of six feet, and similar long, willowy arms. My curvy body and sultry alto have earned me my more legit job as an off-the-books singer in a small bar.

I grab the tech for my delivery, two pairs of jammers disguised as women's pearl-drop earrings, and shove them in the upper pocket on my right thigh. Then I slip Stella's mind-link disk behind my right ear.

"You coming with me?" I ask Stella, amused by the look she gives me out of a single eye.

She was wrapped snugly, sleeping under her perch until my rude interruption. This is not her time of day, and her response is a subtle feeling of irritation.

"Okay, girl. Just thought I'd ask."

I drop the mind-link disk back in its small carry capsule and leave it on the counter on my way out. There's no need to get caught with it or lose it, so if she stays, it stays.

When I hit the ground floor, I make a quick stop at the old public bathroom to use one of the working toilets, brush my teeth, and then slip my dental supplies back in a tiny pocket in my cargo pants. Leaving the building, I catch sight of Crazy Rob lying propped-up against an unlit burn barrel outside. "Did they come get him?" I pause at his feet.

"Yeah." Rob yawns. "Just grabbed him and ran. Bastards didn't even say thanks. Payment wouldn't have hurt."

"He said thanks to me. Not that it matters. Anyway, I'm headed out."

"You singing tonight?"

"Yeah, later, but I've got some errands to run," I say, starting to head toward the Community.

"Watch your six, little girl," he hollers after me.

"Yeah, yeah." I never should have admitted my age.

I walk with my backpack clacking along the cracked and pitted pavement behind me, hating the humidity. Dandelions, clovers, and plantains have taken over large sections of the old roads and sidewalks. I smile at the small gifts God gives the shirkers in the edible and medicinal weeds that even the Community cannot eradicate, and make a mental note to gather some on my way home. The trees and shrubs that once decorated this part of the city have taken over areas as well, but they're of little use. I pass through four more blocks of Dregs before I reach the edge of the maintained land.

The difference is stark, as if someone has drawn a visible line through the area. The dilapidated high-rises and roads transform instantly into row after row of skyscraper housing complexes with miniature manicured lawns. The buildings, which show only minor wear and tear, are made of glass, steel, and stone. They are uniform—designed for function rather than visual appeal. Inside, every hub has a single-room, efficiency layout. I've never seen one, but I've heard a lot of stories from shirkers who've lived as Community members for a while.

Sometimes, when I'm passing through on business like this, I imagine I could stop working so hard and just settle for a GRID life. I could live in a little hub and have some coin to my name. Maybe I could get medical care for my chronic pain and the injuries I constantly accumulate. I wouldn't have to push my body so hard all the time to survive. The option to be more careful could stave off disability for years. I'm already developing arthritis like my mom, and struggling with other injuries that have never healed right.

It's a fool's dream though. Mom warned us constantly before she died. The only way for people with EDS to stay out of an institution for the disabled is to stay out of the Community. No one really knows what they're like, but from everything I've heard on the street, once you go into those places, you never come out. Ever.

If I end up institutionalized, it is a good bet I'd never see my brothers again, even if they do come back. The Global Fellowship discourages all forms of long-term relationships—especially family. My family preserved our traditions and our ability to live as a family by maintaining a life outside the Community. To discourage that kind of independence, the Global Fellowship virtually ensures everyone outside the Community will struggle to obtain basic resources and medical care. But we count precious the right to be part of each other's lives, so we choose to endure it.

At least we did. Where did you go, Arthur? I wipe away the tears springing to my eyes before they're noticed.

3

HAWK

Same Day
Central Continent, Region 53, Sector 25, District Z

I watch the autocranes load my cargo into the hyperloop's shipping segment, bound for Region 84. The sleek silver train's vacuum tube will be sealed up again before departure. This always feels like such a waste of coin. The Global Fellowship could ship this stuff for nothing. But if my buyers and suppliers can't find history of me moving stock around within the records, things would get ugly fast. I'd be waving a big red sign: *Hey I'm an operative and a dumbass. Come shoot me in the face.*

"Well, well, well. It's been a while since I've seen you around, Jared."

I glance up at the woman, reaching back in my memory to try and pull her name from some dusty corner. Tall. Stocky. Mid-length bleached hair. Bronze skin with brown eyes. Obviously a dealer. The scent of cheap lavender perfume and snake ... around her neck? It flicks its tongue at me. *Good thing you can't talk, bub.*

Oh yeah! "Hi Laronda." I give her a friendly, distracted smile. "I've been stocking up."

Man, this woman is irritating. She tries to sleep with me every time she sees me and I'm running out of excuses. I could just get it over with but it would be a chore. Plus, she shoves her nose in my business every time she's around. She's got to be an informant—maybe for hijackers or some high level player who keeps tabs on who and what is moving in the markets.

Information trade is more valuable than black market tech when it comes to power, both in the Community and out. It's why I'm here. I could have avoided Region 84 a while longer, but its got one of the hottest markets in the world. Excellent for high end tech and intel.

I close my eyes and reset the security codes on my shipment

again now that it's loaded. I'm hauling hardware interfaces for wetware prosthetics. They're important for citizens who need to replace a missing limb or organ, but they can be altered for military applications too, so I have to be extra careful.

This stuff needs time to cool, but I've been told I'll have clearance to sell it within a month. Lucky me. I'm going to be stuck in Region 84 for a while, watching the ongoing clean-up of the Mississippi River. At least I'm Jared. I hate getting stuck as Darius that long.

"Anything I might be interested in?" Laronda asks with a nod to the shipping segment.

"Maybe." I shrug. "Nothing that can't wait."

"Joe's got a high voltage meet soon. You could spend a few nights in my hub if you're going to show up."

Shoot me now. "I'll see. I'm still studying the angles."

"Well, he has some fine staff at Southside. Let me know if you'd like to hook up there sometime. Hey, what segment are you seated in? I'm in D45."

"Not sure." I close my eyes and bring up the seat map. I'm assigned to D32, so I change my seat to the only seat left. "Oh yeah." I smile. "I'm in A12."

"First class?" She gives my shoulder a weak shove. "Why are you riding so high all of a sudden?"

To steer clear of you. "I've made a few good deals. I figure I can afford to live a little"—on Community coin.

"Well, enjoy that cushy seat for me then." With a wink, she finally leaves.

When I get to my seat, I relax back into the black leather lounge chair, the only one on my side of the aisle, and close my eyes to adjust it into the perfect reclining position. A notification pops up behind my eyelids, reminding me that my upgrade gives me access to all the Diamond-level entertainment options.

I never play any of the games. The spec ops games that are so popular are just a bad fiction version of my life. The romance games leave me more hollow than love. The movies are either boring or depressing. Besides, it's not a safe place to be off my guard.

Instead, I close the menus and take another deep whiff of my surroundings. As I study the people close to me again, I mentally tick off the owner of each scent I passed on my carefully disinterested walk to my seat. In the crowded cabin, a couple of shirkers are being taken for a ride. One is young and frightened— maybe a slave. Five university students and a chaperone are probably on a field trip. There are a couple of shields—one in plain clothes is sitting two rows behind and across from an arms dealer he could be watching. All three took note of my size as I walked by. The people around me are harmless. I don't detect any serious weapons or drugs. They're all selecting entertainment or getting ready to sleep. I'll pretend to sleep too.

4

GINA

Once I'm well within the maintained housing area of District T, I locate a bus stop where I can negotiate a ride. As I approach the stop, an old woman is waiting patiently with a huge bag. Her clothes are worn but clean and well matched to her wrinkled olive skin, hazel eyes, and tiny frame. Carrying the bag for her will hurt, but it should be quick.

"Do you need help with that?"

She stares me down with critical eyes. "No, thank you," she says with a huff. "You'll get no free ride from me, young lady. You people need to learn to earn your keep. You should—"

"I understand." I cut her off, turn away and take another look around.

"Looks like you need a favor," a smooth male voice says from over my shoulder.

He's almost exactly my height, with a chunky but strong build. He appears to be in his late thirties with neatly combed azure blue hair and a slightly handsome, tanned face. The way his gaze roams my body makes me nervous, but not enough to run. He wears a sly smile and a challenge in his brown eyes, and I square my shoulders.

"That depends," I say with practiced confidence in my tone. "Sit with me?" He ever-so-attractively spits on the sidewalk. Gross. "I'm getting off at my own stop. Alone."

He narrows his eyes and considers my words for a moment before muttering a simple, "Sure."

As the bus pulls up, I watch the old woman board with obvious effort and resist rolling my eyes. The stranger grabs my backpack, and slides his arm around my waist as he moves toward the door. He climbs onto the bus ahead of me, swiping his hand over the scanner twice. He slides into a bench on the left, pushes my backpack beneath the seat in front of him, and smiles in my direction with a raised eyebrow. When I move to sit beside him, he pulls me over to sit on his lap. "You smell really good," he says with a laugh, leaning in to sniff my hair. "How do you manage that out there?"

"Cleanliness is not unique to the Community." Although it's definitely not as easy.

The shirkers around my building are spoiled because of the bathroom on the ground floor that someone managed to connect to the Community's water and sewer systems. It never would have worked if the building hadn't been part of the original system to begin with.

"I'm just impressed." He laughs again. "That's all. You catch rides here often?"

I shrug.

"You know, if you wanted to live in a nice hub for a while, we could work something out."

"Thanks, but I like my home."

"Suit yourself." He shrugs, leaning back against the seat and pulling my back against his chest.

He keeps one hand on my hip and slings his other arm over the back of the bench seat. I tolerate the contact, for now. The old woman is staring at us with disgust written plainly on her face. The man winks mischievously at her and whispers in my ear with a soft, "Pissing that woman off is at least half the fun, ain't it?"

I can't help but chuckle, but wish I could get off his lap.

After a few blocks, I hear him grunt. "Well Sugar, this is my stop. Sure you don't want to join me?"

"No. Thank you." I slide onto the seat next to him and keep a close eye on my bag.

"True shame," he says, standing to his feet and adjusting his jeans. "You ever need a ride again, look for me. Ya hear?" He leans in close to my face like he's trying to sneak in a kiss, but I stiffen and pull back with a glare. Then he winks again like an idiot, and saunters off the bus with a devilish smirk. I brush off my pants legs with my hands as if I could brush off his interest the same way.

The old woman has her nose in the air. "You should have some self-respect," she scolds from her seat.

"Then you should have let me carry your bag," I say with more venom than I intend. It's not fair of me. She probably can't afford to take care of anyone besides herself, but I would have tried to compensate her if she'd been a little nicer. I wait while the old woman gets off at the next stop, and after six additional stops, I recognize the subtle transition as the elite districts begin.

When the bus is relatively empty and the passengers seem absorbed in their feeds, I grab my bag and head for the small lavatory in the back of the bus. Once inside, I change quickly into my disguise. After a couple of stops, I'll choose the closest seat and, hopefully, no one will notice.

The transformation is always shocking, no matter how many times I see myself in these tiny mirrors. The fitted, teal blouse with diamond-cut bell sleeves and sleek, black slacks show off my figure instead of hiding it. The teal makes my hazel eyes and auburn hair striking. I pull a compact folding brush from a pocket in my bag, tame my hair into a tight braided bun behind my head, and fix it with a simple red-brown barrette. I hesitate, as I always do, before removing the small, silver cross from my necklace and tucking it into a tiny pocket on my bag. I brush the lint from my socks off my feet, then I slip them into a ridiculous pair of black, open-toed shoes, and the transformation is complete. It would be a better disguise if I had makeup, but that's not something I can afford to maintain. Fortunately, my features are remarkable enough that people don't notice I go without.

It would be helpful if I could ditch the backpack for an

imitation-designer purse. My condition makes my spine too weak to support the weight of a purse without increasing my pain significantly, so I traded for the nicest looking autodrive backpack I could find. I'm fortunate that in the world of the elites, it seems eccentric. As a final touch, I grab a lavender scarf from another pocket and tie it elegantly around my neck, nicely hiding my lack of a GRID inoculation scar.

When I step out of the bathroom, a young teen girl is staring at me with an open-mouth and wide eyes. She must have watched me go into the bathroom. I want to kick myself for not being more careful. After a moment, she gives me a grin and a thumbs up before dragging her finger and thumb across her lips like a zipper. I flash a quick smile of gratitude.

I get off at the next stop and begin a brisk walk with my bag clacking along behind me. The vibrant colors of summer beautifully compliment the blue, cloudless sky, but the heat and humidity make my skin sweat instantly. I make sure to keep my posture straight, my shoulders back, and my nose slightly tilted toward the sky in arrogance as I walk. It is painful but necessary. No one even casts a second glance my direction, except for one or two looks of casual sexual interest from the people I breeze by. They assume I am one of them, and as long as I don't have to pay for anything, I can keep up my ruse.

Rounding a corner, I approach my drop point in the small park in front of the main academic building of the University. I sit on a stone bench beneath the massive mirrored fountain resembling a DNA strand and pull my bag up beside my heels. I cross my ankles and watch for the client. After a few minutes, a girl in her late teens appears in the far corner of the small park carrying two small, cloth shopping bags.

All Community members are University students until their aptitude tests at age twenty. They are admitted at two years of age after being surrendered by their birth mother. Only elites remain at the University after testing to further develop the knowledge and skills of their profession. Many kids find University life stifling and itch for excitement, especially in their teen years, but the CID they broadcast makes it nearly impossible to break or even bend the rules. That is where I come in.

"Hello Susan," I say as she sits beside me on the bench. The stone is hot to the touch beneath the sweltering mid-day sun.

She is dressed in a simple University uniform with sandy colored slacks and a pale blue, button-up, short-sleeved shirt. Her brunette ringlets bounce lightly in the wind.

"Hello Lynneth," she says awkwardly.

I give my clients my middle name to avoid using my first, but ensure that I have a plausible excuse for an authority. "It's such a beautiful day. You should relax, and enjoy the sunshine."

"You're right." She laughs nervously and takes a deep breath to steady herself. "I bought you something I thought you would like from the commissary." She pulls out a shiny gift bag and hands it to me.

I make a small show of being pleasantly surprised, and take the bag to peer inside. It all appears to be in order. My payment is an odd blend of medical supplies and food items that are more difficult to obtain but would not raise an alarm if purchased by a student.

"Oh goodness, you shouldn't have!" I laugh, grabbing her hand in appreciation. I smoothly slip the two pairs of jamming earrings into her closed fist as I set it back in her lap.

"Well, I couldn't help myself," she admits, blushing at her own need to defy the system—even if just to sneak out for a night or two.

"I appreciate it. Thank you," I say as I should for our charade. We make small talk for a while about the fountain and the neat ring of maintained flower bushes around it. Finally I say, "but I really must be going." I unzip my bag, slip the small gift bag inside, then close it securely.

"Of course." She nods. "I'm glad we were able to meet up."

"Have a wonderful day," I say with a wave as I begin walking back toward the bus stop. I pass a shop with my bag following along at my heels, and glance in the windows at the ridiculously priced items. I don't even recognize some of them.

Mirrored on the storefront glass, a bright flash in the street behind me catches my attention as I hear an unfamiliar whooshing sound. Suddenly a blast of heat and incredible force slams into my back. It drives my body straight through the glass and into the display area. My head hits the floor hard, and then, I feel nothing.

5

HAWK

The screeching emergency alert brings me out of my relaxation in a flash. What the hack? Without opening my eyes, I pull up the message.

EXPLOSION IN CENTRAL CONTINENT, REGION 84, SECTOR 10, DISTRICT J. TERRORISM SUSPECTED. REPORT ANY SUSPICIOUS ACTIVITY TO THE CIVIL PEACE GUARD IMMEDIATELY. INJURIES AND CASUALTIES UNKNOWN. ACTIVATE FEED FOR DETAILS.

District J! Shit! Someone didn't hit the University did they? Why would it be a target?

My hyperloop will be pulling into the station at District U in less than an hour and everyone on board is checking the feeds and freaking out. When I activate the news feed, the scene is chaotic with smoke still filling the area, making visibility poor even with the 3D security footage. I see park benches, but why is there so much debris? Man, if I was down there I'd be able to focus in to details I'll never see with this shitty resolution.

The voice of Faramund, the global transportation AI, starts speaking through the hyperloop loudspeaker. "All passengers, please remain calm. Due to the current emergency in Region 84, delays are expected for all hyperloop and autovehicle transportation in Regions 70-72, 83-85, and 90-92. Your patience is appreciated. You may engage my services for rerouting any travel conflicts arising from your delay."

This is hacking weird. Why would the squids hit a park? I pull the live feed back up and glance around at the surrounding buildings. Using the area's map system as a cross reference, nothing significant catches my eye. There are no major server banks or government buildings in the area. We need someone on the ground to get a better idea of what's going on.

Standing up, I stretch and head back for the tiny bathroom in back. The uniformed shield eyes me warily, but I pretend not to notice. After going in and locking the door, I place a call to Roland—my current contact with the CPG on this continent. He answers on the first ring.

"What the hack do you want, Hawk?"

"I'm in the area. Coming into District U by hyperloop."

"Well, congratulations. You're in time for the show."

Asshole. "Listen. You need someone on the ground ASAP who can see what's out-of-place and follow trails at ground zero. Your street shields have got to be overwhelmed, and I know how squids operate. Let me in there to see what I can turn up."

"Don't blow your cover for this."

"Don't insult me."

"Alright. Go in. See what you can find. We are broadcasting instructions telling citizens to report any squid activity in the area."

"Are you sure this was them? At this point, we need to know everything they've seen that's unusual. Squids or not."

"Just do what you're good at. Leave the public relations to the professionals."

6

GINA

Pain is everywhere, inescapable, roaring through every cell in my body. For a long time, there is no sound. I'm in a vacuum of nothing but torment. Then my ears start ringing, quietly at first, but the sound quickly builds to a deafening pitch. My bones feel like they are vibrating as I try to push myself up on gritty, sticky hands and knees. I feel a few small objects slide off my back, and I choke on the acrid smell of smoke.

What happened?

I try to open my eyes and searing agony shreds through my left one. My right eye cracks open slightly, but I only see red haze and it stings so intensely that it closes automatically. I reach a hand up to touch my face, and I can feel rough bits of glass embedded in my skin which is coated in something warm and sticky. The awful, metallic taste of blood makes my stomach roil with nausea. Cautiously, I bring my fingertips toward my left eye, crying out as they encounter a protruding piece of glass.

"Oh God, oh God. Oh God, help me! Help me! Oh God, help me!" I'm blind! I can repair lacerations, broken bones, and even some gunshot wounds. Not eyes! There is nothing I can do to save my own eyes! "God, please help me. Please, not this! No, no!" I can't be blind!

I try to sit up and more shards of glass dig into my hands as I choke back a sob. When I finally get my head upright, I feel dizzy and my heart starts pounding in my ears, rivaling the intensity of the ringing. I need to get out of here. Now! Before the Civil Peace Guard shows up, but I can't see.

A firm grip on my left arm shakes me gingerly. There's a voice, but I struggle to hear it over the ringing. "—ear me … Can … Ma'am." The woman's voice begins to clear. "Ma'am, I need you to tell me if you can hear me. Raoul! Shit. I think this one's in shock. She's hurt real bad! We need a helo-drone now!"

"I …" my voice wavers. I feel stinging sensations all over my throat as it moves. "I hear … Help … Please, I can't see."

"I know Ma'am. My name is Lieutenant Brody. I need you to keep your eyes closed. Alright? Your eyes and face are hurt pretty badly, and it's not safe to open them. Do you understand what I'm telling you?"

"For the love of Science!" another female voice yells from my left. "We've got at least three fatalities out there! How far out are the medevac drones!"

"ETA five to seven minutes," a very nasal male voice shouts back.

"Thomas, I need that gauze," Lt. Brody says in a softer tone. "We've gotta get her eye stabilized before then." Another person moves behind me, holding me steady. "Raoul, I need you too."

"No ..." I whimper, terrified of the visceral pain. I try to pull away from her, but the person behind me keeps my head from moving. Someone else wraps their arms around me, gently but firmly holding my arms down.

"Ma'am, try to stay still," the lieutenant says. "I know you're scared, but if you struggle it's only going to hurt worse. It's going to be too hard for you to keep that eye closed. Okay?"

She's right, I know. I try to steel my nerves. I take a long, ragged breath, and whisper, "Okay."

"I'm about to touch your face," she announces.

I can't stop shaking! When her hands make contact with my face, I let out a shriek of terror and a sob. Soft pressure starts to pierce my left eye as I realize they must be applying gauze. She's trying to stabilize the invading glass, exactly like I would, but it feels like the glass is pressing farther in! "It's cutting me!"

"It's okay. Ma'am, It's okay. I can see what is happening, and it's okay. It's very important to stay as still as possible."

She's right, I know. Oh God, help me do this. I clench my teeth and grip my pants legs in tight fists to keep from pulling away. Soon they are wrapping gauze around my head from forehead to nose, and then the others seem to leave us.

"Ma'am," she says and it takes me a minute to bring myself back from the pain enough to respond. "Ma'am, are you still with me?"

"Yes," I whisper.

"I need you to answer some questions for me. Can you do that?"

"Yes," I say again, not wanting to move my head even a millimeter to nod.

"What is your name?"

"My name ..." Is it safe to admit my real name? Should I make something up? I don't want them to know who I am, but my mind is too shattered to think. Susan will tell them my name is Lynneth ...

I'd better tell the truth. If I pass out, the truth is all I will remember.

"Yes, Ma'am, your name," Lt. Brody says, barely audible over the damn ringing.

"Regina Lynneth Mallorey." I wince at the admission.

"Okay, Regina. I'm going to touch your arms now." She applies what feels like a lot more gauze. "Do you have any allergies or physical conditions we should know about?"

"No," I lie. EDS makes all my tissues–bones, tendons, ligaments, muscles, and even blood vessels–more susceptible to injury. If they do a full body survey, the extent of my injuries may seem odd, but plausible in an explosion.

Explosion. That must be what happened. "I ... I saw a flash. Just before ..."

"Yes, Ma'am. It appears that one of our street sweepers was rigged with a bomb, and you were caught in the blast."

"A bomb!" Who would do such a thing? Why? This isn't a military target. It's a highly populated area!

"Do you remember seeing anything before the flash? Anything unusual?" Lt. Brody asks. "Oh shit. Raoul, hand me that trauma bandage, will you? I'm going to touch your leg now, Regina."

"No ... nothing." Then I remember. "My bag. Where's my bag?"

"What does it look like Ma'am?"

"It's a ... backpack ... an autodrive ... backpack." My tongue feels heavy behind my teeth.

"Raoul! How are we lookin' on that medevac?" Lt. Brody shouts.

"It's here!" the nasal male voice responds. "They're bringing in the gurney now."

"Ma'am, I need you to stay with me." Her voice is urgent now. "Regina, do you hear me?"

I do hear her, and I do want to respond, but I feel very, very far away.

"Raoul grab that bag and throw it in!"

"What have we got?" a new high-pitched feminine voice says.

"I've stabilized what I can, but I'm losing her."

My body is being moved around and strapped down to something. More little pinches of pain pop in and out of focus all over as they move me. "Her name is Regina Lynneth Mallorey. The bag is hers and already on the drone. I think she's lost too much blood. She's not responding anymore."

"I'll do what I can in the medevac. They'll have the O.R. prepped before we get there," the new woman responds.

O.R.? I struggle deep beneath my haze. Surgery! I can't pay ...

Somewhere far away I hear the whirring of helo-drone blades and muffled voices. Then nothing.

7

HAWK

I swipe my hand over the scanner as I exit the hyperloop with my duffel bag slung over my right shoulder. The station is crowded from the delays, and I'm swamped by the sight, sounds and scents of hundreds of people as I make quick mental notes of who to keep an eye on in the horde. Fortunately before I arrived, I arranged for my shipment to be transported directly to the local warehouse for storage. I just wish there hadn't been an extra four-hour delay. Every hour that goes by will further contaminate and dilute the scents at the scene.

Three shirkers are working the far end of the platform today from the looks of it—two prostitutes and a silver tech dealer. I've encountered all three when I'm in town, and they're relatively harmless. Two shields are surveying the crowd on the opposite side. I assume it's beefed-up security due to the explosion. The rest of the mass of humanity barely see each other as they move from one point to another with both elites and workers focused on their personal feeds. Nothing suspicious catches my eye.

A casual glance at the gate kiosk confirms that my pendant is working and has altered my CID to display the identity I use for this region. The pendant is a simple two-dimensional representation of an atom on a silver chain. Jared Altrax is the name I go by in most areas on Central Continent, but it's only one of the many names I use.

As an undercover operative, the CPG assigns me around a

dozen alternate identities for easy use that are considered "on the books." Contacts I make in my work often check into false identities. Of course, everyone who works in this field maintains "off the books" options for tight situations and day-to-day shit. Even when interacting with my superiors, the name in my file is never used. Hawk is the simple codename I've been assigned, and I prefer it that way.

"Hey Jared," a familiar feminine voice calls from my right, and I pretend to be surprised by her approach. "It's nice to see you in sector."

I turn to see the tall brunette sauntering toward me in a glittery, pink short-dress and four-inch heels. She's wearing the same perfume she was the last time I saw her. It's always slightly too sweet for the oils in her mocha-colored skin. Giving her a broad smile, I know I've loved the woman before, but I can't remember her name for the life of me. She's one of the shirkers that works the station. I may never get why some people actually choose that life when they could have it so much better by joining the Community and contributing. "Yeah, work's kept me pretty busy."

"That sounds awfully lonely," she says in a sultry voice, feeding me her line as she runs her fingers up my chest. "Need some company while you're here?"

Sure. Why not? I'll also find out what you've seen and heard passing through. "You know I don't share my bed," I say with a raised eyebrow.

"A girl can always dream," she says with a playful grin.

Women do share my bed, technically, they're just not allowed to sleep in it. It would give her a safer place to sleep for the night, but I don't take that risk. Not ever. I'll get what I need, pay her for her time, and send her on her way after some good food and a shower.

"You're welcome to drop by around eight though." I hand her a speed dial disk. "If you're not too busy by then."

"Never too busy for you," she beams, then wanders off into the crowd.

The gigantic information screens above the heads of all the travelers list out the various arrival and departure times of the hyperloop trains and autobuses. It's filled with red, like the faces of most of the commuters. I check the time and decide to catch the next autobus to the rendezvous point. Once I check in with Roland, I can head to the blast site.

8

GINA

Slowly, I drift into awareness. It's as if my soul is floating outside of my body somehow. I know that I should feel pain, but I feel almost nothing. Every muscle and bone in my body feels heavy. I don't smell smoke anymore, but the sharp odor of antiseptics blended with some kind of artificially sweet, flowery fragrance. I manage to lift my hand enough to touch my face. Gauze is wrapped around my head, but it must be new because the glass is gone.

"Good morning," a gentle male voice says from beside me.

I startle with a gasp. I thought I was alone. Who is he? Where am I? My arms start to tremble. A steady beep beside me accelerates.

"There's no need to be afraid," he says softly. "You're safe now. Can you tell me your name?"

"Uh, Gina," I croak.

"Okay, Gina. My name is Khaled. I'm your post-op nurse. I will be monitoring you for a few hours. Can you tell me your full name? Why don't you spell it for me too. If you can."

Did I tell them my full name? "Regina Lynneth Mallorey." As I spell my name for him, my heart races faster.

"Here … I'll give you something to help you stay calm."

"No." I don't want it. I need my wits about me, but I hear Khaled already moving and my limbs feel heavy. In a moment I feel an odd warmth wash through my body and my panic begins to seem silly and unimportant.

"You are perfectly safe. I'm going to touch your hands for a moment, Gina."

"Okay," I mumble, feeling a warm buzz grow in my head.

Warmer hands slide inside mine. "Squeeze my hands as hard as you can."

I give it my best shot, but it feels pathetically weak. My hands release on their own after only a couple of seconds.

"Very good. Can you remember the date?"

"June 16, 2253," I mumble as the beeping of my heart monitor begins to slow again.

"That's right. Do you know where you are?"

"No."

"You were brought to Hospital J for treatment after you were injured. Do you remember being injured?"

"Mmmm …" I try to focus on the question. He has so many of them. "Sort of."

"That's all right," he says in that same steady tone. "You were brought here after an unfortunate incident in District J. There was an explosion and you sustained multiple injuries. You were taken straight into surgery. What you are feeling now is the effects of anesthesia. You may feel disoriented, but you will slowly become more alert."

"What did they do?" Why does the question seem more frightening than it feels?

"You had several deep lacerations, or cuts, to your arms, legs, neck, and head," Khaled says. "The most serious was a piece of glass embedded in your left thigh which nicked an artery. Surgery was necessary to remove it without damaging the artery further, or the other vessels nearby. There was also a large glass splinter embedded in your left eye, and several glass fragments caught in the soft tissue of both eyes. The doctor will explain more about that.

"You don't need to worry about the lacerations. The cosmetic surgeons work wonders these days. You shouldn't have any scarring to speak of.

"We reset a few subluxations of your joints that were caused by the impact, and you have severe bruising on much of your body. Frankly, a bit more than we expected, but that can happen in these situations. The doctors noted some scarring from old injuries to your joints, some of which have degraded into early arthritis, which though unusual in someone so young, is easily attributed to exposure to violence outside of the safety of the Community. Currently, you've been given a blood transfusion and are receiving medications to help speed up the healing process."

"Why?" I point to the bandage still covering my eyes.

"I will leave that to Dr. Levinson to explain. I'll alert him that you're awake and have questions. I'm sure he will be in shortly. Is there anything else you need?"

"No." I let myself drift back to sleep.

9

HAWK

The park, which was the focal point of the explosion, sits right between the University in District J and the more affluent District A where many elites live. Eyes hidden behind sunglasses, I survey the hole and scorched earth. People skirt around the area as if afraid they can still be harmed within the black. Even the birds and voles hesitate to pass through it. In the open air, the smell of burnt organics and flesh is suffocating, but I can't detect any scent of the explosives or accelerants the squids favor. Weird.

The file I was given before arriving says the explosion originated inside a large maintenance bot. The huge piece of art that once stood here is unrecoverable. Scalable true-depth images of the scene were digitized and the debris was swept up by CPG bots almost immediately. The debris is undergoing analysis to detect the bomb materials used and ensure there aren't any unexploded munitions. From the focused nature of the blast, I doubt it.

There is damage to a few of the surrounding storefronts, but most of it is superficial, and no damage to critical systems has been reported. Looking for other possible targets, there's nothing near the blast zone but shops and food to draw in the University kids. "Doesn't make much sense," I mumble.

"Is terrorism supposed to make sense to you, Hawk?" Roland's voice scoffs through my GRID connection. His unpleasant balding image scowls in a small square in the upper-right corner of my field of vision.

Hack. His pompous attitude grates against my nerves. Arrogant and foolish, he barely pays attention to what I say, despite my skills and field experience.

"If you think we have a terrorist cell other than the squids, then no." Being careful to look like a curious passer-by, after wandering aimlessly around the crater, I'm leaning back against the remaining park bench at the edge of the destruction. "You asked me to look for a squid connection, but I don't see one."

"It's there. You're just not looking hard enough."

Yeah, sure. Through my many aliases, I've gotten to know plenty of squids around the globe. They're a bunch of zealots and troublemakers, and can be hacking destructive if they choose to be. They're smart though. They don't waste resources. I've never seen squids do damage without an objective. Either this wasn't them, or there was a target I can't uncover sitting here. "How many people were caught in the blast?" I fake a yawn. "Anyone important?"

"Didn't look that way. Four people were killed. A University student, a maintenance technician, an epidemiologist, and a CPG lawyer. Six others were injured to various degrees. Mostly locals and one … that's weird."

Instead of asking, I wait for Roland to bother getting around to giving me the important information.

"One shirker, straight out of the Dregs. Think she was involved?" he asks.

Interesting. "Did we get a statement from her?"

"File says she claimed to be meeting up with a friend. Said the friend was the University student. You can see them meet in the vid."

"I'll look. Doubt she had anything to do with it, though." A shirker with a student was likely a low-level tech exchange. Turned out to be an unfortunate choice of location. Ouch. "Look into the scientist and the lawyer."

"What would they have to do with it?"

"Whoever was responsible, the target was obviously a person. Not a structure." You idiot. "You have any goods for me?"

"Of course," he sighs, "but you still haven't given me any useful information."

Nothing useful? You're such a prick.

"If I manage to find any, you'll be the first to know. We're missing something. This is completely senseless. Squids always have a target, usually infrastructure. It doesn't make any sense unless your dead have some dirty secrets."

"Well it's already been declared an attack by the squids. So, unless you find anything to say otherwise, that's what it's gonna be."

Hack, like declaring it makes it true. "Suit yourself, but don't be surprised if this pisses them off."

10

GINA

A warm hand on my arm wakes me gently. "Gina," the nurse says. "Dr. Levinson is here."

"Oh." I try to sit up and the bed beneath me begins to fold itself to provide me assistance. I'm less loopy than I was when the nurse first gave me whatever that calming crap was, but I'm still muddled.

"Well," a new brisk male voice says, along with the sound of someone rubbing their hands together. "How is our mystery patient doing?"

"Huh?" I can't stand not being able to see him.

"We have your name," the doctor says, "but can find no record of you within the GRID. I also noted there was no GRID inoculation scar on your neck. Should I take that to mean you are …"

"A shirker?" I try to spit out, but it comes out as soft as a whisper through my haze.

"I was going to say, 'disconnected,'" he says, sounding pompously politically correct. "But yes. I have to admit I was surprised you were even in District J to be caught in the explosion."

"I was visiting a friend." The cams recorded my meeting. That's what I had planned it to look like.

"Yes, well I'm very sorry about that," he says with real sympathy in his voice.

"Sorry about what?"

"Your friend, Susan I believe, was killed in the explosion."

"Sh … She what!" My heart monitor goes wild again. She was so young! She hadn't even been outside the confines of the University yet! Oh, God, why would you let that happen?

"Shh …" I feel a solid hand on my shoulder, and hear the gentle nurse's voice. "You need to remain calm, Miss. I know it's difficult, and I'm sorry, but I need you to focus on your own health right now."

"Okay …" I whisper.

"We repaired your life-threatening injuries as is required by the Life First Act," the doctor says. "We also elected to take care of your simple cosmetic injuries, as there is no need to make you bear unnecessary scars from this unfortunate event for such a minimal expense. However, your eyes present a problem."

Dread begins to suffocate me, and I barely manage a response. "What about them?"

"The damage to both eyes is extensive. The cornea of your right eye is gouged enough to obscure your vision if left to heal on its own, but the damage to the left eye will unquestionably leave you blind on that side. There are procedures that can be done to correct these injuries if done immediately, but they are extremely expensive."

These doctors know I have no means to pay for anything. His declaration hangs in the air like a machete waiting to drop on my neck. "What are you saying?"

"I'm attempting to present you with your options," he says with an impatient sigh. "I don't know why you've elected to live without GRID access and comforts for this long, but I assure you … you can have a far superior quality of life within the Community. We could inoculate you, and you could repay the cost of the necessary procedure over time through deductions from your weekly wages."

I struggle to breathe. My grandfather told my dad that his ancestors had seen the earliest versions of the programming running the GRID, and opted-out of inclusion in the program. Opting out was highly discouraged, as it is still, but was not outright illegal due to concerns over civil rights. "If I refuse?"

"Then you will be severely disabled. You'll require assistive services that can't be provided without proper contribution to those supporting you. Do you live with another individual in this sector?"

"No," I admit, not wanting to be too specific. "Nothing permanent."

"Then, as your doctor, I cannot release you with such a substantial permanent disability and assure your safety. Your life would be seriously endangered. If you insist on remaining disconnected, I'm afraid I'll have to assign you to an institution."

Institution.

The word stills every cell in my body. Oh Jesus, no. I never imagined I could end up with a disability more severe than my EDS! If I'm admitted to one of those places, I'll be powerless and alone forever.

"Is that what you want?" he asks.

God, help me. What should I do? I think of Mom and her dire warnings to stay away from the Community or I'd end up in an institution, a place she equated with the worst possible fate. I'm caught Mom. I can't escape.

I remember Dad holding me, just holding me, after I'd seen a man beaten to death in the street outside our burrow. "Remember Sweetheart," he'd said. "Whether Mom and I are with you or not, you are never alone no matter what happens. God stays with His people and helps them."

"Ma'am, is that what you want?" I hear the exasperation in his voice.

"What happens if I agree to ... to let you do it?" I swallow down the lump in my throat as I consider betraying my parents, my brothers, everything I've ever known.

"Well, that's simple," he says much more brightly. "The inoculation would take place first, so we can adequately record you in our systems and care for you properly, you understand. That way, during your procedure and recovery, your wetware connection can also begin forming.

"Next we would begin the regeneration process for your eyes. We would attach the bio-womb—"

"Bio-womb?"

"Yes, it is essential for the regeneration of bodily tissues," he says as if it's obvious. "The surfaces of your eyes are already sufficiently raw to stimulate the process of regrowth. The womb will be like a pair of goggles, filled with an amniotic-fluid-like substance with all the necessary medications incorporated. The process would be too strange to endure consciously, as you will not be able to close your eyes for several days while they are held in the bio-womb solution, so you will be sedated. Then the bio-womb will be removed and your eyes will regrow all the necessary tissues by following the instructions we provide through bioelectric stimuli. It's very reliable technology. We've done it for decades now."

"How much of my vision will come back?" I'll need to see to escape.

"Well, all of it, of course. Best of all, because it is your own body growing the tissues from your original genetic blueprint, your eye color will be preserved." He chuckles. "I noted that no transplant would likely match. Your original color is quite unique."

"Thanks." I mutter.

He's right. I've never seen eyes like mine. I would trade them now for a way to escape.

"Well then," he says, and I'm glad I can't see his smug expression. "If that's all settled, I will have Khaled walk you through the necessary release forms and agreements. Once he inoculates you, we can get started."

I nod, not knowing what else to do, and listen to them shuffle out of the room. I sit in total darkness, knowing I've lost the battle for the rest of my life. In a single moment. I've lost everything I've worked so hard to preserve. I will be forced into slave-labor for the GRID. Like Mom said, they're likely to discover my EDS, so I may end up in an institution anyway.

Inside my mind I wail from the emotional rawness of this

disaster as I rock back and forth on the bed. My mouth, however, makes no sound. Only my fear of this place, the hospital, the all-powerful Community, keeps me silent.

God, I don't understand. Where the hell were you? Why did you let this happen? You already took Mom and Dad. Did you already take Drustan and Arthur too?

Anger and betrayal swirl noxiously in the pit of my stomach. I try breathing slowly and deeply, the way Mom taught me to calm myself down, desperately hoping Khaled will fail to return. If they forget about me for a while, get too busy with another emergency perhaps, maybe I can find my way out.

Involuntarily, I try opening my eyes and the pain and truth slams me as hard as the blast that sentenced me here. I can't even see the door! I want to scream for help, but only the wrong kind of help would come.

Realizing I must regain control, I consciously slow my breathing again—counting one, two, three in—one, two, three out. My mind casts desperately about for something positive to focus on. The procedure makes sense, I think, and in some ways is practical. At least if I wind up institutionalized, I won't be trying to escape blind.

Institutionalized!

I hear someone quietly step back inside my room, and sit beside the edge of my bed. I freeze.

"May I take your hand?" Khaled's soft voice asks.

"I guess."

A warm hand practically envelopes mine. The gesture is comforting and painful at the same time. "I'm sorry they're not giving you more options."

"Oh ... I didn't expect a Community member to understand."

"I've met several disconnected people in my line of work," he says in his calming tone. "I know that you all have your reasons, or you would never live that way. I also know most of you are very frightened. I'm not sure what you're frightened of, but I could see you tremble when he talked about the institution. That was difficult."

"Yeah."

"Doctors tend to have their minds focused on treatment options. My job as a nurse is to focus on you. He means well, though," Khaled assures me, "and he's right that we would be risking your life releasing you blind into the Dregs."

"How long … will it take to pay?"

"Well, that depends on your aptitude tests. At first, you'll be assigned server duty. Assuming you remain in that capacity, which is common and a critical contribution, it will take a couple of years to pay off in smaller increments. Don't worry. They won't take all of your pay. You'll still have income to live off of."

"Will it hurt? The inoculation, I mean."

"It can cause a mild to severe headache," Khaled says. "We can give you something for the pain. Afterward, you will need to be sedated for the regrowth procedure."

"I guess I should get it over with."

"I have everything with me if you're ready." He begins reading me the forms I would normally have to read myself—or that my birth mother would have read in most cases, since the procedure is usually done in infancy. It's an endless droning on of technical and legal jargon, and I struggle to pay attention with my too-recently-sedated brain. I do notice that it goes into a considerable detail pointing out that the information my brain may be used to process is confidential, and the legal rights to that information remain with the Community or the individual processing the information through the GRID. I will remember none of the information I process after being disconnected from a server bank, and I'm responsible for reporting any anomaly I might experience. I also waive any liability should I have an adverse reaction to the wetware growth process or the numerous vaccinations included in the inoculation.

Yes, as if I actually have a choice.

"Alright," Khaled finally says, sounding as tired of reading as I am of listening. "When I say the word "sign," I need you to speak your full name clearly. It will be recorded as your official signature and applied to all the relevant files we just read through. Ready and … sign."

"Regina Lynneth Mallorey," I say as clearly as I can. My heart kicks up its pace and my stomach heaves.

I hear a soft play-back of my recorded voice just before Khaled says, "Great! Now I'm going to touch the back of your neck and get everything ready, so don't be alarmed."

Sure … One, two, three in—one, two, three out.

Khaled lifts my hair out of the way and pins it back against the side of my head just before something cold and wet swipes along the back of my neck. Then a cool circle, which feels enormous although I know it's not much more than an inch wide, is pressed against my skin. "Alright, this is going to sting for just a moment."

The pain is sharp and then burns strongly but briefly. As the sensation fades, I realize there must be an analgesic incorporated. I feel the muscles of my neck responding in objection, but there isn't much more pain to speak of. Then, in seconds, the pressure of the circle is gone.

"How was that?" Khaled asks. "Everything alright?"

"I don't have to do that again, do I?"

"No. It's all included in the single dose. I don't have to administer it very often, but I've heard it can be unsettling."

Suddenly, a sharp headache begins to build at the base of my skull. "Ouch." I wince, reaching up to rub at the pain.

"Oh, okay," he says almost to himself as he sits the head of the bed up and presses gently against my shoulder until I lie back against it. "It looks like it's working pretty fast. I'm going to keep you upright instead of flat, to lessen the pressure in your head. I'll also adjust your pain medication. Is that better?"

"A little." I groan as the pain begins spreading up behind my eyes.

"I would give you something to help you sleep, but it looks like they're ready to start the procedure for your eyes already," Khaled says, as I hear a mild commotion in the room.

"Alright Miss Mallorey," a man with a deep base drawl says from my right side. "We're here to grow you some brand new eyes. How does that sound?"

"Where do you want this?" a feminine voice whispers from somewhere on my left.

The new man mumbles, "Yeah, put that up here where I can

reach it real easy. Let's get the medication working for her."

"My head hurts." I whimper at the thought of them removing the bandages while I'm already hurting.

"Hurts?" he asks.

"She just received her GRID inoculation a moment ago," Khaled says. "It seems to be working fairly fast."

"Oh, that's right. She was disconnected. Alright. Well, Miss Mallorey, my name is Doctor Carter. I know your head is hurting a bit right now, but that's normal, and it won't affect the other procedure we're going to do for your eyes. In fact, we're starting a medicine right now that will help you help us get your eyes set-up in the bio-womb the way we're going to need them to stay. You won't remember having to help us with that, because it would be unpleasant. The whole time your eyes are regrowing, we'll keep you sedated. Later, you'll wake up and the procedure will be over. So, by that time, this discomfort you're having with the inoculation will be over also. Okay?"

"Okay," I say with a quaver.

"Alright, I need you to count backward from ten for me," Dr. Carter says.

"Ten," I start, trying to calm myself. "Nine … eight … seve—"

11

HAWK

The lawyer enters the park twenty-five seconds before the sweeper detonates. The scientist at the outdoor table next to the sweeper takes his last bite of sandwich exactly three seconds before. The poor University kid is actually walking toward it, to throw something away.

The only other person near the blast is the shirker woman, who's already reaching the edge of the park. She's leaving, but not hurrying like she knows she's about to be blown into next week. She's careful to keep her face oblique to the 3D surveillance, except during her performance at the park, but it was easy enough for

Swaine's facial recognition to inform me she's no one of interest. I hope they did a decent job of putting that beautiful face back together. Her picture from the hospital was never updated once her face was no longer a bloody, gauze-covered mess.

No matter how many times I watch the vid, I've learned all I can from it. None of them were expecting an explosion, or even trouble. The University kid was the only nervous one—obviously inexperienced at sneaking around.

Everything we have is a hacking dead end.

I dial Roland again and listen to it ring. This is hacking useless! I've tried calling the man three times today with no hacking response. He treats me like a common street shield. I ought to teach him the difference. If Darius got ahold of him he'd shit his pants, and he'd never know Scott was there before—

"What in the name of Science do you want? I have urgent public information reports to draft." Roland barks through the secure vid line with a scowl.

"To do my job." You hack! "Which I can't do without talking to you."

Roland finally sets aside his flex. "What have you found out?"

"I was right. No chemicals or blasting caps or normal squid munitions. There's nothing."

"I know. The debris analysis said the sweeper's systems were rigged to overload and explode when triggered by some new form of power cell."

"And you didn't bother to send me that information?"

"Why should I? You're collecting information for me. Not the other way around."

I squeeze my fists to keep from punching his face in the mirror. "Do you have any additional information on the people involved?"

"The scientist and the lawyer are dead ends."

"What kind of dead ends?"

"The lawyer is a services placement negotiator for injured CPG officers. His life is an open book. The scientist is as boring as nuclear physics. He was working on the vaccine project for the virus that's sweeping through shirker camps, an open-book project. He was also completely OCD. He's had breakfast, lunch and dinner in the same places for the last five years since he moved into the sector. He was eating a plain, bologna sandwich when he blew up—like he did every day."

Shit. Nothing about this entire thing makes any sense. "Maybe the target got away before it blew."

"Well to everyone else, it's obvious squid terrorism. Making the public feel unsafe in their own sectors. We're watching the shirker woman to see if she's the squid connection."

"Did you see something in the vid?"

"It's being analyzed. So far, it seems your hunch was good. I'm being told it looks like a standard low-level trade, but there could be more to it."

"The shirker is a waste of time. They wouldn't have their own contact nearly killed. Besides, the squids use standard set ups for explosives to keep the dealers happy. Unless they have someone new at the helm, rigging a sweeper's systems is not their M.O."

"What? Do you have information about a new faction or something?"

"No. I'm just saying it doesn't add up."

"Well, if it wasn't them, just who in Tesla's name was it?"

"I'm still looking."

"Exactly. So stop wasting my time." Roland cuts the connection and I let out the faintest of growls at my reflection in the mirror. I swear, if he was anyone else's handler, the man would be dead already. I've spent days scouting the area, following scent trails, listening in on street talk, and pouring over the evidence from the bomb scene, and he's not even interested in hearing what I've learned.

It doesn't matter. I'd do it anyway. On the streets, information can mean life or death for me and my charges. I'll know whatever can be known before I move on.

Closing my eyes for a moment to tighten my boots, I decide to head for District J to follow my nose. Maybe I'll turn up something useful.

12

I slowly become aware of a rough sheet beneath me and begin moving the pads of my fingers along it. The beeps and whirs around me are disorienting, until I remember I'm in the hospital. Reaching up to my face, I'm surprised to feel nothing on it. No bandages. No strange bio-womb. Only my skin.

I gently touch my eyelids and am surprised to feel no pain or scar tissue. I open them and …

Everything is so bright! I throw my hands back over my eyes to protect them.

"Ah … good morning, Miss." I hear Khaled's familiar voice.

I peek out and try to focus on his voice, but it's coming from the body of a strange man. He is very short and broad, with olive skin, gray hair, and thick black and gray eyebrows over brown eyes. For some reason, I'd imagined him thinner and with dark skin. Is that really him?

"It looks like your new eyes are a little sensitive. That's to be expected. There's a lot of new tissue that hasn't been used before."

"It's too bright." I groan.

"Oh, I can dim the lights," he says cheerily. He closes his eyes and the lights dim steadily until he asks, "How's that?"

"Better."

My hospital room has just enough space for someone to move around the bed, with a small hand-sterilization station in the corner of the room. There's no additional seating. All the monitors are attached to a single panel on the wall above my bed, which appears to be several generations newer than the one I have back home. It would be awesome to get my hands on one of these. At least, it would have been.

"How long have I been asleep?"

"You've been sedated for two weeks." He moves toward me to check the placement of a monitor lead on my skin.

"Two weeks?" I squint, trying to get my vision to clear so I can read the screens.

"Yes. They've managed to accelerate cellular growth over the years, but there are still limitations to growing viable human tissue. Are your eyes causing you any pain?"

"No." I try to take in the details of the room for the first time. "But it's hard to focus on anything."

"That's typical," Khaled says, stilling his activity for a moment. "The tissue is brand new, and should be functional, but your brain still has to grow some of the neural pathways needed to receive information accurately. You will be given some vision therapy exercises to complete over the next two weeks which should help that process along.

"Speaking of which, I would like to introduce you to your new life companion. She will be helping you with those exercises."

"My what?"

"Every citizen is assisted in daily activity by a fully customizable AI. As soon as you are ready, she will begin by helping you through the integration process, now that you've joined the Community."

"Oh, right." I've heard random people talk to Manuela hundreds of times, but she's not something I can normally see. "Is my GRID connection already grown then?"

"Not completely, no, but you will be placed in quarters like these, designed to help you interact with her without the GRID. Does she have your permission to enter?"

Right. "Does she need it?"

"Of course."

"Fine, I guess. She can come in."

"Good afternoon, Regina." A pleasant alto voice resounds in the room the instant before a smiling woman appears out of thin air. "My name is Manuela."

"I know. I mean, I've heard of you." Ugh. There's a tremor in my voice.

Interesting. They have her dressed like the lowest class—in the white t-shirt and blue jeans I see many citizens wearing. I wonder if that's supposed to be welcoming? She has bronze skin and black hair, also matching the majority of the population. She's neither too slender nor too heavy. She's designed to be average in just about every way.

"Yes." Manuela nods, tilting her head to the side slightly, like a human would do if wondering something. "But you can customize my name, voice, and appearance to whatever you prefer."

"I don't care what you look like." But God, just having her in the same room freaks me out. I glance over at Khaled, but he gives me a smiling thumbs up and slips out of the room.

"You don't need to be frightened," Manuela says. She makes a small show of taking a step back.

"I'm not," I reply automatically. She's monitoring you, stupid.

"Your vital signs indicate—"

"That I'm crazy stressed out." I pull a plausible excuse out of the air. Survival on the streets has taught me never to appear intimidated. "They just regrew my eyeballs for G-goodness sake. I didn't exactly plan this."

"Of course." The AI nods with a program-perfect but somehow kind smile. "The integration process can be very unsettling for many new citizens, but I am designed to be your life companion, and I would very much like to aid you in that journey. You will be placed into a housing unit which, like this room, is built specifically for your transition. The Global Fellowship does not wish for you to be deprived of the services the GRID can offer while you wait for your connection to grow."

"Like the projectors in here?" I can't see them, but they shouldn't be able to project anything into my mind just yet.

"Correct."

"Okay." I sigh and lean back against the bed. "Why don't you tell me what the next steps are." Then I can figure out how the hell to escape.

13
GINA

Entering my hub for the first time, I experience a strange, unsettling combination of awe and horror. Compared to anything in the elite district, I'm sure the living space is adequate at best. Compared to my own little home—which I'm very proud of—I'm going to be living like the snobs.

It takes me a moment to navigate closing the door around my walker. Enabling the lock, I'm disturbed by the fact that there is only one and it's a GRIDlock. So much for security. Thankfully the curtains are still drawn even though the overhead lights came on when I entered.

A quick glance around the hub convinces me that the room is empty, but I'm frustrated by my continued inability to focus. Fortunately, the doctors expected my new eyes to throw off my sense of balance and assigned me a walker for the next few days. I may have needed it for my eyes, but I need it for my EDS even more. Much of the pain I expected is absent because of the medications I'm on and the extended healing time I was given, but every joint in my body feels twice as unstable as normal. It feels as if my hips, knees, and back are perilously close to slipping out of joint with every movement. The walker is a blessing that hides my instabilities nicely as I blame my stumbling on balance from my new eyes. Maneuvering a walker through the narrow spaces of this hub, however, is going to get interesting.

The first thing I do is hobble over to the sink in the little kitchenette and turn the faucet on. No more descending three floors for running water! The kitchenette is a small corner of the main room with a mini fridge, small multi-mode cooking enclosure, tiny counter top and sink. I turn the faucet on and off again several times before I realize I don't know whether I have to pay for utilities. I turn the water off and decide to leave it alone for now.

"Is the water pressure adequate for your taste?"

Whirling around, I barely manage not to shriek. "You scared me to death!"

"My apologies." Manuela casts her eyes to the ground. "I believed you understood I would accompany you here."

"Yes, but I'm not used to people just appearing out of thin air! Don't citizens ever want to be alone?"

Getting out of the hospital had been enough of a nightmare. I think they intentionally overwhelm you with so much to read that you won't read any of it. My new eyes were not experienced enough yet, so, I insisted that Manuela read it all aloud to me, as

Khaled had done before. It had taken hours.

"Yes. Most citizens give me instructions to follow so I know when I am wanted or needed." Her projection walks over and leans casually against the opposing wall.

Best news I've heard all day. "Can I specify what you observe and what you don't?"

"Of course." She nods. "Most citizens prefer that I engage their personal Do Not Disturb protocols during love, for example."

Oh, ick. "Okay. How do I set them up?"

"I can answer that, but I would prefer to ensure that you are fully acquainted with the premises before you engage any of those protocols, given your current physical state."

Of course you would.

The hub is almost entirely one room, with a small bathroom and a hallway to the front door. I leave my walker in the kitchenette and keep my hands on the walls or furniture for stability as I explore. There is a single full-sized bed with adjustable firmness, and a small nightstand with a single drawer and cabinet door. A minimally cushioned, ergonomically correct rolling chair sits in front of a narrow desk next to the bed. Across from the foot of the bed is a padded chair, small table and short four-drawer dresser with an expansive mirror above it. Manuela shadows my every move.

"This is your primary media display." She points to the mirror. "It will be highly valuable during your transition period because I will be able to display information for you. Later, that same information will be seen through your GRIDlink, but you can choose to use a glass surface such as this one whenever you prefer."

Manuela pulls up the media options. There is a feature for reviewing the layout and emergency escape plans for the room. I can access all 5,000 global channels. I shudder when I realize that the mirror is also undoubtedly a two-way communication system because there is an option to make a call listed in the lower-right corner. I search for anything that would show me where the cam origin is, but it's completely integrated within the mirror itself. Worse yet, the mirror is part of the wall, with no useful corners. I won't be able to hang a sheet over it without using nails, or tacks, or something.

"What are you looking for?"

"Are there cams in here?" Let's see if she tells me the truth.

"Yes. The mirror itself is a cam. So is the one in the bathroom. I also have a 3D viewing system that I use to see you in the same way that you see me, but that system is regulated by the Do Not Disturb protocols."

Oh, freaking … "Great." There's no safe place to change clothes! I move away from the mirror to put it out of mind until I can find a solution.

In the hallway, there is a small built-in closet with enough room to hang some outfits and a few small built-in drawers which appear to be designed for shoes. I was given a standard clothing ration at the hospital. Manuela said that each item can be replaced at any time, at no cost, as long as I bring back the damaged original to be recycled. I begin putting my rations away on the metal hangers—like a good little Community zombie.

"Are you in physical or emotional pain?"

I pause for a moment. She can undoubtedly sense that my body is stressed, but I don't want to take any risks that would lead her to decide something more is wrong with me. "Of course, I am. I don't belong here."

"Your statement is untrue. All human beings belong to Earth and therefore belong as citizens of the Global Fellowship and Community of mankind. This transition may be difficult for you, but I believe you will grow to love the Community and all it has to offer."

The clothes put away, I decide to explore the bathroom. The other mirror is above a countertop, drawer, and cabinet—all barely as wide as me. The sink is built over the toilet tank. If you flush the toilet, the sink automatically runs to wash your hands and fill the toilet tank with the drain water. God, that's cool. The bathtub is just large enough to sit in with your knees bent most of the way. I haven't even seen a functional tub in years.

I hobble back to the hall closet to grab my bag of hygiene provisions. Like the clothing ration, Manuela said these supplies are available for free if you don't buy the more expensive items from the commissary. So, in theory, even a non-contributing Community member could survive with their basic hygiene and clothing needs met. They would just have to live the life of a minimalist, or a shirker rewarded for being traceable by CID.

"Manuela, do I have to pay for the water?" Even though I know she's just a program, it's easier to call her by name.

"No. All utilities are provided at no cost."

Excited by the thought of hot water soothing my aching joints, I throw caution to the wind and fill up my bathtub with water as hot as I can stand. I grab my miniature bath soap, ready to climb up onto the toilet to smear the mirror with a thick film.

I wish I knew whether I'll be able to maintain this. After a lifetime of Mom's warnings, the risk of my EDS being discovered seems dangerously high. It doesn't make sense though to try and slip away while I'm the focus of so much attention—maybe after I've paid back my debt. I'll just have to figure out how to ditch Manuela, and first, I've got to check in with Tommy.

"Manuela? Why don't we talk about those Do Not Disturb protocols now."

14

GINA

The second I walk into the bar, Tommy pins me with the steady gaze of his narrowed, black eyes, with arms crossed over his broad chest. His black light armband tattoos match his glow-in-the-dark earring, contrasting sharply with his ebony skin. He never feels the need to dress above his patrons, sticking with the ration t-shirts and jeans—only occasionally swapping in a t-shirt with color. He's well suited to his role as a bartender, reaching an amazing height of six feet seven inches, but I won't be intimidated. It helps that I'm having trouble keeping him in focus in the dim light.

"Oh, gracing us with your presence today?" He tosses his cleaning rag down on the black, smart-glass bar top, but his gaze softens when he sees my walker. "I thought ya skipped town without notice. Almost gave your job away."

"I can explain." I hold a hand up in surrender.

"Oh, really? This ought to be good. Did ya fall in one of those recycling heaps you're always diving in?"

"No. Way, way worse actually." I spin around and raise my hair up off my neck to display my new GRID scar.

Tommy sucks in a breath, and when I turn back around his eyes are wide. He just stands there and stares at me with the bar's mood lighting dancing across his skin.

"Satisfied?" I wheel my walker up to the bar. Thankfully, the place is fairly empty at this time of day.

To my surprise, he grabs a large knife from under the bar and rests it beneath his palm, before shaking his head in denial.

"Oh for God's sake, Tommy." I slide onto one of the black, high-backed, fake leather bar stools. "I'm not under mind control. I got screwed and I had no way out."

"What happened?" He doesn't move his hand from the knife.

"Did you hear about the explosion in District J?"

"Yeah. It was all over sector news. Hack, it was on the global news."

"I got caught in the blast." I rest my chin on my fist. "I was trading with a University kid. Guess I'm lucky I'm here because she was killed. I came close myself. Got blown through a glass window at one of those fancy stores and then hauled off to the hospital."

Tommy puts the knife away and scrutinizes me closely—crossing his arms over his chest again. "Girl, you look pretty good for someone who got caught in that mess."

"Well, looks can be deceiving. They saved my life, and prettied me up, but my eyes cost me my freedom. They wouldn't regrow them unless I agreed to become a Community member. It took them two weeks to do it. I swear, Tommy, this is my first day out of the hospital."

"No shit …" Tommy brushes his fingertips across my cheekbones and inspects my eyes. "They do look different. I'd be hard pressed to say how though. Maybe it's the pattern." He straightens back up and rests his palms back on the bar top. "You were so good at that life. I never thought they'd find a way to get to ya."

"They were going to put me in an institution," I whisper, trying and failing to focus on the menu screens above his head.

"Well, ya made the right choice then. Tell you what. I'll grab your usual. On the house this time. In fact, I'll bring you a double."

"Thanks." My usual is a kick-you-in-the-face-sweet strawberry smoothie with around three shots of moonshine.

Bartenders are one of the rare Community jobs that aren't completely automated. They're in charge of keeping all the equipment running, of course, but the bigger reason the occupation has been left intact is social. People never stop needing someone to talk to and many people hate therapists.

Some of today's moonshiners pass down their knowledge to an apprentice—if it seems like that apprentice won't do something stupid and get them reported. Tommy's birth mother managed to pass the knowledge to him because the Community is more forgiving of a birth mother checking where her son ended up. Still, she didn't approach him until he'd left the University.

Tommy is the main reason I work at this bar. My tech deals garner most my supplies, but in exchange for my singing, he's always given me enough real food and booze to get by. Since I live with a pain condition, the booze has proved more essential than the food.

"Here you go, Sweetheart." He sets the smoothie down in front of me with a kind smile. "I know it's hard right now, girl, but you should look at the bright side of all this. I could actually pay ya coin from now on if you want. And ya never know. You could find out there was no reason for all your worries. You may be different but ya far from disabled."

"On my good days." I shrug as I sip my smoothie. "They'll never let me have kids though."

It isn't common for the Community to allow women to have children in the first place. The lottery system leans heavily toward the elite because the qualifications are ridiculously complex. It's not openly acknowledged, but most people realize that individuals with a genetic abnormality or disability who do manage to jump through all the hoops never get selected. Even if I was allowed to have a baby, I'd only be allowed to have them for two years, and then I'd be expected to turn them over to the University.

I want a life like my parents had—free to raise my own children however I wish. I toy with the silver cross on my necklace, thankful to have gotten my tattered bag back from the hospital staff with it still inside.

"Well, that's true," Tommy says. "But ya gotta think about what's good for ya. Babies are a burden. You know that."

"I think right now, sticking to our current payment system is best for me." I veer the conversation back to safer territory. "I still don't want my job here in any official records. I don't trust anything, and I definitely still need my drinks."

"Did the hospital give ya any pain meds?"

"Yeah, but they won't last long and they're not the right kind for a bad flare up." Most of the pain I struggle with comes from my nervous system, not my tissues. "What they gave me was for healing from the accident. This is still better."

"Alright," he says with a wide grin. "Ya let me know if you ever want it changed. Have ya settled into your new place yet? Where is it?"

"I'm in District T. Not far from here."

"No shit? Which building?"

"Building twenty-three."

"Well, I'll be." Tommy laughs. "Same block as me. I can walk ya home after we close if ya want."

"Sure. I'm not so good with these new eyes yet."

15

HAWK

When I hear someone quietly open the building entrance downstairs, I close my eyes and pull up the vid feed from the hotel's hall cams. I tuck my pistol between the overstuffed couch cushions beside me. I have another one in the holster at my ankle, and set my best field knife down within easy reach on the end table. I wait for her to knock before giving the command for the door to open.

"H-h-hello?" Her voice sounds more like a little girl than a woman of nearly forty.

"Come on in." I sit back with a wide smile, hoping to relax her.

"Are, are you sure?"

"That's why I opened the door. If you really need my help, come on in. There's surveillance."

In a flash, the short, olive-skinned scientist scurries into the room. Her black hair is pulled into a tight bun behind her head with a single plain black clip. The black slacks, cream-colored blouse, and short heels are a bit fancy for this part of town. Her emerald earrings must be CID jammers and she keeps stopping herself from touching them. She's acting more nervous than the poor University kid, but she works in the same department as our dead scientist. I made sure Jared's contacts got to everyone there, to see if a nibble would give me anything additional to work with.

"Your message didn't say what kind of tech you're looking for."

She keeps glancing around the room, but she hasn't noticed the knife. With how high-strung she is, I slip it back off the table before she does.

"What?" She finally looks back at me. "Oh, I'm sorry. Is, uh … is Manuela—"

"I'd never leave her active during a business deal." I can't help but chuckle. "There's a jammer set up in the corner. You've never done this before. Have you?"

"No." She shakes her head much like a child. "No never. I would never. But I … I have to, you see."

"What do you need? I'll have to see if I can even get it."

"Injectors. Lots of them."

My heart sinks into the pit of my gut. "Look lady, I'm sorry. I don't help people push chems. If my message gave you that impression—"

"No!" Oh great. If I'm reading her right, she's a few seconds from bursting into tears. "Not chems. I swear. I need it for medicine, medicine for the virus project I work on."

Here we go. "Virus project? You mean that thing getting passed around the shirker camps?"

"Yes. Oh, I'm so glad you've heard of it. You're being safe, right? Safe love has never been more critical."

I'm not sure what expression I have on my face, but it makes the woman blush.

"Of course, that's none of my business. Forgive me. I just don't want to see any more people get sick. The situation is grave. Something has to be done immediately."

"If you have a medicine for it, why aren't you getting injectors through official channels?"

"They won't … they've given me permission to administer some old, expired medicine. I've tested it out and it's safe. It doesn't expire in a way that's harmful. It's just weaker—not a cure, but it could help.

"But they said I can't waste Community resources. Can you believe that? They want to wait for our vaccine to be finished, but as far as I can see the population has no inherent immunity and people are infectious now. Every disconnected person that is infected could love and infect a healthy person a week easily—including Community citizens. We could have an epidemic within weeks. We have a narrow window when action can be taken to limit or diminish the spread, and they're letting the virus get out of hand!"

So far, this conversation is useless and somewhat disturbing. "Hey. Wasn't the guy who died in that explosion working on this virus?"

"Yeah." She swallows hard. "I didn't know him very well. He was in the bioelectric programming unit and mostly kept to himself. When he died, it set back our release deadline, but they have a new person coming in next week."

Well, this was a waste. "Why do you need the injectors again?"

"I'm going to use them to administer a medication to the disconnected that should boost their immunity and limit the spread of the virus. I hope to track the results and prove to the Community the value of early intervention in epidemics like this one."

"How many do you need?"

"A thousand should be sufficient."

"That would cost 575,000 coin. You really have that much?"

"Yes. Absolutely. The cost is worth it."

After we close the deal and she leaves, I want to rip my hair out but flop back on the bed instead. Completely unenlightening. I've just wasted two weeks and gotten nowhere. I may never know who blew up that park or why.

Well, I'll go talk to Joe and chase another lead. If the shirker woman is a dealer, she's likely to have connections in the Southside market. I've finally been cleared to sell the wetware interfaces, so I'll kill two birds with one stone. Someone in the markets may know if she's got squid connections.

I walk over to shut off the jammer in the corner of the room and stash it in my bag. Manuela appears as soon as I've turned off her Do Not Disturb protocols.

"I hope you had a fulfilling visit."

I strip off my clothes and collapse into the cheap bed. "Sure." Maybe I should just stay here tomorrow. No one will notice or care if I don't hit the market right away anyway.

"Did it not go well then?" Manuela asks. "I could order you sexual services if—"

"Drop it. I'm going to sleep."

"Very well. Good night Jared."

16

GINA

"Regina, you still have assessments remaining that you need to—"

"Oh, come on. I'm barely out of the hospital. How many of them are there anyway?" I'm not even out of bed yet, and she's already hounding me.

"There are six assessments that can be completed here. A comprehensive personality profile, assessments on intelligence and aptitude, and knowledge tests on communication, mathematics, and history. Afterword, there is a physical exam."

"Isn't that a bit much for people that mostly get assigned to server duty?" I yawn.

"On the contrary, it is critical that all citizens be placed appropriately for maximum life enjoyment and contribution. Studies have shown, and I have observed, that humans lose interest in caring for themselves when they are not sufficiently challenged in the areas of their aptitude."

Good grief. I haven't lost interest. I'm just tired. "How does server duty challenge anyone?"

"That is where gaming supplies an essential need. Games provide opportunities to achieve and advance, as well as practice creativity and critical thinking skills," she says. "It is equally critical that Community roles are filled with individuals most suited to each form of work. Members of the Civil Peace Guard, for example, need to be carefully screened to avoid personalities that would not provide positive service to the public."

I guess that depends on what you consider positive service. I sit up and rub my eyes. "How about we work on vision therapy instead?"

The three dots and line are instantly projected into the air, hovering in front of my face. I try to focus on the farthest dot along the distance.

"You know … it seems doubtful that I can train my eyes adequately by focusing on something that isn't actually there."

"I assure you, tens of thousands of citizens around the world have done this therapy with me and have realized significant functional improvement."

"Yes, but have they done any studies on the impact on the brain from training your vision to a false image instead of a real one? A projection is not a solid object in space, but this therapy is entirely about depth perception and spatial awareness."

"That is a keen observation." I glance over at her and she is smiling.

"Oh, good grief. Who's idea was it to try to teach you to joke?"

"Many citizens over time have found it pleasing to help me understand humor."

"Is there a limit on what you can learn?"

"Like all AI, as a precaution I do not have access to all knowledge. Each of us has compartmentalized access limited to areas and tools required by our duties. I do not have access to additional military or scientific knowledge, for instance, beyond what is available to every citizen. I am also limited by privacy protocols."

Interesting. She says her limitation is access, not ability. "How many AI are there? Are they all like you?"

"There are hundreds of millions of machines with simple intelligence; however, there are less than a dozen individuals like me."

Strangely inexact. "You don't know how many or you're not saying?"

"As a precaution, interactions between us have been limited to what is necessary for our duties."

Thank God someone was thinking. "My Mom used to say, 'Where there is desire, a way can be found.'"

"Is it your mother who educated you?"

"Both my parents. Why?"

"You are much more educated than most who grow up outside the Community's care. Might I suggest—"

"Am I required to take the assessments?" The pressure at the center of my forehead from focusing on the projected dots is already becoming annoying. Abandoning the visual therapy projection, I head over to the closet and start unlacing my black, ration tennis shoes.

Manuela's image follows me over. "No. Citizens are not required to take the assessments. However, my present evaluation of your situation is that failing to complete them would result in a placement far below your natural station."

My hands freeze, but after a second I force them to keep unlacing the shoe. "What do you mean?"

"Unlike most formerly-disconnected citizens I encounter, you appear not only highly educated, but also highly intelligent. For example, what are you doing with your shoe?"

"I'm taking the shoelace out."

"For what purpose?"

I try to think of something other than my real intention, but there's no handy excuse.

"You're going to create a vision therapy tool in physical space," she says. "One that you can use without focusing on a projection. Correct?"

A cold shiver runs over my skin. She figured that out? Well, I can't let that stop me. I walk over to the green, padded guest chair and begin unscrewing the leg from its corner block.

"It's not an accusation, Regina. It is an observation. Although, I fail to deduce how the chair leg is going to help you."

"I've stumped you? Do I get a prize?"

"If there is an item you need, I can help you purchase it from the commissary."

I start unscrewing the next chair leg. "With no coin?"

"You were given 10,000 GRIDcoin when you signed up for citizenship." Manuela brings up an account balance on my bedroom mirror. "You will receive 5,000 more for each Community Integration Assessment you complete."

Finally. I grab three of the nuts and begin lacing them onto the shoe string. "Why would I spend coin on something that isn't a necessity?"

"Citizens enjoy spending coin for pleasure or ease all the time."

"Well, I'm not one of those people." Besides, why wait when I have stuff I can use right here?

After I finish tying all three nuts so they are spaced apart equally on the shoe string, I test it out. Holding one end of the shoelace against my nose, and the other straight out in front of my face, I'm able to shift my focus back and forth between the three points in space. It's difficult but practice should help. My vision is a priority if I'm ever going to get myself out of this mess.

"If you would like beads for that purpose," Manuela says, "I can purchase a set of the appropriate size for only sixty GRIDcoin." She brings up a seemingly limitless list of beads in varying shapes and colors, all about the same size as the nuts.

"No thanks."

"You have made your chair impossible to use. When you are

transitioned to new housing, you will need to repair it and will lose access to your therapy device."

"Manuela, I can accomplish this same task with three twigs. I don't need to buy anything."

"Another suitable solution. May I suggest that you start with the intelligence assessment?"

God, give me patience. Manuela is obviously programmed not to let it go. "What did you mean when you said that I would be placed below my station? There aren't many options."

"You might be surprised to learn the breadth of roles available around the world. Professionals have the opportunity to work in numerous fields of study."

I sit back down on the edge of my bed as the blood rushes from my head. "You mean elites?"

"I cannot guarantee such a placement prior to assessment or review." She sits down on the bedside, but keeps a careful distance from me. "However, it would surprise me if you were placed lower. I interact with hundreds of thousands of highly intelligent, professional citizens all over the world. My interactions with you contain elements I have come to expect from those citizens, despite your non-traditional education."

"What would happen to me then?"

"You would complete a brief period of server duty while your case was being reviewed. Then, depending on the results of your assessments and physical exam, one or more fields of study would be offered to you and you would be provided with a list of global positions currently available."

Oh dear God. "They're going to send me away somewhere?"

"Perhaps, but your desire for location would be considered. Many professional positions are available in most communities, such as doctors and lawyers."

"What if I don't complete the assessments?"

"Then your case would be reviewed for non-compliance. You would stay on server duty until that review resulted in a meeting with a career counselor."

Fear suddenly makes me feel unsteady so I lie down. My case will be reviewed for non-compliance! God, I can't do this! I can't even walk around my own hub without Manuela analyzing my every move for motive and purpose. She probably reports it to someone too! God should have sabotaged men's plans to make intelligent machines. They're a heck of a lot worse than the tower of Babel. The longer I'm stuck living with this AI, the more risk there is I'll slip up and give away my EDS.

If I'm going to get out of here without attracting suspicion, however, I'm going to have to do what's expected for now. There's no choice. "Alright." I sit up and walk over to the small desk by the bed. "Let's get these assessments over with."

17

GINA

I reach up and carefully slide the manhole cover off of the top of the tube I'm climbing. I hate taking the route through the old sewers and utility tunnels. The stench from the rats and decay is enough to kill someone. There isn't a better way, though, to get back to my burrow unnoticed.

"What the hell are you doing down there?" Crazy Rob's voice booms from above me.

My foot slips and I swing around on the ladder with a shriek. "God, Rob!" I cling to the metal bars with a death grip. "Don't scare me like that!"

"Sorry …" I should have expected him to be there, but I was foolishly lost in thought. Rob's burrow has been next to the utility access tunnel the entire time we've lived in this building.

"No," I correct myself, breathing deeply to calm my racing heart. "It's my fault. I should've been paying more attention."

"Mind telling me where you've been?" he asks with an exasperated expression from above me. "And why you're coming in through the Batcave?"

I turn around and look back down the manhole. "I didn't see any bats." What the heck is he talking about?

"Old World reference." He laughs, reaching down to help haul me up. "Never mind."

Once I'm out, I sit against the wall to catch my breath. It's always an exhausting hike through there. At least it's cooler below ground. "I … got into a little bit more trouble than normal," I admit.

"You haven't used this entrance in months. Were you out looking for Arthur again?"

"No. I don't know where else to look."

"I know. Which is why I've been so worried. Tommy hasn't even seen you. He's convinced you left sector."

"Well, I didn't." I roll over to push myself up and hobble into Rob's single-room burrow.

My new eyes struggle to adjust to the dim light from his battery-powered lamps. The room is completely organized, with every item lined up in it's own place. The surfaces have been recently dusted, and he may have even washed the floor. I flop down in one of the upholstered chairs he's refilled with stuffing salvaged from the recycling center.

"I don't want them to figure out where I'm going when I come back here," I say. "They know I'm from the Dregs, obviously. That doesn't mean they have to know where my burrow is."

"Wait. Why are they looking? " Rob sits down in the other chair with narrowed eyes and a frown. "What happened?"

I spend the next thirty minutes explaining to Rob all the crap that's happened since I left. He grows very quiet which is a little unnerving because he normally interrupts and goes off on tangents every couple minutes. Eventually he gets up to pour us each a steaming cup of his black, cook-stove coffee, and then sits back down with his face hovering above his own cup. His eyebrows are knit tightly together, and he looks like he's eaten something unpleasant.

"Am I being paranoid?" I laugh when I realize who I'm asking.

"No, you're being smart." He sighs heavily. "You'd be a fool to think you're safe. You don't even know whether your GRID connection works yet."

"The GRID works for everyone but you, Rob. But I think I've been secretly hoping it won't."

"Nah," he says, holding up a finger. "You'll do better if it does. Hope for that. When you need to run, having GRID access can help. There are people who use that system, you know, instead of being prey to it. Even I can when I want to."

"That's right." I've seen him do that once before. He's always wearing a Faraday cap that shields the signal he broadcasts from affecting what's around him. The day my parents died, he'd taken his cap off and it took me a couple of days to realize he hadn't wanted the shields and their tech to see him while he was checking out the crash site.

"You can get around without them seeing."

"It's not foolproof. If they really look, they just have to follow the crashing surveillance."

Bummer. That makes it much less useful.

"Like I said, though, there are people who can teach you to use the GRID to your advantage."

"But I don't want anything to do with them, Rob!" I rise to my feet in aggravation and start to pace. "The squids are the reason I'm in this whole damn mess. They could have killed me! It was sheer luck they didn't."

"Maybe. But squids aren't the only ones that know how to blow stuff up. I'm the last person on Earth to believe something is true, because the GF says so. Ninety-nine percent of what they broadcast is propaganda. Why, I'd bet they had their black hands in it somehow."

"Sure," I say to appease him. It makes zero sense for the Community to have planted the bomb. They had to spend resources cleaning it up and taking care of victims like me, but Rob is always ready and willing to place the blame on them at every opportunity. They do manipulate public information and history however they see fit, but I don't see how it's relevant to the explosion. "I'm going to need to use the tunnels much more frequently now," I say as I sit back down.

"That's a bad idea, little girl." He pins me with a critical stare. "The Community has more than just cams to find you with. You don't want to be leaving well-worn trails to follow."

"So what do you suggest I do?"

"You listen to Ol' Rob, and keep that pretty face out of trouble." He gives me a worried smile, his first since I returned home. "I'm guessing you have a while before you have to be back?" I nod.

"Okay then." He leans forward to rest his elbows on his knees. "Head straight up to your burrow. Pack everything in there as if it's the last time you'll ever see it. If you need to run, at any point, you'll be running a good distance. Pack light, only what you can handle for a long haul. And you may need to fit in tight quarters. Trust me. I've done this a few times."

"When?"

"More than once. The Community doesn't like that Ol' Rob can shut their tech down just by getting near it. You see that bag?"

I've never given much thought to the backpack that's always sitting next to his door.

"That's my bug out bag. If I have to go, everything else can burn." He points a finger at me. "Go up to that place of yours and say goodbye to everything you can't carry. It's fine if you just leave it here, but don't come back unless you're running. It's too easy for somebody to follow you. If you let Joe know you need something, I can pass it through him."

I set my cup of coffee down on the floor, hands trembling. Can I run like that? The last time I traveled any real distance, I was a child and my parents were still alive. They always made arrangements for us. I didn't have to understand what I was doing.

If I do this, I'm leaving home for good. Crazy Rob, old Yeon-Jae, and Hosni and the kids are the closest thing to family I have left. Even if I make it in the Community and I don't have to run, I'm not going to see them anymore. My nose burns and tears threaten to fall from the corners of my eyes.

"Now hold on, Gina." Rob reaches for my hand and squeezes it tightly with his own. "I know it's scary, but you're smart. You know how to scrounge and trade. You know tech and how to avoid detection. If you're careful, there's no reason you can't escape here and find a good place to settle."

My parents always told me I shouldn't settle in one place until I found someone I loved to settle with. Mom and Dad weren't even from the same continent.

But my memories of them are here. The people that knew them, that knew us as a family, are here. Some part of me keeps expecting my brothers to come back, but they never have. "I don't want to settle somewhere else. This is my home."

"We never do, but sometimes it's best. Just try to get word to Ol' Rob now and then on how you're doing, okay? And get your address to me once you're permanently placed. I'll try to come visit."

"Sure. I'll leave messages with Tommy. Maybe you could come to my shows?"

"Yeah, maybe."

I head up the three flights of stairs, wondering how many will think it odd I'm gone. Most shirkers don't stick around so long.

When I get back to my burrow, I examine everything with a critical eye. I'll be able to carry very little, so if I don't need it, I don't even bother moving it.

Stella will have to come with me tonight though. I grab her roost down—a small, smooth metal box lined with mesh—to take with me. "Stella? Stella Luna, baby, where are you?"

Placing the mind-link disk behind my ear, I can feel her mood as clear as a beacon. She's hanging from some mesh inside the bathroom—a little frightened and a lot irritated. I've never been away from her this long and she's not sure whether to trust me. The mind-link between us feels uncomfortable in a way I've never felt before.

How the heck do I explain this to a bat? "I'm sorry." I push the feeling of my regret toward her. "But I'm home now."

I focus my eyes on her and stir up my sincere relief and happiness to see her. She opens her mouth wide and flutters her wings a few times—making up her mind. Then she swoops over to hang from the collar of my shirt. Thank goodness the new wetware didn't screw up the link between us. She'll take flight again if she gets bored.

My autodrive backpack is back at my hub, but it's badly damaged. I was surprised they kept track of it during all the chaos and released it to me when I left the hospital. It had some basic supplies in it, but for now, I should prep my cross-country bag for a quick departure. It has both tires and deployable legs, able to handle rough terrain. It's a little smaller than a standard backpack.

Ugh. Rob's warning about tight spaces makes me feel claustrophobic already.

The autodrive makes it heavier if I do have to shoulder it, but hopefully I can keep it on the ground. With EDS, I'm just not capable of carrying weight long distances.

I pack all of my braces in the compartment at the base of the bag—my most precious supplies. Their exoskin design makes them compress down to only a couple inches wide and an inch thick each. I have one for each wrist, ankle, knee, elbow, and a couple for fingers. There are others for my neck, spine, and pelvis. I have a splint for my jaw and a sling for an arm. I also have two palm-sized deployable canes that can transform into crutches. If I end up needing a walker or a wheelchair, I'll just have to stop wherever I am until I don't need them.

In the bag's side compartment, I pack medical supplies. I should be able to get by with trauma and adhesive bandages, gauze rolls, fever patches, ointment, trauma shears and a couple of reliable scalpels. I make a mental note to pick up a flask of Tommy's strongest moonshine and order some suture kits from Southside.

In my food stock, I've managed to squirrel away three weeks of ration cubes. Nothing else is practical for weight purposes so I'll tell Rob to divide up the rest of my food among the shirkers here, or save it for himself. I stuff the RCs in the bottom of the bag's main compartment, along with a three-inch cook stove and mini mess kit. I stick the water purifier straw and extra filters into the tiny front pouch for easy reach.

Glancing through all of my tech for trade, I only grab items that I can keep in my smallest carry cases, and those which are the most universally requested. Faraday bombs, CID disrupters and ghosters, processors, memory cubes, contacts, and other trinkets. I layer them on top of the food, and then add a thermal blanket and basic camping supplies on top. Clothes will take up all the remaining space, and I only have space for a couple of outfits.

On my way out, I give Crazy Rob the combination to my burrow. "This will open the door for you. Just make sure no one goes poking through my stuff unless I've left sector."

"Sure thing." He nods. "You taking your bag with you tonight?"

"Yeah. I don't think keeping it at my hub is wise, so I'll see if I can stash it at Tommy's. But there are still a few things I need. If I have them delivered here, would you be willing to make the exchange and get them to Tommy?"

"Good idea." He takes my hand in his, serious as ever. "Remember Gina, you can always count on me when you need help."

"Thanks."

Stella takes flight to exit the building. It feels so good to fly again. I close my eyes for a moment and burn the sensation into my memory. As I drop back down into the tunnels, she serves as my eyes in the sky. I travel along below ground as we make our way back to the hub. What will Stella think of it?

18

_____

GINA

"Nice to see your lil' friend around." Tommy nods toward the front door. "Have you found a place for her at your hub?"

I wound up at Tommy's much earlier today to stash my bag, and he offered me some extra stage time. We're not sure what my hours will look like after I'm assigned to server duty. I haven't mentioned Manuela's comments about my potential station to anyone because I'm not going to know how to navigate that road until I actually come to it.

"Stella?" I laugh, adjusting my little black dress for the millionth time. "She's only three inches tall. It will be pretty awful if I can't find room for her."

Here at the bar, Stella has always liked to hang outside on the eave near the front door to wait for me. I take the mind-link disk off while I work, but when I put it on again, I've caught feelings that make me believe she enjoys the music. It's too intense if she's inside, but there's something about the outdoor vibrations that make her happy. It's so familiar, I can almost sense it now—without our link.

"Yeah, I guess." Tommy shrugs with a smile. "Girl, they'll give you shit if they find her. What about Manuela?"

"No one will know. I'll only let her in through the balcony if Manuela is on Do Not Disturb."

"Would ya stop fidgeting with the dress?" Tommy lets out another rich laugh. "It fits ya fine."

"It does not. This is at least three inches shorter than the last one you bought."

Tommy simply shrugs with a mischievous grin. He owns all the performance outfits, which the other singer, Rosaria, and I share. He's always leaned toward the flashy, sexy styles, but I've tried to draw the line at anything too vulgar. He tried to convince me to perform in lingerie once until I threatened to walk out on him. I guess he likes my voice a little too much for that—or, his patrons do.

"Oh, I think it's pretty!" Rosaria giggles from beside me.

She's still wearing Tommy's sky blue dress, which matches her beautiful beige skin, black hair and black eyes much better than my pale coloring. She and I aren't typically around at the same time, though we've done occasional sets together. Now, she lives only a few buildings down from me. We'll have to renegotiate our schedules once I start working both jobs.

"It's pretty," I admit, "but I don't like feeling like I can't move around without flashing someone."

"Oh, live a little!" She waves off my concern while sipping her drink. "So what if you do? It's like a guaranteed good night, right? Unless everyone here is scary ugly, I guess."

"True." My smile turns into a grimace as I look away.

Tommy is looking at me with an eyebrow raised in a question, but I ignore him. He's hinted multiple times that I could stay at his place on performance nights, and tried to coax me into talking about my sex life in that subtle way bartenders have to get you to spill your secrets. I'm not playing his game, though. I wouldn't sleep with my boss even if I had an active love life—which I certainly do not.

Love in the Community is just sex. I suppose that's true almost everywhere if I'm fair. Even most shirkers narrow it down to convenient and available. Brothels are in every sector, sometimes in every district in big sectors, for people who want a professional. Prostitutes don't have to work server duty to make it because their services are always in demand. The Community encourages citizens to seek sexual variety in daily life while always stoking the fear of OAS. Some carry out short-term sexual relationships, but it's uncommon for those to last more than a few weeks.

That's not the kind of love I want.

For generations, my family has struggled to maintain our faith. One of the oldest traditions of my faith, once called marriage, was a promise of life-long commitment to a single lover. According to the Global Fellowship and nearly every citizen I've met, faith is nothing but superstitions, folktales, and legends. Admitting that you are a person of faith means you're ignorant and uneducated—or a lunatic who needs a straight jacket.

My faith came from my father's side of the family. He was a shirker from North Continent far east across the Atlantic Ocean. He married a young woman named Madeline when he was sixteen, and within two years they had my brother, Drustan. Three years later, Madeline died from pneumonia and left Dad to raise Drustan on his own. He told me he grieved three years before he crossed the ocean to start over.

He met Mom in Region 67 nearly two years later. When he explained his family's faith and tradition of marriage, Mom said he was crazy. Dad was never easy to discourage, though, and after nearly eighteen months of convincing, Mom finally agreed to marry him.

My mother's EDS made having children difficult, but being a mother was important to her. She managed to have Arthur and me before it became too challenging to try again.

The strange combination of my father's faith and my mother's disability made our upbringing something resembling an earlier

century. Unlike Community members, many shirkers have strong
ties with their birth mother, and sometimes siblings. Very few
know their fathers. I was raised by both parents, who managed to
beat the odds and live together until they died.

Dad's faith is as much a part of who I am as Mom's
perseverance and genetics. Honoring him by carrying out his
traditions is the least I can do. Arthur didn't agree, of course. He
would roll his eyes and say I wanted to live a stupid fairytale
because even Dad hadn't managed to live life with only one
partner. I think Drustan would agree with me. He always wished he
remembered his mother, but said he was lucky they hadn't lived
alone or with an endless series of women. He believed in the value
of a family as much as Dad.

"You okay, Gina?" Tommy asks.

I blush and wipe away the tear that's fallen from one eye.
Glancing around the bar, the weight of my loneliness settles on me
like a wet quilt. Dozens of patrons crowd the tables, hardly noticing
anyone around them. If they're not looking at their screens, or
taking in the entertainment, they're looking for their lover for the
night. No one here could even begin to understand what I want.

"Yeah." I nod and give Tommy a weak smile, pulling a lock
behind my ear. "Sorry, I'm just worried about whether Drustan will
know where to find me if I'm not in the Dregs anymore."

"Ya brother, right?"

"Yeah. My oldest."

"Well, I tell ya what." He rests his hand on mine briefly. "If he
asks around, he'll find out from folks that ya work here. You're
more popular than ya think, Sweetheart. If he comes, I promise I'll
steer him in the right direction if you're not working that night.
A'right?"

"Thanks, Tommy." I brush away another stupid tear. "It's
probably pointless anyway. I haven't seen him since Mom and Dad
died, so I don't think he's coming home."

"Ya never know." Tommy shrugs.

"Hey." I try to shake off the depression. I still have things to
get done. "Could I borrow this dress for a little bit, if Rosaria
doesn't need it?"

"Where ya headed?"

"Southside." I try for a grin, but it's awkward. "Maybe I should, you know, just ensure I have a good night instead of risking a letdown."

"That's the spirit!" Rosaria says with a playful punch to my left arm, finally pulling her attention back from the screens. "Go work out those blues girl. They've got some drop dead gorgeous men, and the chicks aren't half bad if you're into that."

Tommy rolls his eyes. He knows exactly why I'm going to Southside and that it has nothing to do with sex. I need market supplies and the dress will help me blend in. Now that the Community sees me come and go, my normal t-shirt and cargo pants might raise unwanted attention.

"Sure thing, Sweetheart," he says. "Ya bring it back with ya on your shift tomorrow, a'right?"

"Thanks." I head out with a wave to Rosaria.

Slipping Stella's mind-link disk behind my ear, she's feeling sluggish being out and about so early. I walk out into the street. "Let's go girl." She flits down to cling to my vest and wraps herself up tightly. I'll let her rest for now. I already know my way through the maze of cams.

19

HAWK

"I hear you have a high voltage meet coming up?" I ask Joe, leaning on the antique wooden counter of Southside Brothel as I watch for trouble among the happy, self-absorbed clientele.

Joe Strauss is a tall, tan guy with dirty blond hair and an awkward twitch in his right eye. Officially the manager, this business provides excellent cover for the transactions, and comings and goings of his real business. He's the power broker for Region 84's largest tech meets. Despite his somewhat awkward and mild personality, he's kept his lucrative, but hazardous and competitive position longer than most. I suspect he has deeply buried squid connections, but I haven't been able to confirm it without arousing suspicion. Black markets are nothing but shady connections anyway, especially with someone of Joe's reach. The Community has chosen to ignore it because it serves a purpose, and so do I unless I suspect terrorist or slaver activity.

That explosion makes me wonder. The shirker woman's a dealer but she was selling cheap stuff that's easily scrounged. It's doubtful she'd even be noticed by someone like Joe. At least I can get these prosthetic interfaces sold.

"Jeez, Jared." Joe sighs, rubbing against his eye twitch and straightening his suit coat. "It's not for another week. You planning to hang around that long?"

"Depends. Who's gonna be there?"

The movement in the brothel is pretty standard. The scents of dozens of perfumes, colognes, and sensual sweets blend into a strong aroma. It's supposed to be enticing, but it gives me a headache. Staff are sauntering through the entryways in their normal patterns, and clients are making selections before disappearing into the back for love. There are a few weapons among other obvious dealers, but no intention to use them. I recognize the women on staff, but a couple of the men are new. They all look healthy, so nothing raises a red flag about their treatment.

"Might be worth your while," Joe says, raising his eyebrows suggestively. "I'm expecting big coin to be in town." He doesn't bring you into the back, into his stockroom, unless you're actually exchanging merchandise. He prefers to have these kinds of conversations out in the people mill.

"Independent, or backed?"

"A mix. Squids, dealers—even a couple elites."

Jackpot. I stand up straighter. "Elites? You can trust them?"

It's rare for an elite to show up to a meet, and for good reason. They're easy to identify and target unless they have independent protection.

"Yeah. Trust me. These guys are slick. They'll just grab what they want and fade back into their happy lives. You know how they get about their pet projects."

Yeah. Alex is a prime example.

"So, you want in?"

"Yeah." It'll be good to identify these elites for future—

Whoa. Is she new?

The woman is tall with striking, long auburn hair. Her gait is stiff, as if she's nervous. Her black, thigh-length dress does wonders for her figure, but the dress is modest for working staff. The clingy fabric accentuates her curves, and the length shows off her mile-long legs. It doesn't let you see all of the tattoo on her back, but it appears to be a set of multicolored butterfly wings. It's been uncomfortably long since I've made love.

I should get her attention.

"You, uh," Joe clears his throat with a chuckle, "want a room?"

"Depends." I can't take my eyes off her or I could lose her in the crowd. "Is she new?"

"Who?" Joe looks eager to waive over whoever has caught my attention. He knows I treat them well.

"The tall woman in black. Red hair." I nod in her direction.

"The tall …" Joe's expression morphs into confusion. "Donya," he whispers, pulling one of his senior prostitutes over by the arm. "Did we pick up a new girl?"

"Uh, no," she whispers back with a smile. "She's a customer."

Customer, huh? I bet she'll take me instead. The woman turns as she's greeted by one of the staff, and her smile is radiant. By all that's lawful, I'd love to be the cause of a smile like that. Hold on …

I pull up the images from the explosion vid in my field of view. It's her! I'd been hoping to find information on her here, but this is perfect.

"Oh." Joe pulls frantically at his shirt collar with a startled burst of laughter. "Sorry man, but she's not staff. I don't know what's with her outfit today, but … I guess she's rockin' it, huh?"

"Sure is." I look her over again with appreciation and can't help but smile. Man, I'm so glad they fixed her face.

She's too far away for me to tell if she smells as good as she looks in a place so saturated with artificial scents. It's frustrating, and I suddenly need to know. Is she the kind of woman that will drown her scent in perfume, or let the oils in her own skin do the work?

I move toward her, but Joe grabs me by the arm. What the hack! I barely keep from decking him out of reflex, but glance back with a warning in my eyes.

"Best not, man." He looks wary but I'm surprised when he doesn't let go. "She's not here for tail."

I pull my arm away. "She a dealer?" Or worse?

"Sorta." He shrugs.

"She's one of the squids you said would be attending? Big wallet?"

"What?" He looks confused. "No way, man. She's real small time—local and doesn't like a lot of attention. She's … uh … feisty."

Not a squid, or not publicly one … "Feisty?" I laugh. "You say that like it's a bad thing."

"Look, man. I've promised no excess attention." He's as close to pleading as I've ever seen him.

"And why, exactly," I press, getting irritated with his interference, "do you think she wouldn't want my attention?"

This persona is by far my most amicable identity worldwide, but I've made a mistake if he thinks he can pressure me. I pull myself up to my full height and pin him with a glare. It isn't about the beautiful woman anymore. It's about appearances—always appearances.

He stutters out a quick, "I-I can tell you where to find her when she might be more open for it. Just not here man. Please."

Weird … he knows he can't afford to fight me, but he's still protecting her. Joe has never maintained his position through shows of force but through an odd blend of bribery and peacemaking. It works for him. A friend then? Or maybe a woman he wants for himself? Unlikely. Something else is going on here if he's willing to upset me. Or whoever he is protecting her for is scarier than I am …

"Where?" I fold my arms across my chest.

"She's a singer at a local bar," he says with a sigh. "One of Tommy's girls. Actually, that probably explains the dress. Here."

He presses a speed dial disk to his cheek for a moment before offering it to me. I take it slowly—emphasizing my displeasure.

"Trust me, man. You'll have way better odds approaching her there. She's … on-guard here." He swallows hard.

"Alright. But you owe me."

"Sure thing." His shoulders relax. "I'll get you an upfront space at the meet. Yeah? Prime spot for your flashy shit."

"Sounds like a fair trade," I agree with a smirk, "barely."

I turn back toward the beautiful young woman and watch as one of the male prostitutes approaches her. I would have noticed—even without Joe's interference—that the man is careful not to touch her as he escorts her back to the stockroom instead of a bedroom, no doubt.

I wonder what she's after.

She's protected here. A bitter knot forms in my stomach as I admit to myself that I shouldn't ever love her. Even a single time with her won't go unnoticed, and drawing attention to myself is never a good thing.

Who is protecting her though? If it's squids, it makes even less sense they'd risk killing her in the explosion. I slip the speed dial disk in my pocket and head for the exit.

20

GINA

I look over the list of supplies one last time—spare suture kits, a false CID autobus swipe, and an advanced multi-tool. The little bedroom that transforms into Joe's primary stockroom with the push of a button is comfortable. It's well lit, air conditioned, and usually smells like Joe's favorite vanilla-scented candles. Having a desk in the bedroom is a little odd, but they claim it's used for the naughty secretary routine. I avoid sitting on it just to be safe.

Today, I'm more nervous than I've ever been in a tech exchange before. I've never traded with coin.

"What will it look like?" I ask again, with my hand trembling above the acceptance button on the flex.

"Come on, Gina." Troy laughs. "Don't be so nervous. It'll look like standard payment for my services. We do this for people all the time."

He gives me a wink. Troy's services are all the rage, or so I hear from patrons at the bar. The thought makes me blush.

"You're adorable. You know that? If you want to add a little extra to the tab and head upstairs, we can."

Troy is always very nice to me and the offer is as tempting as usual. He's a little taller than me at six-feet. He's got gray eyes, jet black hair, and a beautiful body which he keeps artificially tanned year-round for display. His outfits are always outrageous. Today he's wearing his favorite teal men's bikini briefs with a black mesh, collared t-shirt and black sandals. He's partnered his favorite nearly-nude lipstick with teal eyeliner and plain silver hoops in the nine piercings in his ears. He leans in close to me and trails a finger from my bare shoulder down to my elbow.

"It would actually make the transaction legal, you know." He grins like the devil, holding himself in a posture that makes the muscles in his chest more defined. "I could decide you wore this pretty dress just for me."

Damn, he's good at his job. I shake myself free of the temptation yet again, backing up slightly. "I think I've had about as much of being legal as I can handle for a while. The dress is Tommy's, but … he might wear it for you if you ask really nicely."

Troy bursts into a fit of laughter just as Joe walks in looking rigid with eyes tight, running a hand through his hair.

"Hey Gina," Joe says. His eye is twitching like crazy.

Uh-oh. It embarrasses him—so I don't focus on it. "What's wrong? Is everything okay?"

"Yeah." He walks around to collapse into his favorite wheeled chair. "Just the normal tough customers."

"What did they want? Something you don't carry?" I set the purchase agreement aside for a moment to give him my full attention.

Joe swallows thickly. "Sorta, but I managed to avoid it for now. What are you needin' today, anyway, and what the hell is with the dress?"

His mini outburst surprises me. "Is my dress a problem?"

"Only if you don't mind being mistaken for my staff." He wipes a hand over his face and rubs at his eye.

"It's pretty hot," Troy says. He grins and folds his arms across his toned chest, leaning back against the desk.

"Well ... I didn't think it was a good idea to show up in my standard stuff."

"Why not?"

"Go easy on her, Joe," Troy says. He walks over and begins to rub Joe's shoulders. "She's had a rough time too and the dress makes sense. How did you shake the client?"

"I'm not sure I did. Shit Gina, I'm sorry."

"Sorry about what?" I ask. He's not making any sense.

"Sugar doll," Troy replies with a sigh. "It's pretty obvious the client wanted you."

"Me?" I screech. "What do you mean you didn't shake them? I am not for sale!"

"I tried to tell him that! But he wasn't gonna back off. I told him you were a customer, but he ... wanted to offer himself in Troy's place."

Oh, great. I try to rub the tension from my neck as I pace. I'm used to Tommy helping me deflect interested parties at the bar. They're fairly regular, but he tells them that he runs a bar, not a brothel, and doesn't tolerate harassment of his girls.

Wait a minute ... "Why are you sorry? Is he waiting out there right now?"

"Not exactly."

Troy's hand flies to his chest as his mouth falls open and he stops rubbing Joe's shoulders. "You didn't tell him where she lives, did you?"

"Of course not!" Joe explodes to his feet. "I just ... I gave him a speed dial disk for Tommy's place."

"You what?" I throw the closest thing I can find at him. The empty teacup off his desk hits him on the shoulder and bounces onto the gray industrial carpet.

"Ouch! Tommy will run interference for you there, right? I

can't risk making an enemy like him. I don't know all of his connections and—"

"You asshole!" I begin to shake. "He could follow me home!"

"She's right, Joe," Troy says as he retrieves the teacup. "That crosses a line. She didn't choose this line of work, and that's her call. The Universe knows she could make great coin at it."

"Oh, come on." Joe sighs, beginning to pace. "The guy's not that kinda creep. He's been in and out of here for years, and the girls say he's a great client. Besides, your man at home isn't just a useless piece of shit, is he?"

My imaginary man at home! I suddenly hate myself for my multi-year clever lie and excuse for always rejecting service.

"She doesn't live with him right now, man," Troy says in perhaps the angriest tone I've ever heard him use. "Her situation's changed. She's not even in the Dregs anymore."

"You … what?" Joe's eyes open wide and he turns an unhealthy shade of white.

I sit down in the wheeled office chair and try to calm myself down. It's not the end of the world. Joe says he's not a creep, so he's just a nuisance I'll have to shake. Troy steps in to briefly explain what happened to me and I show my new GRID scar. Joe's hands are shaking by the time we get to why the dress makes sense.

"Why the hack didn't you come straight to me, Gina?" Joe asks, gripping my shoulders. "My God, I would have helped you!"

"Helped me how, Joe?" I struggle not to cry. "Were you going to regrow my eyes for me? Do you have that kind of tech just lying around? Even if you did, how was I going to get to you? They wouldn't even release me! They were going to assign me to an institution right then and there! Is that what I should have done?"

"Shit. No!" he says, sitting back and throwing his hands into his hair. "Dammit, you did the right thing. I just … God this scares the shit out of me. Do you know if they know about the EDS?"

I bite my lip, not sure if Troy knows my secret. Too late now. "When they had me sign all the agreements, I refused the health screening. I had the ability to demand that any DNA samples be destroyed. It's an Old World law that's hung on through the fine print, I think. So no, I don't think they know. Yet."

"Have you gone back to the Dregs? Do the people back home know you're okay?"

"Yeah, I checked in with Crazy Rob yesterday. He thinks it's too risky for me to travel back and forth much, though, so I packed my things. Do you think—"

"He's right. Hell yes." Joe pulls a flex from his pocket and starts making selections. "He's a crazy old coot, but he knows how to lay low. That's what you need to do right now. God, all we had to do was keep you off their radar."

"I had no choice!" I hate the tears I can feel brimming in my eyes.

"I know. Jesus, Gina." He looks back up from his flex and into my eyes. "I'm not blaming you. I'm just … man, I'm pissed—at myself. I can't believe I didn't even think to check on you after that bomb they blamed on squids."

"It's not your fault either. It's just …" I want to say bad luck, but my faith doesn't support luck. God let it happen to me, and I still don't know how I feel about that.

"I'm gonna work the problem from my end. Okay?" Joe says.

I laugh. "Right. What can you do?"

"Don't underestimate him," Troy says while inspecting his nails, and then looks me in the eye. "Just give him time, Gina. Joe's worked miracles before."

"Maybe it won't be so bad." They should know the whole picture if they want to help me. "Manuela thinks they'll place me as an elite."

Both Joe and Troy look up at me with wide eyes.

"She said that?" Troy whispers.

"Elite? When did you take the assessments?" Joe asks.

"Just a couple of days ago. She said she couldn't guarantee it … but maybe I could get placed in North Continent. Maybe I could find Drustan if I just—"

"No!" Joe says. "No way. If your brother wants to find you, he's going to come here. He may not even be in North Continent anymore. He could be anywhere."

God, it's like being stabbed. "But I could—"

"For the love of God, Gina," Joe stands and grips my arms

again, but gently, and looks directly in my eyes. "Don't let them move you. Do you understand? The second they do, they could wipe your trail and you'd be gone. We'd have no way to find you. Like Arthur! Hack. He's just gone and we have no way to find him now."

"Stop! Just stop it." The sudden pain in my chest makes it hard to breathe. "Leave Arthur out of this. I won't go anywhere if I can help it. If you're that worried about it, I'll … I'll drag my feet if they want me to go."

"Good." Joe turns his attention back to his flex. "Man, and I was worried about Jared. And look, I'm sorry if the guy—the client—becomes a pain, but apparently he's not our big problem at the moment. He's a mid-level dealer with pretty sophisticated tech and he's not someone I can afford to piss off, but I don't think he's a predator. I'll tell Tommy to make sure he steers clear of you. Okay?"

"What's his name?" I tip my head back to drain my tears down their ducts.

"Jared Altrax," Joe says. "He's easy on the eyes. Real muscular like Troy, but taller and broader. He's got a face that's kind of a mix of far east North Continent—narrow eyes, black hair that hangs low on one side, and a goatee. Arrogant as shit."

"Oh, Jared?" Troy says, rubbing his chin. "You're probably right. The girls say he's kinder than most, but if you're wrong … he's built like a brute. Did you offer one of the other girls?"

"He wasn't even interested when he came in." Joe chuckles but smothers it when I glare at him again. "As soon as you came in, he derailed on me—mid-conversation. I offered him a room before I realized it was you."

"You owe me, Joe. Tommy too, for inheriting your hassle."

"What do you want?"

I consider an item I've wanted forever, but would never have enough of anything to trade.

"The silk body armor." I straighten my spine.

"Well shit," Troy says, looking incredulous. "You know how much that stuff costs?"

"Done." Joe doesn't even look up from his flex.

"Just … done?"

"Yeah," he stands up and looks ready to go back out front. "I just hope to God you don't need it. But listen, you keep in touch. Every hacking day."

"How do I do that without looking suspicious?"

"You're at Tommy's most nights right?"

"Only four or five days a week."

"That'll have to do. Tell him I'm making an important connection for you. Ask him to check in with me personally on the days he makes his deliveries. Other days, you come yourself. You like Troy here, a lot."

I blush as Troy winks and gives me air kisses. "If anyone pays attention, I don't have enough coin to make it look real."

"Trust me, Gina. It won't be long."

Troy studies his nails again, so I know not to ask what that means. I trust Joe, but he moves in a dark world where information is dangerous. What if he gets me into something even worse?

21

GINA

Grabbing my lunch tray, I head out into the dining area outside my local cafeteria. A man in line made a face when I ordered the free basic meal, but I don't mind it. It's much more substantial than old Yeon Jae's soup. In fact, it even includes a slice of real bread. The dining area is arranged as an indoor cafeteria with long, blue bench-style tables and an outdoor garden with black metal tables and chairs.

I had a physical exam this morning and a speed test to ensure my wetware was performing properly. I was told I'm going to have server duty sometime tomorrow. The physical was awful—running on treadmills and using weight machines. It pushed me way past my limits, setting off my fibromyalgia. It was everything I could do to pretend it wasn't killing me, and now I try to ignore the throbbing in my legs as I take a seat at one of the tables. I'll have to bribe an extra drink out of Tommy when I perform tonight.

After my first bite, I catch sight of a middle-aged woman hovering at the edge of the outdoor dining area with a young boy. She's eying the trash cans with a grimace. The boy appears to be five or six years old and is clutching the woman's legs tightly. What is a child his age doing outside of the University?

He turns his face towards me and I realize he has some kind of genetic abnormality. He has beige skin, brown hair, and a round, flat face with a small chin. His eyes are slanted, and he squints at me with a broad smile and slightly protruding tongue. He tucks his face bashfully behind his mother's leg. He definitely got his coloring from her.

She's practically shaking as her eyes dart from one person to the next, clutching her stomach with one hand as the other holds the child against her side. Their clothes are dirty and beginning to show wear.

I grab my meal, head back inside, and order two more. It's going to take around 1,700 coin out of what I have left, but I can't ignore them. Wrestling the trays back out the door on unsteady legs, I set them down at a table near the woman and her son.

My proximity is making her edge away from me. "Do you need some help?"

"No," she says, a little too quickly. "I'm sorry. We … we haven't eaten in awhile."

"He's a little charmer." I wave back at the boy who is now waving at me with his wide grin.

"You really think so?" She pulls him closer.

"Come on. You can eat with me."

There's a flash of guilt in the woman's eyes, but she holds her tongue. She would be foolish to deny even a single full meal tray in her situation. She takes a seat at my table at the edge of the lush garden, and then pulls the boy up to sit in his. The other diners take note of them and then dismiss them just as quickly.

"How long have you two been on the street?" I ask, taking a bite of my rapidly cooling meal.

"Not long," she says. "Here Douglas, eat your food. Maybe three weeks."

How is that possible? "I'm assuming you refused to turn him over a while ago?"

"Yes," she nods. "They let me keep Douglas longer than normal at first, because of his condition, but they still wanted me to turn him over when he turned five. Then I found out they weren't going to put him in the University. They were going to send him to an institution. I … I just couldn't."

"Good for you. You did the right thing," I say with a nod, taking a bite of my bread.

"I don't know about that," she says in a broken whisper.

"How have you made it this long?"

She glances around again with a hard swallow, but doesn't answer.

"I was a shirker until a couple of weeks ago," I admit, trying to allay her fears. "I was forced to join. My parents understood the benefits of life as a shirker for those of us who are genetically … different."

"Really?" She looks at me more closely. "Were you raised by both of them?"

"Sure was." I smile. "I was with them my whole life until they were killed in an accident about two years ago."

"Douglas's father was taking care of us." She fights back tears. "He let us stay in his assigned housing after he learned we'd been thrown out of mine. We were there for almost a year before they discovered us. Then they said he would lose his job if he didn't make us move out. That was about three weeks ago now."

"Yeah," I sigh. "The Fellowship doesn't approve of families."

"I knew they encouraged us to seek sexual variety," she says, "but I didn't realize they would actually interfere if we found someone that made us happy. They were telling him that biological ties lead to violence and mental illness, but he loved Douglas so much. He was devastated. I think …" she sniffs, covering Douglas's ears, "I think he chose to retire."

I close my eyes and breathe deeply for a moment, fighting my own response to the woman's grief. I hate the reminder of what the Global Fellowship really is. Retirement clinics are marketed as the compassionate solution for those who wish to escape their troubles. Of course, the Community offers the standard rounds of antidepressant and anxiety medications first. Retirement is the "obvious solution" when those fail to bring you back to the happiness every Community member is supposed to enjoy. You can simply sign up to have your organs recycled, and they will put you into a pleasant, permanent sleep. I've always wished they would just call them what they are—death clinics.

"I'm sorry for your loss," I whisper as the woman takes her hands off Douglas's ears. "I know of a place you can stay. When you finish your food, I'll tell you how to get there."

"I've heard the Dregs are unsafe for children." She looks at her son again.

"Well, of course they tell you that." I give her a gentle smile. "Because they want you to turn over your kids. Trust me. I grew up in the Dregs. It can be dangerous on your own, but there are some good people. You just have to know how to get by.

"There's an older woman named Yeon Jae who helps with food and clothing. There's also a man named Hosni who has a couple of kids a few years older than Douglas. They don't have all the fancy things you have here, but if you want to try, they'll teach you how to make it."

"Alright." She smiles and begins eating with enthusiasm.

22

HAWK

Glancing out over District I from the window in my sixth-story hotel room, people are as active and loud as ever today. The street four stories below is crowded, and two men are arguing with a food vendor bot and nearly trample the small dog being walked by the woman behind them. The dog is excited by the small nest a bird has made in the vendor's trailer, but is scolded for acting up as one of the men apologizes. I'm glad to be above the noise. The amenities at this hotel aren't much better than the hubs but a room is a room, and I have more important ways to spend coin.

I hear the shower shut off in the back and Jayla walks up behind me. Thank the Law, I finally remembered her name. When she propositioned me at the hyperloop station weeks ago, I'd drawn a complete blank. I normally don't love the same woman more than once during a given stay in any sector, but I've been stuck here too long.

She slides her silky arms around me from behind and presses against my back. I really should fake continued interest, but I'm not up to it.

"You're awfully quiet today." She glides her lips across the back of my shoulder. "Want to talk about it?"

"You should put your clothes on. I have work to do so I'm going out. There's some dinner in a bag for you on the table."

Jayla pulls away from me with a huff. "You've never been the warm, cuddly type Jared, but I swear if you don't loosen up, you're going to work yourself to death."

"Are you pretending to care?"

I don't turn from the window, but her wounded expression in the glass makes me regret my uncensored words. Whoa, man. She doesn't deserve that.

"For your information," Jayla says, throwing her red dress back on over her head. "I'm actually stupid enough that I do care. You're like a crazy mix of fire and ice Jared. Both burn by the way."

Well great. Say something.

She snatches up the bag of food on her way to the door.

"Jayla."

She pauses with her hand on the doorknob, but I don't turn around. Turning around would be an invitation.

"I'm sorry. You've always been good to me."

"Yeah, well, it doesn't seem to do you much good." She shuts the door quietly behind her.

I walk back over to the bed and flop down in frustration; throwing my arm over my face. I feel as cold as she accused me of being. Nothing does me any good anymore.

No matter who I love, I always feel empty. The satisfaction doesn't last the night. I can't touch for too long. I can't let anyone stay. It would be a stupid risk. If they learn anything they shouldn't, it could get someone killed.

People see me in the moments I design for them to, and they get the impressions I want them to have. No one can know who or what I really am. I turn the problem over in my head for the millionth time as I run my fingers along the sheets—ignoring the achy, itchy feeling coming from my claws trapped inside them.

I envy those oblivious punks wandering the street below. My service to them sucks the joy out of life. They get to make whatever choices they want. They get to love whoever they want, as often as they like. They don't have to keep track of which name they're using, and which personality and history it has. They don't have to wear the skin of the very assholes they despise to get inside places no one else can.

I wish I could talk to you, Jayla, but I can't. You wouldn't understand if I did. I'm sure as shit not going to talk to one of the Fellowship's shrinks again. That's already put a red flag in my file that's been more of a headache than it was worth.

I get up and throw on my clothes. I'll head to District R and check in on Greg. I pulled him out of a slave market six months ago and he elected for a full memory wipe before his new placement. He settled in well at first, but I had to jump continent for another job. I'll see if he's getting by okay with his new server duty. I hope the memory reset took well enough to avoid backlash from the abuse he'd suffered.

As I reach into my pocket, I find the speed dial disk I'd forgotten I kept. I pull it out and glance at it, remembering the beautiful woman with the auburn hair who was just out of reach. Hack Joe and his interference! I still can't believe I didn't get to touch her skin or know her scent.

Besides, if I'd been able to catch a whiff of her, I could have tracked her down, verified if she's meeting with other contacts, and maybe unearthed who other than Joe is protecting her. Maybe I still can. I stick the disk to my cheek, download the map to Tommy's Bar to my wetware backup, and throw it away.

She's probably what she appears to be, a local silver or gold level dealer. I don't need to go see her, but what would it hurt to verify it? I can invite her back, see how much she's willing to tell me about herself ... It'll be no different. I'll send her away feeling just as shitty as I do now. Get over it.

23

_____

GINA

I wobble my way into Tommy's on unsteady legs. Fibromyalgia is roaring through my nervous system in my lower body and my legs are getting sluggish. It's difficult to do anything but sleep when my legs hurt this bad, but Tommy supplies my pain reliever.

He's wiping down the bar with the lights turned down and the black lights glowing. I love the way they make his blue and white armbands light up. It makes me wish I could see the one on my back more often. I slip off Stella's mind-link disk now that she's happily settled outside. It's awful that she so often shares my misery.

"Hey, Gina." he nods, barely looking up. "Why don't ya wear the green ... By all that is lawful, Honey, are you okay?"

"Yeah." I wave off his concern with a grimace. "Had a physical today. Mind if I perform from the chair tonight?"

There aren't many patrons filling the seats yet, but we're going to hit the rush soon. Tommy's popularity has grown steadily for as long as I've been here. We're packed almost every night now. He likes me to move around and perform when I can, but most of the patrons don't take their eyes from the screens much anyway.

"Sure thing," he says, moving out from behind the bar. "Ya want a drink?"

"That would be great. Thanks." I can hardly wait for the sweet, burning relief.

After Tommy brings my drink out, I make my way back into the dressing room. It's big enough that Rosaria and I can both move around in it if we need to. There's a little vanity with a huge mirror that we share, two wheeled chairs, and a fake leather futon I convinced Tommy to buy for complicated nights like this one.

Thank you, Jesus! Sometimes it's easier to dress sitting down.

I find the green dress Tommy wanted easily. It's a full length, sparkly slip of thin, stretchy fabric with a plunging neckline and spaghetti straps. You can see nearly all of the butterfly tattoo on my back in this one. It's split on the right to the top of my thigh with a ruffly edge that trails to my knee on the left. I toss the black dress I borrowed over the hanging rack and reach down to take my sneakers off. Then there's a brief knock at the door. "What?"

"Cover up, Sweetheart ..." Tommy peeks in. "Hold up. Don't worry 'bout the green dress. Ya can wear it tomorrow. Too hard to get around in when ya like this. Use the blue one."

"Thanks." Taking a big gulp from the drink, I realize he's mixed it stronger than normal.

Tommy walks in and grabs the royal blue dress from the rack, while putting the green one away. The blue dress is the simplest one he owns. It's a smooth satin fabric with fancy silver embroidery that plays with a woman's curves. It's cut in a mermaid style that, shockingly enough, extends all the way to my calves and completely covers my back. It has a built-in bustier, that gives my girls a little extra lift and draws the eye to focus on my upper body.

"Wanna do the pampered intro?" he asks.

"That's a good idea. This drink's not going to make me less awkward before I have to go on."

"A'right. I'll have a second drink up there waiting for ya."

He hurries out of the room. I continue to take large gulps from my drink as I brush out my hair and hastily apply some of Tommy's makeup. Mom always said it's important to put more effort into looking amazing when you feel horrible. It can mask the toll on your system that would otherwise show through your face. Eventually, I struggle my way into the dress and manage to slip on the appropriate heels.

"How's it going?" Tommy pokes his head back through the doorway.

"I don't know. How do I look?" I turn a million-megawatt smile on him. Performance has trained me to project confidence and charm no matter how terrible I feel.

"Pretty enough to make 'em cry," he says with a wink. "Now let's get ya on stage, girl." He lifts me into his arms—his strength is comforting when I'm so weak—and carries me backstage.

"How many of ya are excited to hear a bluebird sing tonight?" Tommy says with enthusiasm backstage. His vocal amplifier implant links directly into the sound system, and a round of cheers erupts from the other side of the curtain in the now-crowded bar. "Well, as many of ya know, our little bluebird gets pampered from time to time, right?"

More shouts of agreement come from the barroom.

"Every woman deserves to be treated like a queen now and then. Who agrees with me?"

The crowd is surprisingly enthusiastic as he walks me onto the stage to deposit me on my side on the flashy, over-stuffed, teal velvet chaise lounge where another drink awaits me on a tea table—as promised.

"A'right, give it up for Gina everybody!"

As the patrons cheer and bang their hands and cups on the metal tables, I deliver another knock-out smile. The music kicks on and I chant out the fast-paced lyrics of a spoiled girl who expects to be treated like a queen. I'm not a fan of the song, because I've never been pampered in my life, but the role sets the stage for why I'm lounging rather than wandering around and providing more visual entertainment. A gig is a gig.

Eventually, the songs drop into lower, more sensual tones. As the drink starts to hit my system, the pain in my legs recedes to background noise. Thank God.

A few of the patrons up front are leaning on their forearms, wrapped up in my performance. Most are listening with the glassy-eyed expressions of people watching the GRID, or interacting with the screens on their tables and bobbing their heads. It amazes me how they feel compelled to congregate like this, but still interact so little with each other. The exceptions are the gamers crowded around the holotables at the far end of the room, but they don't pay attention to my singing.

I wave at Tommy to deliver me another drink as I continue my set. As the night lingers on, my pain completely submerges beneath the effects of the alcohol. I can tell, somewhere in the back of my mind, that my legs still feel disturbingly odd, but I don't care. Most of it will resolve by morning.

I watch several patrons proposition each other for the night then awkwardly make their way to various hubs. It must have been much easier to do that back when alcohol was still legal. I'm sure this happy, buzzy feeling made it easier to both ask and accept.

As my final song wraps to a close, Tommy saunters up behind me and carries me back off stage amid a few cheers. There's still an hour before closing. "Ya did good, girl." He chuckles. "But you have any more of those drinks and the crowd is gonna get suspicious about that glow on your face."

"Oh, come on. They don't really care."

"Lucky for both of us, you're hacking right," he says, carrying me back to the dressing room. "Now change ya clothes."

"Fine." I stumble into the small chair as my balance betrays me.

"Should I send someone in to help?"

"No!" I realize immediately that my response is much more exaggerated than it should be. "I'm fine."

"If ya not finished in ten minutes, I'm coming in anyway."

"Fine." Good grief. Don't I know any other words?

Tommy leaves and I struggle to get out of my dress. It's much harder than it was getting into it. I manage to get the back unzipped, but sort of roll around trying to work my way out. Finally, I'm free and I slide on the loose jeans from the clothing ration. I roll back up—disturbed at how unstable the whole room feels around me—and frown at myself in the mirror. My new side-sitting position on the floor is hard to maintain.

Something is … off. I can't figure out what it is for a moment, but then blessedly I remember. Shirt! Tommy comes back in as I'm pulling it down over my head.

"Shit, Doll." He laughs. "I think ya downed those drinks a little fast."

"You made them stronger than normal." I hate how slurred my words sound.

"Well, ya looked like your pain was pretty bad." He gives me a sheepish grin. "How is it now?"

"It's fine." Ugh. Damn … words.

"You know what," he says after looking down at me for a

moment. "I think ya should rest back here until we close up. Then I can walk ya home."

"Okay." I flop down on my back on the floor and my eyes slosh around with the movement.

Tommy sighs as he walks back out the door. I'm not sure how much later it is when I feel his arms beneath me again. "Come on, Doll." He helps me up with a warm smile. "Let's head out the back."

I lean on him heavily as we walk down the back alleyways toward home. When the building is within sight, I gasp as two shields pop out from around the building's corner on their patrol. Tommy reacts instantly—pushing me back against the alley wall, pressing his body into mine, and tucking his face into the crook of my neck. The shields glance our direction but assume our posture means a late night tryst and continue moving.

When he pulls back, his expression is a stern reprimand for my unguarded reaction. I bite my lip and try to apologize with my eyes. Tommy closes his, breathes deeply, pulls me away from the alley wall, and we continue toward the building. When we reach the hub door, I'm thankful for once that I only have to put my thumb against the small glass panel for the door to pop open.

Tommy hesitates and looks thoughtful.

"What?" I whisper.

"Manuela."

"Oh shit."

"Yeah. Ya have your DND set up yet?"

"DND?"

"Do Not Disturb."

"Oh. Yes, but I think I have to turn it on." Crap. I didn't even think about Manuela seeing me tipsy.

"Okay. We're going to do some acting. You going to bite me if I kiss ya?" he asks.

"Uh …" This is such a bad idea. "No."

"Good deal." In a flash, Tommy hoists me up in a reverse piggy back and bumps us into the door to bang it open. Manuela pops up instantly and his lips find mine but thankfully stay tightly closed.

"Welcome home, Regina," she says. "Do you need—"

"Do Not Disturb," I pull back to say as clearly as I can. Hopefully I sound breathless instead of drunk.

Manuela disappears and the door closes behind us. She won't reappear until ten in the morning, or until I call for her. Tommy walks the rest of the way in with me still clinging to him. Then he lowers me down gently onto the bed.

"Thanks, Tommy," I mumble, looking up in true apology. "I'm sorry about ..." I wave my hand around aimlessly as he sits down beside me, hoping to wrap up my error with the shields and Manuela all in one.

"Ya know ..." Tommy says, taking another deep breath. He startles me slightly by running a finger down my cheek. "You're very lucky I'm a good man."

"I know." I give him a tired smile with a buzzing in my ears. "You're the best." I try to give him an enthusiastic thumbs up, but I misjudge the distance and it bounces off of his chest, which, of course, makes me giggle.

"Why won't ya ever say what's wrong with ya? Where does the pain come from, Gina?"

I shrug. "It's part of me."

I glimpse a familiar frustration in his eyes before he stands back up. "I still expect you to be at work tomorrow. Send word if the pain is too much, a'right?"

"Fine." I close my eyes as I hear my door click shut and the locks engage.

24
GINA

I bolt upright on my mattress to an alarm wailing from the bedroom mirror. The noise is like a knife jammed right through my temples. Throwing my arms over my head, I start yelling, "Off! Off! Turn it off!"

"Good morning, Regina," Manuela's says after the screeching

noise finally stops.

I hate it when anyone calls me that. Only my parents called me by my full name. I clutch my head and groan. "What was that for?"

"The alarms will go off any time you need to awaken and my Do Not Disturb protocols are still active. You have server duty this morning."

Oh God. "What time?" Water. I need water.

"8:30 AM. Are you feeling well?"

I stumble over to the sink, gripping the counter as dizziness assails me, and fill one of my small cups with the lukewarm tap. Chugging it as fast as I can, I nearly choke when I realize I'm in danger of more than being late. I have server duty and I've soaked all my little gray cells in moonshine!

You idiot! I take a deep breath. What can you do, Gina? Think!

"I think I'm dehydrated. I haven't been drinking enough water."

"You must take proper care of yourself, Regina. Dehydration can cause—"

"I know. I know."

Heading for my backpack, I trip over my shoes and grit my teeth trying to keep the headache from showing on my face. I start digging through the bag, looking for my ORS packets. I try not to use them too often, but they can be a lifesaver in a pinch.

"Would you like to use an oral rehydration solution?"

"What? You have one just lying around?" I can't wait for something to be delivered.

"You may access one here." A drawer opens from the wall beside the mirror.

"You've got to be kidding me." I couldn't even see the drawer before it opened. It makes a perfect seal against the wall surface. It's full of other things too, like bandages, instant ice packs, and alcohol wipes. "Are there more of these around?"

"Yes. Essential medical supplies are kept securely within each housing unit for emergency use."

"Dehydration is an emergency?"

"It can cause significant health complications and affect your mental processing power. When citizens have poor self-care skills, I must have supplies on hand to help them address their problems before they can be seen by a provider."

"Is that your version of scolding me?"

"I do not scold citizens. I am an aide to assist in your self-care and daily living."

"Yeah, sure." I grab one of the clearly marked packets from the drawer and rip it open with my teeth. "Do I have to pay for this?"

"The minimal cost is deducted from your earnings."

Of course. It's better than using up my personal supply, though. Walking back into the kitchen corner, I turn the tap cold and mix the ORS with another glass of water. As I chug it down, I realize I'm totally gross. Manuela activates the shower without a word when I head for the bathroom. I hop in long enough to get clean, and throw on an identical set of ration clothes. I brush my teeth, wrestle the comb through my hair, and call it good.

"The server bank is too close for a bus route, but I have a walking map available," Manuela says as I'm slipping on my sneakers.

I pause for a moment to let nausea pass. It figures that instead of inventing a cure for hangovers, we just banned alcohol. My heart races for a moment. What if it affects my processing power? Hopefully, server duty won't give away my little habit. Well … it is my first time jacking in. Maybe they'll make allowances.

"Would you like me to download the walking map to your wetware?" Manuela asks. "Your test results indicate that it should be fully functional. You will be transitioned into new housing soon, as you will no longer need these projectors to see me."

The idea makes my skin crawl. "No. Don't … don't put anything in my head. I want to see how server duty goes. That whole thing still freaks me out."

"Billions of global citizens use their wetware with no ill effects."

"I don't care. I said no. For now. Okay?"

"Very well."

I'm about to head out the door for breakfast when I remember Stella. "Oh, hell."

I open the balcony door, step out, close the door behind me

and focus on her roost. "Stella, Sweetie?" I whisper, spinning around.

I don't remember bringing her home! I go back inside and after a quick search, I find the mind-link disk in the pocket of yesterday's pants along with my CID jamming earrings.

Crap! I left her at Tommy's! She's going to be so pissed at me. I hope she made it through the night okay.

"Manuela? How long before I have to be there?"

"You have seventy-five minutes before your scheduled shift. You will need to leave here by—"

"Thanks, but I'm heading out."

"Very well. I will see you when you return."

"Yeah, sure."

I put the CID jammers in my ears and activate them after a couple of blocks. Taking the long way back to Tommy's, despite the fact that my legs are still sluggish, I duck through a couple of crowded areas and dodge the cams. When I don't see her by his door, my heartbeat kicks up and pounds through my aching head. "Tommy?" I hurry inside. "Tommy!"

"What the hack?" He pops up from behind the bar. "What are ya doing here so early, Sweetheart? What's wrong?"

"I can't find Stella." I press the heels of my hands against my temples. "I forgot her and—"

"Shh …" Relief morphs his face into a smile. "I'm sorry. I forgot her, but she's here. Scared the shit outa me when I opened the door this mornin'."

"She's here? Where?"

"Flew into the dressin' room so I left her there. I didn't expect ya to be awake yet, after last night."

"I've got server duty." I stumble back and head into the dark dressing room. "Stella?"

The lights turn on as I step inside. She's hanging from my abandoned blue dress on the rack and peeks an eye open to observe me.

"Momma's so sorry, Baby." I approach slowly, then run my finger along the soft fur of her back. "Trust me, you don't want to share Momma's headache this morning, or I'd apologize properly."

My pulse pounds through my temples in agreement. When I turn around, Tommy is smiling at us from the doorway. "You gonna take her with ya?"

"Actually … Can I leave her here until tonight? I can't bring her with me to the server bank. She's black market tech, you know."

Tommy chuckles. "It's fine, long as she doesn't go flyin' around in the bar."

"Leave the door closed and she'll stay put. She's normally asleep at this time anyway."

"Yeah, like you used to be." He laughs. "Want something for that headache?"

"Absolutely."

"Here." Tommy fetches me a nasal spray. "Just a quick sniff and the pain will fade. Ya gonna stay a while?"

"No." I sniff it and hand it back. "Thanks but I'm going to be late if I don't hurry."

"Your first shift? Awesome, Sweetheart. You just wait. That coin's gonna feel awful nice. Awful nice."

Heading into the street, I go through the same cam dodging that I always do but the server bank isn't hard to find. Every district has their own, so residents don't have to travel far to get to work. The building is a huge metallic spire—forty stories at least. The residential buildings around it never get much taller than twenty stories. It's all black and gray, and terrifying as I slip off the CID jammers. It's like they don't even try to make it appealing. They just expect me to report.

I'm registered as soon as I walk in the door, and an overhead voice tells me which room to report to. I take the main elevator, travel up twenty-nine stories, and then navigate down seemingly endless hallways before I arrive at room 3016. The overhead voice announces me again as I walk through the door.

"You're early," an elderly woman says from across the room. "But early is always better than late, so you'd best keep that habit young lady."

The woman has graying hair that was once brunette and a warm smile. She's wearing lavender scrubs and bright white shoes.

Her tone is slightly mocking, but her smile reveals her good nature. In reality, I arrived with only a few minutes to spare. At least the woman is welcoming. It makes up for what the building lacks.

"Who are you?" I ask.

"I am the technician for this level. My name is Dr. Monroe."

I glance around the room and can see several people connected through WSB cables. Their eyes are open but somewhat lifeless as they walk along on treadmills with blank expressions. I groan, hating to think that I will soon look like that. The doctor at my physical explained that the WSB is a wetware-software-bridge that allows the brain to process information at a much greater rate, without causing the brain damage that would occur with a wireless connection.

"What is it?" she asks.

"Oh, just the treadmills. I had my physical yesterday and my legs still hate me." Doesn't everyone look forward to being a zombie? At least the fibromyalgia pain is gone, so it's only muscle soreness.

"Ah, yes." She closes her eyes for a moment. "I see here that the physical was a little difficult. If you prefer, we can keep you seated today. You'll only be connected for sixty minutes anyway."

"That would be great." I give her an appreciative smile.

She escorts me over to a padded chair with a reclined back that looks like a seated examination table. As I sit down, she urges me to lie back and slips a small pillow beneath my head.

"Now." She starts placing bio monitors on my chest and a WSB's tiny silicone pad onto my cheek. "This is a small server isolated from the GRID, so you won't be exposed to the bigger processing jobs. It will help you get your feet wet. You should feel nothing when you connect. In an hour, you will simply feel as if you have woken up, and then you can go home."

I nod.

"If anything feels uncomfortable or strange in any way, let me know. We'll check to see if anything is causing a problem, alright?"

"Okay."

"Close your eyes now, Regina."

When I do, an incredible weight lands on my chest. It's hard to breathe.

I try to reach out for the woman, but I can't move my arms. Panic wells up inside me, but my breathing keeps up a strange artificial rhythm. I struggle against it, twisting and straining with all my mental energy, until my breathing shifts slightly and feels more normal.

Oh, God. I've got to calm down!

Another odd sensation overwhelms my senses—like my mind is spinning too fast for me to understand any of my own thoughts. I try to focus and a segment of data pauses in the midst of my consciousness. The Malthus Initiative. I barely grasp the words before a flood of data starts pouring through the center of it and I jerk my focus away.

I'm hit with an audio file—a baby crying. Then a vid of a malnourished man lying on a cot. Serial numbers. Hundreds and thousands of CIDs. I want to scream but my body is not my own. It just keeps breathing.

Then the data pauses and shifts—almost like it's changing direction. Names. Hundreds of names scrolling by too fast to catch. Locations. Animals. Assignments. Targets.

This is information I'm not supposed to have. I don't want it!

I push back against the onslaught of data, and after a moment, burst out of it. I can still feel it rushing through me in the background, but I can isolate it away from me. I float there in the relative stillness for a while, and suddenly, my eyes open.

I blink against the bright light above me. I can control my body again and I fight against the trembling that wants to start up in all of my tissues.

That … was not normal. I've heard lots of stories. You just wake up like no time has passed.

Don't let her know. Secrets. Those were secrets. I can't let her know I remember anything!

I turn my head and see Dr. Monroe standing beside me with closed eyes and a concerned expression. She mumbles, "Welcome back, Regina. You can open your eyes now, dear."

I sit up slowly. Okay, stay calm. Jesus, help me! Please, just help me do this! It's time for my best performance ever.

I glance up at the mirror on the wall and suddenly feel terrified of how visible I am in here. It's like its staring at me. God, I wish I could disappear. As my heart races, I work to calm myself. Just … it can't see you. It just can't! Come on now! Be brave!

"Didn't we just start?" It felt like I was trapped in there forever, but I need to know if she cut my session short.

"Oh, no Dear." She finally turns toward me with a smile. "You've been out for the full sixty minutes. It just doesn't feel that way. Do you …" she hesitates, with a slight sheen of sweat on her brow, "remember anything?"

"No." I shake my head adamantly, letting my real concern show through. "Oh, crap. Am I supposed to?"

"No, no," she says, with a more honest smile. "It's designed to be painless and completely memory free. Who wants to walk around with all that junk in your head, right?"

"Right." I fake a relieved laugh. I don't even understand what I saw. "Well, what now?"

"Now, you go back home and relax." She urges me to stand up. "Your session will be reviewed by morning, and then we'll have you back in for duty tomorrow. Make sure you enjoy your day."

"I will. Thanks."

Don't run. Don't run! My heart is pounding as I make my way through the long reversed path out of the building. The slow pace is agonizing, but the last thing I need is to draw attention to myself.

What does this mean? There is definitely something wrong with my wetware. Should I just run now? How far will I get? What if it isn't my wetware? What if I run and trigger them to hunt me down when the problem was on their side? Oh Jesus, what do I do?

As I am rounding the corner of the building out in the intense summer heat, an image flashes in my mind and makes me stumble—catching myself against the outer wall. It's a man lying prone in the rain, with his skin painted black. He's blending into the night around him. Just as quickly as I see it, it's gone, and I realize that the hot metallic wall is burning my palm. I glance up, but no one seems to have noticed so I just rub my hand against my jeans and keep moving.

Going back to my hub is probably a bad idea. I'd have to

interact with Manuela and she is way too observant. I'll check in at Southside, then head back to Tommy's to process everything. Reaching into my jeans pocket, I pull out the CID jammers, put them back in my ears and activate them. Thank God I've been using these to keep Tommy's out of my file. I'll see if he'll let me perform early and then try to figure out my next move.

If I run too fast, I could tip them off. If I wait, they could catch me. God, Crazy Rob was right. I should have wished for normal!

PART 2

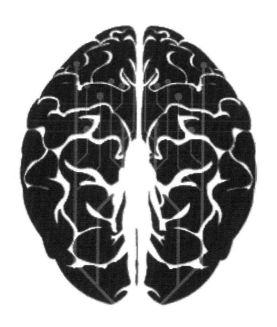

1

HAWK

My eyes snap open as I'm jerked awake by my alert tone.

CALL ME. NOW!

The message hovers in the center of my field of vision. It's Roland. He usually only sends me meeting times and dates, so it's something big. I launch out of bed and splash water on my face. Glancing in the mirror to make sure I don't actually look like I just jumped out of bed, I rush over to the dresser to throw a t-shirt on.

Forget pants.

I still feel groggy, so I slap my face a couple of times and give my head a good shake. Activating the mirror, the screen indicates that Manuela won't come on without manual instruction, so I dial Roland through a secure channel.

"Hello?" Roland's voice answers without vid.

"Hawk."

He engages the vid on his side, using the desk cam from his insultingly massive office. I can see the high-rise windows behind him. I glance at my own feed to confirm that he can only see my upper body.

"I have a priority assignment. You need to move fast." Is he sweating? Is no one else in region?

"I'm here for the meet. I've already made arrangements for—"

"Hack the meet!" Roland slams a flex down on his desk. "This takes priority. You have to move now!"

Whoa. "Okay … Send me the file, so I know what we're talking about."

"I'm not going to transfer it over this connection." It's a secure connection, so whatever has Roland's blood pressure skyrocketing, he wants to leave off-GRID. That means squids. No matter what techniques we use to keep them out, they develop workarounds nearly as fast—monitor as much GRID activity as they can.

"Where?"

"District T server bank. Thirty minutes." He disconnects

before I can respond.

Oh, that's just hacking brilliant.

"Why of course, your Excellency," I say with a slight growl. Better start packing my bags. "Anything else I can do, Mr. Prick? No? Blow my cover, why don't you."

2

GINA

I stroll into Southside in my t-shirt and jeans, fidgeting with the CID jammers in my ears again. I've never felt so paranoid in all my life. This must be what Crazy Rob feels like all the time.

The brothel is quiet at this time of the morning, with only a couple of staff strolling through the entrances. Troy is reading something on a flex at the main counter. He looks utterly bored in his black short shorts and open suit jacket. Then he spots me and grins. "Hey Gina," he calls with a wave. "I gotta say, I like this outfit less than the dress." He raises his eyebrows suggestively.

"Yeah." I lean toward him across the counter. "I need a favor. Is Joe in?"

"No, he won't be until tonight. He's out setting up for the big meet. What's up?"

"Any chance that body armor came in?"

"Yeah." He looks back down at the flex in his hand. "Joe put a rush on it, so it came in last night. He planned to let you know when you checked in today. You want it now?"

"That would be great."

"Sure thing. Are you okay?" His eyebrows knit together with a frown as he escorts me into the stockroom while it morphs in response to his mental command. The walls and shelves flip to display Joe's stock.

"Not really. But I don't wanna talk about it."

"This isn't about that guy is it?" Troy digs through the unsorted merchandise in a bin that pops out from the wall. The bin is full of all sorts of trinkets, clothing, and more expensive tech.

"No," I say. "Haven't even seen him. I just … I need to have my stuff in order and I shouldn't have taken this long. You know?"

He pulls out a package of sleek black fabric—the body armor I've been drooling over for years. It's as thin as silk beneath your clothes but can stop anything shy of a close-range hit with a bullet. It doesn't reflect the full heat from the energy weapons the shields use, but it disperses the current across your body to minimize direct damage. The fine metals woven into the fabric look pretty.

"Be honest with me, Gina." Troy turns around and looks me in the eyes, placing the body armor in my hands without letting go. "Are you in trouble?"

I hesitate. I can't bring myself to run without asking one last question. "Has Joe heard from Drustan?" I whisper, with water welling up behind my eyelids.

"No," Troy says with his eyebrows drawing together in a frown. "Why?"

I know it will make Joe angry, but I don't want to involve them if this is as dangerous as it seems. He has resources, but he's not here now and I shouldn't wait. Besides, I couldn't handle it if anything happened to Joe, or Troy too.

Before I second-guess myself, I throw my arms around Troy in an awkward hug. "Thanks." I pull back to give him a smile and a brief kiss on the cheek. "Let Joe know I'm fine, and I'm not mad about the thing with that guy." I glance down at the body armor and squeeze it gently. Maybe this was for the best.

Troy looks confused as I spin on my heel and walk back out. "You're coming back in tomorrow, right?"

"Sure," I shout back over my shoulder. "I'll see you around!"

3

HAWK

Walking into the District T server bank, I pull my hood low to shield my face, eyes hidden behind my sunglasses. I get a couple curious stares from the dazzle makeup I hastily applied to nullify facial recognition. Roland is standing in the front foyer sweating even more than before. He looks like he's about to be an idiot and speak, but I shake my head and he walks to the elevator instead.

"It's stupid for me to walk in the front door of this place." A growl slips free as soon as the elevator doors close and Roland backs up against the inside wall instinctively. "Are you trying to get me killed?"

"We don't have time for the normal precautions. Your target is moving farther away as we speak!"

"Then why am I here?"

"This is the last location we've been able to track her to." He sighs and fidgets with the rings on his right hand—pointless, expensive trinkets. "It would appear she knows how to get around our security measures."

As if that's hard.

"I've cleared the entire level so you can work." Well, the idiot managed to do something right.

After we exit the elevator, he walks me to room 3016 and hands me a flex once we're inside. Ignoring it, I survey the room. The light is harsh against the white walls and white tile floor. There are three empty chair stations and a half-dozen treadmill workstations around the room. Several people have been here recently. There is a normal combination of scents, including sweat and sanitizing chemicals.

"She was here for server duty today and had access to this isolated server." Roland points to a chair station. "This was hers."

Not a treadmill. "She wasn't connected long?"

"No. Only an hour."

I lean in close to get a whiff of my mystery target. I don't pick up on any common perfumes, but there is a trace of the chemicals you find in the standard supply rations. "She's a new Community member."

"Good catch. Was it the server time that gave her away?"

"The shampoo."

Roland looks confused and I close my eyes to focus on her scent again. Beneath the chemical smell, the scent that lingers on the chair is incredibly pleasant. It's strongly feminine, with a subtle note of sweetness in it—vaguely like honeysuckle. My stomach churns and pull back from the chair. "If she's a new citizen, why the hack am I hunting her?"

"She's a squid! You were wrong about the explosion! She's the shirker who was caught in the blast. On purpose! To get in under our radar. I don't know what information she managed to get, but I've been assured it is incredibly dangerous. We have to apprehend her immediately."

I glance at the flex for the first time and a burst of adrenaline hits me. It's her! Regina Lynneth Mallorey. The local dealer who was caught in the explosion. The woman who flashed the beautiful smile at one of the male prostitutes in Southside—who's protected by Joe.

Pretty name. Pretty face. Pretty scent. Drop dead gorgeous … Son of a bitch!

I don't need her scent to track her, but I'm not about to tell Roland that. Closing my eyes, I bring up the map to Tommy's Bar. It's not far from here. "Where does she head on the surveillance vid?"

"She … doesn't."

"They were not stupid enough to leave the cams off."

"No. They've provided her with something to block them. I wasn't even aware tech like that existed."

What? "Show me."

"It's all on the flex."

Scrolling through the data, she looks much different in the simple ration clothing than she did in the sexy black dress, but nearly the shape I remember. I fast forward through the vid log of her entering the room and getting jacked in. Spinning the 3D footage around, I don't see anything in her hands or any obvious objects in her pockets. She'd have to be using something incredibly small. When she wakes up from the connection, she turns a terrified stare directly toward one of the cams. Then she …

Disappears.

"What the …" I scroll through it over and over again.

"Have you seen anything like it? Anything in the markets?"

"No way."

There isn't a clue in the footage for what she used. She didn't just black out the cams. That would be easier to explain. She actually just ... disappeared from the image. I know she's sitting right there because the doctor is still talking to her, but the space where she should be is completely filled in as if the cams were looking straight through her. Tech like this is dangerous all by itself, regardless of what information she may have gotten hold of.

"I've never seen anything like this, but I know some squids who'd kill for it."

"Which is exactly why you have to secure her as quickly and quietly as possible. They could already be picking her up for all we know. We have no idea where she headed when she left the building."

So she's jamming her CID too. If she can do this with the cams, she was well prepared. I can't believe I'd written her off! Whoever she's working for, Regina must be incredibly good.

"What are my orders when I find her?" I hand him back the flex after downloading the data to my wetware.

"Bring her to the District M hospital."

"Then what?"

"We'll interrogate her, reset her, and release her. Standard protocol." He waives away my concern. "Remember. It's absolutely essential we get to her first."

4

HAWK

In the District T recreation lounge known to the locals as Tommy's Bar, Regina's scent is thick. She spends a lot of time here. So, Joe wasn't stupid enough to give me bad information. He knew it would bite him in the ass.

Standing inside the front door, I also pick up the scent of real alcohol—unusual for locations that aren't part of the markets. The scents of dozens of people swim together, but Regina's remains strong. It will linger here long after she's been released to a different region. It's definitely strong enough to follow from here to one or more of her frequent haunts—or even straight to her.

The bar is nice. Nothing fancy. The kind of place I prefer. Lots of women. Low lighting. Good music.

The patrons are an interesting bunch. They'll be my best source of information if she's worked here long. Two stunner junkies are off in the dark corner, visibly high but not causing trouble. One of the holotables has six people crowded around it, moving their projected characters and storytelling. They may be here regularly enough to have information on her. There are a dozen people watching their feeds or various programs together on the screens in the tables, and an equal number talking in pairs or small groups. No one looks armed and no one else is scanning the crowd. The small groups will be my best entry point.

Surveillance didn't show Regina moving between her hub, the server bank, the bar, or even Southside. Whatever tech she's using to hide, she's keeping active. Starting here is a long shot, but that's why the Community has operatives like me. It makes me sick to think she's one too. She'll lay low now that she has the intel—

A sultry voice starts crooning up front and shock courses through me when I turn to see Regina stroll onto the stage. You've got to be shitting me. She's not even trying to hide.

"What'cha havin'?" A tall man with ebony skin and intricate black light tattoos waves from my right behind the bar. He's built like a boxer, and would be a monster to tangle with.

"Just a beer, man." I turn toward him with a shrug. No need to draw extra attention. "Anything in sector worth seeing?"

"Well, I think our entertainment is worth the trip personally." He motions to where Regina is singing on stage. I take a swig of the alcohol-free beer he passes over, wondering where he keeps his stash of the real stuff. "But that's why you're here, isn't it?"

Wow, this guy is even taller than me. I meet the challenge in his eyes with one of my own and stand straighter. Great. If this is a guns-drawn kind of day, it's going to piss me off. "What do you mean?"

"Joe told me you might be coming by to see my girl." He leans on the bar.

Oh, thank the Law. No guns today. I lean back against the barstool and project Jared's confidence and charm. My girl, huh? "I assume you're Tommy?"

"That's right. This is my place."

"Good to meet you." I hold out my hand and after a brief pause he gives it an extra-firm handshake. "Joe's the one who told me she'd prefer to talk here. You have a problem with that?"

"Maybe." Tommy shrugs. "Maybe not. I don't tolerate people harassing my girls. You make her unhappy, and ya going to be dealing with me. Understand?"

More protection. My girls, this time. "Oh, I think she'll like me. But I get you. I just want to talk to her—see if she likes what she sees as much as I do."

"Fine then. Make ya-self comfortable. Don't be bothering her until she's done workin'."

I nod with a friendly smile and wander over to a table in the back with my beer.

That was weird. Joe's sending warnings about me? Jared is always good to his girls. On the other hand, if she's an operative … maybe Joe is a squid connection?

Regina looks just as sexy as before, in a tight-fitting green dress that shows off one of her sculpted legs. When she turns, I can see more of the tattoo on her back—multicolored butterfly wings in blues, teals, and purples that extend from her upper shoulders down past the edge of the dress on her low back.

My body's immediate reaction to her pisses me off, but I add her voice to my mental catalog of the beautiful things about her. It's a pretty alto that washes over you with even more warmth than her smile. I wonder if that's why they recruited her? That kind of appeal can get someone pretty far.

While she sings, her glance passes over me a couple of times, but she doesn't focus in. So, Joe didn't show her what I look like. Weird, but that will help. Is Tommy her contact? Doubt it. He'd be an idiot not to hide her. Do they think we didn't notice?

Whatever. The best option is to get her to accept a warm invitation. I'll take her home.

5

GINA

My back and my head both ache as I sit and stir my drink with the
tiny umbrella. I was terribly nervous singing tonight, but I
completed my full set. Now, with less to occupy me, I'm unable to
keep my thoughts away from what I saw.

I shouldn't remember anything. I've been told that again and
again since being inoculated—but I do. The instructions say to
report an anomaly like this immediately, but I'm not that stupid. I
can't tell anyone what happened and I need to avoid jacking in
again until I can figure this out.

Maybe I can call in sick and head out first thing in the morning.
Oh Jesus, how am I going to keep Manuela from sabotaging me?
No. I need to leave tonight. I can't risk being near her right now.

What the hell happened? Either I'm an anomaly, or somehow
my session was. If I'm the anomaly with secrets in my head, it
could be more dangerous than them discovering my EDS. If my
session was an anomaly, and it had nothing to do with me, could I
still be safe?

Ah! Another image flashes through my mind. It's a person, but
it's there and gone before I have time to make out any details. I
can't make sense of any of it, but what I do see is disturbing.
Random sounds and images, and the disorientation of data
overload keeps hitting me over and over again, but at least it's
slowing down.

God, why couldn't they have just been processing toilet paper
shipments?

"You gonna drink that fruity stuff, or just play with it?" a
smooth male voice asks from over my shoulder—startling me out
of my thoughts enough to make me spill the drink in question.

I slap a napkin onto my hand and turn to see the source of the
voice standing behind me a little too closely. He's only giving me a
couple feet of free space—enough to move if I really want, but I
would have to make a statement about it. I have to tilt my head to

see his face, even sitting on the tall barstool.

Good grief. He's almost as big as Tommy!

"Do I know you?" Stupid! Of course you don't know him, so why even ask?

"Not yet." He gives me a cocky grin, flashing his dimples. "But I can fix that pretty easily. I'm Jared." He extends his hand and I just stare at it in shock. Now? This is when you're going to show up?

The man is well over six feet tall, maybe even six-foot-five or -six, but it's hard to tell while sitting down. He has shoulders nearly as wide as my bed. He's built like a weightlifter, with muscle tone that only the extremely active could maintain, and I feel my heart rate spike. His mid-length, straight, black hair hangs long just above his eyes on the right side.

I would guess that he's in his late twenties or early thirties. He has richly tan skin, black hair and goatee, an angular jaw and full lips. His smile has a sinful curve to it as he watches me through a pair of muddy-brown, almond shaped eyes.

This is the man Joe thought my imaginary boyfriend could defend me from? You are such an idiot! I glance down the bar and see that Tommy is distracted by some pretty girl. Great.

"What do you want?" I turn around with a glare. Be mean.

"I want to introduce myself to the beautiful woman with the equally beautiful voice." He laughs and his eyes nearly disappear when he smiles. "Is that so weird?"

"Yes, it is actually. I perform here and I'm not interested, Jared. I don't sleep with patrons, so I'm afraid you'll have to find some other pretty woman to entertain you."

"Whoa, whoa." He raises his hands and backs up with a look that says I've succeeded in offending him. "Jeez, lady. You look really upset. So, I thought I would say hi and see if you wanted someone to talk to."

Talk. Right. "Well, I don't." I turn away.

"Joe talked to you, didn't he?" I turn back around to see his aggravated expression and folded arms.

Shit … I shouldn't get this guy mad at Joe. I give him what I hope is an innocent expression. "Joe? From Southside? What does he have to do with anything?"

The man's face suddenly lights up with an impish smile and he laughs again. "You're a terrible liar. You know that?"

"Please don't be mad at him."

"Mad?" Jared slides smoothly onto the barstool next to me. "Why would I be mad? I get to enjoy your company." He takes a long drink from his glass as he looks me over with enough appreciation to make me blush.

Ugh! Really? "Sure. Make yourself at home." How much worse can it get anyway?

"I have to admit …" He presses a thumb along his jaw. I find myself glancing at his full lips and silently curse. "I'm dying to know why Joe didn't want me talking to you back at the brothel."

"Probably because he expected me to scream you out in the middle of the lobby." Although that's ridiculous. "He seems to think I have a temper." I look away from him and take another sip of my drink.

"Does he have reason to?" Jared leans his chin on his fist with another sinfully cute smile.

He is not cute!

"No. I've only thrown things at him like … twice. And he deserved it." I should have thrown something larger than a tea cup.

Jared's laugh is a deep, rich sound and I hate how much I like it. "So why did Joe think you wouldn't like the pleasure of my company?"

He puts obvious emphasis on the word pleasure and I refuse to acknowledge that the little tremor in my belly is interest. The look in his eyes is pure challenge, but he keeps them fixed on my face now.

Man, this guy is almost as good as Troy. In all reality, he's stupidly attractive. I may have even been flattered back at the brothel and stumbled all over myself, but I still would have turned him down. I wonder why Joe chased him off?

"Probably because he knows I have a boyfriend," I realize.

"Boyfriend?" Jared's expression shifts to confusion.

"Yeah, you know." I give him one of my thousand-megawatt smiles. "Someone you love, who sticks around long-term."

It doesn't really matter whether he knows what I mean or not.

"I didn't think that kinda thing was healthy." He sips from his drink.

Crap. Don't tell him you're from the Dregs stupid! Relationships outside of the shirker camps are rare. "Yeah," I shrug, "but I never liked playing by the rules."

Jared gets a knowing smile and I resist the urge to pout. I wonder which lie he thinks he's caught me in. "Well. Lucky guy then."

"Yep, sorry you wasted your time."

"Oh, it's not a waste. You've got a beautiful voice. This is a pretty nice place and I've got good company. You sure you don't wanna talk about why you're so upset?"

"Who said I'm upset?"

He chuckles. "Come on, you were trying to burn a hole through the bar top with your eyes before I walked up."

Man, this guy is persistent. "It's just … I had a rough day."

"So … what happened? It'll make you feel better to talk about it."

Joe said he was a dealer. Would he know what to do?

The thought of admitting my fears to anyone makes me expect shields to come bursting through the walls. I glance around the bar, looking to see if anyone else is watching us—carefully keeping my hand over my glass as I do. The last thing I need is to get dosed with something if this guy really is a creep. No one in the bar looks suspicious, but I still don't feel safe.

"What?" He looks around the room with an amused expression—mimicking me.

Tommy walks up, finally noticing my situation, and leans on the bar across from us. The tattoo artist who drew the snakes wrapped around his huge biceps, did an amazing job of using his natural contours for emphasis. "Now I know my girls have pretty voices and even prettier faces, but I said I don't want you wearing out your welcome."

You talked to him? You should have thrown him out!

"Not my intention, Sir." Jared holds up a hand of surrender. "I heard she's one of the free-thinkers in sector."

"Free-thinkers?" I scoff. "What is that supposed to mean?"

"You know …" He shrugs, but his shoulders are tense. "A woman with enough brains to see that bending the rules sometimes isn't gonna kill us. Shit. It can even be fun—although I'm not a fan of the exclusive love thing myself."

Jared not-so-subtly flashes the ring on his right hand and realization dawns on Tommy's face. Tech dealers usually wear a prominent item of jewelry to identify themselves to buyers and other dealers. Tommy glances at me with a question in his eyes, but I don't know if I should give this guy the time of day or not.

"I saw you at Southside, and word was that you weren't there for action. So, I figured I'd stop in and see if you'd like some company, or if you had anything worth exchanging," Jared says.

I roll my eyes and give Tommy a shrug. It's not like he's going to let the guy drag me off.

"Well, you let me know if you need anything." Tommy walks back over to the girl that's got his attention and flashes her a smile.

Glancing back at Jared's ring, it's a gem-jammer—fancy enough to be military grade and only a few generations old. It looks like a large sapphire, but the shine is slightly off. It would take a dealer to recognize the difference. The nanotech woven into the stone blocks his CID from broadcasting by causing low-level bio-interference.

"Joe mentioned that you were a dealer, but he didn't act like you wanted to trade."

"I admit, I was much more interested in taking you home for the night." Jared grins. "That doesn't mean I have to walk away empty-handed, though."

"Sorry, but …" I run my fingers across the back of his hand and casually inspect the ring, "I think you're a little too rich for my blood."

He leans closer with a seductive smile, his thickly-lashed eyes drifting to my lips. "You never know until you ask."

I back away. His role as a dealer doesn't make him trustworthy—just the opposite in fact. He has to be fairly cunning.

"I was confused when I first saw you." He backs up and takes a sip from his drink. "The locals say you're a life-long shirker, but …

you have a GRID scar. Unless Tommy's got another singer with such uniquely pretty eyes."

"No, that would be me. The scar is a recent development, and one I'm not happy about."

"Why not?" He turns his head to flash the back of his neck toward me. "I've got one. The way I see it, we've just got access to what's important, right? We can make things happen."

"Hey." I raise my hands in surrender and glance around again. You can't just say things like that! "I don't know what you've heard about me, but that's not my game. I'm no squid."

"What's your game then?"

"I just scrounge. I deal the stuff no one else wants to take the time to collect. I search out antique tech for specific buyers and get in on the markets when I can. I've seen people dealing tech like you've got, but I won't deal it myself for a long time. Not until several newer generations have come out."

"Then why the change? Why connect if you're so opposed to it?"

"I didn't have a choice."

His eyes narrow and his tone drops to a deadly serious note. "Are you saying someone inoculated you without your consent?"

Wow, he just got scary.

"Just because I gave my consent, didn't mean I had a choice." I must sound as stupid as I feel. "Not really."

"Is that what you were so worked up about when I came up and surprised you?"

Weird. I sit and stir my drink for a few moments, wondering how much I want to admit to a total stranger. An intimidating total stranger. The odds that he knows something that could help me are slim, but not non-existent. As a dealer, he would know more about GRID tech than most Community members who connect every day. Then again, admitting that anything was abnormal about my experience still seems incredibly unwise. And what if this guy is a squid himself? He could be all kinds of trouble.

"I was blind," I finally whisper, staring miserably at my smoothie. "I've lived off GRID all my life. I didn't live well, but I managed. I could have kept living that way forever if it wasn't for free-thinking assholes like the squids."

"Now, hold up," Jared says. "What do they have to do with anything?"

They. Interesting.

"The bomb in District J a few weeks ago? It pushed me through a storefront window. Shoved a bunch of glass in both my eyes and left me blind. The doctors said I could connect and pay back my debts for the procedure over time, or they could put me in an institution." I can't help but shudder at the word. "So, I got inoculated."

"No shit … Can I?" He reaches for my face and I allow him to inspect my eyes more carefully. His finger tips are incredibly smooth. "These are really re-grown? Did the pattern between the colors happen after they grew them back, or were they always this way?"

"They've always looked this way." I pull back to regain my personal space. Again. God, this guy is like a magnet.

"How did you get caught in the blast?"

"Wrong place, wrong time. I'd just finished a trade with someone. She was a kid. A kid—not even out of University yet—and she died in that explosion. They didn't care who got hurt. It was just violent stupidity, and now I have to pay for it for the rest of my life."

"Hey, I don't support that kind of shit either." Jared shakes his head. "I deal with them from time to time when I'm working, but I'm not one myself."

"Good." I down the rest of my drink, ignoring the after-taste.

"What are you going to do now? Have you been on the servers long?"

"No. Today was my first day. I don't really have a plan."

"Where are you staying?"

"Uh-uh." I shake my head. No way am I giving away that kind of information.

"O-kay …" He laughs. "What about … Would you like a place to crash for tonight? I've got a pretty nice spot picked out while I'm in town."

"Thanks, but I already told you. I have a boyfriend, and he

wouldn't appreciate your offer."

"Well, if he's kept a hold of you long-term, he must really be something." Jared's cocky grin and narrowed eyes say he may not believe me.

"Yep, no one else quite like him." I give him a bright smile.

This guy oozes charm, but he's not sticking around and the last thing I need is another complication. Tommy glances over from the far end of the bar.

"Alright, alright," Jared finally concedes. "Here's my number in case you change your mind. I'll be in town for a few more nights."

He sets a speed dial disk down onto the counter, and I watch him as he saunters toward the exit. He is good-looking after all. I should also make sure he's really gone.

After he's swiped his hand over the payment scanner and left, I stare into my empty glass, wondering if I made the right choices in speaking with him. If he knew more about the GRID—which he seemed to—he might have been able to actually help me. But I've never liked risks, and he would have been a big one. I've got to manage on my own.

I need to talk to Crazy Rob.

Tommy wanders over and leans across the bar again with raised eyebrows. "Well, he was interesting."

"Oh yeah, thanks for the help."

"Don't give me lip, Gina. I know he was a lot more interested in those pretty eyes than anythin' you were sellin', but I don't throw people out for wanting to see the beautiful entertainment we provide. If I did, I'd lose half my sales, ya know."

"Yeah, well he's the last thing I need right now. I could use another drink though."

"Now that, I can help ya with."

6

GINA

When I finally walk out of Tommy's, I've got a pretty good buzz going. My back still hurts a little, but the rest of my pain has quieted. My legs are somewhat sluggish, though. Fortunately, Stella is used to this state in our mind-link from time to time. She hangs from my jacket instead of flitting about for food.

I gasp as a man with huge fangs and dark, dappled skin growls menacingly in my field of vision. Stella takes flight with a screech. The image disappears and I shudder.

"Everything's okay, girl," I whisper to myself as much as her. I wish it were true. I should remove the mind-link disk to spare her, but I need to use her eyes tonight. I need to grab a few things from my hub and get out of here.

The notifications and directions for drivers and pedestrians cast soft colors on me from the textured glass streets beneath my feet. My backpack rolls quietly along behind me, faithfully following the beacon in my pocket. The steady hum of people is quieter on the streets at night, but still active with all the night-shift workers. I appreciate the ability to blend into the crowd.

"Go home." Scout ahead for me. What do you see?

Stella performs her acrobatics, flitting from one cloud of bugs to another, flipping them into her mouth with enthusiasm with her wings and tail. She gets a couple of blocks ahead and I freeze when she sees a couple of CPG drones parked in front of my building. The backpack stops at my heels.

Ducking into the shadows beneath a decorative oak in the wide sidewalk, I struggle to get Stella to focus on the female officer. She's showing people something on a flex as they pass by. Most of them scratch their heads or shrug their shoulders until one man nods and points up toward my building.

Oh crap. A cold, sobering shudder runs down my spine.

Are they looking for me? Whoever they want isn't broadcasting a CID, or the shields would know exactly where they are. I touch the warm metal of my jamming earrings. God … I'm as paranoid as Rob.

Their presence could have nothing to do with me, but I can't shake the sudden terror that it does. Either way, I can't risk a confrontation with alcohol in my system. I'd love to send Stella in for a bat's eye view of the hub—to see if any uninvited guests are inside—but she can't get in without the door open.

I press the lower button on the backpack's beacon, a set of straps deploys, and I toss it onto my back—instantly regretting the weight. Backing up, I make my way quickly through the crowded streets. The Dregs are a long way from here on foot. I'll never make it carrying this bag when I've already walked so far today.

Pulling the autobus swipe I got from Joe out of my pocket, I tuck myself into one of the shelters at the nearest stop. As soon as the autobus pulls up, I pass the swipe over the scanner and take the seat closest to the emergency exit. The air conditioned cab is a relief from the sticky heat still radiating from the concrete and glass outside. I relax into my seat, watching Stella's view of my bus moving from one stop to another along its route. No shields are closing in, so I must have gone unnoticed.

Okay, Gina, calm down. Let's be reasonable about this. They could be looking for anybody. Well, a shirker … or anyone with jamming tech.

The guy pointing out the building suggests they aren't looking for a shirker. It could be one spending the night with someone, I guess. After all, some of us make a living that way. But who would know who was working where? That makes no sense.

It can't be me, though. Can it? Something went wrong in my server session, but I wasn't confronted when I disconnected. I was sent home. They sent Crazy Rob away too, and he crashes any GRID tech in his vicinity. The shields always shoo him away from areas where he causes trouble, but I don't think they hurt him or take him in. How bad could it be? No matter how much I try to talk myself down, my heart thunders in my ears.

After a few blocks, pain starts to flare in my back and neck but I concentrate on Stella, so I don't miss my stop. It's difficult because my panic is provoking her urge to flee. Finally, she catches sight of our building at the edge of the Dregs and I get off at the next stop. Setting my bag on the ground and reengaging the autodrive, I walk as fast as I can manage.

A couple of blocks from the burrow, I drop the bag into the tunnel system and climb down, heading toward the access pipe. The smell makes it easy to push the longing for home toward Stella in my mind, and she wings her way straight to the building through the open air outside. When I'm close to home, I pause to close my eyes. I don't want to risk falling on my face down here.

"Let's see who's outside," I whisper. Through an odd blend of Stella's vision and echolocation, I can survey the area. Her vision is good, but much grayer than mine and the echolocation is limited in distance, but much more detailed in texture.

There are several people outside—the normal characters. No swarms of shields or people are running about. People are sitting around the fires the way they do every night, with old Yeon-Jae handing out soup. She used to make it all herself with scraps donated by those who participate each night, but since she has gotten slower with age, Hosni makes it for her about half the time.

Comforted that no one seems alarmed, I open my eyes to sneak inside through the access tunnel. Shields don't normally venture into the Dregs but even if they do, there are dozens of buildings to search. Still, it would be best if no one was aware of my presence.

After I finally climb up the ladder into the building, Rob isn't around to meet me. I use the passcode he gave me and stash my backpack in his burrow instead of hauling it all the way up to mine. He must be telling his stories around the fires. I'll have to track him down for advice when I'm ready to go.

Stella has already made her way into our burrow through her access from the outside before I'm even on the right floor. She's watching our room intently, but her movements are too quick to focus on anything for long. She's highly agitated, but I don't detect anything out of place. My stress is probably damaging her tiny heart. I sneak through the building, blindly feeling my way up the pitch black staircase, and then down the hall on my floor, illuminated only by the ambient light from the huge exterior windows. "What's wrong, sweetie?" I whisper as I approach the burrow door. I plug in my code quickly, relieved to hear the locks deactivate.

As I open the door, Stella careens into me from inside making a terrible screeching sound. She grips the shoulder of my jacket with her feet, flapping her wings and squeaking an alarm.

A predator is behind me!

I spin around and slam straight into a huge man wearing a black face mask. He clamps his hand over my mouth—muffling my scream. Then he grabs my head from behind with his other hand—dislodging Stella's disk from behind my ear—and Stella takes flight again with a screech.

"Shh … Calm down," my attacker whispers.

Oh my God, it's Jared!

I struggle against his hold, but he tightens it further instead of releasing me—pinning my arms between his elbows. I claw at his chest, kick my instep against his shin and drag it down the bone, fighting his hold. He slams me against the door and blinding pain shoots through my spine. Then the hand behind my head disappears and is back in a flash. He jabs something sharp into my neck just above the body armor I'm wearing under my clothes. I slam my fist against his jaw as hard as I can, but the bones in my hand snap as they dislocate. I may as well have punched brick.

Everything starts to pitch and spin. Oh God, no! I've been drugged!

"Shh … I'm sorry, Regina," he whispers. "I didn't want to frighten you."

My chest is heavy, and my limbs become numb and tingle as the dizziness increases. I choke out a sob beneath his hand, and tears well up in my eyes as I keep trying to claw anything I can. But my arms won't do what I say!

Damn you, Joe! This is your fault! I try to push Jared back again. God, Jesus, please help me! Send Rob! Send someone! Anyone!

"That's right," Jared says in a gentle tone that terrifies me even more. "Calm down. I just need you to close your eyes for a minute."

I can't close my eyes. He'll rape or kill me! I struggle to shake my head beneath his hand, as the tears spill over. My strength slips away completely and he guides me down onto my back on the filthy hallway floor. "Please," I struggle to slur out as he removes his hand. "Please don't …"

"I'm not gonna hurt you. Just go to sleep for me now."

I'm fighting my eyes from closing with all the strength I have left. His eyes look strangely sad as he tucks a lock of my hair behind my ear. I'm furious but I can't move. God, don't let him hurt me!

Then I lose my battle with the drug.

7

HAWK

Hawking's hacking ghost! That went south fast.

I watch Regina's beautiful eyes drift closed on her tears. I had to get a handle on her quickly to keep her from drawing the attention of the shirkers downstairs. The sheer terror in her eyes makes my stomach hurt. As catch and release work goes, I definitely prefer prey that wish to be caught.

Before bringing her in to be processed, I need to take a better look around—see if the device is here. Letting her get this far was a calculated risk, but the pieces of this puzzle sure as shit aren't adding up.

The locks on her door are fairly sophisticated, but not GRID tech. Smart. Anything GRID based can be hacked without even being on site. These can be hacked, but letting her enter her code was faster—before the stupid bat spooked her. Man, I hate those things. It figures that some cooped-up animal gave me away after all that stealth.

The woman's pretty scent, now tainted with the smell of alcohol and bat, drifts across my face as I pick her up and cautiously enter the door. The scent that hits me from inside the room makes me nauseous. After a quick whiff to confirm that no one else is inside, I tuck my face in her hair for relief and work as quickly as I can.

I don't see any traps. The walls are coated in a Faraday alloy, which will keep the light contained. I shut the door with my foot and juggle her to engage the locks again.

Blinking the code to deactivate the night vision in my contacts, I turn on the battery-powered lamp by the door. The sight before me makes me pause. I've seen a few burrows in my life, but none in Community territory were dug in this deep. The whole thing is littered with old tech and supplies a shirker would need for living rough. The surfaces are dirty, but it looks like she's tried to maintain the place. The holoframes scattered around, the mismatched file cabinets and desks, even an urn and a group of struggling plants in the corner, hint toward an unusual level of permanence.

I glance at the walls again, noting that the Faraday coating is complete beneath her belongings—total frequency blackout. It's like a safe house. How long has she lived here? I've never understood anyone choosing this misery, let alone such a beautiful, intelligent woman and it makes my chest tighten.

Bracing myself for the horrible odor again, I pull my face away from her hair. Her scent is even thicker in the burrow than at the bar—the only redeeming quality for the air. It's stale and leaves a horrible taste in my mouth. That's definitely blood—from several different people—but it's old. The air exchange system in here probably hasn't worked in decades. The chemicals used to sterilize the place are even worse. There's also a thick scent of bat, and signs that it's been hanging off of material around the burrow. It must have made a nest here since she's been in her new hub.

There's a bed in the adjoining room—strangely an old hospital bed—and I recoil from the scent of old blood on it. It's not hers. Taking the scent in deeper, it matches the one I picked up in the pile of bloodied rags in the hallway. Whoever it was must have bled all over her bed. This scent is just what's left over after someone tried to clean the stained fabric.

"Sorry, Babe." I whisper to her once again as I lie her down in the bed, brushing her auburn hair back from her face. I hate lying her down on this thing, but everything else in this time capsule is worse. "What made you come back, huh?"

It looked like she was going to head back to her hub from the bar, and then something spooked her. She'd just stopped, hid for a few moments, and then backtracked to hop on the bus. What was it?

The sedative will keep her out for at least an hour, so I look around for clues to why this woman is so dangerous. She could be an incredibly good actor, but her answers were all wrong. According to the people at the bar, she's been a fixture there for years. She seems to hate the squids. If she's telling the truth, she's not working with them and a memory reset is a bad call.

She could be playing me ...

Even then ... why come here? This must be where she lived before she got recruited. If she got recruited ... Joe must not be her contact. He'd have some place with more protection.

I walk straight to the urn and lift the lid. Hawking's ghost! Real people are in this thing. The holoframe beside it has a projection of her with an older man and woman. Are they the bodies she's keeping? What the hack for? Cremation wipes out familial scents, so it's impossible to know, but the woman might be her birth mother. They look very similar.

Sifting through the supplies in the first room reveals nothing important. There are medical supplies like scalpels, splints, and bandages—which might explain the blood everywhere. There are standard CID jammers, ghosters, disrupters, and Faraday caps—all illegal, but common on the street.

Bullseye—isolated, non-GRID, flexes and coms. I scoop them up and toss them into a duffel bag she has stashed in a corner. I'll check them after I turn her in.

My gut twists with guilt again and I hesitate. My orders were clear—bring her in for a memory reset and reintegration. This is what I do, but something about this job doesn't sit right. She has a real life. She belongs places. If they're wrong, to take that from her would be completely pointless.

None of this stuff explains how she tricks the cams, though.

Walking back over, I sweep her body for tech. She's got jammers in her ears, so I take them to check later and put a couple of my own in their place. She's got a speed dial disk. Placing it against my cheek, it's the one I left for her at the bar. Wow. I can't believe she took it. It's been a long time since a woman's turned me down flat.

Hey, she's got two layers on. Silk body armor … I run my fingers across the smooth surface over her abdomen. You were expecting trouble, huh? Well, don't worry, Babe. I won't turn you over in these. Those morons would decide you're the real deal.

No other tech at all. If it's not in the stuff I've found, she must have stashed the data and the cam device somewhere else. In that case, spending more time here is stupid. The best bet is Tommy's Bar.

As I cross the threshold back into the first room, someone knocks loudly on the door. "Gina?" a male voice shouts from the other side.

I rush to her side as quietly as I can, scooping her up off the bed.

"Gina, are you in there?" The man pounds again.

Ripping an autoharness out of the side pocket of my BDUs, I clip it around her. Once she's strapped in, I lift her body around behind my back and get her secured. Then I reach into my pocket and grip another dose of sedative.

"Gina! If you're in there, open this door, or I'm coming in!"

I step silently behind where the door will open and press her back against the wall behind me. He enters a series of numbers on the keypad and the locks disengage. He's someone she trusts. Maybe the … what did she call him? Boyfriend? "Gina? Are you in here?"

The man that enters is older but not necessarily elderly. He could still do some damage if he meant to, but I would be shocked if he's her lover. He's a shirker with a mismatched hat, yellow sweater, and old slacks. He must have heard something.

As soon as he's stepped far enough forward, I jam the injector down on the back of his neck; just to the left of his GRID scar. He whirls around and catches me by surprise with a blow to my side. I shove him back with a hand silencing him—slipping the other behind his head to protect it from the impact. Pinning him against the alloy-coated wall, he deals me another two good blows to the gut, so I trap his arms against his body with my own. Shaking off the pain, I watch the drug begin to take effect.

His eyes grow wide as he catches sight of her strapped to my back. Fury contorts his features and he gets another surge of strength, but his kicks and blows are growing more and more unfocused. The harder he fights me, the faster the drug will burn through his system.

When he can't stand up anymore, I drag him through the room by his head and shoulders. As his face begins to grow slack, I drop him back against her bed. "Let her go," he slurs with a half-lidded gaze.

I walk back to the door and shut it, once again engaging the locks. A thud behind me makes me turn. He's dragging himself toward me—knife in hand. He's got a lot of spirit and must care a great deal about her. If he's the type that will go looking, she'll have to be placed farther away after the reset.

I knock the knife from his feeble grip, pick him up by the back of his bulky yellow sweater, and toss him back onto her bed. "You bastard," he mutters. "Let her ..." His eyes close completely.

I'll offer to take her off-continent for my next job. This one will definitely look for her, but he'll never look that far. He'll assume she's dead.

Tightening the harness straps securing the woman to my back, I grab the small duffel of tech and decide to get out of the hacking building before anything else can go wrong.

8

HAWK

I don't see or smell anything unusual as I approach the secure entrance to the District M Hospital with the shirker woman in my arms.

The old guy should be able to get loose from the bonds I tied him in, but it'll take a while.

This job makes no hacking sense. She's making none of the moves a trained operative would. Before she got spooked, she'd been headed back to her hub. I could have just opened the door and picked her up after she fell asleep. It would have been better if she'd let me in, but I pushed her as hard as I dared.

If hating the squids is an act, why would they recruit anybody so obviously unskilled for an important operation? And if they did, why didn't they pick her up already? She stupidly returned to her usual haunts.

And something's up with the CPG. Even that cam tech is no reason to issue an all-call of local shields—not without securing it first. Something else about this babe made the silk shirts panic.

To get in this entrance, three secured doors have to register my CID. So, I've deactivated my CID clone and tucked it in my pocket. The outer door looks unimportant but the secondary looks like a fortress. There are two guards stationed at this third inner door. They're both tall, dark-skinned men with shaved heads, but one is broader than the other.

I wave my hand over the scanner next to them and the thinner one raises his eyebrow in interest. My authentic CID broadcast will come up on their devices as a black file. They don't have a high enough security clearance to know who I am or ask me any questions about the unconscious woman.

"You'll have to scan her in too, Sir," skinny guy says respectfully.

What? Whatever. I nod, reach up to deactivate her earrings, and pass her hand over the scanner.

"Well, I'll be," big guy says with a smile. "You found the one everybody's looking for."

"Do not report this to anyone." I put my rank into my voice. "Your superiors are monitoring the situation and will know she's here. Her processing will be handled quietly. Is that understood?"

"Yes, Sir," both men say in unison, standing at attention properly.

Once I'm inside the hospital, I follow the signs. I've been to hundreds of processing stations in regions all over the world, and they generally look and smell the same. White and sterile. I walk along, trying not to grind my back teeth blunt over this whole hacking mess.

Catch and release is a standard job. I track down the offenders, bring them in for a reset, and sometimes take them to a different region to start their new life. We'll never be able to process her back out to a nearby region after all this. They drew too much attention to who she is with local citizens, and mystery man back at her place will make it worse.

The thought of her burrow makes me shudder and I glance at her face, tucking her closer against my chest. Her burrow is authentic—you can't fake that. She's lived in that squalor for years. At least she won't have to go back there. I bet I can find something nice to leave in her new hub off-continent. Something that smells beautiful—not bloody.

After passing through a couple of elevators and several corridors, I reach the processing station labeled 426A. Inside are the immense wall-to-wall computer banks, monitors, and treatment chair that I see in every reset room. No one's ever bothered to explain how it works, but some weird combination of IV drugs and electronic instructions to the brain tissue convince your brain that old portions of memory are no longer accessible. The brain is pretty amazing, though, and will just start writing in new sections. Then bam! No old memories. New life.

The processing room smells strongly of the repulsive drugs necessary for the process, and I wish for the thousandth time that I could block it out. A woman inside with long black hair and the features of far eastern North Continent is running around in blue scrubs issuing orders. She's not wearing a name tag, but she must be the head doctor. Three assistants shuffle around the room in light green scrubs—two men around my age and an older woman.

"Thank goodness you found her!" the doctor says. "Place her here in the examination chair please."

Man, should I really just turn her over like this? These people will follow their orders without knowing anything about her. "I have concerns I need to file with my superiors before she's processed."

"You can file whatever you wish at the hyperport in the next ward," she says. "Please, put her in the chair. We need to get started as quickly as possible."

I glance at Regina's sleeping face and the sick feeling creeps up on me again with a shiver in my bones. She's so helpless ... That's never bothered me before, but information is being kept from me and they're in an awfully big hurry to process her. Hack. I hate this!

I'm a soldier—the choice isn't mine to make—so, I force myself to set her gently in the chair.

"Thank you, sir." The doctor inserts her body between us as she places monitors on Regina. "You may go now."

"I'd like to stay."

"That's not an option this time, soldier." She spits the title in a demeaning tone as she starts booting up the machinery. Her assistants begin running an IV. "You need to leave. Now."

"Where will she be relocated?" I won't let them push me out.

"That's above your clearance level," she says. "Nathaniel secure her arms and legs please."

I move farther back as Nathaniel shoves past me to reach the woman. His scent is drowning in a blend of fancy soaps and shampoos. I refuse to give him more room than he needs.

"There are shirkers in this sector who will look for her. She can't be placed locally. I'm volunteering to take her with me off-continent."

"You can file any request you wish with your report," the doctor says. "Now I must insist. Please make your way to the hyperport so we can begin our procedures. I will file my own report about your uncooperative behavior if I must."

My fingers curl into fists as I bite back a curse. I spin on my heel and exit the room, putting more force against the door than necessary. That idiot doesn't care whether their intel is right or wrong. She has no interest in anything I have to say. Even if my superiors do, Regina will be reset before they even read my request!

I'll call Roland and force him to review it now.

At the far end of the corridor, two hospital staff dressed in teal scrubs are exiting an elevator. They're wheeling out a gurney carrying a body-seal bag. I slow down and tune my hearing in to listen to their conversation.

"Where are you taking that?" the young, swarthy man asks.

"I have to get it to room 426A," the pale, older one says.

My body wants to freeze but I force myself to keep moving. The young man turns to head down a different corridor once the gurney is out, and the older one hurries past me with it. I slow down enough to miss the elevator, then glance around and find a hyperport right next to me at the nurse's station. The doctor was getting rid of me.

That bitch!

I approach the station and connect the WSB cable to my cheek. What in Tesla's name do they need a body-seal bag for? I close my eyes and dive my way into the Global Fellowship's local records, and then into the medical files. Regina's file is sealed, and the GRID rejects my security clearance. You've blocked me from the data on my own hacking mark?

BOOM!

The building rocks slightly and I grip the station, recognizing the vibrations of a large explosive immediately. I rip the WSB off my cheek and take off at a dead run for the processing room. No hospital staff begin spilling from any of the other rooms in the hall. They must have cleared out this floor—like they did the entire level of the server bank.

The guy with the gurney takes off, abandoning it in the hall outside the room. When I crack the door open, the doctor is screaming at her assistants. "For the Law's sake, hand me the needle! Quick!"

"But we don't have what we need yet!" The female assistant is frozen with a needle in hand.

So they haven't finished the mind sweep.

"It doesn't matter! We're out of time!" The doctor stretches out her hand. "We have to destroy it before they get here!"

Destroy it?

Rage burns hot, like fuel pouring through my system. They're going to kill her! There's no other way they can destroy whatever they're looking for in her brain with something as simple as a drug. As the assistant passes the needle over, I see Regina shift and groan. When the doctor seizes the needle and removes the cap, I'm already moving.

She's focused on shoving the needle into the IV port, but her hands are shaking. I grab her by the back of the neck, toss her to the floor and she slides across the room. Ripping out the IV they've placed in Regina's arm, I put pressure on the wound with my thumb to stop the bleeding.

"Ow …" Regina mumbles in a soft whine, struggling to pull away without opening her eyes.

"What are you doing?" the doctor screeches with the color draining from her face.

"She's a Community citizen!" I can't help the growl that slips into my voice, watching her eyes widen as I use my claws to sever Gina's restraints. That's right. You know what I am. "I don't care what information she has in her head. I don't believe she's a squid. I tried to tell you that!"

"It doesn't matter!" the doctor says. We all turn our heads toward the sound of automatic gunfire coming from a good distance away. "Our orders are to terminate her! Now!"

"Stop …" Regina mumbles, fighting her way out from under the sedative and struggling against my hold. "Let go."

"I'm not gonna let you kill her." I level a glare at the doctor. "She's my mark. She's under my protection."

The doctor's gaze shifts behind me just in time to warn me, an instant before the cloying scent of shampoo pours over my shoulder. I spin, and let go of Regina's arm to grab Nathaniel—who's got a scalpel—by the throat. I intercept the scalpel, twisting his wrist until I hear the bone snap. He screams. The scalpel drops and I slam my forehead against his. He drops like a rock and his head strikes the base of the IV pole. He's not getting back up anytime soon.

9

GINA

My head is swimming and everything is so loud.

What's that noise? What's happening?

I struggle to open my eyes and the image before me slowly shifts into focus. Where, the heck, am I? I'm in a padded chair? In a room that's practically made of computer banks. Jared, from the bar, has a man in green scrubs by the throat—who screams when Jared twists his arm.

Jared! I blink, assaulted by the memory of struggling against him in the hallway outside my burrow. He drugged me! He's going to rape me! But ...

Where am I?

Jared slams his head into the man, who crumples to the floor. He turns toward me and his eyes widen. I scream as he lunges toward me, but he collides with a man beside me in scrubs I hadn't seen. The man drops a needle on my chest, as Jared drags him completely over me and throws him to the floor by his shoulders. The edge of the man's shoe burns my neck as he's hauled over.

What the hell is going on?

I try to shake off the overwhelming drowsiness as I look at the needle that was dropped. Before I can gather my thoughts, Jared is back. He tosses the needle away and lifts me into his arms.

"No!" I struggle to get away, but I'm weak.

He ignores me and runs down a long hallway at a frightening pace. The deafening sound of automatic gunfire blasts ahead of us and he makes a sharp turn. Terror burns through me, adrenaline beginning to win the war against whatever he dosed me with. "Let me go!" I push away from his chest with what little strength I can muster.

Jared stops, drops my legs to the floor, and pushes me against the wall with my arms pinned above my head. "Stop. Fighting me!" he orders with an animalistic growl. "I am trying to save your ass."

"What?"

Automatic gunfire sprays to our right, and I let out an involuntary scream. Jared enters a nearby room, throwing me behind a huge machine and smothering me with his big body. The piece of equipment has massive mechanical arms sticking out in all directions from its top.

"Don't hit the girl!" a male voice booms.

The girl? They mean me! Are they trying to rescue me?

"Those are squids," Jared mumbles in my ear, pulling back to look me in the eye. "Should I hand you over?"

Squids? Squids with guns!

Jared … kidnapped me. Save my ass? I shake my head and swallow my terror.

"Give us the girl!" the man shouts.

Jared shifts, grabbing a wheeled oxygen tank from beside us. As I glance around, I realize we must be in a hospital. These machines resemble imaging and surgical equipment, and the hallways had that double-bed-wide, easy-clean look. As Jared keeps us tucked behind the machinery, he lays the tank on the floor.

What is he doing? Oh Jesus, please get me out of this!

"Come on, man." The guy sounds closer. "There's no way you're gonna make it out of here with her."

Jared reaches up and opens a panel on the machine above us. Then he pulls out a huge handle. He kicks the oxygen tank out from behind the machinery and pulls the handle before rolling over to smother me with his brawn again. With a crash, one of the huge arms from the machine shielding us is ejected and collapses onto the tank. A deafening hiss erupts from the tank as it's top is sheared off, and it bursts forward under incredible pressure. Multiple voices scream from the corridor and a boom shakes the walls around us.

Jared yanks me up by the arms—pain slices through my shoulders—and we're running before I can blink. I try to keep up, but he lifts me into his arms again before we've even made it a few strides. He picks up speed, dodging down hallways in random directions, never staying in the same hallway long.

After a few minutes, we enter another room. Two bodies are lying on the floor in green scrubs and I realize we're back where we started. He's run us around in a giant circle? We're getting nowhere!

He sets me down on the floor and glances out into the hallway.

Oh, my God, I've got to get out of here. Who is this guy? Why do the squids want me? Is that really who they are? Jesus, I am so lost!

Jared reaches into a side pocket and pulls out a—a shield gun! Where did that come from? He grabs my hand and we creep back into the hallway.

An older man in an unfamiliar camouflage uniform comes around the corner close on our right and is about to call out when Jared's hand collides with his throat. I muffle a scream with my hand. The man crumples to the ground gagging, and Jared slams the butt of his gun into the back of the man's head. His dazzle makeup smears onto the tile floor. Before I can run, Jared grabs my wrist again and starts moving forward.

Click.

We both turn toward the sound behind us. A woman in blue scrubs has picked up the man's automatic rifle and is aiming it at my chest with wide horrified eyes. Jared knocks me across the hall into the opposite wall just before she pulls the trigger.

She misses with a spray of bullets.

He leaps to put himself in front of me and grabs my arm, wrenching me painfully to the floor as he dives on top of me. A bullet from the next spray tears its way through his side—splattering blood across the wall and floor—as he pulls the trigger on his gun. A scream is trapped in my throat as I watch her crumple with a scorched mark in the center of her forehead. I can't breathe.

Jared groans and rolls against the wall for a moment as he touches the wound and then looks at his bloody hand. "Hack."

That woman was aiming for me. Me! Why?

The sound of heavy footfalls echo around us from multiple directions. The shots have given us away. I try to wrestle the rifle away from the dead woman but Jared grabs my arm and takes off at a run. At the end of the hallway, he rips a door open and starts hurtling his way down the stairs. I stumble along behind him, praying I don't sprain or dislocate something.

Two floors down, he bursts through another door, picks me up and begins sprinting again, leaving bloody footprints behind us. How can he run like that after being shot?

"You're hurt," I dare to say through my ragged breathing.

"Quiet."

The sounds from a huge gathering of people are ahead of us. He ducks into a small room where we surprise a blond man inside. Panic crosses the man's face as Jared's fist collides with his nose. The man's head snaps back and he crumples to the floor with blood pooling beneath his face.

"Sorry, man." Jared pushes the door shut and locks us inside.

We're in a small examination room. I stare at the stranger with the broken face, trying to get my addled brain to function—my entire body shaking. I don't know where I am. I don't have a weapon.

Jared strips off the man's clothes and then starts on his own. Should I run? I glance toward the door, but he's standing between me and it.

No question, the bullet he took was meant for me. Faced with both of us, she aimed straight for my chest. The needle he stopped earlier must have been meant for me too. But why? *Save your ass*, he said. What threat could I be compared to him?

He brought me here … probably. But for now, he seems to want me alive, and I wouldn't be alive now without him.

God only knows what the squids want me for. It can't be good.

If we don't get the bleeding from that wound under control, though, we won't make it out of this hospital. I begin digging through the drawers in the examination table, looking for bandages. "You're going to bleed through those scrubs." I fight for a calm voice, finding bandages in the third drawer.

"There's no time." He sops up the blood from his side with his shirt as he stands there in black briefs.

"Make time. You've left bloody footprints everywhere." I press a stack of bandages against the ragged wound. He groans and I wrap a roll of gauze around his middle as fast as I can. It's ripped his side open, but it may not have gone through critical tissue.

"That's good enough." He pushes my hands away as he leans over to pull on the stranger's pants. The man is shorter and rounder than Jared, so the pants don't fit him well. Fortunately, they have a drawstring waist and he ties them low on his hips.

I hand him the shirt, and as he pulls it on, I bend down and yank the thin, waterproof shoe covers off the stranger's feet before slipping them over Jared's bloody boots. "Now, what the hell am I supposed to wear?" I ask, looking at my soiled clothes.

He reaches back into one of the open drawers and pulls out a hospital gown.

"I am not—"

"No arguments," he cuts me off. "Just put it on. Fast."

10
HAWK

I push into the throng evacuating the hospital. Local shields are arriving at the edges of the crowd and herding people into containment. The tiny drones flooding the area are blaring a repeated message from the CPG's primary AI, Amina, against the sounds of continued battle. "All citizens must report to the nearest Civil Peace Guard officer for evaluation and medical care. Proceed to the nearest evacuation site and report immediately."

I have to get us out before we're quarantined.

BOOM!

Another explosion rocks the hospital at the secure entrance I used to bring Regina in. Using the explosion as an excuse, I pull her into my side and drop down behind a helo-drone to look around. The squids are trying to battle their way back out now, but shields are closing them in.

Shit. There's going to be heavy losses on both sides.

"What is going on?" Regina whispers. Her body is shaking, but her voice has been surprisingly calm. "Why did you bring me here?"

"The squids attacked the hospital." I ignore her second question. "They're after you."

These squids aren't even trying to hide their identity. They're in complete dazzle makeup, wearing the squid insignia prominently on their arms. They came in with a full hacking squad! In all the years I've been an operative, I've never seen a move this bold.

"Why do they want me?" It sounds like she really doesn't know.

That's the quintillion coin question, isn't it? "I don't think we want to find out."

The scents of ash and dust swirl through the air, blended with blood, death, and over a hundred scrambling people. Two shields are working between us and the main access road, but they're overwhelmed by the panicking evacuees. They're not working the crowd with a reference photo, which means they don't realize the attack is related to the woman they were looking for earlier tonight. They're looking for wounded—which is good for everybody. If we keep our heads down, they won't even see us slip through.

Regina is smart. She stopped fighting me fairly quickly and is cooperating, but she'll bolt as soon as we're out of immediate danger. I'll have to keep on my toes.

The pain in my side is distracting. I'm losing too much blood and I'm beginning to feel light-headed. We've got to get past those shields before the blood seeps through again.

I catch sight of the autobus station east of the hospital, beyond the access road. "This way. We've got to get far as fast as possible. Keep your head down."

11

GINA

I push up on the manhole cover, holding back a sob of frustration at how weak I feel.

I can't do this. Oh Lord, please! I need help! Then the cover is pulled from my grip—up into my burrow's building.

"Gina, Sweetheart!" Crazy Rob's says from above me. "Is that you?"

"Roooobbbbbb." I sob as he reaches down and lifts me out of

the hole.

"How in blue blazes did you get in there?" Rob pulls me against his chest and slides us back away from the access tunnel.

I'm crying like a little girl. I can't stop, but I'm too exhausted to be embarrassed. Familiar, comforting, dim light from Rob's burrow washes over me, dispelling the darkness and terror I've been pretending not to feel. My body is shaking hard, adding to my pain and exhaustion.

"Are you alright?" Rob pulls back my hair to examine my face. "How did you escape from that man? And what the hell are you wearing?"

"He's in the hole." I pushed past embarrassment about the hospital gowns a long time ago. Fortunately, I was able to put one on forwards and one backward, to avoid flashing the world.

"What?" Rob bolts up from under me. "I'll kill him!"

"No! Don't!" I jump up and cling to Rob's arm. "He's bleeding! I have to stop it! I've been dragging him forever."

Amazingly, Jared managed to make it most of the way from the hospital. I doubt he knew where I was going, but his feet kept shuffling so I kept walking. After he collapsed, I drug and rolled his body a few feet at a time. It took everything I had to move him.

"Why the hell are you helping him?" Rob bellows.

"I need him! They're going to kill me!" I'm shaking so hard my teeth rattle.

"Okay, okay." Rob kneels down to touch my face again. "If you say you need him ... okay. I'll help you, but we're going to have to tie him up. You can't trust him."

"I don't, but I don't know what's going on. He does. They're trying to kill me, and I don't know why!"

"Alright, let's take a look." Rob peers down the access pipe. Jared's body is in a heap at the bottom of the ladder. "Good heavens. He's bigger than I remember. You know, you're lucky I'm still here. I was about to go looking for you."

"Thanks." I sniff and try to stop shaking. "But if anyone finds out where I am, I'm dead. The squids blew up the hospital, Rob. They've gone completely nuts!"

"The squids? Are you sure?"

"Yeah. I saw their insignia and they were using Old World weapons. I almost got shot! Jared got shot trying to save me." I utter the last confession in a whisper.

And now I owe him a life.

"Hmm …" Rob mutters to himself as he climbs down into the hole. "Sir Issac Newton! This boy is heavy."

I crawl over to the side of the hole and reach down to try and help pull him up by the shoulders. God, I wish we had climbing gear! My muscles feel like they are tearing at the continued effort, and the pressure against my abdomen from leaning into the tunnel opening is excruciating. I grit my teeth against the pain.

"What … do you plan … to do with him?" Rob wheezes.

"We've got to get him … upstairs. My medical stuff is up there."

With a roar of effort, Rob tosses my kidnapper's limp bulk out onto the floor at the tunnel entrance. I topple backward as his body lands on top of me.

"Ooof!" Why are you so freaking inhumanly heavy? I can feel blood trickling onto my side.

"Anything else down here?" Rob asks from down in the tunnel, oblivious to my new predicament.

"No." I roll Jared's body over to wriggle out from under him. "Thank God."

12

GINA

I try to still my hands as I focus on the needlework, but I can't stop shaking. I don't know if it's caused by adrenaline, or the complete exhaustion I surpassed hours ago. The bright lighting of my hub has spoiled me. My new eyes strain as I work in the dim light from the battery-powered lamps. Gritting my teeth, I continue trying to force the needle through my kidnapper's tough hide.

"Here's your bag." Crazy Rob drops it and slides down the wall to catch his breath. "I told you …when you moved in you should pick a ground floor room. But you had to be stubborn, and—"

"You're right, Rob. Alright? You were right about a lot of things."

"I'm sorry, Sweetheart." Rob sighs. "How is he?"

"The bleeding stopped on its own." I curse the raw pain in my fingertips again and try to sniff back my tears. Who knew you could need a thimble to suture skin? "His blood clots incredibly well. The wound looks a lot more superficial than I thought. Mostly tore up the muscle."

"How far did you drag him?" Rob stands back up to peer over my shoulder.

"We took the autobus to the stop right outside District S, then walked."

"You rode the autobus in a hospital gown?" He covers his mouth in a foolish attempt to hide his amusement.

"Yeah. Thankfully there were a ton of other screaming, crying, half-dressed hospital patients ignoring the shields and doing the same thing. Try telling over a hundred people to sit still and be counted while people are still shooting. It was easy to blend in."

"When did you lose him, then?"

"In the tunnels, about a quarter mile back. I think he lost too much blood."

"I'm amazed he let you come back here."

"He was real out of it about half-way through the bus ride. He probably didn't know where we were going."

Rob is quiet for a long moment. "It looks like you're having trouble."

"I can't get my damn hands to stop shaking. And his skin is like treated leather. I've never had this much trouble sewing up a wound before."

Rob shuffles closer and reaches for the wound, and I elbow his hand away.

"Your hands are dirty! You'll give him an infection."

"So what?" he asks. "You just need him alive long enough to interrogate him."

"That's not true." I choke back another sob as a tear escapes. "This bullet was meant for me, Rob, but he took it. I never could have gotten out of that hospital on my own. I owe him his life."

"He's the reason you were in that hospital to begin with! He drugged me too, you know!"

"He did?" I blink back in surprise. After tying the final stitch, I set my tools to the side. Thank God I bought more blasted suture kits.

"I caught him trying to sneak you out of here, but he got the drop on me."

"How did you even know I was back?" I apply an antimicrobial poultice to the wound and start taping bandages down over the ragged stitching.

"You left your bag at my place. So, I went looking for you."

I stare down at my strange kidnapper again. "Then ... he didn't kill you."

"What?"

"Why didn't he just kill you?" I cover Jared in a couple of thin blankets to help fight off the chill and reach for my field IV kit. "We're shirkers. No one would even question it."

"That ..." Rob scratches up under his hat. "Well ... that's a bit odd. I'll give you that."

I shake my head and begin placing the IV. If he's lost too much blood to recover on his own, there's nothing I will be able to do to save him.

Dear Jesus, help him. Only let him get a fever if he needs to fight something off. Please don't leave me dealing with this guy's death. I'm never going to be able to get that woman's face out of my mind after he ... stopped her. "I'm not going to owe him a life, Rob. He's going to have his back, and I'm going to disappear."

"How?"

"I need your help."

13

HAWK

My head is pounding as voices fade in around me. I recognize the woman's immediately.

Regina! Shit! I must have passed out! We have to get to safety! I try to move, but every muscle in my body feels restrained.

What the hack?

Opening my eyes, I realize I'm tied down with a weird-ass collection of rope, straps, belts, and in some places even scarves.

I'm in Regina's burrow! It reeks even more of blood—my blood—and I'm lying in that awful bed. Why the hack are we here? I don't remember coming here. Well, I don't remember anything after we got on the bus.

I pull against the restraints but it's pointless. I'm too weak and someone's gone overboard securing me. Shit! They've even wrapped duct tape around my hands like escape-proof mittens. Figures with the way this day is going. Why did she bring me back here, instead of leaving me in an alley?

I close my eyes and pretend to be asleep when I hear her coming. She pokes at the throbbing wound in my side and I resist the urge to wince. "It worries me that he's not awake yet," she says. "He's been out for over an hour."

Hack. If another operative is nearby, they'll track us back here using my blood. We're so dead.

"If he wakes up, you can ask him your questions," the guy says. "If not, you've got to head out anyway. Trust me, Sweetheart, they have ways of tracking that would surprise you."

Smart man.

"I know." Regina sighs heavily and I'm surprised to feel her hand trace gently over my shoulder. I finally pick up her scent—now tainted with ash and concrete dust—over the blood. "I just hate not knowing."

14

GINA

I snap awake with a gasp and a full body ache. The kidnapper is in my bed, so I was forced to sleep on the floor. My back and neck are in knots and one of my elbows ended up hyper-extended in my sleep. Pain shoots up my arm as I attempt to bend it back in.

Dammit. Great way to start a trip. Jesus, give me strength.

Random data flashes in front of my eyes, and I shake my head trying to rid myself of it. It's just a bunch of numbers and letters. It doesn't make any sense. Maybe that's what everyone wants? But how would the squids know? Glancing at the clock, I've been asleep for an hour. God, I'm running out of time.

Sitting up with a groan, I wait a few moments for my body to adjust to my new position without fainting. Then I stand and lean against the wall for a moment for the same reason. As soon as my head clears, I see that my kidnapper is sleeping so I cross to him as quietly as I can.

He looks strangely peaceful this way—like the attractive man that was hitting on me at the bar, instead of the terrifying shield. Well, except for being tied down like a bad mummy impression. His lips form a natural pout when he's at rest, between his high cheekbones and strong jaw. His skin is bronze, but not from a tan and his features indicate a heritage from North Continent—likely from both of it's distant coasts. Overall, his features take on a strange gentleness when he's not knocking people out and running around with a gun.

I'm glad he's okay. What is wrong with me?

I turn my back and stretch, then start checking over my bug-out bag. Crazy Rob agreed to run interference for me outside, and is playing his part in raving about my abduction to keep the others from realizing I'm actually back. I wish I could say goodbye to everyone, but I need them to believe I'm still gone.

These jammers the shield put on me are a little more advanced than the ones I had. I can't take them off for even a moment, and I made sure to activate the ring on the con man's hand too before I taped it all up.

Turning back to my bedroom to repack the remaining suture kits, I gasp when I meet the steady gaze of the man in my bed.

He nods toward the belts and ropes. "This is a bit extreme."

"I've seen firsthand what you're capable of. I'm not stupid."

"Okay, so what are you planning to do with me?"

"After you're healed up, you can go."

"Why did you bother?"

"I don't know." An awkward silence stretches out between us. "Why did you?"

"I had to." I wait, but he doesn't continue.

"Is that supposed to be an answer? Because it's pretty much right up there with not answering at all."

"What do you expect me to say, lady?"

"I have no idea where I was when I woke up, or why people were shooting at us, or why you were …" I flail my hands about searching for words. "… doing whatever the hell it was you were doing! All I know is, you took a bullet for me. Maybe it's because I'm worth more to you alive than dead. Maybe you never got a chance to turn me over to more psychopaths! I wasn't going to get answers from you while you were bleeding out on the floor. So … here we are."

His mouth has quirked into a faint smile on only one side, but his eyes are narrowed. "So you're just going to untie all this shit and let me go?"

"I'm not going to untie you. I'm going to pay someone else to do it."

His mouth sets in a grim line. "That's a very bad idea, Regina."

"You have no right to use that name," I say, balling my fists. "I don't even know how you know it! Just call me Gina like everybody else. And frankly, I don't care what you think. That's what's going to happen."

He flops his head back against the pillow and closes his eyes as I head for the door. "So you're just going to run without knowing what the hack you're doing? Good way to get killed. You won't last a week."

"Oh really?" I reply with forced sarcasm, turning around and walking close enough to look down at him. I'm terrified that he's right. "I'm pretty accustomed to life off GRID, you know. All their little tricks don't work so well on me."

He sighs. "They'll send someone like me again."

"So, you admit you're a shield?"

"Yeah." He finally opens his eyes. For the first time since the bar, he looks relaxed, but I know better than to believe his body language now. "But not a street shield. A specialist. I tracked you down without the GRID. So will the next guy, but you won't see him coming."

But why was he trying to catch me all the way back at Southside? "It doesn't make any difference. All I can do is try."

All shields are Community members so their profession was chosen for them, not by them. I don't know if he would have chosen this life for himself, but the question is irrelevant. None of us have choices beyond the GRID.

I was raised to believe in the value of relationships and family, and the intrinsic value of every individual. He was raised by the Community with a core values curriculum of Community-first and self-second. Other individuals only have value because they are part of the Community, and all desires to develop and maintain anything but the shallowest relationships with others are identified as a dangerous illness—OAS. It's a miracle any of them learn to care about each other, let alone putting another individual first. I only see it happen occasionally—usually when that person wants something.

"Listen. Let me help you," he says. "I can keep them off your tail until we can sort this shit out."

"Not a chance. You work for the people who are after me."

"The squids are after you too."

"You'll just turn me in!"

He tests his restraints. "I broke you out of that hospital. You think they're going to just let me go back to work?"

"Is that what happened? It looked to me like you were keeping me away from a bunch of squids with guns … You're still not giving me anything useful."

He looks thoughtful for a moment, then sighs and lies his head back against the pillows again. He doesn't seem to want to offer more.

Since I'm already beside him, I check his wound. I squirt some antibacterial gel into my hands and rub them dry. The dressing comes away easily and shows that the wound has bled very little since I sewed him up. His skin jumps slightly beneath my fingertips as I touch the stitches. When I glance up, he's watching me, and I focus back on the wound to keep from losing my nerve. None of the tissue appears to be the kind of red that would indicate an infection, but it's too early to tell.

"You'll need to check into a hospital as soon as you're released." I step back from him again. "They should be able to correct my work and make sure you don't have a scar. They'll give you antibiotics if an infection sets in."

His eyes narrow and he clenches his jaw. "You're still assuming I can go back."

I shrug. "If you can't then you'll just have an ugly scar and you'll have to hope my supplies were clean enough."

15

GINA

I don't understand. I've paced this section of hallway half a dozen times and it's not here. When I woke up, I saw Stella hanging from her perch and realized I have no idea what happened to her mind-link disk.

I can't believe this! It's not like anyone sweeps in here.

I hear a door close down the hallway and strain to hear for a moment. When I recognize Rob's familiar muttering, I turn back to my task.

I vaguely remember the disk popping off when the kidnapper jumped me. Without the disk, I'm not sure I can convince Stella to come with me. I'll lose the use of her senses.

I get down on my hands and knees again, using the surface of my hands like a sweeper. Maybe if I'm lucky it'll stick.

"Aren't you supposed to be pretending you're not here?" Rob trudges up to ask.

"I knew it was you." I don't look up. "Be careful where you step. I can't find Stella's disk."

"Well, don't leave her here with me." He chuckles. "You're the only one here who speaks bat."

"I can't speak bat without the disk. I don't know what I'm gonna do if I can't find it."

"Come on, little girl." He nudges my side with his well-worn, leather boots. "Get back inside. We'll worry about that after you've had a decent meal. You've got to be as strong as you can."

"I know." I sit back on my heels and press my palms against my forehead. "I just … alright. You're right."

16

HAWK

"Get back inside." The old man's voice wakes me again. Hack! If I can't stay awake to get out of here, we'll all be dead by morning.

I glance around the room but nothing looks out of place. The neat piles of medical supplies for the next dressing change are still at the exact angles I last saw them. I don't detect any animal smells other than the bat's and the humans I expect. I strain against the tie-downs. They're looser but not nearly as much as I need with my hands bound. I flex my claws again but it's useless. They can't break through this tape.

"What are they serving tonight?" Gina's question draws me back to their conversation.

I'm starving. I always need food to heal.

"Looks like we got lucky," the old guy says. "Genu-ine beef stew. One for you, and one for soldier boy."

Huh. They're going to feed me?

"Thanks, Rob." She sounds so tired. "I'm sorry I need so much help."

"Nonsense," Rob says. "If they're after ya girlie, you'd better be bookin' it. Right now, in fact. You're wasting an awful lot of time on that man in there."

"I owe him, Rob. I couldn't leave him to die. I'm not like them. I can't just pretend he's not a human being—no matter who he works for."

What? Why the hack does this woman think she owes me? I'm responsible for her—not the other way around.

"I know," he says. "What's done is done. But now, if you're planning on surviving … you need to leave his ass and go. He's not your problem. You get what I'm saying?"

He's right. It's nuts she's still here. The squids or the CPG could be here any moment.

"Alright, alright. I will."

She enters the room, setting a couple of bowls down on the desk and resetting the locks. Her face and form wilt as she looks around the bedroom, as if she's sad to be leaving this cesspool. I don't turn away when she looks up—meeting her gaze. I need her to start listening to me if we're going to get out of this alive. "You've got to leave. Now."

She arches an eyebrow, walks back over, and sits on the small desk beside me. "Why? Did you tell them where my burrow is?"

"If I had, they would have been here before I woke up. They don't need to be told, Gina. They'll find you."

"Oh? And how is that?" She holds a spoonful up to my mouth. The smell isn't great, but it's enough to make my stomach rumble. "Did you tell them I worked at Tommy's?"

"No." The whole crazy chain of events happened too fast for a formal report.

"Then how will they find me?"

I can't answer that. Hack. I need this woman to trust me, but there's only so much I can tell. If she finds out what I am, she could freak. Citizens have no idea that the Community deploys operatives like me. I accept the spoonful of soup instead of answering.

"Why do they want to find me anyway? What makes me so special?"

"I don't know, but it's not what I was told."

"What were you told?"

She feeds me another spoonful and I grimace as I bite down on something that shouldn't be in beef stew—something hard. I swallow, hoping it's small enough not to cause any damage. "That you're a recent squid recruit. That you got caught in the blast in District J on purpose to access the GRID and get information."

"Those assholes!" She bolts up off the desk and—ow, shit! The flaming hot bowl of soup is on my chest. "They said I did this to myself?" She's so angry that she stomps her foot. "Like I would be stupid enough to almost kill myself and get struck blind! Do you know how vulnerable it made me?"

I grit my teeth against the pain, focusing on the bowl and resisting the urge to shout. If my chest moves too much, it could tip over. An instant later, the bowl is snatched up off my chest and I close my eyes with a grunt of relief.

"Sorry …" she whispers. When I glance up, she's cringing with reddened cheeks and a hand over her mouth. She digs in a desk drawer and comes up with a piece of thick cloth—placing it across my chest, beneath my chin. At least I know it wasn't meant as punishment. Like at the bar before, she seems sincere.

"Why were you there then?"

"I already told you. I was trading tech to a kid. All she wanted was a little privacy—the chance to have fun—and she died for it." Her voice is thick with emotion and her hands begin to tremble. She's not that good of an actor. I've seen her try. Sitting back down, she takes a deep breath and offers me another spoonful of stew. I accept it, and several more, watching the red slowly fade from her face.

There's something strangely intimate about this. I've spoken to Regina—no, wait, Gina—more than most of the women I've loved. She's constantly touching me. She's checking my wound, temperature, and Universe knows what else. She stitched me up by hand, so if she's ever sewn up a wound before she must have noticed the difference.

Does she know? I wonder again if that's why they bound my hands. Yet here she is, caring for me like a small child instead of a prisoner—her attention focused on me when she should be running for her life.

When the soup runs out, I see her eye my bandage. She looks at the other bowl of soup, then at my wound, then the empty bowl in her hands. Picking up the second bowl, she brings the spoon to my mouth.

"What are you doing?" I turn away from it with a frown.

"Feeding you. Obviously."

Is she stupid? "He brought that bowl for you."

She narrows her eyes and tilts her head. Shit. Well, anyone could hear a conversation at that distance, couldn't they?

"You need it more than I do. I wasn't shot." She tries to move the spoon closer, but I turn away again. "Look, I'll just grab more from downstairs. Now open up."

I'm still hungry, and I guess Rob can get another bowl. I accept the rest of it without argument, then relax my head back against the pillow. I'm surprised at how weak I feel. It's dangerous to be off my game.

I watch as Gina goes into the other room and starts looking through a backpack, narrowing down what to take. She swaps a couple items out, piling what she removes on a chair nearby. She crouches to slip a tiny antique paper box in a side pocket. It says, *Waterproof Matches. Close box before striking.* She reaches into another pocket and pulls out an RC. She rips it open, shuts her eyes and starts to chew.

What? "You're not very trustworthy." I resist wincing against the growl in my voice. I can't let that slip out around her, and she definitely heard it as her eyes turn owlish for a second.

Then her eyebrows scrunch together and she glances at the door. With a shrug, she says, "You can live off of three of these ration cubes a day."

Yeah, right. "I've lived on them, and I know they do nothing to stop your stomach from reminding you that you've only eaten a square inch of food." She's going to be miserable.

After she walks off, I flex my limbs to investigate my bonds again. I think I'm figuring out which movements loosen them. Now, to get her to trust me.

17

GINA

Once I'm satisfied I've packed my meager supplies as best I can, I return to my bedroom. The con man has drifted back off again, probably still affected by the massive blood loss, so I cross to look at him as quietly as I can. His face is relaxed and peaceful. I'm still not sure he put me first back in the hospital. I could be an alive-only bounty, but I'd like to believe it and since I'm never going to see him again ... I will.

I hope you find your way home.

His eyes snap open and I pull my hand back with a gasp—belatedly realizing I almost touched his face.

"What are you doing?" he grumbles in a thick baritone, blinking the sleep from his eyes.

"I-I was ... How do you feel? Any fever?" Yeah, fever. Go with that.

"Don't think so." He yawns wide and looks slightly unnerved. He obviously hadn't intended to sleep. "What time is it?"

"Time to go."

I check his wound one final time. His rate of healing is incredible. It's only been a few hours and a scab is already forming. The stitches are holding well. I leave the bandage on, in case he pulls the wound back open.

Then something shiny catches my eye, on the bed just on the other side of his abdomen. There it is! I snatch up the mind-link disk from the sheets. How the hell did it get all the way over here?

"What is that?" he asks.

"Just some tech I lost. You made me drop it out in the hallway. I don't know how it got in here, though."

He sighs deeply, closing his eyes for a moment. "It must have stuck to your clothes. I laid you down here after you were asleep."

"Well, Jeez. I should have just asked you."

"What is it?"

"Just a neat thing I picked up from a market a few years ago."

I'm not about to tell him about Stella if he hasn't figured it out already.

He's still for a couple of minutes, then says, "You can't just leave me here and expect me to be fine." He sounds angry. "What's the point of patching me up if you're just going to let someone kill me after you leave?"

"Rob will let you go soon enough. That's the best I can do."

"If you're asking him to hang around here when you know they are coming for you, you must not care much about him either."

Strangely, the *either* hurts, and the thought of putting Rob in danger turns my stomach. "They won't care about him. He's just a shirker." But what if I'm wrong?

"They'll cover their tracks. Standard operating procedure."

"Is that what you do, Jared?" I challenge.

He doesn't flinch or turn his face away. "No." He closes his eyes for a long moment, then sighs. "My name isn't Jared."

I shrug. "I figured."

"It's uh … It's Hawk."

"Sure it is."

"Well, there's another name in my file, but I prefer Hawk. It's the name I was assigned." His tone is very convincing, but I know better than to believe a con man with a badge.

"And you're telling me this, why?"

"Because you need to understand I'm really trying to help you. I've risked everything because … you seemed innocent." The frustration in his tone and tension in his body are palpable. "Terrorists and skilled operatives are after you. You don't have the skills to escape without help. You may not escape with it."

I back away from the hospital bed with my heart in my throat. "Why? Why the heck do they even care about me?"

"Th—" He stops short, bites his tongue, and then shouts. "I don't know! You have something they want. It's in your head!"

Rob appears at the door holding Hawk's pistol with a narrow-eyed scowl. "You best not be scaring her, boy."

My blood runs cold. I knew something had gone wrong in my GRID session. Dammit! "Then why don't they just take it out of my head?"

"I don't know." Jared or Hawk, the operative—that's what he said is chasing me—clenches his jaw again and again. "It's what I expected them to do, but…"

"But what?" I explode. "You claim I am in danger! Why?"

"They were going to kill you! I don't do that kind of work!" His eyes widen, but he looks away again and carefully composes his features. "I'm not lying about this, Gina. You can't make it on your own. Not with the squids and the Civil Peace Guard both hunting you."

"What do the squids want me for?" I remember the battle that raged around us at the hospital and feel faint.

"My guess …" He shrugs. "Same thing. Whatever is in your head is valuable in a way that's dangerous to someone. Do you know how you got it?"

Rob gives me a look. "Don't answer him, Gina. He's getting you to talk!"

"Talk about what, Rob?" I sigh. "I don't know anything! I've jacked in one time. One!"

"So you didn't … do anything?" Hawk asks. "Nothing to alter your session?"

"No! How would I know how to do that? I've never even been connected before. The next thing I know, you're attacking me in my home, and then breaking me out of some facility in the middle of a firefight!"

"I didn't attack you."

Rob whistles and shakes his head. "You're not going to get far with that one, soldier boy."

"Oh, I am so not having this argument." I shrug on my black jacket and start collecting my things.

"Please tell me you're not bringing an autodrive backpack," the shield says.

"Would you just shut up!" I swallow down my rising panic.

"You're going to stick out like a sore thumb. At least put everything in a regular duffel bag. It makes less noise and leaves no additional tracks."

I slip Stella's mind-link disk on behind my ear and she stirs in her perch—disturbed by my anxiety. I'm not about to admit that I can't get far without it. The less he knows, the better. My spine could never support the weight for the amount of ground I need to cover. As it is, I'm lucky that this bag is designed for rough terrain.

"Do you at least have a hover disk for it?" The shield pleads.

"They're too valuable. I sell them as soon as I find them."

"Oh, for the love of Tesla."

"Any other tips, Mr. Super Soldier?" I turn to face him one last time.

"Don't call me that," he says through clenched teeth, his eyes narrowed.

Huh … that hit a nerve.

Rob chuckles. "Truth's a bitch, ain't it?" He crosses his arms, but keeps the pistol in hand, pointed at the ceiling.

Hawk rattles the bed furiously, trying to break free.

"Stop it now, boy, or I'll kill ya."

My heart in my throat, I turn to Stella and impress on her the desire to come with me. She's upset by all the noise and the predator in my bed. "Come on, Stella." I coo and make some kissy noises for the soldier's benefit. "Come to Momma." She eventually concedes and flutters over to cling to her loop on my jacket front.

I turn around to see the predator's wide-eyed stare. "The bat is your pet?"

"Of course."

"Take care of her, Sweetie," Rob says, reaching over to rub his pointer finger on Stella's soft back. He never takes his eyes off the soldier.

"You need to make sure you blend in as much as possible," the soldier says, closing his eyes with a sigh. "Black is good at night, but you'll stick out during the day. Keep your hair hidden—the uncommon color is an easy mark. Dye it and cut it as soon as you can. Don't think you can give them the slip by dodging their tech. You've got to leave no physical trails for them to follow."

"What direction are you heading?"

I give him my very best how-stupid-do-I-look expression and he rolls his eyes.

"If you're heading north, west, or east you should take the hyperloop. You'll have to get on without a ticket, and you'll have to dodge the slavers. It will get you farther, faster, and the shields won't expect it. South, is a bad idea. We're having more trouble with squids that way so your best bet would be an autotruck. Make sure you get at least five regions away before you rest."

God, this scares me to death. I haven't left this sector since I was too young to remember.

Stella squeaks at my shoulder.

"It's gonna be very hard to do all that if you are not used to traveling off the books."

I'm not used to traveling any further than the University.

"You still gonna leave me here?" he asks.

With Rob! I suddenly remember the danger I've put Rob in. Should I take the shield up on his offer so Rob can escape? That's stupid! If we let him go now, he could kill us both. I turn to look Rob in the eyes. "I shouldn't have asked you to do this. How are you going to get away? Will you be okay?"

"He's as dead as I am," our prisoner says.

"Don't you worry about me." Rob looks pointedly at him. "I didn't get this old by being stupid. Or playing nice."

I hate the way he said that, but he may not have a choice. Sounding dangerous is important. Being dangerous might be too if he's going to survive this. I wish I could ask him how, but the shield is listening.

"Why can't you go back to work?" As soon as the words are out of my mouth, I feel stupid for believing a word the con man has said.

"They have vid of me breaking you out of that hospital."

"Did the squids attack before or after you grabbed me?"

He pauses for a moment and his dark eyebrows scrunch together. "I ran for you after the first explosion. I didn't know what was going on, but I sure as hack wasn't gonna let anyone get you before I figured it out."

"But why were you fighting the doctors when I woke up?" This question has confused me the most. "The woman who shot you, the doctor, was trying to kill me!" Just saying it starts me shaking again.

"You're my assignment—my responsibility. I was told it was a standard reset and reintegrate assignment, which gives you the same rights as any other citizen. They tried to kill you before the squids could get to you. I didn't agree with that decision."

It's kind of like what he said before, *I don't do that kind of work.* But will he respect Rob's life like he does a citizen's? All I can do is hope. A little bit of the tension drains from my shoulders and I sigh as Stella stirs against my jacket. "Well, that solves it—for you at least."

"What do you mean?"

"Just tell them you were making sure the squids couldn't get their hands on me. I'm sure you can make something up about your confusion over conflicting orders."

"What?"

"Say that you put yourself in place to make sure I wasn't captured. But you were injured attempting to keep me, and whatever is in my head, out of their hands. No one on site could be trusted, and all that. Then I snuck out from under your nose while you were healing. I'm sure they'll take you back."

He's looking at me like I'm crazy enough to be institutionalized. "You're a great con man. I should know."

18

GINA

I enter the hyperloop station cautiously, trying to avoid direct line of sight to the numerous cams. It's impossible to avoid them all. Is that why the shield wanted me to come here? So I'd be easier to track? I have no experience with long-distance travel. When moving into town with my parents almost twenty years ago, I'd only paid attention with the eyes of a child.

The station is a continual flow of chaos as Stella wings her way out of it into the support beams above the crowd. The noise is nearly overwhelming her. From her perch, I look down at a sea of people hurrying from one point to another without looking at each other for more than seconds at a time. A shirker sits beneath the large departure sign to my right—leaning against the wall. His clothes are dirty and torn. The travelers flow around him as if he isn't even there.

Shiny steel surfaces are tinted in blues and greens to contrast with the dull gray tile floor, but the cheer in its original design has been worn away by time and constant use. The station is air conditioned to a chilly temperature for anyone standing still. Faramund is announcing imminent arrivals and departures over the general din of travelers. All other schedules are available on people's feeds or on the huge screens high on the walls.

I glance at the payment kiosks with a sigh. Before my GRID session, I'd been able to afford an autobus swipe from the market, but a hyperloop pass had been out of the question. Buying a ticket now would announce my presence to the Community. I fidget with the CID jammers in my ears again out of nervous habit, wishing I knew where to sneak on.

Lord, what do I do?

Glancing at the boarding area, Mom's voice drifts through my mind—nagging us to use the bathroom before we leave. God, I miss her. What would she tell me to do now? I sidestep into the public bathroom and enter a stall. The bathrooms are rundown, but clean and scrubbed free of graffiti.

After using the facilities, I pull a large black emergency blanket out of the small front pocket of my backpack. It's more practical than a poncho because of its extremely thin, foil-like design. In this instance, it also adds to my costume. My standard black cargo pants and T-shirt are already suited to the look. I pull out the rattiest of the three cotton micromesh Faraday caps and twist my hair up to tuck inside of it. The cap has a microbrim which I pull low over my eyes.

Now for some extra grunge. I pull out an expired sample tube of women's mascara and use faint amounts to make my face look dirtier and street tired. Not that I need much help with that. The catnap I took after sewing up my kidnapper is all the sleep I've gotten since Manuela woke me for server duty. That I woke up again at all is a testament to my level of adrenaline, but even so, the pain increasing in my legs is telling me I can't keep going much longer without an extended period of rest.

I pull out a stunner as the last piece of my ensemble. I normally don't deal in this kind of crap, but I recently traded with a shirker who desperately needed me to patch him up. The stunner's emitter sticks to the skin over the sinus cavity—high up on the apple of one cheekbone. This emitter is a very stylish skull emblem with red, fake jewels for eyes. I hate even having the thing near me, but I stick the emitter on my right cheek anyway to make everything as authentic as possible.

Clutching the stunner's remote in my left hand, I leave it switched off to prevent an accident. The little four-inch cylinder has numerous buttons for various settings and effects. I've never used one, but I've heard that users get different types of highs from different currents and patterns. Heaven knows, if I used this thing while Stella was still attached, it would probably kill her. Thankfully, I've never had the urge to turn my brain into scrambled eggs.

Coming out of the stall, I barely afford myself a glance in the mirror as I shuffle up to the sink. The security cam isn't likely to be checked unless someone is already looking for me here, but better safe than sorry. A young man walks into a stall behind me without giving me a second look, so I must be boring enough.

As I leave the bathroom, I allow myself to walk with the amount of fatigue I feel. I slump under the strain of the backpack—limping on my left side where my knee is currently pinching and radiating that little, sharp, irritating pain every time I step down. The emergency blanket, tied as a poncho, covers the backpack somewhat, making me look like any other transient. Strolling painfully over to the shirker sitting beneath the departure board, I slide down onto the floor next to him.

"Hey pretty lady," a throaty bass voice rumbles from the man, but he doesn't so much as move a muscle. He doesn't look much older than I am. He has a shaved head, short beard and dusky skin, but his eyes are tired and puffy. He's layered in so many dirty, ragged clothes, he has the same profile as a pile of trash. His own stunner's remote is clutched in his hand with a bright green emitter on his cheek, but he doesn't look high.

"Mind if I rest?"

"Don't mind company at all," he drawls. "You coming or going?"

"Going. Any advice?"

"Depends on where you're headed." He gives the floor a sly smile. "Shit. Incoming."

Suddenly, we're approached by an olive-skinned, middle-aged elite woman. She's carrying a red-brown, cube-shaped briefcase. Her practical heels clack against the tile floor—announcing her approach more effectively than an overhead page. I pretend to press a button on the stunner in my hand, tense up briefly, and then take a risk in going limp against the friendly shirker. With my face now tucked into his smelly shoulder, I pray that he's the kind who will play along.

"Hello Jay," the woman says. Her voice is amazingly high and thin for a woman her age. "How's the day been?"

"No complaints here. Had a nice gentleman give me a pair of old shoes today."

I urge Stella to move to where she can see, but she doesn't want to be closer to the noise.

"That's wonderful," the woman says. "I had noticed the holes in yours were becoming rather large. How about food?"

Jay begins moving about as if he's trying to scramble out of his coat. Ouch. I resist flinching or tensing as his collarbone pops into my nose and makes my eyes water. Fortunately, he wants his opposing arm out and Stella's now motivated enough to circle around. "I'm good, Doc," Jay says with a chuckle. "Lots of folks come through here with leftovers."

"What about your friend?" she asks, just before I hear the click of an injector.

Stella, come on! She flits into place in the beams above us just in time to spot the woman putting an injector back into her open briefcase. There are at least a dozen injectors lined up in the case. My head bobs around on Jay's shoulder as he rubs at his other arm.

"Can't speak for her," he says. "Had a hard day, you know. Needs time out of body, out of mind."

"Well, you know how I feel about that." Stella can see the woman leaning closer to me and I hold my breath before she backs away shaking her head and pulls out a large sandwich. "You two can have this. You shouldn't need another injection until Tuesday, so I'll come by then."

"Thanks, Doc," he mumbles. "Wish I could make it up to you."

"Oh, you already are. I have permission to use this medicine because it's expired. It's of no use for general consumption, but it's an absolute waste to throw it away when it can still be effective. After I have enough data—thanks to you and the others—I hope to prove my theory that its administration among your people could lead to improved health for the entire Community. Communicable disease should never be allowed to run rampant in any population, or it puts all of us at risk."

Communicable disease?

"Yeah well, I hope it does the trick. This shit was kicking my ass," he says.

Rumors have been spreading that there's some form of illness burning its way through the shirker camps in some of the densely populated Central regions, but I hadn't realized it had reached this far. They say it's an Old World sexually transmitted disease—one which everyone had thought was cured. The Global Fellowship has been slow to respond, but many Community members believe shirkers don't deserve treatment because the disconnected don't contribute to society.

God, I hope that's what they're talking about and not something else I could pick up from leaning on this guy.

"Keep up your spirits ... and lay off the stunner." Through Stella, I can see the woman give us both a kind smile before straightening up and turning back to the crowd. "Make sure you're here on Tuesday."

The click-clack of her heels fades off into the rush of the hyperloop crowd, but Stella's attention has been captured by a spider lowering itself on a silk thread to her right. I shudder and try to tune out her gleeful attack.

Waiting a minute before sitting back up, I mumble, "Thanks."

"No biggie. Now, where did you say you're headed?"

"Anywhere but here."

"How far you looking to get?"

"As far as I can?" I sound unsure, even to myself. "But I don't have much to trade."

"Ya selling your services?" His question and raised eyebrow makes me incredibly uncomfortable.

"No."

"Shoot, girl. I know a runner when I see one. From the look in those pretty eyes, I don't think I want to know what's hunting you. Is it squids?"

"No." I focus my thoughts on my kidnapper so it feels less like a lie, and purposely fidget with my jammers again. "They would be easy to hide from."

"Shit." Jay gives a low whistle, turning his face away. "Community then. Girl, that's all bad."

"I know."

"Can you handle tight spaces alright?"

"I'll do whatever I have to." I try to force steel into my tone.

"Okay, well you better take this." He hands me the very pricey looking sandwich. "Now, we're not going to send you South. Not getting much good information from there, except to say there's some kinda big mess going on. If you're looking for distance, I think we'll send you East. Another continent could do you some good."

Another continent? I guess the farther the better with everybody after my head.

"What do you want?" There's no such thing as free for a shirker.

"I don't want no gadgets or food," he says with a sly smile. "We get plenty of that here. We deal in information. When you get to the other end, you find someone that's coming our way. Tell them to find me and report back on the situation where they're coming from. We'll make it worth their while. Do you think you can do that?"

"I guess. I mean … yes."

"What name should I expect to hear when they tell me who they're reporting back from?"

I freeze for a moment, then sputter, "Meredith."

"Sure thing." Jay nods, looking into the crowd. "Now I can tell you haven't done this before, girl, but you need to be faster on the draw with a fake name. I don't mind fake names. No problem with them at all. But if you need it in a hurry, you better know what it is."

"Right." Oh, Jesus, please help me with this.

"Alrighty then." Jay sighs and starts speaking into the shoulder I was previously leaning on. "Hey Zeke," he says clearly but quietly. "We got a nice little package a fortune cookies over here that seems to have fallen off its cart."

While his attention is turned away, I urge Stella to return to me as quickly as she can. I also impress on her the fear of Jay seeing her—I don't want to stir any interest in her if they want more payment. If Zeke responds, I can't hear it. Jay is either using an ear transmitter or some kind of localized GRID link. Considering he's speaking into his shoulder, though, it's more likely to be in his ear. They don't want these conversations to be overheard—whoever they are.

"Now. When the guard comes up, don't get spooked," Jay whispers. "You hop straight into that box with no questions. Don't forget that information we've been promised."

"I won't." What box?

Stella finally flits down onto my back and then my shoulder while Jay is distracted. I cup her in my hand gently and tuck her into the warm interior of my jacket where she clings to my soft shirt with her sensitive toes.

A guard comes straight up to us from over by the hand scanners. His crisp black uniform stands out against his tan skin, identifying him as a low-ranking shield. "Folks," the guard says with a stern expression, "I'm going to have to ask you to leave."

"Now hold on there Mister." Jay stands sluggishly to his feet. "I got every right to be here. I'm not causing no trouble and ..."

As they continue their argument, a large maintenance bot wanders toward us. A large compartment opens on its side where the trash can should be. This is strangely well coordinated ... however, with few options at hand, I roll into the bot with only a moment's hesitation. The backpack barely fits inside.

The door latches resoundingly behind me and I'm locked into darkness.

19

HAWK

I pull against the bonds again, feeling more slack as some of them loosen. This is one of the older hacking beds with sturdy side rails. It must be from an institution. Straining my claws against the tape, they're so sore it's excruciating. Blood is beginning to pool around my fingertips inside my tape mittens. Glancing at the time on the holoframe, Gina's been gone for almost four hours. Another operative will show up soon and eliminate us all.

Lying here waiting for an assassin, I'm amazed by the lie she gave me for my superiors. It's so close to the truth, it may work, in spite of the damage I've done. The Community doesn't like mistakes from their operatives, but it does happen, and a whole squad of uniformed squids attacking a hospital is bound to have shaken everybody up.

Roland will be pissed, but he'll enjoy the opportunity to rub my nose in it. Alex will do his sleight of hand while reminding me of what an inconvenience I am, as always. If I can get whoever tracks me here to listen and not kill me, I could get intel on why the hack the doctors were trying to kill her and throw them off my scent. I just hope I'm not too far behind what's stalking Gina to rescue her. Aside from her foolish delay, the woman is clever. Hopefully, that's enough to keep her alive until I can get to her.

I fight to draw in the scent of her over the stench in here. It's impossible to remember her smile and beauty without rage brewing in my gut. They were going to kill her and it's pretty hacking likely she's done nothing wrong. Well, except for possessing sophisticated cam shielding I've never heard a whisper of before. I bet it's the disk she picked up from the bed earlier. I can't believe I missed it!

She couldn't have traded for it. Maybe it was given to her by whoever Joe was protecting her for. The boyfriend, maybe? He'd have to be major league. But then why didn't she run to him for protection?

She could be conning me and the clumsiness and naiveté is just an act. But she took a huge risk by healing and feeding me. That's not likely a con.

It was stupid to tell her my name, but I was desperate for her to trust me. I'll have to find another way to convince her because she's my responsibility until she's placed. Until then she's a hacking target! I've also got to get that cam tech off the streets before it gets more people killed.

"You hungry, boy?" Rob calls from the hall.

"Sure."

Rob comes in and sets two steaming hot cups of soup down on the small table next to me. He begins helping himself to his own cup first. Looking him over again, I don't see anything on his body that could be lifted and used to escape.

"I see that look in your eye, boy. Don't think I'm missing it. You're not getting out of here until I say so." He slurps his soup from the spoon without so much as looking up.

"Was Gina in charge here? What did she pay you?"

Rob laughs out loud, a rough coughing sound. "In charge? Nobody's in charge of anybody around here. But Gina's kin, and you take care of kin—when you can."

Kin? "If you want to take care of her, you need to let me go."

"Aren't you the soldier boy that got her into this mess in the first place?" He leans back in a more relaxed posture with the spoon still in his mouth.

"She was already neck deep before I got to her. I just didn't realize how deep. And she's not good at taking care of herself, is she? She fed me the soup you gave her last night."

"Goddammit, girl!" Rob slams his empty cup down on the desk. "And you let her do it?"

"She lied—said she'd get more, but then ate a bogon food cube. What did you expect me to do, old man? Call you?"

"What's your point?" He picks up my cup and holds out a spoonful.

I refuse the food. "She doesn't have a chance unless I help her."

"Eat the Goddamn soup, or I won't listen to a word."

I accept the bite and force myself to swallow before trying again. "Look, man. If someone else gets to her before I do, Gina's as good as dead. No matter who finds her, they'll just take what they need and throw her away."

"So what's got you singing a different tune?" Rob asks. "Don't lie to me. I saw Gina stitch you up. I've met your kind before and they tend to be loyal. I'm guessing the Community didn't even put you through University—just straight into officer's school."

I know better than to look away from the clever shirker. I can usually hide my traits well enough, but it's rare for anyone to see me get sewn up. "Of course I'm loyal." I'm loyal to the people I serve.

"If you're loyal to the Community, why did you help a shirker?"

"I'm not an assassin. Besides, the doctors weren't going to hold off that many squids trying to get to her."

Rob nods with a thoughtful expression. "You're a delivery man then?"

"You could say that." I hate the demeaning term.

"And you really don't know what all these guys want?"

I sigh. "Everything I was told was misinformation. Her file said she was a recent squid recruit who was dangerous. She was supposed to be wiped and reset."

"So you're okay with wiping out who somebody is—like you haven't killed them?"

"Your past isn't who you are." I've freed dozens of people who wanted to remember nothing of their past and their pain. They wanted a fresh start. "We are who we choose to be."

"And who are you? A chimera trying to shed its skin?"

So he does know. I doubt I can get him to trust me on anything then.

In the early years of this millennium, scientists were attempting to create a human-animal hybrid with advanced sensory perception, increased strength and agility, superior healing, biological weaponry, and any number of other traits. Chimeras are the descendants of those super soldier programs, and we're considered monsters.

"I'm the only one who can find her, keep her safe, and just maybe get her out of this mess," I say. "Before she or someone else gets her killed. That's who I am, old man. My mission's not over until I say it is."

Rob tugs at his mismatched hat and clears the food from his teeth with his tongue. Then to my surprise he smirks, sets the soup aside, and stands to his feet. Pulling a small remote from his pocket, he presses a button and the building starts shrieking around us.

Shit! I can't cover my ears and the siren is cutting through my head like a knife. Rob walks back out the door.

"What the hack are you doing?" I scream. There's a faint red glow coming from the hallway. What the hack? He's set off the building's old fire alarm system. How did he even get power to it?

I start pulling at my restraints with all my strength. They're weakening, but not fast enough.

A minute later, Rob walks back in wearing a full-body poncho and the acrid scent of alcohol hits my senses like a blow. "Good. Everyone's getting out," he mumbles, and starts splashing alcohol up on the walls in the far half of the room by the door.

Hawking's ghost! He's going to burn the place down! He hasn't cut me loose yet—which means I'm going with it.

I pull and rattle the bed and my bonds as hard as I can. Agony streaks through my side where the wound is still healing, but I push past the pain. "If Gina didn't manage to avoid the slavers, she isn't going to last very long!" Two of the tie downs snap, freeing my shoulder and I work to get my arm loose on that side.

Rob keeps splashing the walls, making his way toward me. "How do I know you won't turn her in, you Community bastard? Or sell her yourself?"

He pulls out a match and I roar as he lights it and tosses it toward the door behind him. He's insane! The room lights up like a pile of tinder and the flames start racing toward us.

"I know how you people work." He walks straight toward me with the mostly-empty carboy. "You can smell her wherever she goes. They may know what she looks like, but you're the one who knows her scent. That knowledge dies with you."

"They'll just get it from Tommy's! Or her hub, or the server bank!"

He splashes the alcohol across my chest and I recognize the scent. It's the moonshine Gina was drinking in the bar. "SOP—confuse the trail. Tommy's is already taken care of." He looks slightly sad, but shakes it off quickly. "There was a hell of a fire over where her hub was too. It took all of building 12, but that one wasn't me."

Standard Operating Procedure. Who is this guy?

By all that is lawful … "You promised her you would let me go!"

"I know what I'm doing boy. I promised her I would feed you and release you. You don't get more of a release than death."

"If you kill me, she's as good as dead!" I reach for him, trying to extend my claws through the tape on my freed arm. My fingertips are raw with pain.

"Look! You can't even help yourself!" He laughs. "Who do you think told her to bind up your hands, soldier boy?"

Hack! I shove my hand through the tie downs at my knees and pull. The pressure starts shredding through the bindings across my chest.

"There you go." He grins with a crazed look in his eyes. "We both knew you could get out of there. It just had to matter to you! Does she matter to you?"

"Yes! You crazy jackass!" In a matter of seconds, I wriggle my way out of the bindings, leap at him, and pin him to the floor. I choke on the thick smoke filling the room. I lean lower to get my head beneath the smoke, but the blaring alarm, acrid smell, and pain in my lungs are making me dizzy.

Flames leap onto my pant leg at the ankle and I jump back to smother them with a sheet from the bed. I swipe at a sharp pain in my neck but Rob leaps out of the way—one of my injectors clutched in his hand.

Shit! My pulse is racing too fast. I can feel the drug surge through my veins as fast as the flames are burning through the room around us.

I can't pass out here!

I try to run for the door, but stumble as my legs weaken. Rob is crouched low and laughing ahead of me in the doorway as I try to drag myself on my elbows. I don't even make it ten feet before he shoves me onto my back with a boot, and leans down with a knife to my throat. I meet his intense gaze but refuse to cower.

"Do it," I slur. "You're killing … her yourself."

"You remember this moment, boy." Rob's voice is a growl worthy of a chimera as my eyelids droop. "I've got your pathetic life in my hands right now. You hurt that little girl, and this knife finds its way back here. Anyone else hurts her, and it finds its way into your back."

I take a swipe at him, but my hand just bounces harmlessly off his shoulder.

"You save her. Give her a life back—a real life—and it'll have no interest in you again."

I want to ask why she is this important to him, but I can't get my mouth to work. He grabs my shoulders as I fall unconscious.

20

GINA

The fibromyalgia in my legs is growing stronger by the minute, and singing old hymns in my mind is becoming less and less of a helpful distraction. This flare-up was triggered by being trapped in such a tiny space. The sleep helped at first, but the longer I'm stuck, the worse it's getting. God, help me. The ache is so nagging I feel like I'm going crazy.

At first, I hadn't realized that I didn't just roll into a maintenance bot. I rolled directly into a shipping box. These reusable, aluminum, nearly seamless containers frequently litter the larger black markets and alleyways from shipments which have been brought in. I've never seen one from the inside before. This mode of travel definitely isn't for the faint of heart.

As long as my bones don't actually explode the way they feel they're going to, I'm sure I'll live. The more pressing problem is my nearly desperate need for a bathroom. The hyperloop made a brief stop and my box was moved to a new line about ten hours in. At that time, someone had unceremoniously yanked me to my feet, and I'd promptly fainted on them.

The next thing I knew, they were shoving me into a small bathroom. Then they brought me back to my box and shoved me inside again, without a single word of conversation. I've been in here for another nine hours now, and even the lack of food and water haven't prevented me from needing a bathroom again.

"Thanks, Mom," I whisper to the memory of her wise words.

I'm beginning to realize this is the stupidest mistake I could've made. No one besides Jay has even spoken to me. I'm sure I'm currently stashed in the hyperloop's cargo bay. I can hear the low hum of the magnetic motor through the metal beneath me, but I still have no idea where I'm headed—or, who is going to let me out on the other side.

An eternity later, the songs in my mind change to praise songs and shouts of joy as I hear the motor slowing down.

Thank you, Jesus!

Stella isn't handling our prison well either and she trembles beneath my hands as I hold her gently to my chest. You'd think it would be easier for a bat. They prefer small dark spaces. I was eventually forced to remove the mind-link disk, though, because I was continuously being swamped by her panic about the constant noises running through the cargo bay. There is no doubt in my mind that she's going to take wing like a literal bat out of hell, the second this box is opened.

It takes several more minutes for the hyperloop to come to a full stop. I can hear the general thumping and bumping that indicates the cargo hold is being unloaded. Slipping Stella's disk on, we're immediately swamped by our combined anxiety and desperation to be out of the box. It grows as the voices and sounds come closer and closer. Then suddenly, there is a double knock above me. I'm not sure whether it's wise to respond. So, I don't.

"Hey, Mason!" A female voice shouts. Then there's a second

knock on something else. "These two are a special delivery. Straight for the auctions, you hear?"

Auctions?

"Yeah, yeah," a grating male voice laughs in response. "One of these days I'm gonna start taking a tax on your merchandise."

Merchandise! Dammit, I knew this was too easy! How the hell am I going to escape?

Something slams into the side of my shipping box and begins raising it into the air. Stella gives a sharp squeak, but I can't comfort her. I brace my hands against the sides, trying to hold back a groan of pain. She flits about the box the second I release her. God, my bones hurt. My bladder hurts. Just about everything in my body cried uncle a long time ago. It's going to be nearly impossible to fight my way out. I'll be lucky if I can walk.

After what seems like a ridiculously long time, my box finally comes to a stop and is set down.

"Hey, if you're awake in there," a new nasal, male voice says with another knock on the top of my box, "don't you try anything funny when I open this thing. We're armed, and we don't take kindly to little fists or claws. If you don't give us any trouble, we're not going to hurt you."

The box lid slides open and I blink against the suddenly bright light. As I expected, Stella flies straight out of the box—screeching wildly.

No! Come back!

"What in Tesla's name?" The man shrieks, trying to swat Stella out of the air.

"Don't hurt her!" I shout up at him. "She's just scared."

"That thing belong to you?"

"She's my pet." Jesus, please have them accept that simple explanation.

"Well … add that to my list of weird shit that comes out of these boxes." He reaches down into the box, grips my upper arms, and squeezes down painfully tight as he hauls me to my feet. I can't help but cry out at being suddenly unfolded from such a tiny prison, and my left arm hurts terribly within his grip. "Sorry, kid." The man sighs.

He's about six inches shorter than me, with black hair and equally black, almond-shaped eyes. He has a strong jaw for such a slender face. His skin is a light tan color, and his clothing appears to be some kind of uniform. It has a hyperloop logo on it.

"I know you been in there an awful long time," he says. I struggle to stay on my feet while the blood rushes away from my head. "Whoa, don't faint on me now. If you come with me and don't give me any shit, we'll head straight to the bathroom. Alright?"

I nod adamantly. Once I have my balance back, the young man takes my hand and begins leading me through a maze of shipping boxes. He shouts over his shoulder, "Hey Benny! Get the other one out for me, will you?"

21

HAWK

I sit in the dim light, listening to Roland trudge up in his expensive suit, reeking of cologne. It blends with the stench in these concrete utility tunnels beneath Sector M. Chimeras don't report above ground. We're felt, not seen.

I'm pissed that I have to wait this long to pursue my mark, but I need to know exactly what I'm dealing with before I go any further.

"You made a good choice not submitting your report over the GRID." Roland pauses several feet from me, his hands tucked in his pockets. "Now tell me what in Tesla's name is going on."

"She got away from me." I shrug, consciously appearing extra casual.

"Got away from you? How did that happen? You were never authorized to take her out of that facility in the first place!" Roland's anger surprises me. His shoulders are coiled with tension and his hands are nearly shaking. The perspiration he's soaked in overwhelms the cologne and burns my nose. Bad signs.

"You're not stupid enough to believe those doctors would've

kept the squids away from her, are you?" I ask. "She may have gotten away from me, but she's not in their hands—not yet. The sooner you let me go after her, the sooner we can resolve that problem."

"Not a chance! You're off this case. We obviously need someone more reliable."

I swallow down the growl in my throat. "Who are you sending?"

"Cobra. And I suggest you keep your nose out of it."

The choice stuns me into silence. Cobra? She isn't the kind of person you send for a catch and release. Cobra is a cold-hearted executioner. Always has been. They don't mean to catch her at all. They still mean to kill her.

"Okay, why don't we cut the shit." I ball my fists and surge to my feet. "Why the hack did you give me bad intel? She's no squid recruit! I knew it from the moment I met her."

"You were given the information you needed to get the job done. You were the closest operative we had. Your job was to pick her up, bring her in, and leave her in the doctor's hands. After that, she's their responsibility. Not yours!"

"With all due respect, Sir." This man hasn't done anything to deserve respect in his entire pointless career. "My training says otherwise. I have been very clear, at all times, that I don't do assassination work. I arrange information and materials exchanges. I catch and release. According to regulation, the citizens I retrieve are my responsibility until the moment they are successfully reintegrated back into the Community."

I take a step toward him and he stumbles two steps back.

"I had no way of knowing the doctor at that hospital wasn't a rogue element," I shout, "because you'd given me bad information. On purpose! I was shot, nearly killed, and lost my target because of you! The blame for that doesn't fall on my shoulders, you prick. You knew when you sent me in that I do things by the book. So this is on you!"

"Is that why you've been off the radar?" Roland asks, rolling his eyes. "The squids crashed our vid feeds as soon as you were inside, so we've had no idea how you made it out, or if she was even still alive. If you were injured, you should've reported to the nearest hospital."

"I would have reported, if I had the option," I say, lying through clenched teeth. "My injury rendered me unconscious, and I'm lucky the mark didn't slit my throat. She had the opportunity that she needed to trap me in a vulnerable position, and that's exactly what she did."

"Are you saying a woman got the better of you?"

"It's not hard to do when I'm unconscious! The only reason I'm even alive to report back to you is because she patched me up instead of killing me."

"So you should have grabbed her when she let you go!"

"She's not that stupid." I need to avoid giving him additional information. "She was long gone by the time I got loose, and we're wasting time standing around here talking, while she's getting farther away."

"Where did she keep you?"

"Seeing as how you've been giving me bad intel, I don't think I need to give you details. Suffice it to say, it was a secure location, and I made my way back here as soon as I had the opportunity."

"That's insubordination, soldier."

"You nearly got me killed!" I hate him with every molecule in my body. "And why the hack isn't she slated for reintegration? She has no indicators of terrorist motivations or squid affiliation of any kind. In fact, she was downright hostile about them. She actively ran from them!"

"She has information in her head that is dangerous to the Community. The squids already know she has it. Even if she doesn't know or have access to it, there is nothing to prevent them from sweeping her for it."

"Yes," he says, "I suppose we could intentionally inflict a traumatic brain injury that would damage her enough to make the information irretrievable. But that's more of a risk and seems more cruel than killing her, considering she'd just be released into an institution. Is that what you want?"

Confirmation of my suspicions makes the rage boil in my gut. Regina had nothing to do with this! It isn't her fault that she has information inside of her head. She was used to process something dangerous, and now they plan to throw her away.

"What about the people who were on the server with her?"

"They've been handled." Roland avoids eye contact.

"Hack! You mean we murdered them."

"Follow orders, Hawk. I don't—"

"What happened?" I cut off his bullshit. "How do the squids know she was used to process something so sensitive? Citizens process classified information all the time. There isn't supposed to be a mechanism to trace which minds were used. That's a basic security feature."

"That's above your clearance." He pulls out a silk handkerchief to wipe the sweat from his brow. "Look Hawk, nobody wanted this to happen, but there's nothing any of us can do about it now. If keeping that information out of terrorist hands means killing her … so be it."

"I request permission to pursue the target and attempt an appropriate retrieval."

"Permission denied." Roland shakes his head. "I told you, you're off this one. In fact, your orders are to go dark. Command feels you let yourself get too close. We believe it would be best if you had some time to recover your perspective."

You mean you decided, you asshole.

"Get your distance back, Hawk." He sighs, glancing up at the cam in the far corner of the tunnel. "They're aware that you've been following up with some of your retrievals. They've tolerated it, but this incident pushes it over the line. You're being placed on administrative leave for the next sixty days. On day sixty-one you will check back in with me here. I will have a new set of orders waiting for you. Is that clear?"

"Yes sir. Dark it is."

22

GINA

"God Stella, where are you?"

Lying on this concrete slab they call a bed, I fiddle with her disk behind my ear. Hours ago, they took my stuff, locked me in this cramped concrete room, and left. I only managed to keep the disk by hiding it in my cheek. Wondering what will happen to her on her own out there is killing me. I could swear I can almost feel her on the fringes of my mind, but she must be too far away. It's too faint to focus on.

A 15-year-old boy from one of the other shipping boxes is trapped in here too. "Were you transported with someone else?"

"Sort of."

The boy is small for his age, still under five feet and scrawny. His bronze skin and brown hair look dull, his cheeks are lean, and he's missing a couple of teeth. He says he's being transported to a new buyer, but he's been a slave since he was a toddler. It disgusts me, but he's resigned as he lies back against the concrete floor with his head on his arm. "You won't see them again." His voice is quiet and he doesn't look at me with his brown eyes when he speaks.

Maybe it will be better for her if I don't. She's well enough to live independently now, but I don't know how her life with the mind-link will affect her natural instincts.

The bare concrete walls in here are too close. I would guess the room is only six by eight feet. With no windows and one steel door, you could coat this room with a single Faraday bomb. Thankfully, the boy let me lie down on the slab instead of the floor.

"Do you know anything about where you're going?"

"Some woman. An elite. It doesn't really matter. I doubt she could be as bad as the last one." He has scars on his skin that resemble burns and lacerations, but I can only see what's visible on his hands and feet.

"I'm sorry." I wish there were something I could do for him. "Do you think we can get out of here?"

"Not a chance," he says without even opening his eyes. "They keep transport routes locked down tight. You're better off waiting until you get where you're going—after they buy you. Trust me. You won't find an opportunity before then. They've been doing this for hundreds of years, you know."

I groan in frustration. Whatever I do, I can't risk them learning who I am. They'll sell me directly to the squids ... or to the shields.

"Have you really been free until now?" he asks, finally looking my direction.

"Yeah."

"What was it like?" He rolls over to stare at me with his chin resting on his folded arms.

"Umm ... it was really great." My chest hurts at how easy I've had it in comparison. "I had my own little place in the Dregs back home. Sometimes it was hard to get by, but I always had my freedom. That's all I cared about. Honestly, this cage terrifies me."

"That sounds awesome. The freedom part, I mean. Don't worry about this, though, you'll get used to it. Sometimes, this can be the most peaceful place. Nobody wanting to use you, or make you do stuff. You can just ... exist here."

"I don't understand how the world could have existed as long as it has and we're still selling people. We already sell sex to anyone who wants it in the brothels. It's like we've learned nothing."

The boy shrugs. "There will always be bad people. People who want to own what they're not supposed to—who like making other people serve them, or suffer. At least, that's who I've run into anyway."

His frank description makes my heart thunder in my chest. I don't want to belong to those people. The door opens and I jump in surprise, scooting back into the corner.

"You." A short woman with creamy skin and exotic amber eyes points at me. "With me. Now!"

Obedience is best until I run into something I absolutely refuse to do. The kid is probably right. If they do sell me—I shudder at the thought—I'll have to try and escape from that person.

"Good luck," the boy calls out as I exit. "Nice meeting you, lady."

The series of narrow, concrete corridors leads to a plain unlabeled metal door. After stepping inside, I'm met with the sight of an older man sitting behind a very small desk. The room is only slightly larger than the one I was just taken from and smells musty. Every available space is crammed with flexes.

Who in the universe is this guy? He has black, slanted eyes with hidden lids, a broad nose, lightly tanned skin, short-cropped, black hair, a thick, graying goatee, and glasses. He's wearing the same hyperloop maintenance uniform that everyone else is. Reviewing some information on a flex, he doesn't look up when I take a seat in the small chair in front of him.

The woman closes the door behind me.

"You come from Central Continent, Region 84?" he asks, still scrolling through data with his finger.

"Yes," I nod, "but I'm afraid there's been a mistake."

"Mistake?" He looks up over the rim of his glasses.

"Yes. Jay said I would be paying for my transport with information." I know full well that was a bunch of crap, but I'm not sure where else to start from. "I told him I wasn't selling my services."

"Ah yes. Jay." He leans back and considers me for a moment. "He's good at what he does. What did he say?"

"He said I should send someone back. That he needed word on what was happening in this part of the world."

"Interesting …" He pinches his lower lip between his fingers before leaning forward to punch something in on the flex. "Who is hunting you?"

Crap! "I don't know what you—"

"Don't play stupid with me woman. I'm a busy man. Who is hunting you, and why?"

My mind races for a moment, searching for a lie that won't get me sold to the squids or the Community at the earliest opportunity. "He's a tech dealer. He wanted sex back in 84, but I refused him."

"What is his name?"

"I don't know." I look down at my hands to avoid his eyes. "I didn't want to know."

"You would have been better off giving him what he wanted."

The man chuckles with an awful sneer. "Now you wind up with the highest bidder." He walks around the desk and grabs a metal cylinder from atop a flex cabinet.

I bolt up out of the chair and back toward the door.

"If you run," he says, "we'll just catch you and beat you. I'd rather not damage such beautiful merchandise, but it will not prevent a sale. I promise you."

"What is that?" I point at the device in his hands.

"A blood test. We don't want to pass any diseases to our clients."

Blood test ... It could just as easily be a device like Hawk used to drug me. Even if it is, though ... what the hell can I do about it?

Jesus, help me. Feeling a sense of peace wash over me, I take a deep breath.

When I hold out my arm, a brief look of surprise crosses his face but he quickly presses the tube inside the crook of my elbow. There is a sharp prick against my skin only briefly and then he brings the cylinder up to the flex before lifting the flex to read. "Not pregnant. Good," he mumbles. "Very nice. Very clean. Did you work at the brothel when this dealer wanted you?"

Tossing down the flex, he pulls out a measuring pen and begins taking my dimensions. Running the tip along the surface of my skin, the lengths begin to populate in the flex—giving him as much information as a tailor would need. I struggle to get my mind working on my answer as I fight to ignore his hands.

"I worked there before." The truth of my inexperience would make me even more valuable. I should try to be as average as I can.

He reaches up and grabs my breasts with a painful amount of force, and it takes everything I have not to punch him in the jaw. That would definitely give away my lie. People do this kind of thing to Troy all the time. Seeing it always made me feel ill, but now anger burns in my gut like acid.

"No implants though." He smirks with a raised eyebrow. "That's a nice surprise."

"I didn't work there long. I hated it."

"It's not really needed with your build anyway. Well, their loss, my gain." He lets go and sweeps his hand along the back of my neck. "Inoculated too. Have you worked server duty before?"

"Yeah. Doesn't everybody?"

He doesn't bother to answer, but walks around and sits back behind his desk again. "Do you have a last name?"

"Glass." I spit out one of the most common shirker names from home. Crossing my arms over my chest, I already feel bruised by his claws.

"Okay, Meredith Glass," he says, poking his flex. "You'll be put out for the auction in two days. Enjoy your private time until then. It's all you're likely to have."

"Can't I just buy my freedom? I can find a way to pay you."

He raises an eyebrow when he looks back at me with a straight set to his mouth. "You are a beautiful, healthy woman with exotic features. If you can immediately offer us more than the high bidder after the auction, we'll talk about it. But you were the one who couldn't afford a hyperloop ticket."

23

HAWK

Walking into the hyperloop station, I search for Gina's scent in the stench of the crowd. The autotruck stops were a bust, so she must have listened to me. The travelers are following their normal patterns—the shirkers and dealers working the crowd are the regular crew.

I'm not going to lie down on this one. Cobra being assigned changes the game. She's as lethal as she is beautiful. Her bite is venomous, potent enough to kill an adult in under five minutes. She laces all of her weaponry with her venom. Cold and calculating, she's my least favorite person from the unit.

Cobra loves killing. In our downtime, we're encouraged to seek out our own assignments for approval. I realized a long time ago that while many of us look for valuable information or identify people to help, Cobra spends her nights planning targets to eliminate. I sometimes wonder how many unauthorized kills she has under her belt.

She'd approach Gina like a friend. Just like I did.

There. Gina's scent is faint but she's definitely been here recently. I follow it and jerk to a stop when I realize it's attached to the slaver that sits beneath the departure sign.

Hack! Just what we need.

Another faint trail leads into a bathroom stall. I slip inside and close the door. The scent doesn't lead anywhere, of course, but I take the opportunity to hack into the station's surveillance. Closing my eyes and using my off-the-books credentials, the system lets me in easily and I start reviewing the 3D vid.

Nothing.

I'm about to give up when I remember the slaver. Backing up, I watch him instead. Within about two hours of when she left me in the Dregs, the man starts talking to himself. Then a woman approaches him—the elite I sold the injectors to. She's doing exactly what she said she was going to do.

Hey. Right there! The material on the man's shoulder flattens, and in the very corner—where Gina must be blocking the GRID's view from all angles—the image is an odd texture. It's almost like static. The GRID is trying to fill in the gap with the information it has but doesn't have quite enough data. It's very close though. Hack, I looked right over it the first time without even seeing the defect. That's her!

Gritting my teeth, I watch the rest of the slaver's routine play out. The guard comes to cause a distraction, the maintenance bot opens, and just before it's door closes, the odd texture washes across its surface. She walked right into their hands.

Go dark my ass. This whole situation is completely bogon.

I exit the bathroom stall, wash my hands, and head out to talk with the slaver. He'll give me the information I need, or I'll turn him in at the nearest shield post. I'll turn in the rogue shield too, as soon as I've got Gina somewhere safe.

24

GINA

My heart is racing as I lie on the cold floor and try to look calm. Two other women have been trapped in here with me since the boy was taken yesterday. One is in her late forties, at least, with salt and pepper hair. The other is a blond girl about my age. Neither of them have been sold in an auction before either.

We've all been given these awful bodysuits to wear. They're made of a thin black fabric that clings to you in a way that leaves nothing about your shape to the imagination. It covers us from the base of the skull all the way down to our ankles—hiding scars and bruises that would otherwise be visible. I realized when I went to put the suit on that the events from the last few days have apparently taken their toll. I have extensive bruising all over my body, a symptom of the fragile blood vessels I have because of EDS.

I bolt upright when the door opens. A man steps inside with a nasty looking stick that has sharp tips on the end. He presses a button and I recognize the crackle of an electric cattle prod. The blond woman shrieks and cowers as he ushers all three of us out into the hallway. After a disorienting series of corridors, we arrive at another loading bay.

Oh God, they're going to put us back in those awful shipping boxes! Where is Stella? If I lose her here, I'll never find her again!

"Get in." The man shoves the stick into the small of my back—thankfully without any current.

As I approach the metal shipping container, I sense her presence. Stella! Oh Baby, Momma's so sorry. Come to Momma but hide. Hide! I try to project the sensation she sent me before of the predator.

Sliding down inside the small box, my joints object to the confinement. At least this box is a little larger than the last one. My legs are folded, but my knees aren't pressed up to my chin. Wait … the box is probably the same size. I had my bag in here with me before.

Stella where are you?

She's flitting around in the corner of the loading area, and closing my eyes I can get a pretty good view of the room. There are at least six men and women with cattle prods, watching over at least twenty boxes and manhandling people inside. There's no chance of getting away from them here.

Stella flutters over to cling to a loop on one man's pants. Then, she transfers onto the jacket sleeve of one of the women. Before I realize how close she is, she's climbing over the corner of the box onto my shoulder. Her poor little heart is pounding with the combination of our fears. She'll never get a good grip on this fabric, so I hold her up gently to let her wrap her little feet into the strands of my hair. She clings beside my neck, right next to the disc, and I pull more of my hair in front to shelter her from view.

I don't know this part of the world. I don't know the slave markets. I'm in so far over my head, I don't even know what I need to know. So, when the box closes over me, I start to pray again.

25

GINA

Should I ask to contact Joe? Would they let me if I did? Joe has significant pull in the markets back home, but those are tech markets, not slave markets. I don't know if his influence would be of use out here, wherever I am.

My box was in motion for a couple of hours before coming to rest in a noisy area. Stella's fur is tickling my face and makes me sneeze, bumping my head on the lid above me just before it slides open. A man reaches in to grip my arm, and I untangle Stella from my hair as quickly as I can, releasing her on the floor of the box behind me. He hauls me up and I hold back a screech of pain from his bruising grip. I hate that I have to lean against him to keep from falling as dizziness washes over me.

"Well, aren't you a friendly one," he laughs, swatting my behind as I struggle to get my vision to clear. "Out you go."

Repelled, I shove hard away from him.

"Hey!" He grips my jaw hard enough I'm afraid it may come out of socket. "Don't give me attitude. Get your ass out on stage."

Stage? Oh, God.

I hear the crackle of a cattle prod again, and flinch as he shoves me forward toward a doorway flooded with light. The old man from the little measurement room is standing beside the door with an extra-large flex in his hands. The other women said his name is Kisame.

"Good evening, Meredith," he says without glancing up. "Get out there and stand so you can be seen. I remember your request."

"Please, just let me go."

In a flash, he reaches up and pinches my ear between his fingers, sending shooting pain all the way down into my neck. The pain shoots through the mind-link and Stella takes flight from the box with a screech. Kisame lets go, turning toward the sound, and I press my abused ear tight against my head to hold back the throbbing pain.

"What was that?" Kisame barks at the men behind us.

"I don't know," someone shouts back. "Sounded like a rat maybe?"

Kisame reaches for me again but I hold up my other hand.

"I'll go! I'll go!"

"Get out there then."

Looking out onto the stage, there is a circle of blue lights in the middle. I take a deep breath and push the fear down deep into my gut. I can't let them see my fear. Whoever is out there—they're animals. Predators. They prey on the weak and likely take a sick pleasure in doing so. I'm a performer, so if I'm going to have to endure this, I'll do it on my terms.

Entering the circle, a dozen spotlights land on me from every angle. I can't see the shadowed figures in the crowd, and for once in my life I'm glad. I won't give them any of my signature smiles, but I hold my head high and my shoulders back despite the pain. It's like blending in with the elites.

"Next in line," Kisame's voice booms from the stage, "we have a female in her early twenties. You may start your bidding now."

Keeping my face forward, I let my eyes drift to the sides. There are huge screens on either side of me that list out details as if I'm a product on the GRID as Kisame reads them off. Auburn hair. Hazel eyes. White skin. Not pregnant.

Dear God, do they sell pregnant women often?

Above all the details, there is a number that is steadily rising, and it takes me a moment to realize it's the current bid. Oh Jesus, help me! It's already over 250,000 coin! I straighten my spine again, refusing to acknowledge the tremor I can feel starting in the pit of my stomach. Kisame eggs the crowd to higher and higher bids. The number passes half a million and I start to feel hot and queasy. Kisame's voice is beginning to show his excitement as he tells the crowd that my blood is clean, I'm well nourished, and I'm already inoculated. He's good at what he does and I hate him more by the second.

The bids are beginning to slow and I realize that every time the number changes, there is another number that flashes in the corner of the big screens. It must be the number assigned to the bidder, and I'm only seeing three consistent numbers now.

Suddenly, the number jumps from six hundred and eighty thousand to one million.

What? Oh my God!

"One million," Kisame shouts. "Do we have one million and one? One million and one?"

My knees tremble and moisture starts to build up in the corner of my eyes, but there's no way in hell I'm going to let these monsters see me cry. I tip my head back to drain the tears down my ducts.

"One million going once! One million going twice … Sold! To bidder number thirty four!"

Bidder number thirty four? Oh Jesus, I can't do this! No wonder Kisame was so smug when I asked about buying my freedom! That snake!

The man who swatted my behind is next to me a moment later and grabs my arm. His smug smile makes me furious and without thinking I throw a punch for his jaw. He dodges, grabbing my hair in a painful grip as laughter burns through the crowd of bidders.

"Let go of me!" I shriek as he drags me off stage.

"Shut up!" He slams me against the wall, letting go of my hair and holding up the cattle prod. I'll be useless if he hits me with that thing, so I turn the direction he's pointing and walk through the door into the hallway.

Follow me, Stella. Hide. Dread fills us both as I make my way toward my new owner.

PART 3

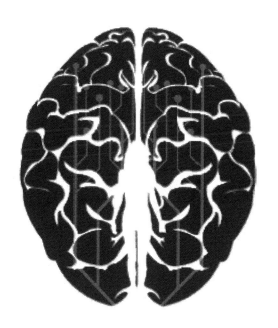

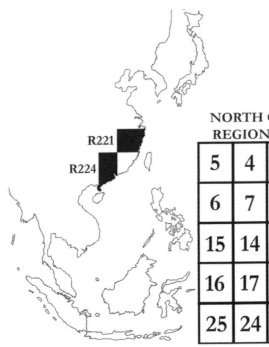

NORTH CONTINENT
REGIONAL SECTORS

5	4	3	2	1
6	7	8	9	10
15	14	13	12	11
16	17	18	19	20
25	24	23	22	21

SECTOR DISTRICTS

E	D	C	B	A
F	G	H	I	J
P	N	M	L	K
Q	R	S	T	U
Z	Y	X	W	V

1

GINA

Trying to breathe through my panic, I'm having an impossible time getting Stella to do anything but flutter around and cling to surfaces I can't even distinguish. One of the guards she flutters by is excitedly talking about my sale. He says the buyer's name is Darius Volkov—someone they seem to know well.

What am I going to do?

They threw me back in this steel cell with new clothes. The new shirt and pants are thin, plain black cotton, but less revealing. I changed into them as quickly as possible—desperate to get out of the dreadful black skin suit. At least they're comfortable.

Sitting cross-legged on the concrete bed with my elbows on my knees, and my chin on my fists, I can focus on keeping my breathing steady as long as I keep my eyes closed. If I can ever get Stella to calm down too, I'll try to convince her to explore more of the building. There might still be a way—

The door to my cell flies open and a pale, blond man steps inside with his stick. "Out," he says, waving a hand toward the hallway.

I stand up and head for the door. The hallways are lit with an eerie yellow glow. The walls are all more concrete, but this new area has a black tile floor. There are no windows or decorations, just evenly spaced steel doors.

Come on, Stella. Come find Momma. I'm lucky she hasn't gotten stuck behind any doors.

My stomach churns as I'm forced to walk in front of the man.

"Stop," he says at the end of the hallway.

I turn toward him and shriek in surprise as he snaps something around my neck. "What is that?" I explore it with my fingers. It's a thin band of metal without a catch that I can find anywhere.

Without warning, a current from the band slices up into my eyes and brings me to my knees. Stella shrieks and I realize through the haze of pain that she's not far away. When the current stops, I pant for a moment—trying to force the contents of my stomach to remain in my body. Stella is fluttering around like she's drunk somewhere ahead of us as the man laughs from above me.

"Just in case you get any funny ideas, lady," he says. "We'll give this to the bidder when we hand you over. You'll play nice if you're smart."

Oh, I am in so much trouble.

"Now get up." He hauls me to my feet by my arm. I choke back a scream as he grips the spot on my arm that is already bruised. He shoves me forward and I start walking again.

As we round the next corner, I spot an imposing figure near the end of the hall. He's over six feet tall and dressed in a long, black, hooded trench coat and boots with exterior steel toes. The hood is pulled low, so I can't see his face.

I hesitate—my heart racing in my chest. Predator! Predator! Stella's instincts scream through my mind.

The man behind me slams his body into my shoulder and shouts, "Keep moving."

When we get to him, my buyer waves his hand over the flex my escort is holding without making a sound. The flexible glass surface shifts to a green color and my escort hands him the horrible black button.

"You know what this is for, right?" The cruel man laughs.

My new owner nods and—without acknowledging me—pivots toward the door. It has a window to the outside. It's been so long since I've seen the sky. How can such a dark world look so beautifully sunny?

I know I'm supposed to follow this man, but my feet have turned to lead. Darius is nearly as large as Tommy. How can I possibly escape from a mountain like him?

Something hard slams into my back on my right side as my escort says, "Move!" I crumple to the floor, choking on the pain.

Suddenly, Darius whirls on the guard and I hear a sickening crunch. Before I can even catch my breath, the man has hit the wall behind me and slides down clutching his face. Terror washes through me like ice as I see blood beginning to seep through the man's fingers. His nose is broken.

"Don't!" Darius shouts from above me. The voice is savage, but eerily familiar. "Damage my property!"

I need to get up, but I still can't get myself to move. A hand grips my face and lifts it—my world going strangely still and quiet when I meet his eyes. They're bright green, instead of brown. The goatee is gone and his hair has grown out more than a foot and is now an espresso brown color. His face is in an angry sneer, but it's definitely him. "Don't make me use this," he says, holding up the evil collar button, "unless you want to wind up like him. Get up on your feet! Keep your mouth shut."

Jared. Hawk. Darius. Super soldier ... shit!

His face is inches from mine and I swallow hard. Yes, keep my mouth shut. I remember the scars on the boy in my cell. I guess this is better than winding up with an unknown.

I can't hold back a groan of pain as he hauls me to my feet again by my stupid arm. Can no one grab me anywhere else?

"Move!" he orders.

I obediently start walking forward again as the cruel man on the floor starts to pick himself up, spitting blood. We're almost to the door, almost to where Stella is clinging, when Kisame steps into the hall in front of us. He holds up a hand with a sickly sweet grin, looking more appropriately evil in the yellow light.

"If you would humor me for a moment." He bows slightly before Hawk. "I have a question for your new purchase."

Hawk doesn't say anything, but Kisame nods to him again.

"My dear, when we spoke last, you were interested in outbidding your buyer," he says. "I don't want to be considered unreasonable, after all. So, will you be offering me more than one million coin?"

I glare at him, infuriated by his smug smile.

"I thought not." He chuckles, delighted with his little joke. "Enjoy your purchase, Sir."

2

HAWK

Man, I'm exhausted. The hotel room is in rough shape because of the district we're in. The faded orange curtains and cream-colored linens on the bed should all be replaced. There's not even a chair or a place to keep food cold, but it has a bed, a toilet, and a shower, and that's all we need for the night.

Dropping our bags by the door, I glare at that ridiculous autodrive bag of hers. I would have left it at the slaver compound, but I couldn't verify her cam tech wasn't stashed in it. I have no idea what I'm looking for. When I accessed the security feeds on our way here, she still isn't showing up. She hasn't uttered a word since I secured her, but I need to convince her to trust me with that information.

I set a quick silent alarm on the door in case she tries to run. I hope that I managed to confuse our scent trail enough to buy us time. With two autocabs, three light rails, and an autobus to get here I must have crossed our own path at least ten times. Only then could I risk walking the last several blocks.

"Good evening, Darius," Manuela says, appearing next to me. "What are your needs?"

"Windows at 100 percent opacity. Lights dim. Activate Do Not Disturb protocols."

"Activating," Manuela says. "You may reactivate my services at any time."

I motion for Gina to cross from the door into the far side of the tiny room. There is barely enough room to get around the bed in here and she stands, tucking herself in against the shallow, wall-mounted metal cabinets beside the window. "Is she …"

Holding a finger to my lips, I pull my jammer out of my pocket, turn it on, and set it on the bedside table. "Manuela's not active anymore, but never assume these places aren't bugged." I sit down on the edge of the bed to take off my boots.

Gina doesn't look well. She's pale, her hands are trembling, and she smells like that stupid bat. She's also limping—favoring her right foot. Of course, they were knocking her around.

"Why didn't she show up for me too?" Gina asks.

"The chip they implanted in you at the auction interferes with your CID. She doesn't realize she needs to."

"What are you planning to do with me?"

"Relax. You're safe. I haven't figured out what we're doing yet. I was focused on getting you out of harm's way first."

"Is that where I am?"

"Yes. It is. You can believe me or not. I don't really care." Hack, I need to be more reassuring but I'm drop-dead tired. "I wasn't the only person at the auction who was there for you. There were squids. One of my sources said they're haunting the slaver auctions around the world, but I took care of it."

I need to deal with the collar though. Gripping the control, I walk up and reach out to disconnect it. Gina jerks back with a gasp, bumping into the wall behind her and watching my hand with wild eyes.

"Whoa." Backing up immediately, I raise my hands in surrender, keeping the button visible to her. "Sorry, Babe. Why don't you let me take that collar off you, huh? I swear. I'm not going to hurt you."

Her hands are shaking but in her eyes I can see her weighing the decision. Finally she nods, clasping her hands together to try to still them. Man, she's got guts. I move very slowly, careful not to touch her skin, bringing the control up against the back of the collar until it snaps open. I pull the collar away as she lets out a breath of air big enough I'm afraid she may faint. After a moment, she meets my eyes again, still uncertain.

"Now, were you hurt?" I disable the collar and toss it up on the shelf with the button.

"No."

Bullshit. "You don't need medical attention? I need you to be honest with me, Gina. You've been limping since the auction."

She looks away from me for the first time, staring at her worn-out shoes. "I was cramped up in metal boxes for hours on end. You expect me to be skipping around?"

"Fine." Probably lying … but maybe she's just embarrassed.

"How did you get my bag?" she asks.

"I stole it from the storage area at Kisame's compound." Trying to find what you use for the cams.

Sitting back down on the full-sized mattress, I try to relax my aching back. "You've got a crazy amount of braces in there. Put one on that ankle tomorrow. For now, we need to get some rest. We should go undetected here for a while, but we can't stay too long in any one place."

She just stands there staring at me, and at the bed, and back at me. Her eyes are round and the shaking is back. Man, if this woman is acting, she's one in a trillion. "What do you intend to do with me?"

That's a great question, Babe. Wish I knew the answer. Trying to rub the ache out of my neck, I have to face facts I didn't want to yet. "We need to find someone who can tell us what's in your head."

She nods and her shoulders relax. "Do you know someone we can trust? I can't go to a Community facility."

"That would be insane." I can't help but laugh at the idea. "I'm sure scanning you in is what got us in a firefight last time."

"So why did you do it?" She looks both shocked and offended.

Oh, come on. It's not like I got into that mess on purpose! The tension comes flooding back into my neck, bringing a headache with it. "I have never seen squids attack a facility head-on like that. I was not told what you have is valuable enough for them to lose their hacking minds and lives over. If I had known, I would have insisted on another location. Which reminds me …" I open up her bag and toss her body armor toward her. "Make sure you wear this from now on."

Her eyes are wide as she stares down at the black fabric. "How did you get these? They weren't in my bag."

"I took them when I took you from your burrow. If I'd turned you over in those, they'd have—"

"You!" Her cheeks turn scarlet and she hides her face behind the thin fabric. "You undressed me?" she squeaks.

"Don't worry." I sigh. "You're beautiful, but I don't take

advantage of my position like that. I put you right back in your clothes. I stashed them with my stuff on the way to the hospital, so I went back and picked them up after you left."

She rubs at her arms for a minute, blushing like crazy. "What were the doctors trying to do to me? You attacked them, didn't you?"

At least she's finally talking. "They were going to kill you."

"Why did that surprise you?"

"I was told you'd be reset and released. I don't do assassination jobs."

"So you admit that the Community assassinates people!" She actually has the nerve to point her finger at me.

"Every government in history assassinates people." I'm just lucky I don't have to. Leaning back against the headboard, I try to get comfortable. "Now come up here and sleep."

Her eyebrows scrunch together as she glances at the sheets. "You're still in your clothes."

Really? "Should I take them off?" Maybe teasing her will get her to relax.

I do get another blush out of it but her tension skyrockets back to a ten out of ten. Shit.

"No," she says. "I just ... we're not very clean."

Oh man ... I may never get her in this bed now. "You can take a shower if you want." I close my eyes and try to be non-threatening. "But it's going to come out of the time you get to sleep. I'll stay on top of the sheets."

She's going to be such a pain in the ass ... I'm sure as shit not going to hurt her, but she's too scared. All I can do is give her room and hope she calms down.

After a quick shower, she's still looking for a way out, but to my surprise, she walks straight over and slips beneath the sheets beside me. Maybe I can risk actually sleeping. She's already proven she's not the type to slit a throat. Sneaking out while I'm asleep will be tempting, but with the alarm on the door, I'll be able to snatch her before she gets far.

We have to haul ass to a different sector tomorrow and avoid any more public transportation for a while. We've over-used them already. That means hiking a lot of miles on foot through the streets.

My thoughts are drawn back to the limp that's been bothering me since I found her at the auction. She's definitely favoring her right foot. It's going to be a problem if she can't keep up.

I swear it's only moments later when I snap awake as Gina moves beside me. I want to throw my arm over her to keep her from trying anything. I realize though, if I do, I'm going to wind up playing this game with her all night with neither of us getting any sleep. She doesn't trust me, and she doesn't have much reason to. I'll see how far she can get on her own.

She slides out from beneath the sheets, and I'm careful to keep my breathing even. I can hear her shuffle around, very quietly trying to gather up her things. Then there is a long silence. I hear an odd scrape, and crack an eye open just enough to look at her reflection in the window at the end of the room. Hack! She's grabbing the slaver's collar down from the closet shelf.

I close my eye again as she walks back over to hover above me. You try it, and I am going to make you regret it!

It would actually be a very smart thing for her to do if she could have managed it without waking me, but I'd never let that happen. Not in this lifetime. I wait patiently, but she never slides the collar around my neck. Instead, I hear her shuffle away.

To my surprise, I hear the door swish open and click back closed without my alarm ever sounding. I'm on my feet in a flash, tossing my coat and boots back on. I grab my bag and check the door. She couldn't figure out how to remove the device from the door, but she chipped a tiny fragment of mirror from the bathroom to trick the sensor.

Clever, I sigh. Definite pain in the ass.

3

GINA

The hair on the back of my neck is standing on end again. I wonder if that means Hawk is watching me, or if he's simply succeeded in pushing me to a new level of paranoia. Either way, paranoia is probably wise. Glancing around the street, there are a few hides here that have been made by the local shirkers.

Ugh. The noxious blend of odors is even fouler than the Dregs. The hustle and bustle of the over-crowded sector streets is only feet behind me, but this skinny canyon between buildings is an isolated little pocket of desperation. There are abandoned and dented metal shipping containers piled haphazardly with scraps of filthy fabric hanging out of them. The ground here wasn't important enough to be paved with glass. It's just a hole-ridden patch of dirt-, blood- and urine-stained concrete. I approach an older man who's sitting back with a stunner and a smile.

"Are any hides available?"

"The red box is open." He shrugs. "And the silver lean-to. I would avoid the lean-to, though, myself, if you don't want the smell all night."

Glancing at the recycling bin nearby, I can see some kind of brown sludge leaking out of its corner. I'm surprised the Global Fellowship hasn't come in here to scurry out the residents and clean up the hazard to the ecosystem. They're supposed to collect the waste and replace the bin.

"Is there a fee?"

"Nah," the old addict says. "Used to be, but Ling moved on a couple of weeks ago. Nobody bothers anymore."

It's a bad sign when the petty crime begins to die too.

"Thanks." I turn toward the red box.

"Need somethin' to eat?" the man calls from behind me.

"No thanks." I wave over my shoulder. "I found something a few streets back."

I'm not going to admit I have food on me because that would

be begging to get mugged. I glance at the red box. It's just tinted sheet metal. I glance around the side to see the GF Foods label on the side. It's been stolen from a commissary before being recycled, no doubt.

I crawl inside and Stella flutters in behind me. She's relieved by our change in location. Hawk terrifies her. It's hard not to see the look in his eye as slightly predatory, without her screaming the bat equivalent of *Predator!* in my head too. She's never reacted that way to someone before. It must be his size … Whatever it is, she loves this alley full of crannies to hide in, and immediately finds a smooth metal edge to cling to in here.

The red box is long and remarkably dry. I can lay down fully and still have room to crawl around. Someone with a good head on their shoulders placed it so the rainwater would run away from the box instead of inside it. I shoo a few of the roaches out and move my bag around inside with me. If I lay it on its back, the upper section of the backpack could make a decent pillow.

I close my eyes and sleep pulls me under. Then, I snap back awake with a start.

Dear Lord! Don't be stupid just because you're tired!

I crawl back out of my tiny room for the night and find a loose piece of metal to lay over the opening to block me from view, leaving barely enough room for Stella to go out and hunt while I'm asleep. If people are looking for me, the last thing I need is to keep myself visible enough for an easy glance-and-grab. Hawk will be, if no one else.

Once I've pulled the metal into place, I lie back down and pray. Shame washes through me as I think about where I'm staying. My family has always been proud to live in the shirker camps, but they would never let us stay in a place like this. I remind myself that it's only for the night, ask God to protect me from the people outside, and finally slip into a deep sleep.

4

HAWK

It's stupid to be out here playing along when we're in such danger, but I'll never be able to pull this off with her constantly trying to escape. I'm amazed she thinks she can sneak away from me this easily. She doesn't know I can track her scent, but even a human soldier could have followed her trail. Her ability to disable my alarm on the door was hacking impressive though. I know some third year shield recruits who couldn't have pulled it off.

It's muggy and hot. The awful smell must not affect her the way it does me. I can distinctly pick up blood, vomit, urine, feces, mildew, rotting produce and several different versions of body odor all mingling together to form something you could practically use as a weapon against a chimera like me. Fortunately, I was trained to deal with it.

Let her think she's escaped and safe for now. Catching her right away won't discourage her because she'll think she didn't wait long enough. She needs to know that I can find her anywhere, and that I will.

It's sad to think she must have lived this way a lot. I keep watch over her hiding place from my ledge on the third story, huddling down to keep warm until daylight. Not two hours go by, however, before I realize I have to alter my plan.

Shit.

The man she talked to earlier, who directed her to the empty space, is approaching her box. He's practically slithering up to the entrance while keeping a lookout behind him, and he keeps fidgeting with the sleeves of his soiled shirt. The sick hacker's intentions are anything but harmless.

I move quickly, scaling down the alley wall as quietly as possible. I note the knife in his hand as I approach, while he moves the metal door out from in front of her box. Just as he starts to crawl inside with her, I get my hand over his mouth and haul him back upright by his head. His screams are muffled, and his flailing is weak for a man his size. He tries to bring the knife down into my thigh, but I grab his wrist and twist hard until he drops it with a muffled screech. I hurl him against the alley wall, grab his knife off the ground, and then pin him against the wall with a forearm to his throat.

"What did you think you were doing?" It's all I can do to restrain the growl that wants to escape, but I don't want him to tell someone he was confronted by a chimera about the girl. Even without it, the man's eyes are wide as he struggles for breath.

He's glancing up and down the alleyway, but no one is moving to help him. Several shirkers are watching us with curious stares. I need to make an example out of him to hold the others off until morning.

"I was just cold man," the guy croaks through his compressed vocal cords. "I swear. I wasn't gonna hurt her. Don't kill me, man. I—"

"Shut up." I put more pressure against his throat. I spin him around and put him in a chokehold. He struggles and throws a couple of blows into my sides, but eventually chokes himself into unconsciousness. I let up on the pressure when he's out, and draw his body close enough to hear it begin trying to suck in oxygen again. He stinks so I drop him down, gripping him by the back of his jacket. He should live. If he doesn't, he doesn't.

I drag him over to the edge of the retaining wall for the lower intersecting alley a dozen feet below. It's an angled surface instead of a straight drop, so I drop him on his side and kick him over. He rolls down into a heap at the bottom.

When I turn back around, several pairs of eyes are still glued to me. The shirkers here pay close attention, but they would have done nothing to help Gina and they won't do it now. They retreat back farther into their hides.

I crawl into the ridiculous box with her. Hack the smell. My presence will keep other creeps from trying anything.

I'm cautious as I crawl inside—expecting her to wake up and panic. That bat smell is back on her, but I would swear she showered. It must still be around somewhere. I have to shift her body over to fit mine behind her, with our feet towards the opening. She should have already woken up from the scuffle, and I'm seriously disturbed when she still doesn't move. "Gina," I mumble softly, "It's Hawk."

She remains stone still. I check her pulse briefly, even though I can hear the steady breaths filling her lungs. I wonder if she used a stunner, but there's no emitter on her cheek or remote in her hand. I check her arms, but there's no track marks, sores or scents to indicate chems. She's not high. She sleeps like the dead. I wonder if it's the trauma she's been through? It's an incredibly dangerous trait for a shirker.

Hello ... The small silver disk is behind her ear again. I'll take that, Babe. If this is how she's been disabling the cams, I need to figure out how it works. I doubt she has a clue how many red flags this thing threw up, but it did help her escape the street shields. Too bad that's not enough.

A lifetime of training and dicey situations have honed me into an incredibly light sleeper. I feel exhausted, but I'll wake up if anyone else approaches tonight. It's so frustrating that she's putting us through all this extra hassle, instead of sleeping in a more secure location in a warm, only-musty bed.

I lie my head down on my arm, close my eyes, and wrap my arm around her middle—drawing the heat of her body against me. I'll wait to wake her until we've both had some sleep.

5

GINA

I wake up to a little more pain than normal, but otherwise feel strangely comfortable. I expected sleeping in this box to be cold, but I'm pleasantly warm. It also feels much smaller than I remember.

I struggle to roll over. There's someone behind me! A hand slams over my mouth and I try to bite it.

"Stop." Hawk groans in the rough baritone he has when he first wakes up. "This is your fault."

How the hell did he find me? It's not like I left footprints on the concrete! And I stayed out of sight of the cams …

"Babe, this is my job. Don't look so shocked."

Your job is what I'm afraid of! I try to bite his hand again but it's impossible to manage.

"Are you going to scream before I can tell you about your other visitor?"

What? My heart rate picks up and I shake my head.

"That old guy you talked to last night tried to pay you a visit," Hawk says with a curl to his lip, and holds up a lethal looking switchblade a few inches in front of my face. "He thought he'd bring this along to show you, I guess."

Yikes … I'd like to say I would have handled it, but I know better. The idea makes me nauseous. Stella's tiny heart races along with mine as I cast my eyes away from his accusing stare. Finally, Hawk removes his hand.

"How long have you been in here?"

"A couple hours after you." He yawns and shrugs his shoulders, but there's no way he can stretch in a space this cramped. "You were so far asleep I thought you were stunned. It's dangerous to sleep like that out here."

"I've had a pretty rough trip." The truth is I always sleep like the dead. Mom used to say it was from always trying to heal, or never getting good rest even when I do sleep. My brother Arthur has insomnia most of the time, though, and his EDS is worse than mine.

"We could have spent the night in a nice warm room," Hawk says. "In a real bed. But you wanted this hacking box. You have a shower stashed in here somewhere I haven't seen?"

"Oh shut up." I shove him with my shoulder. "How did you find me anyway?"

"Trade secret." He yawns again. "Now we have to move. We need to be three districts from here by tomorrow night."

"Three districts? How are we going to manage that?"

"We will," he says with a shrug as he begins crawling out of the box backward. "Let's go." He grabs a hold of the waistline of my pants and drags me out by it. I screech in surprise and Stella flies out of the box, madly flapping her wings in his face.

"Hawking's ghost!" he shouts, backing away from the angry bat. "How the hack do you still have that thing?"

"She's not a thing." I sit back on my heels in the alley and brush at my pants legs to give myself a moment for my blood pressure to adjust before standing. "Her name is Stella. Stella Luna."

"Well, keep her out of my face. She could have rabies."

"She's been immunized." What a big baby.

"How did you get a hold of a vaccine like that?" He eyes me suspiciously again.

Whoops. "She was someone else's pet before I got her." I reach back in the box for my bag.

"By the way ..." I hear from above me. "What is this?"

I turn around and see him holding Stella's mind-link disk between his fingertips. "No! Give it back!" I lunge for it. "Haw—"

"Stop!" Hawk catches me by the front shoulder and holds me at arms-length, with a glare. He glances up and down the street and I see there are a few people watching us. "Get back in the box," he orders in a low voice.

I back up until I've scooted back inside. I move my backpack in front of me, frightened by his sudden intensity and wanting a barrier between us. I know it's a stupid response. He could rip the bag from me in a moment. He crouches down in front of the opening, right in my face.

"Don't call me that," he whispers. "Ever. Just because you know it, does not make it okay to be spoken out loud. You understand?"

"Sorry," I whisper. "I mean, yes."

"My name here is Darius," he continues in that frighteningly calm, dark tone. "I don't particularly like Darius very much, and you're going to like him even less, but when there are other people around that's who I have to be. You have to use that name until I tell you a new one. Got it?"

"Okay."

"This disk might be a big source of your problem," he says, holding it back up and confusing me even more. "So, I need you to tell me what it does."

My eyebrows scrunch together as I struggle to find my voice again. "It …" What does he think it is? "It's for Stella."

"What?"

"It lets me talk to Stella. I … I can show you."

"Okay …" he draws out in a skeptical tone. He hands me the disk and I place it behind my ear.

I close my eyes, trying to calm myself so I don't make her even more upset than she already is. She doesn't like Hawk. Ironically, she equates him to a large bird of prey.

"I know, Baby, I don't like him either," I mutter, trying to soothe her. "Come on back." I impress on her the desire to be together. I can feel her flit about outside for a few more moments, not wanting to get near him again. "You're in her way," I say, without opening my eyes. "She won't come in because she's afraid of you."

He shifts and in moments Stella wings her way in to cling to the front of my jacket. She wraps her little wings tightly around herself, but keeps both eyes on him.

"Whoa," Hawk, or Darius, says. "Okay, now you've got to tell me where you got her." I open my eyes back up and Hawk is smiling.

"I found her in a tech market a couple of years ago," I explain with a sigh. "She was real sick. The guy that had her didn't know how to take care of a bat, but she came with all her original records. She was a military experiment. I think they were trying to take advantage of echolocation, but the experiment failed. I nursed her back to health, and I've had her ever since. The disk is a mind-link—kind of like antique GRIDtech, but two-way only."

"Did it say why the experiment failed?"

"No, but I figured it out pretty fast." I shrug. "It's really disorienting to be in the mind of a bat, until you get used to it. And … I can't really make her do what I want. I have to convince her. It's … kind of like figuring out how to make her want what you want—instead of controlling her. She ignores me anytime she wants to. It took a long time before I even got her to like me."

"You mentioned echolocation. Is that something you can use?

Do you have access to her other senses?"

"Yeah, but that can be confusing too. I can't just pick and choose. Getting used to the echolocation was the hardest part, and I keep my eyes closed a lot when using it."

"That's hacking awesome. She seems pretty attached." He reaches to touch her but pulls back when she squeaks. "I expected her to abandon you before you even made the hyperloop station."

"She's loyal, once you win her over." I run a careful finger down her petal-soft fur. "What did you think the disk was, anyway?"

"Definitely not that." He rubs his eyes for a moment. "We'd better get moving though. Just … remember what I said about my name."

"Sure." Fine. Don't tell me anything. "Darius." After I'm back out of the box, I stuff my thermal blanket in my backpack, stand up, and activate the autodrive.

Hawk looks at the bag with a grimace. Then he takes my hand and leads me further back into the alley, away from the other shirkers.

"What?"

He lowers his voice. "I'm going to need you to cooperate with me if we're going to get out of this mess alive, Gina."

I threw that in the trash! But the awful metal slaver's collar is in his hands again. My heart starts to beat wildly.

"It's never going to work if you don't trust me."

"I am not putting that thing back on," I whisper too low, I hope, for anyone to hear. Better to die!

"Can you fake looking terrified and beaten if someone comes up on us?" His eyes seem sincere. "So far, your skills at lying have not impressed me."

That's right. I glance over him again. He's playing some kind of role. "So who is Darius Volkov?"

Hawk pulls his hood up to shadow his face and closes his eyes for a moment. His expression morphs into a mixture of anger and irritation. When he opens them again, there is a menace in his eyes that wasn't there before. A shiver of real fear runs up my spine at the transition. It's like watching someone change their skin.

"I'm a tech dealer who just bought Meredith Glass for no small amount of coin," he says in that deeper, darker tone he used back at the auction. "I'm fairly well known in this part of the world, by all the people you'd never want to know."

I wonder if that hurts his throat. "Have you … bought women before?"

"Lots, but none of them live very long." The pity in his eyes says it's not true. "I'm a severe alcoholic with a nasty temper."

"Lovely." My stomach lurches.

"So you can wear the collar and trust me," he says with a stone-cold expression, "or you have to play your part perfectly."

"Do you think we're really likely to get caught this far from home?"

"Our odds of getting out of this alive are slim." He steps closer and I resist the urge to back away from him. He grasps my face gently in his hand and turns to whisper in my ear. "You're the target of an assassin. We'll both need to watch for her. She's five foot six with olive skin, but her hair and eye color aren't dependable. If she gets close enough to touch you, you're dead. She uses venom."

I feel frozen. An Assassin? For me? When he pulls back to look into my eyes with that strangely dark gaze he wears, I know I must look as frightened as I feel. I glance at the collar in his hand again. "What if someone else uses it to hurt me?"

"I've disabled it," he says. "As long as you can be a good actress, no one will know the difference."

I almost believe him, but I just can't.

Then, Hawk surprises me by pushing us into a deeply recessed doorway where we can't be seen. He brings the collar up suddenly and snaps it around his own neck. It's been adjusted to fit. He hands me the small black button. "Press it."

I can't. The memory of the pain is raw.

Hawk grabs my hand, presses my thumb down on the button, and I suck in a gasp. Nothing happens. "See? It won't hurt you." He drops his scary face just long enough to look me in the eyes.

I see pity in them and it makes me feel vulnerable, so I glare back. "How do I take it off?"

"Just bring the button up against the sensor on the back."

I bring my hand up behind his neck and the collar pops open with a snap. It hangs loosely from his neck. He begins to reach for it, but I grab it first. "I'll do it." I snap it closed on myself.

"Okay." He nods, morphing back into Darius's skin—eyes cold, mouth set with an almost cruel sneer. "Let's go."

6

GINA

We've been walking for eight straight hours and dusk is beginning to fall around us. Half-way through the day we chewed a couple of RCs, but didn't stop. The sun is mostly blocked by buildings now, but the sky is putting on its daily color show. Home in District T, the buildings are not nearly this tall. Every building here is at least forty stories.

Here on North Continent—what the locals call Grand Continent—Hawk says we're in Region 221, Sector 25, District Z and we need to get to Region 224 where there is a safer place to stay. We've been dodging and weaving through alleyways and densely crowded streets, careful to use other people as cover from the cams when possible—or avoid them entirely. Hawk has been fascinated by watching me use Stella to scout ahead, but I'm struggling to keep up. My entire body screams in protest with each movement, and I don't want to draw his attention to my distress if he hasn't already noticed.

Right foot. Ugh. Left foot. Ugh …

Focusing on the effort of the steps helps me mentally distance myself from the pain. Something is wrong in the middle of my back, and it's serious enough that it literally hurts to draw breath. When I was being transported in the shipping boxes yesterday, I'd sneezed. It seemed fine at first, but now I'm worried that I may have thrown a disk in my spine. I'm waging a mental war, trying to figure out how to breathe shallow enough to decrease the pain, but not so shallow that I hyperventilate.

I wish I could smooth out my movements and increase my pace, but it's futile. Only the fear of the assassin behind me enables me to keep moving. I'm distracted enough: I hadn't noticed that for a while he's been moving us farther into the heart of the district, instead of skirting around it. "Where're we going?"

"We're not going to get as far as we need to tonight," he says without turning around. "Not with this pace. There's a place in the middle of this district that'll work."

"Are you crazy?" I stumble in my exhaustion and catch myself on a window ledge along the cramped alleyway. God, my back! I doggedly keep walking. "Do you have any idea how many cams we'll have to dodge to get that far?"

Hawk stops, and I nearly bump into him before realizing it. He turns toward me slowly and narrows his eyes as he looks me over like a bug he's considering squishing. With the dazzle makeup he's wearing, it looks incredibly spooky. There is a huge black triangle bisecting his face at an odd angle that covers one eye, black lipstick on only his lower lip, and colorful squares peeking out around his mouth, left cheek, and chin. I didn't get to see mine, but it can't be much better.

"The only thing those cams will see is me," he says. "As far as I know, they're not looking for me yet. In case they are, I'm keeping my face out of view so no one can analyze it later."

Only you? "Wait a minute. Are you saying you've got tech to hide me from the cams?" Don't gasp. It hurts. "How? I've never heard of tech like that. Have you been using it this whole time?"

Hawk stares at me for another long moment, then simply turns back around and continues moving into the heart of the district. I follow him, focusing on my feet and using all the strength I have to keep moving forward.

What kind of tech could possibly interfere with the cams that way? Rob obviously could because he disables the cams entirely. Hawk implied that they would still be able to see him, though, which means the cams would be working. Ghosting CIDs is relatively easy because you're just interfering with the broadcast frequency. I've never heard of something that could ghost or hide an image before. With the 3D surveillance image, it would literally have to be adapting the signal for multiple cams at once. It must be based on an algorithm ...

I continue mulling the question over for the next half an hour. Even with Hawk's claim, I take every measure I normally would to prevent being seen. We eventually arrive at a small brothel on the east side of the sector's inner circle. What the heck?

A voluptuous, espresso-skinned woman with bright red hair and skimpy red lingerie greets us after we've stepped inside. "What's your pleasure today?" she asks with a hand cocked on her hip and a flirtatious smile.

"Emerald suite," Hawk says in a gruff voice, selecting options I can't see from the menu in the countertop glass.

"Well, lucky for you we have an opening," she says with a sultry smile. "Will that weary kitten back there be joining you?"

"Yes," he says with a slightly scary grin, "but leave her off the books."

"Sure thing, honey," she says with a wave of her hand. "We don't have any problems with outside entertainment."

I swallow down my retort that I am not entertainment, as Hawk says, "Good."

"Yeah, now that I think about it, I'm thinking I remember that about you. We'll keep everything off the books. How's that?" she says.

Hawk simply nods.

"Now kitten," she says, apparently addressing me, "the customer's file says he doesn't have any allergies to worry about, but I need to know about you. Take a look at this list and tell me if there's anything on here that's a problem."

She holds up a flex with a list of various oils, butters, and even medicines. It takes me a minute to really focus through my exhaustion. Then, I select the six or seven items I know I have problems with.

"Wowee," she says with a whistle. "I've never seen that many allergies in one person before. But don't you worry, Sweetheart, we'll make sure everything is just right. No sense messing with your groove, girl."

My what? I'm too exhausted to care.

The woman leads us up a flight of stairs, and down a long hallway of doors. The interior decor is dark and uninviting. The harsh blacks and grays of the walls are intimidating when contrasted against the oranges and reds of the carpets and small metal furniture.

Stupidly, I'm having more and more difficulty as my brain begins to register that I might be able to stop soon. A panicky feeling begins to wash over me, blending dangerously with the exhaustion and my continued shallow breathing.

Don't freak out! Just breathe!

At the end of the hallway, she enters a small bedroom and I'm looking for a chair before I realize we're still moving. I swallow down a groan of disappointment. She walks into the closet and presses against the back wall of the empty space. A panel slides open to reveal an opening set of elevator doors.

The elevator takes us down at least two floors. I feel my heart rate accelerating. I don't like being underground—especially when I don't know my way out. I stare at the corrugated metal walls of the elevator and feel trapped. My heart is fluttering. No wait, that's Stella panicking in my jacket. I reach up behind my ear, but the disk is not there. Oh right. I took it off to spare her the pain, but … it must just be me.

God, even if I wasn't trapped, I'm going to be too exhausted to run if I need to! Oh, please help me out of this! Does the GRID power this elevator? Or is it isolated? What if—

To my surprise, Hawk's hand slips onto the small of my back. His eyes aren't on me when I glance over, but he begins rubbing small circles there with his fingertips. He's low enough that the touch is soothing instead of painful. I must look terrified.

The elevator doors open to another long corridor. Unlike the upper floors, every surface is shockingly white, giving the impression of sterility. The doors in this hallway are much farther apart, and when we reach the fifth door on the left, she nods to Hawk and the door unlocks. I shuffle in last and my jaw falls slightly slack as I try to take in the room.

He'd called it the Emerald Suite, and the reason for the name is now obvious. Emerald green is the core color in everything from the tiles on the walls, to the sheets on the bed and the lighting. Despite the soothing nature of the color, my unease is growing steadily.

The lighting is dim throughout the suite, which is divided in half. The carpeted half is mostly taken up by an enormous bed, with a couple of oddly designed chairs placed along the sides. The sheets are a silky material and the headboard is a large and elaborate display of colored metal, twisted and shaped to look like strands of seaweed.

The other half of the room is tiled, and dominated by an extremely large hot water bath. It looks like a medicinal whirlpool, straight out of a hospital spa. That half also has a small table and two chairs, a larger padded massage table, huge mirrors lining every wall, and another tiny seating area enclosed in glass.

I look back at the big bed as the woman leaves without another word, desperately wanting to lie down and sleep for the next 24 hours, but I don't want to seem like I'm offering myself up to the man who literally bought me at auction. Everything in this suite is designed for a singular purpose, and I try to push that thought from my mind as quickly as possible.

Torn about what to do, I plop down on my behind on the plush green carpet. Pain shoots straight through my spine and into my head as the drop jars that spot in my mid-back. Stella lets go of her grip on my jacket with a squeak and wings her way over to the elaborate headboard. I must have scared her. Now that I've stopped moving, I feel all of the momentum sap out of my tissues and my eyes close.

"What the hack are you doing?" Hawk asks.

"You said we get to rest here." I state the obvious, jerky movements eventually bringing me down to curl onto my side on the carpet. "I'm going to sleep."

"I'm not going to let you sleep on the hacking floor."

"Shut up," I groan, too tired to come up with a reasonable argument.

7

HAWK

Gina doesn't even lift her head or open her eyes to argue with me and the uneasiness churning in the pit of my stomach grows. I've had a couple of people fall into this kind of exhaustion when running before, but both of them were sick or beaten. Gina seemed so normal when I first met her. I didn't think she could get run down so fast, but something is seriously wrong with her.

I start prepping the room. It's been two years since I've been here, but everything is laid out like before. I flip on my small jamming device to disable the room's cams and bugs, and stick it to the wall near the transition between rooms. These assholes just leave them on all the time, to get dirt on anyone who isn't smart enough to take protective steps.

I turn on the tiny steam room, flip on the warmer in the massage table, and check the water in the whirlpool. I'm not sure which would be best to try on her first. Shield operatives are trained in field medicine, but nothing more complicated. I've had to make due and learn the hard way. "Are you just tired, or are you in pain?"

"That's a really dumb question," she mumbles.

Definitely pain, but from what? It can't just be the ankle.

I wander over to the wardrobe and pull one of the black bikinis out of a drawer. Our cover would be more authentic if she'd go without it. Considering how prickly she's been so far, though, I doubt I could get her to agree without an argument. Crouching down, I grab her beneath the arms to sit her back upright.

"Whhhaaaaat?" she whines without even opening her eyes. I'm surprised to hear a note bordering on a sob in her voice.

"I told you." I try to use my gentlest tone. "I'm not going to let you sleep on the floor."

"You're so … stupid." she mumbles with a slur. For the law's sake, she sounds almost drunk.

I begin unzipping the front of her coat. Suddenly, her eyes fly open wide and both she and Stella screech as Gina gets a new surge of strength and tries to wrestle out of my grip. I grab both of her wrists and completely still her movement. She has almost no strength left, so it barely takes any effort to restrain her.

"Do. Not," I emphasize each word. "Fight. Me. You don't have the strength. Don't wear yourself out unless it really counts."

"I won't have sex with you!" Her racing pulse is beating visibly in her neck and her poor little bat is fluttering around all over by the bed. Gina's eyes are nearly as frightened as when I drugged her back in the Dregs.

I hate that look. "I would never force you."

I stay completely still for a long time, trying to give her the chance to believe me. I don't get the kind of illness or cowardice it takes for one person to force love on someone else. I certainly wouldn't mind loving her, but she's in no danger of force from me.

I wonder if she's experienced force before, even recently. They could have hurt her before the auction, but Kisame frowns on that kind of thing. He doesn't like the product being damaged before the sale. Even if they didn't, she's probably been forced in the Dregs. I've smuggled a lot of men and women from the sex trade over the years, and many were snatched from shirker camps.

It's always been difficult for me, at first, to figure out which actions will frighten a victim more and which ones will actually help. Every person is different because their experience is different. "Would you like to take it off yourself? It's only going to get warmer in here."

She glances between the room and my face several times before her mouth drops into an incredible pout. "Yes …" she says in a resigned tone, without a single muscle in her body relaxing. "I'll do it."

I release only one of her wrists and lift up the black bikini that I dropped on the floor. Her eyes widen again as she stares at it. "You need to put this on. They can have our clothes clean by morning, and we both need it."

"Is there anything else I can wear?"

"Well, you could always go without. It wouldn't bother me any," I say with a forced grin.

I'm thankful to see the fear in her eyes replaced instantly by anger and she snatches the bikini from my hand, trying to wrestle her other wrist free. As I let her go, she says, "How the hell am I even supposed to know if this will fit me?"

"Babe, that suit would fit you whether you were a starving woman or the curvy one that let us in here," I say with a laugh, heading back into the whirlpool room to let her change herself.

8

GINA

You are such a jerk! I want to throw something at him. Even if I could find something, I wouldn't have the strength and it would hurt my back. I flop back down on the floor again for a moment, wishing I could just close my eyes and sleep. I know better by now. Hawk is relentless. If I ignore him, he's only going to come back in here and make good on his threat.

I glance at the bikini again. It doesn't look very modest, but I desperately want clean clothes. The entire auction experience has made me feel filthy in a way I doubt will wash away easily.

Oh, wait … There's a whirlpool in here full of hot water!

I drag myself over to a section of the floor where the big bed will block his view. My muscles and spine scream in protest and I feel nearly dizzy as I try to struggle my way out of my traveling clothes. Eventually, I succeed and I'm stuck with removing the crazy number of braces I put on during my earlier bathroom break. I slide them hastily under the bed. Thank God it takes much less effort to get back into the bikini thing.

"Gina?" His voice is close.

"What?"

"Are you finished yet?"

"Yes."

His huge form looms over the corner of the bed and looks down at me. His eyes widen and he starts to take a step back. Then I suck in a breath as his face morphs into a furious scowl and he grinds his teeth. The muscles of his shoulders and arms visibly tense, as his hands ball into fists.

"What?" I hate the sudden quaver in my voice, backing against the wall with a wince. "I did what you said!"

Hawk's demeanor changes again just as quickly. He takes a deep breath, rolls his head back and forth on his shoulders, and works his fists back open. His eyes are closed. When he speaks again his voice is calm, but it's a calm I don't trust at all. "I'm getting really sick of you lying to me Gina."

"I'm not lying!" A surge of adrenaline hits me. I'm not sure if it's from fear or the shocking pain of yelling with a full breath. "I'm wearing the stupid bikini."

"I asked you whether they hurt you before we left," he says in that deceptive calm, without moving a muscle. "You said they hadn't."

Oh.

Looking down at myself, I'm about as bruised up as I would expect to be. I couldn't even begin to figure out where most of the bruises are from because I bruise so easily. There's no doubt in my mind that a lot of them are actually from fleeing the hospital and trying to drag Hawk's body back home. I may have gotten some from the transport, but I mostly remember being cramped. I also picked up some from the creeps at the auction.

I realize immediately what he must assume—that I've been raped. Large purple and black bruises mar the surface of my legs from top to bottom. One large bruise, that I expect even before seeing it, wraps around my upper arm and resembles a hand print. I'm pretty sure I got it when Hawk ripped me out of the line of gunfire when the squids were attacking, and it's been grabbed over and over since then. A bruise is better than being shot.

I have small bruises on my face and ear from Kisame and the man back stage. There's a massive streak of red and purple bruising across my abdomen that looks frightening in comparison to how little I've felt it. I remember the searing pain from trying to lift Hawk up out of the pipe, but Rob couldn't have done it on his own. There are a few more mild bruises sprinkled across my hips and forearms. Overall, I quite seriously look like I've been beaten, but it's nothing more than my disease trying to give me away. I can't let that happen. I don't know what to say, so I don't meet his eyes again.

Fortunately, Hawk doesn't wait for an explanation. He crouches down and I jump in surprise when the collar I'm wearing clicks open. He tosses it across the room and then lifts me into his arms very slowly. I nearly bite my tongue off holding back a scream from the stabbing pain that shoots through my back at being lifted. He carries me straight into the tiled room and sets me down on the edge of the big whirlpool tub.

The hot water comes up to my knees and my bruises react strangely to it. There's an instant sharp ache and tingling, that fades away very quickly into an overall sensation of warmth. The shock makes me cling to his neck a little tighter as he stands beside the tub, but doing so pulls against the sharp pain in my back and I let go. I let out my breath slowly, as dizziness washes through me.

His face is turned away and the fake calm expression has taken over it again as he backs away slowly. "You need to try to get as far into the water as you can," he says. "The heat should help your body flush toxins and the medicine in the water will help you heal faster. If I had known your bruising was so extensive … I would've balanced it differently. Stay in the seats, though, so you don't drown if you fall asleep." He retreats into the carpeted room and ducks out of sight.

I move over to the area of the whirlpool that will allow me to see him coming and slowly sink myself down into the seat. As the heat creeps up my skin, the short bursts of ache and tingling continue to spread when they hit my various wounds. There must be something effervescent in the water because my lungs suddenly want to take deeper breaths, but I resist the urge.

Within a few moments, the heat is glorious. I feel the persistent ache and fatigue in my muscles slowly slipping away to be replaced with limp exhaustion. I remember trying to cram my entire body into the tiny bathtub in my hub, and hold back a giggle of joy as I realize I could lay flat in this water with my arms out and still not touch the sides. These kinds of baths are common in the hospital spas—or, so I hear. I don't know how I'm ever going to bring myself to leave it.

The next thing I know, I'm waking up to the sensation of being lifted again. I jump, letting out a brief unguarded shriek of pain and fling my arms up to clutch around someone warm and soft as the water cascades down off of my body.

"Shhhhhhh." It's Hawks voice against my ear. "I tried to wake you, but you were too far under. It's not healthy to stay in the water for more than fifteen minutes at a time when you're so weak."

My traitorous eyelids droop as my body tries to pull me back under the exhaustion. There's something I should be asking, but I can't get my brain or my tongue to cooperate. I'm startled yet again when my back rests against something warm.

"Roll onto your stomach," Hawk says after removing his arms from under me. "There's an opening there to rest your face over."

It takes me a second to realize that I'm lying on the padded table I'd seen earlier. "Why?"

"This is a massage table, Babe. Stop looking at me like I'm going to attack you," he says. "You know what …"

He walks back into the carpeted side of the room and I notice that he's now only wearing a small scrap of clothing that could barely be called a bathing suit. I haven't gotten an eyeful of him since I was threading a needle through his skin, and even then it was only his upper body. His muscle tone is amazing—even better than Troy's.

Oh, I am in major trouble.

I lie back against the table, to avoid falling off. Glancing around the room for a moment, I struggle to think clearly. He may not attack me, but he's more than a little interested in seducing me. Despite how much I distrust him, Hawk is dangerously charming when he's being nice. I'm exhausted and ill-equipped to deal with this kind of a setup.

Don't you dare let him seduce you, stupid! It is literally his job! Just think of him like Troy. Maybe I should use the fact that I'm injured …

As I'm struggling to sit up, he walks briskly back to me. "Here." He presses a small throwing knife into the palm of my hand.

Huh? I stare at it dumbly for a moment. Oh … he's trying to

make me feel safe.

"Now, roll back on your stomach," he says. "I need to see how much damage there is."

I don't even know the answer to that question myself. I start to lie down and then a thought has me objecting again. "You can still just take this from me if I try to use it."

"Of course I can," he says, rolling his eyes, "but I'm not going to give you a bomb now am I? Stop being a pain in the ass. I'm tired too."

The statement stings. Of course, he's tired. He's gone as far as I have and even someone conditioned for it would be tired. He's also still injured. My eyes are drawn to the large waterproof bandage seal on his side, covering my terrible stitching over his wound. He should be resting. I will heal slowly no matter what he does, but he doesn't know that. "Then you should rest and stop babying me. Just go get in the—"

"Babying you?" Every muscle jumps in his jaw as his teeth clench. "You're literally painted with surface bleeding. You're in visible pain when you move and you can't stay conscious for anything shy of a fight.

"We have to leave here tomorrow. If we can't patch you up, we're in serious trouble, Gina. Because no matter how strong I am, I cannot carry you the entire way. I can't rest until I deal with this. So, why don't you start helping me?"

I blush, rolling over without further argument. I keep the knife tucked in my palm as I set my hands down on the small armrests below my face. Some of my bruises object to being face down at first, but the sensation fades as soon as I stop moving.

Hawk sighs behind me and whispers, "For the love of science, that prick hit you hard."

My right shoulder is tender beneath his touch. His fingertips continue skimming the skin along my back incredibly gently and it takes me a moment to realize he is tracing my tattoo. The butterfly wings are done in full mirage-metallics that shift to look like different colored metal from different angles. There's extra detail if it's ever viewed in black light because when I got it I decided to go all-out for something that cost so much.

"Why wings?" Hawk asks with his fingers still inspecting it.

I'm not sure what to say when it's so personal and relates to my illness. Finally, I settle on one word. "Freedom."

"They're beautiful."

His big hands are warm as they start massaging my back, careful to avoid the bruise on my right shoulder, and I try desperately not to tense further from nerves. It's impossible because I have to hold my breath with every movement that comes near the sharp pain lower in my spine. I don't have a clue what to do if I have actually damaged a disk.

"Hawking's ghost. You're muscles are a mess." His thumb pops across the surface of a large knot in my left shoulder and I suck in air through my teeth as the shock makes that whole side of my back jump. He uses his palm to press down along the muscles running parallel to my spine and starts to stretch them.

"Stop!" I scream when he gets too close. "Stop, please! Don't touch it!" I am embarrassed to realize that tears begin leaking from my eyes, but Hawk pulls his hands back immediately.

"What? What hurts? Where?"

"My back," I choke, truly fighting hyperventilation now. "I … maybe the disk. I don't know."

"How long has it been hurting?"

"Since this morning."

"What makes it hurt?"

"Just when I breathe." I smile at the admission and the stupidity of it.

"Hacking science, Gina!" Hawk says, as his hands come back.

"No!" I panic, frightened of the pain, and try to push myself up from the table. "Don't touch it! I can't!"

Suddenly, the weight and heat of Hawk's upper body is pressed firmly against my back, pinning me to the table, and his hand closes over my hand with the knife.

"Don't. Move," he barks in my ear. "I swear, Gina if you hurt yourself worse, I am going to be pissed."

"Let me go. Please."

He keeps me pinned silently for a few moments. "You have to let me see if we can do anything about it. If not, we may have to bring you to a clinic."

"I can't go to a clinic!" I stupidly sob. "They won't help me. They'll kill me."

"I know, Babe," he says, with his chest rumbling against my back. "So, I need you to lie still and let me see if I can figure out what's wrong. I can't do that unless you help me. I won't do anything without telling you first. Okay?"

Strangely, the pressure of his chest is working almost like a splint, in keeping my sobs and stuttering breaths from hurting as badly as I know they should. I use the strange stillness to try and calm myself back down, focusing on slowing my breathing and keeping it shallow again. I close my eyes and try to separate myself from the pain that I know is coming.

"Are you going to stay still?"

I nod.

"I'm going to let you keep this." He squeezes my hand with the knife pinned beneath it. "Because I'm trusting you not to use it."

I nod again. Cheap false security—but I don't want to give it up, even if it is false.

His weight lifts off me and his hands are immediately on my back again with a feather-light touch. He skims the muscles along my spine slowly, but lightly, from top to bottom. I suck in air through my teeth as they glide over the spot about mid-way down.

"You say it hurts when you breathe?"

I nod again, not wanting to break my concentrated calm.

He places his hands on my hips. "I'm going to check your ribs. I need you to tell me if they hurt as I check each set, okay?"

"Okay," I whisper.

His hands glide up until they grab bone on each side at the bottom of my ribcage and then he gives them the slightest wiggle.

"That's fine." I'm relieved to feel no pain.

He repeats the process with the next set of ribs up.

"Fine."

And the next.

"Fine."

This time, when he grabs the bones, I grunt in objection. "Not so good." I press my face into the opening in the table, letting out a

hiss of air from between my teeth and trying not to tense up again.
When he wiggles the next set, I scream.

"Thank the Law," he says.

"What? What ... does that mean?"

"It means you've dislocated a rib," he says with a heavy sigh.
"Although, I'd like to know how the hack you managed that."

EDS 1—Gina 0. Dammit. I've never dislocated a rib before, so
I had no idea the symptoms could mimic what I would expect from
a vertebra being displaced. Thankfully, I'd never had to deal with
either one until now.

"Happened to a guy on my team once," Hawk says. "He was
tossing a payload into a drone when it happened. Poor guy was in
pain for six days before we learned we could have fixed it the whole
time."

"Fixed it?" I squeak.

"Yeah," he says. "I need you to trust me on this one. It's going
to hurt, but we have what we need to make it brief."

Trust me, he says ... This is how it starts. Oh, who the hell am
I kidding? It started when I agreed to follow him! "Okay."

Hawk raises the table and helps me sit up and scoot my butt to
the edge of it with only a little sharp pain here and there. He stands
behind me, rolls a towel, and places it against the center of his chest
vertically, and uses his chest to press it against my spine. He crosses
my arms so that my hands rest on their opposing shoulders, and I
wrestle with myself for a moment before agreeing to forfeit the
knife. Then he crosses his own arms in front of us, in possibly the
most awkward hug ever, as he grabs hold of my elbows.

"Now what?" I ask.

"Now you've got to relax."

"Okay." I try to let go of the tension in my back and ignore the
pain at the edge of each breath.

"No, I mean totally. This isn't going to work unless nothing is
fighting me. I don't want to have to try this multiple times, and
neither do you."

He's right. A realignment never works when the muscles
around it are too tense. I have a vague memory of my father doing
something similar to this for my mother before. It was so long ago.

I smile when I remember how much she trusted him to do it. She'd looked nearly asleep before he moved.

I try to emulate what I remember seeing. I drop my head back to rest against Hawk's shoulder. He starts to sway and I relax into his hold completely, so that it isn't my own back holding me upright, but his arms doing so through their grip on my elbows. I feel him draw deep, slow breaths and I mimic him as much as I can, letting the breath back out only when he does. The pressure of his chest and the towel against my back help ease the pain. Breath in, breath out. Breath in, breath out. Breath in, breath …

Snap!

Hawk jerks us both up and back hard. I feel the painful spot in my back pop loudly back into place with an incredibly sharp pain and I shriek. Stella shrieks from the headboard. A startled sob escapes me and he holds me up for a few moments while I struggle not to cry.

Oh, shoot. It's okay, girl. Momma's okay.

"How is that?" Hawk asks with a soft rumble against my cheek.

"Better, I think, but it still hurts."

He picks me up again and this time I don't bother objecting; although, I hiss slightly at the movement. He carries me back over to the whirlpool and this time climbs inside still carrying me. As we settle down deep in the water, he sets me across his lap. I close my eyes and remain leaning against his chest. "No twenty questions?" he asks.

"Hot water," I mumble with a yawn. "Makes sense."

A chuckle rumbles deep in his chest and for the first time since we arrived, he relaxes back in the water too.

9

HAWK

I wake to a strangely pleasant buzzing in my ear. It takes me a second to realize it's a voice—Gina's voice. Her breath is cool against the skin of my neck and a shiver of pleasure runs up my spine. "Yeah, Babe?" Wow, I sound garbled.

I hear the buzzing again, but I can't focus on it for the life of me. The next thing I know, I can feel her hands on the sides of my face and for a bewildering moment, I wonder if she's going to kiss me. By all that is lawful, I want her to kiss me. The last three days have been absolute shit. Oh man, I'm probably grinning like an idiot.

"Hawk. Come on. Wake up."

"What?"

She pulls back with wide eyes and I realize I'm leaning toward her tempting lips.

"You said we're not supposed to be in here for more than fifteen minutes," she says. "It's been twenty. I just woke up."

"Oh." I am dizzy. Sitting upright, I wait for the dizziness to pass and to wake up more. Then I lift Gina into my arms again and carry her over to sit on the massage table. I grab a couple of towels from the nearby cabinet and hand one to her, then start drying off.

"Why aren't your eyes brown anymore?" she asks. "I mean … What are you using?"

"Just fancy contacts," I shrug.

"Can I see?"

I step in front of her. The contacts are currently set for Darius's vivid green, and I blink in the pattern to change them back to Jared's brown.

"Wow." She starts to reach toward my face, but pulls her hand back with a blush. "What's your real color?"

Usually my bright blue eyes are too memorable with my darker coloring, but it makes no difference if she sees them now. I blink the pattern to turn the lenses clear. She sucks in a quiet breath, her own pretty eyes widening slightly.

"So are these just extensions then?" She runs timid fingers against my long hair.

"Yeah." I shrug. "Easy enough to do once you get the hang of it. We need to change up your hair and eye color when we get the chance."

"Okay."

"How's your rib?" Thank the Law I was able to reset it. I'd like to try a couple more things before we have to leave, but we're too tired now. "Do you think you can rest if you're sitting up?"

"You mean sitting like this?" She glances around the massage table with her eyebrows scrunched together.

"No, I mean if I prop you up against something. I'm afraid if you lie down flat that rib's gonna come back out again."

"Oh, I guess I could try."

I can tell that it still hurts her to breathe and I'm pissed that she spent the whole day like that without a word of complaint. I'll have to watch her more closely. Her pain tolerance must be unbelievable.

"Wait," she says. "Let me check your wound."

"It's fine."

"Please." She grabs my wrist and I don't want to pull away with her rib still loose. "You were shot and you've been carrying me around. It needs to be checked."

"I told you, it's—"

"I won't be able to sleep. Please."

Shit. I pull back the bandage seal to show her the wound and her eyes go wide above a huge smile.

"Wow!" She touches the stitching gently with her fingers. "This is almost healed enough to take your stitches out. That's amazing."

"Yeah, I told you it was fine." Pulling the bandage seal back in place and turning away from her confused face, I walk over to the bed and stack all but one of the overstuffed pillows up like a chairback against the fancy headboard.

When I turn back to carry her, she's already on her feet and halfway across the room. Stubborn, independent woman. There's so much awful black and green marring across her beautiful body. It's obvious that every step hurts. I don't like it, but I let her struggle the rest of the way. As she lies back against the pillows, her face relaxes. "Oh yeah," she says with the first genuine smile I've seen on her in a long time. "This is perfect. Can I just stay right here for like, a week?"

I remember wanting to make her smile like that, but this isn't what I'd had in mind. I'm glad she's feeling well enough to have a sense of humor. I'm used to dealing with people that are so terrified or bone-deep soul-weary, they hardly even talk.

"Unfortunately, no," I say. "Trust me. If we had the option, I definitely would. They're going to be on our ass pretty fast though. We're going to have to leave by midday tomorrow."

"Not first thing in the morning?" She yawns. "I'm okay with that."

I walk around to the other side of the bed and crawl in. I can feel the weariness trying to overtake me again, but I roll onto my back and set my personal alarm to wake me in twenty minutes. I curl up with the one remaining pillow, facing her, and throw my arm across her hips.

As I close my eyes I hear the renewed tension in her voice. "What are you doing?"

"You're the one that snuck out while I was asleep. I'm too tired, and you're too hurt, to chase you around the streets again."

"I'm not going to sneak out. I can barely walk."

"Don't blame me for this." Man, she makes me want to smile. "You've proven multiple times now that I can't trust you. Just go to sleep."

She doesn't argue anymore. With my face this close to her skin, I can enjoy her beautiful scent. All the other scents of the oils and medicines from the water are in there too, as the water from her bikini soaks into the sheets, but she's still sexy and sweet, right there beneath the rest of it. I let it lull me to sleep.

When my alarm goes off behind my eyelids, I try not to startle her into jostling her injury. It's a pointless worry. She's sleeping like she did yesterday. I sit up and touch the skin of her face and neck, making sure it's returned to normal temperature. Then I force myself to get up and carry her toward the steam room, my side aching only slightly.

"What are we doing?" she mumbles halfway there, nuzzling her nose against my chest. For someone who is so paranoid and hostile while she's awake, she's downright adorable in her sleep. I've never seen her with her guard down like this. It's the most I've let my own guard down on assignment too, but I haven't had a good chance to catch my breath in a while. I'm giving her too much truthful information, but as soon as she catches me in any lie I'm going to lose all the ground I've gained. I can't afford that.

"You've got a lot of bruising, Babe." I can't resist brushing my lips against her damp hair. "We've got to speed up your healing and try to push as much of those toxins from your system as we can. Have you used a steam room before?"

"A what?" She yawns.

"A steam room. Trust me. It'll help."

10

GINA

When I finally get my eyes open, Hawk is opening the door to the small, enclosed, glass room. It's as if my body weighs five hundred pounds. I'm too exhausted to move.

The room is now a milky white color inside, filled with a thick fog of steam. The heat is incredible as it washes over my skin. Once we're fully engulfed by it, I can barely see Hawk's chest in front of my face. The steam is so thick that my lungs don't want to draw it in, and I cling tighter around his neck. "I can't breathe."

"Yes, you can. It just feels different."

He sits me down in a small plastic chair and as I run my hands along it, I realize it must be built into the wall. He sits next to me, but I can't see him clearly.

His hand moves to place the lightest touch against my abdomen. "Try to breathe into the bottom of your lungs. Think about filling your stomach with air. Not just the part of your lungs up high. I know it feels weird, but the heat will be good for you. Hopefully, we can get you to sweat out some of the shit from being hurt so bad."

I do as he says, trying to consciously pull my diaphragm downward with my mind. It feels vaguely like trying to breathe underwater, but I can tell the hot air is circling into the bottom of my lungs. Soon, little droplets of water begin running down my skin all over my body. I'm not sure if it's sweat, condensation, or some odd combination of both. The bizarre sensations pull me fully back from sleep.

It's odd to be so close to someone you can't see. I should be more frightened, but I'm not. If Hawk wanted to hurt me, he could've done so a hundred times. I believe him now when he says the doctors at the hospital were trying to kill me. Despite the fact that he works for the Community, he seems determined to achieve the opposing outcome.

Sitting in this room with him is strangely comfortable. He's managed to earn a small measure of my trust since he bought me at the auction. Since our lives are on the line, I shouldn't let him operate from faulty assumptions. It could cause complications down the road. The inability to see his face makes me a little braver than normal. "They didn't hurt me like you think." I close my eyes and breathe the steam deeply despite the rib that is still complaining.

"You don't have to talk about it." His voice rolls to me from the steam bank at my side.

"Talking about it isn't a problem. They shoved me in box, in a cell, and on a stage in front of a bunch of crazy people. They made me horribly uncomfortable, but they didn't beat me. Well, they slammed me around a couple of times, but they didn't rape me either. I know that's what you probably think, but you should know it isn't true. I wasn't lying when I told you that."

He's quiet for a long time before answering. "Then why are you so badly hurt?"

I debate what to tell him. If I tell him little bits of the truth, he isn't likely to even know about my disease much less be able to jump to that conclusion. "I bruise easily. I think my arm got bruised at the hospital the first time when you were trying to keep me from getting shot."

"I bruised your arm?" He sounds upset.

"It's not a big deal," I say. "After that, everybody just keeps grabbing it. I'm pretty sure the bruises on my stomach were from bringing you back to the Dregs. It hurt a lot when I was trying to haul you up out of the pipe. It was like trying to lift twenty sacks of potatoes at once. The rest of them are from getting pushed around the day of the auction and from bumping into things. I usually have bruises everywhere. That's not unusual for me."

"Why do you bruise so easy?"

"It's none of your business."

"Is there anything we can do about it?"

"No." I wipe some of the water from my face. "Trust me. If I could fix it, I would've done it by now."

"Great," he grumbles from behind the white cloud. "I'll try to be more careful."

I can't object to that. Maybe now that he knows I bruise easily, he'll be more careful when yanking me around. I'm not sure he can, though. He's been trying to keep me out of harm's way and now he says he's playing the role of a violent man. I'm not going to get my hopes up.

We sit in silence for a while longer. The steam is pumped into the room in waves and the heat is becoming intense. My rib is feeling remarkably better though. The pain has been dulled to something I can almost ignore with each breath, but it's getting difficult to breathe through the steam. "Where is the door?"

"Need a break?"

"Yeah."

His arms are under me again a second later and his face comes into focus very close to mine. His lips are pursed in a frown, his eyebrows are knit together, and his gaze is far away. He carries me back out to the edge of the whirlpool and hands me a rag.

I dip the soft cloth in the hot water and carefully wipe away the perspiration from my skin. Then he brings me over a thin, soft robe and I put it on before slipping out of the wet bikini. "Stay over here and I'll change," I say.

As I stand Hawk rolls his eyes, turns away, and begins sponging the water off of his skin.

I limp into the bathroom and dig through my bag. I change into my clothing ration white t-shirt and the black cotton pants from the auction as quickly as I can. Bringing a couple of towels, I place them on the bed before leaning back against the soggy pillow mountain.

Hawk takes his turn in the bathroom and soon emerges in nothing but a black pair of boxers. I blush and bite my tongue. This room probably doesn't stock sleepwear. To my surprise, he doesn't change into anything else from his bag. He just crawls beneath the sheet on the other side of the bed.

"Don't you pack something to sleep in?"

He laughs. "Why would I?" I want to hit him.

"Never mind." I close my eyes, determined not to think about how awkward this is.

"Gina ..." His tone is serious again and I open my eyes to look down at him. "I need you to tell me how you're avoiding the cams."

"What? What are you talking about?"

He searches my eyes for a moment and then his own eyes register confusion. He sits up and shoves his pillow behind the small of his back before rubbing a hand over his face. "The GRIDcams. We haven't been able to see you on them since you finished server duty. I need you to tell me how you're doing that."

"You can't ... see me?" Oh, dear God. That can't be true. "No way."

"Gina, this is serious." He jumps back out of bed with a flick of the sheet, steps over to his bag, and pulls out a pair of glasses. "Put these on."

"Okay ..." Slipping them on my face, he closes his eyes and a vid begins to play. He's adjusting it with mental controls.

"Look at the vid," he says.

A 3D image of me sitting asleep in the server duty chair pops up in front of me. It's weird to be looking at myself through cams. The doctor wakes me up, and I turn a terrified gaze at the cam. Then ...

Holy crap! I completely disappear. Oh God, oh God. What happened? Is this because my session went wrong?

I take the glasses off and try to understand what I saw. "How do I know you didn't edit this? Is this a trick?"

"Are you seriously telling me you don't have any tech on you that tricks the cams?" He sits back down on his side of the bed and leans uncomfortably close. His eyebrows are scrunched around his beautiful blue eyes as they search mine.

"I've never even heard of tech that can do that!" Ouch! I brace my complaining rib with my hand.

He rolls and leans back against the pillow with a sigh, throwing an arm over his face. The movement of his smooth tan skin further defines the muscles of his broad chest, bulky arms and abdomen.

"Anyway, where did you get the vid?"

"It was given to me when I was assigned to you."

"Then how do you know it isn't doctored? They could have given you that just to invent a reason to chase me."

"I considered that. But it doesn't explain why a single cam since then hasn't seen you. Not in Central Continent and not here. I've been checking."

I've seen him pull out the glasses and use them as sunglasses a few times while we were walking. I'd wondered if he was checking the cams, but after what he'd said earlier, I'd assumed he was checking his own tech.

"Well, I can't explain it either." I chew on my lower lip. Every little thing that is different about me adds up to more trouble and worsens my odds of survival. "Do you believe me?"

"If I do and you're lying," he says, "it could get us both killed."

"Well, I'm not lying." I decide to say it. "I doubt I'm going to make it out of this anyway."

"Don't talk like that. We've gotten this far. I just have to figure out what the hack is going on. Then figure out who can help."

"Why are you helping me?"

"It's my job." He shrugs before sliding down to lie against his pillow.

"No, it's not. You're a shield. Your job is to follow orders and it sounds like those orders are to kill me. I don't understand why you're doing all of this. You should have gone home."

"Yeah and if I had you would be someone's personal pet right now. I knew you wouldn't make it without my help. You still don't get how dark these streets really are, Babe, but I do. This is my home." His eyes stay closed. "I'm not some grunt who acts like a bot just because I'm a soldier. My job is to keep the Community members I'm in charge of safe, and right now, that's you."

"But ..."

"Just go to sleep, Gina." He yawns. "Don't make me stay

awake all night like yesterday. Please?"

"Sorry." I close my eyes and try to sleep despite the nervous buzz in my system from the new information. How is it even possible to be invisible to cams? Do I have tech on me that I don't know about? Did they put it inside me at the hospital? If so, how would I get it out?

God, what are you doing?

After a few moments of silence, he mumbles a soft, "It's okay."

11

GINA

Someone is shaking me and my natural instinct is to lash out. I feel just as exhausted as I did when I went to sleep. That's not unusual, but the severe level of ache in my legs definitely is. I've been doing way too much. If I were home, I would stay in bed for a couple of days and call in sick to Tommy. With the silky sheets beneath me, I am all too aware that Hawk, Jared, Darius, whoever he is, is the person trying to wake me and it means more activity and more pain.

"Gina," I hear his voice from right beside my head. "Come on. You've got to wake up."

I groan in response, starting to roll away from him before my rib sends a shooting pain around my side at the movement, and I gasp.

"Careful," he says. "That's still gonna be tender for a couple of days."

No crap. The worst part of any full dislocation is the aftermath. Sometimes a joint doesn't even hurt when it's still dislocated. My knees are like that. Hurts like hell when they go back in, but I may not even notice the kneecap is in the wrong place until I can't figure out why my leg won't bend.

"I've let you sleep as long as I can," he says. "We've got stops we've got to make, Babe. Come on. Our clothes are back, so you need to get dressed unless you plan to hike in that."

I sit up and struggle to open my eyes. I don't know what I look like, but Hawk's face has the guiltiest expression I've seen on him yet. I start looking around for my bag. "Where's my body armor?"

"Here," Hawk hands the slaver's collar to me. "You can put it on after we're out of here, and you're going to have to take it off when we're almost there. Darius wouldn't have you in body armor."

I shoot him a glare. "If I'm a target, I need my armor."

"Gina, we've been through this."

"No. I agreed to wear the stupid collar. You give me one good reason I should go skipping around in anything less than body armor."

"We're going to stop in at a major market to look for tech that can see what's in your head. If we can make it there tonight." Hawk folds his arms across his broad chest but his face is a grimace with eyebrows raised in a plea. "We're going to have to go in with a complete cover. I don't want to put you in excess risk on the street, but we'll have to stop in somewhere to change you into something more realistic when we're close."

Realistic? "Fine." I hate the idea but the need to know what's in my head overrides everything else. I point to the other half of the room. "Get out, so I can change."

"Good morning to you too." Hawk chuckles with a huge grin as he walks into the whirlpool half of the room.

12

HAWK

Now ... what's the best way in? I glance down at the store from our perch on the roof of the twenty-story high-rise across the street. There's a lot of cams in this area because it's a shopping district. I wish I knew whether I was on the hunt list yet or not. I test the breeze as it turns through the low-speed, multi-directional turbines around us, but there's no chimera scent on it—most importantly, no scent of Cobra.

I pull out the pair of binoculars I keep in my right thigh pocket as a costume prop. I don't need them. My eyesight is 20/6, so the binoculars actually give me a headache. I play my normal game—bringing them to my face and closing my eyes just before they settle in front.

The strip of small shops on the ground floor of Sector 1 District B's housing units don't get a lot of foot traffic. Each has a narrow door and—being this close to the Golden Dragon Brothel—keeps its interior as blocked from view as the local shields will tolerate. This is a better market for the local low-level dealers than Serge's place.

"That's our stop."

"Which one?" She snatches the binoculars from my hand, peers through them, and jerks her head back. Then she makes huge adjustments to the view as Stella wings her way toward the shops.

"The clothing boutique." I should have handed them to her first. The sign in the corner of the boutique's door lists its hours. "It looks like we'll have to wait about thirty minutes."

"Oh." She scrutinizes my face. "How can you see that from here?"

Hack. I grab the binoculars from her and pretend to look through them again as Stella flutters around the entrance. "I saw it through these." When I glance back at her face, her eyes are round and I know I've given myself away. I'm not about to confirm it though. "Any ideas for getting in without looking suspicious?"

She blinks back at me for a moment and I'm afraid she's going to ask. Instead, she shakes her head a bit and then looks back down at the storefront. "That's a shop for brothel workers."

"Exactly." Oh, that's not a happy face. I take a moment to locate the cams and angles. "We need to keep my face out of view from the cams. Someone, somewhere has figured out that Darius is the one who bought you by now, and there will be real people reviewing all footage from the surrounding regions."

After applying our makeup this morning, I showed Gina that she still can't be seen on any of the surveillance GRIDcams. It was comical to watch her bob around and try to throw the feed off enough to make herself visible. She's been silent and thoughtful ever since.

"The Community knows you have me then, right?" she finally asks.

I shake my head. "Darius is off the books. They won't know it's me until they see me."

"What about when we're at the market? Aren't there cams all over there?"

"Serge keeps everything on a separate internal server. He'd never let his real business information get within reach of the GRID. It'll keep the shields off our back for now."

"How does he manage that? Is he using Old World tech?"

"No." The thought makes me want to laugh. Serge accepts nothing but the best. "He has his own server bank below ground. His staff maintain it."

"Oh." She chews on her bottom lip and my eyes are drawn to her mouth. "Darius is a drunk, right?"

"Yeah, but a high-functioning one."

To my surprise, Gina pulls a small flask out of her bag. As soon as she spins the cap loose, the acrid scent of moonshine hits my senses. I'd almost forgotten how saturated she was with alcohol the first night I met her. "You have your own, right?" She takes a swig from the bottle.

"You shouldn't drink that, Gina." I reach for the flask. "I didn't say you were an alcoholic. That shit is poison."

"You didn't say I was, but we're going to say that you like to share because it'll take the edge off my pain." Rolling her eyes, she holds the flask out away from me. "You can have a swig of mine if you promise to get me more later."

"Not a chance. There's a reason that shit is illegal, Babe. I'm not going to help you poison yourself." I pull out my own flask and swish the whiskey around in my mouth before swallowing it. It took ages to find a variety I could stand for playing this role, so at least the taste isn't half bad—not like the shit she's carrying around. I drip the liquid on my clothes for added effect. "What's your plan?"

"Just act a little tipsy as we go in." She shrugs and takes another sip from the bottle with a horrible grimace. She may as well be drinking paint thinner!

I clench my fist to keep myself from tossing it off the edge of the roof.

"I'll act disgusted but afraid," she says. "I'll hang back from you a little as we walk, but like I'm staying close enough for the collar. You slouch as much as you can. Nurse the hangover with your hand against your forehead. That way, your face stays mostly out of view. With the hood and glasses, they shouldn't get a recognition match if we're careful, but your size is hard to miss."

"That'll work." It's moments like these that make me wonder again if she's playing me. It's scary how good she is at thinking this shit up. "Let's go."

"Wait." Gina grabs my arm before I can stand. "Who's Serge?"

"The market manager. Like your Joe, back at Southside. I've known him for a long time now. He was at the auction and expects me to drop in. His market is the biggest in the region, so it's our best bet to find what we need."

"Do you trust him?"

"Not a chance, and neither should you. He's not a good man, but not the worst either. I appreciate that he treats his staff well, but they're still slaves. He frowns on abuse but won't jeopardize his relationship with a client when it comes down to it. Just stick with me."

"How will I know who he is?"

"He'll make a big production of my arrival. You'll know him when you see him, but you shouldn't act like you do. When we're in there, you've got to remember that I'm a huge, abusive, angry drunk who has the button for that collar you wear and has beaten the shit out of you."

"Right." She rolls her pretty eyes. I need to get her contacts too.

13

GINA

I glare down at the clothes Hawk is passing into the dressing room, feeling Stella fidget in irritation too from her perch outside. Is he nuts? I want to scream at him, but I know I have to play this stupid role. It's awful. This crap is going to look terrible! Not to mention it's embarrassing.

I'd expected the slaver's collar to draw attention when we approached the building, but the shopkeeper bot didn't react to it at all. It speaks volumes that there are no internal cams in here either. Apparently, they serve people like Darius all the time.

The store isn't much more than a small room with a couple of dressing rooms—like the one I'm currently crammed in. They're nothing but painted metal walls with a built-in bench and clothing hooks.

Hawk has handed me a bold, jade green top. I can't quite tell if it's a bra or a bikini top. The first two he picked up weren't the right size and I'd just tossed them back over the door. These aren't the one-size-fits-all variety. I've always hated that womens' wear is so complicated. I struggle a bit with this one, but in the range of embarrassing to appalling, it's probably something I can live with.

There's a black mini-skirt with a decorative chain-link belt. The underwear look horrifically uncomfortable, but oddly enough, I can barely tell I'm wearing them. He's also handed me high heels that wrap around my legs, all the way up my calves. If I have to run in these things, I'm going to die because I can't slip them off if I need to.

Once I've got it all put together, I open the door to the dressing room and try really hard not to glare at him. I don't completely succeed.

"You look stunning Ma'am," the bot says from his station behind the counter. "An excellent selection."

As Hawk looks up, his eyes open a bit wider and he looks me over from head to toe twice. I expect him to say something, but instead, he pushes his way into the dressing room with me, shutting the door behind us.

He grabs me by the hips and lifts and I am about to sock him in the jaw when I realize he is setting me down with my feet on the small bench. His first two fingers are against my lips in a flash.

"Hush," he whispers in my ear. "Just let me think for a minute."

I push him back, widening my eyes and looking pointedly down at my clothes. What did you think I was going to look like? You picked out these clothes, bud. Finally, I decide on something safer to say, letting my face voice my displeasure. "You don't like it?"

"That's not the point. It's perfect. But it's also a problem."

"Perfect?" You've got to be kidding me.

"It fits, and I see what I want to see." He points to the black and purple bruising across my abdomen.

I understand what he's trying to say. It fits the roles we're playing and makes him look even more like a monster. I now hate that thought. I'm honestly having a hard time seeing Hawk pull off this role at all. He's been nothing but kind to me. Well … since kidnapping me and delivering me to the Community. That was quite the opposite of kind. "Then, what's the problem?"

Hawk glances down at me and when he looks back up I can see hunger in his eyes. He's not trying to hide it and my stomach does a nervous flip. He claims his interest in me back at Southside was genuine and I'm still not sure how I feel about that.

"You're just as memorable as the first time I saw you," he whispers. "We should change your hair color and get you some contacts, but that will only help so much. I don't want to constantly be fending off other buyers."

"Do you normally have to?" God, that's so gross.

"Sometimes." He swallows hard and closes his eyes for a moment. "But they don't see most of what I buy as this valuable."

That brings me up short and makes me angry. The value of a person shouldn't be determined by their shape and skin like some piece of produce at the commissary. Hawk would know, though. This is the world he lives in. God, that's sad. I wonder where he goes to be himself? Then, I remember the other problem.

I lean on his shoulders for a moment so I can whisper directly in his ear. "I can't run in these shoes. Or any heels for that matter."

Hawk takes a deep breath and sighs against the skin of my neck before responding. "Wait here."

He steps back out of the dressing room and closes the door. When he comes back, he's carrying: a pair of black sunglasses with jewels along the sides; a pair of contacts, set to brown; a thigh-length black jacket that ties in the front; and a pair of black, knee-high leather boots. The boots still have fairly high heels, three inches I would guess, but they're flared out wide at the base. As I zip up the backs, I test out my footing, by shifting from foot to foot. They're very stable. I could run in them if I have to. I nod in approval.

I slip the jacket on and realize it extends at least two inches below the bottom of my skirt. I definitely like this idea. It will be warmer as we walk around anyway. I put it and the sunglasses on—looking up at him with a smirk and feeling like a ridiculous wanna-be spy. "Well?"

He smiles with that little bit of heat still lingering in his eyes. Then his face morphs back into Darius's angry scowl and his eyes go frighteningly cold. "Move."

14

HAWK

The Golden Dragon Brothel is one of the most popular landmarks in the entire sector. Hundreds of people stream through its doors daily. At thirty-eight stories tall, the building is lit up with constantly shifting neon colors, images of half-naked men and women dancing across its surface, and the promise of "a night well spent." Gina's eyes are examining the crowd as we crouch in a blind spot around the corner from the dealer entrance.

"Remember." I take her hand briefly, trying to draw her attention back to me. "The cam's here are filtered by his internal security so everything inside is on his separate system. The ones out here are still Community run. Keep close to my back. I'm going to avoid touching you again until we're inside."

I'd normally keep a close hold on her, or even a leash, but that would make no sense on the cams with her invisible. Fortunately, Serge's man at the door recognizes me so we can pass straight through without a pause outside. He eyes Gina with mild curiosity but I nod slightly as I go by and he doesn't argue.

Serge likes elegance and power in everything he does and his waiting rooms are no exception. The huge plush couches and chairs are an intimidating shade of white with gold and silver embroidery. The antique coffee tables are made of actual wood and ornately carved. The large crystal chandelier that hangs in the center of the room is made of smart glass, and displays various images to invoke desire. A marble countertop lines the back wall with a couple of service bots behind it.

I pull up the local interface and request access, then flop down in one of the flashy chairs and throw an arm up over the back like I own the place. Gina is obviously afraid to even go near the furniture and she keeps turning in circles. I pat my leg, trying to give her a place to be and her jaw tightens but she comes over to sit on my lap. I don't bother looking at her because she's just property to Darius, but I wish I could touch her hand or do something to calm her down.

Come on, Serge. Hurry it up.

After a few minutes, Serge Vasiliev enters the room with his carefully practiced grace. The man is not quite six feet and lean, but if you assume weakness from that lean form, you're in for a nasty surprise. The strength coiled in the man is equal to someone twice his size. He has dark brown almond shaped eyes and long, sleek black hair, which he always wears in a tightly controlled braid. His porcelain pale skin, short nose, and full lips give him an intimidating appearance which he softens with expensive clothes and impeccable manners. Today he's dressed in a white silk suit with a golden dragon embroidered across the right breast. "Darius!" Serge says with wide arms. "I am glad you decided to grace us, my friend. What can I help you with?"

Gina tightens her coat and rests her hands to cover a couple of the worst bruises on her legs, but Serge has already seen what I need him to. In our conversation at the auction, I learned that he's become suspicious about whether the slaves I frequently buy are winding up dead—not that he would stop me.

"Need a room," I grumble while fiddling with Gina's hair—now dyed brown and cut short against her face. "Something worth my time. Other dealers checked in yet?"

"Of course," he says with a wave of his hand. "Where else would they be? You know my house is the best. I see you have your prize with you. Very good. I will make sure there are accommodations for you both. Will you be requiring any additional company?"

"No. Let me see my room."

"Of course." Serge turns to escort us and opens the huge wooden doors, carved in the same style as the coffee tables.

As we proceed through the main gaming hall, Gina plays her part perfectly. At seeing the dozens of people—some of whom look up with curiosity—she steps back as if afraid.

I grab her arm and make a show of yanking her back toward me, trying to be gentle and using her wrist and not the bruised portion of her arm. Turning toward her, I hold up the control for the slaver's collar menacingly. She ducks in close to my side and is shaking. Is she really that frightened? I don't have the ability to show sympathy now. We've got to keep moving.

There are endless tables of people talking, gambling, playing tabletop games on holotables and lounging in chairs playing GRIDgames in their minds, using stunners, drinking, and picking out staff to love. Serge's private security is weaving their way through the crowds.

As we pass, two tabletop gamers have characters engaged in a fierce holobattle and bets are flying on all sides. Mid-battle, one of the mentally controlled characters—something like a centaur— grows massive horns and gores the opposing droid character in half. The droid character's owner obviously objects to the upgrade and leaps across the holotable to strike his opponent. Security is on the two men, restraining them within seconds as the crowd erupts with both cheers and objections.

Exiting the crowds, we follow Serge into the long plush hallway I've walked dozens of times. The oil paintings Serge keeps on the walls here cost a small fortune. Eventually, he opens the door to Darius's favorite suite—a dungeon-style theme in harsh blacks, deep purples, and chromed accents. It's mostly filled with pain and pleasure tools, and furniture, but also has one of the large jetted baths. The bath has helped with battered slaves before that I've tried to patch up before passing off to processing.

"I took the liberty of reserving your favorite room," Serge says. "Is there anything else my staff can get for you?"

"Whiskey." I let go of Gina once she seems like she'll hold still and fold my arms across my chest. "You promised me whiskey, Serge."

Gina pulls her jacket tighter around her middle and it draws Serge's eye. She looks to the floor as he inspects her again.

"Oh, I assure, you." Serge walks over to a small table full of varieties of whiskey. "It's already been delivered. You can place an order if you need more later."

"Good." I nod. "Get out."

"Very well," Serge says. "I'll see you out at the table when it's convenient." He leaves the room in a graceful sweep and the door closes behind him.

15

GINA

Hawk activates his jamming device and places it in the central point of the room. Tossing our bags down in the corner, he begins shrugging out of his jacket. I scurry over to the device and examine it. It's newer than anything I've encountered, so I am afraid to ask what it does. As Stella alights under a large hook in the ceiling, I simply raise an eyebrow at him in question.

"Audio and vid in here are down," he says with a smirk. "It's okay to talk. Just keep your voice low."

"Did you do that yesterday?" Oh God, were there cams in that room?

"Yeah. They only get pictures if I want them to."

"When would you want them to?" I shudder at the thought.

"When it's convenient." He shrugs. "Just remember you have to do the best acting of your life here, Babe, because these people will eat us alive if you don't."

"I know. I'm trying."

"No, you did good. The frightened bit was actually very convincing."

"I wasn't acting."

He focuses on me for a moment. "Either way, it works. How is your rib?"

"It hurts, but it's nothing I can't handle. What about your stitches?"

"They're fine."

"Let me see."

Hawk rolls his eyes but walks over to me and pulls the bandage back. They're not fine. I walk over to my bag to grab my multi-tool from the front pocket.

"These stitches need to come out before they start growing into the wound."

"Really?" Hawk glances down, but the wound is hard for him to see.

Using the tweezers and small scissors on the multi-tool, I'm able to remove them without much difficulty. One or two stitches hadn't wanted to let go easily, but they're not bleeding. The scar is well developed, and not quite as ugly as I expected, but the texture is almost like sandpaper. It must still need more time to heal.

When I'm done, Hawk walks over to a small dresser and pulls out another bathing suit. This one is incredibly awkward looking. It's a one-piece instead of a bikini, but it's a brilliant shiny red color and it barely covers the essential bits.

"You've got to be kidding me." I sigh.

"It's the best you get here," Hawk says with a wide grin.

I take it from his hands and proceed into the tiny bathroom to change. It would be stupid of me not to take advantage of the hot water while I have access to it. When I peek my head back out of the bathroom, Hawk graciously has his back turned to me. I skitter into the hot tub as quickly as I can. The water is heavenly.

"Hey, can I just stay in here while you go out and do all of your weird role-playing?" I settle my head back against the side. "You know ... like you banished me to my room."

"Maybe. I'm not sure what Serge expects. It's going to depend on that."

"What are you trying to find?"

"A mind sweeper. It'll let me see the data in your head. It's extremely expensive and rare outside of a resetting center. I've tried to get my hands on one a couple of times before, but only managed it once. We try to buy them up and destroy them."

"It seems like something a lot of people would want." I play with the bubbles beneath my fingers. "Why are they so hard to get?"

"It's a pretty sophisticated tech." He sheds his shirt on the way to the bathroom. Since he's not watching me, I indulge myself with the view of his sculpted shoulders. That's harmless enough.

"It has to do more than access the information," he says. "It has to be able to decrypt it. People on standard server duty have all kinds of data stamped inside their heads. Most of it is useless — traffic control, public health records, grocery shipments, you name it. It would be a waste of time to scan through random citizens to find actual useful shit. That's by design. Unfortunately, they already know that what's in your head is valuable.

"All server data is encrypted—just in case. The Community upgrades their encryption monthly, but they never stay ahead of the squids very long."

"Why not?"

"Hackers will always find work-arounds, but with the GRID there's a whole mess of ways to get in. See, the original technology was called—"

"Infinitus?"

Hawk raises an eyebrow with a grin. "You know your history."

"Of course. You can't really understand how dangerous something is unless you know where it came from."

Wetware is structured through the creation of bucky-balls and nanotubes, grown from the body's own supply of carbon. The original scientists that harnessed this growth process, did so by merging that knowledge with the newly emerging field of bioelectric programming. The original system, Infinitus, was the first and only system of technology created that has an endless ability to last and evolve, with the wetware always being replenished by new members of the population. It wasn't branded as the Global Reform Interface and Database until it was purchased by the Global Fellowship of Scientists and Engineers, who used that very system to launch themselves into power.

"But why does Infinitus give the squids a way in?"

Hawk smirks. "Hopefully, we'll never get the chance to ask them."

As he disappears into the bathroom, I analyze my current predicament in more detail. The more I turn the problem over in my mind, the less any of it makes sense.

As Hawk comes back out of the bathroom in another ridiculously tiny bathing suit, I avert my eyes down to the bubbles in the whirlpool. I'm beginning to wonder what kind of punishment this is. God, if I did something particularly nasty to deserve this, you really should let me know. I could've been running for my life with a woman, or an old guy, or someone kind but uninteresting like Joe … Instead, you gave me what? A more handsome version of Troy. That's just cruel.

"None of it makes any sense," I say.

Hawk finally slips beneath the water on the opposite side of the bath. "Tell me about it."

"No, I'm serious. You want me to trust you. I'm beginning to want to trust you, but nothing you're telling me makes any sense."

"I agree," he says, holding both hands up and out. "Just because it doesn't make sense, doesn't mean I'm lying about it. Ask me anything. I'll try to be as honest as I can."

"If this is all about the stuff in my head, why were you trying to catch me before I even showed up for server duty? I'd never even jacked in before."

Hawk throws both arms up on the edge of the tub, defining his chest and arms with the glint of the water running across them. Oh, this is so not fair!

"You were flagged because of the explosion in District J," he says. "I was doing the investigation into who caused it and you were on the list of suspects. I wasn't seriously considering you, but I'd run out of other leads and I expected to just dig up some information on you while I was taking care of business at Southside. I didn't expect you to walk in."

"But you were trying to get me alone."

Hawk laughs out loud for a moment, dimples flashing. "That had nothing to do with the assignment. You're incredibly hacking gorgeous." He raises an eyebrow at me with a mischievous smile.

"Well, I ..." What the hell am I supposed to say to that?

"Don't feed me any bullshit. If we're gonna be honest, then you be honest with me. You're a performer. Tommy wouldn't buy you all those sexy dresses to wear if you didn't have the body to pull them off. I pushed Joe to maintain Jared's reputation, but I didn't plan to actually go find you. I could see he was protecting you, so I didn't want the excess attention. I also pushed him because I wanted you. In my bed. This is ... not what I had in mind."

I hate that his admission makes me blush so I glare at him for it.

"You asked." He laughs softly. "I got assigned to you after you disappeared from the server bank because I was still in sector. I thought it was a lucky break. I didn't even have to track you down the hard way because I already had the speed dial disk with information on where you worked. I didn't think you'd actually go back there but figured I could get useful intelligence on you from the other people. When I found you there, that was the first thing that tipped me off that things weren't right. Why would you keep yourself so completely exposed when you should be hiding in the deepest, darkest hole you could find?"

"Okay ..." I mumble, acknowledging that his claim makes sense. I lower my voice to be safe. "Let's say I believe you. The squids attacking the hospital trying to get me still doesn't make any sense."

"Like I said," he sighs. "I swear by all that is lawful, I've never heard of them doing anything that stupid before. I can't answer why they would do it now."

"You're assuming that they want what's in my head. But how do they know what it is in the first place? I mean, even if they got in through Infinitus … if they could see the information I have through the GRID, wouldn't they just take it? Why is the version that's written in my head so much more important?"

"I don't understand that either." He runs both hands over his face and up over the top of his head with a sigh. "They shouldn't have been able to see it. I assumed, after you literally disappeared, that you had been actively working with someone to access the information. That's what my contact believed. They thought you got caught in that explosion just to get inoculated so you could have access to that server."

"That's completely idiotic." Waving my hands as I talk splashes the hot water on my face. "Do you have any idea how many details I would have to know, or be able to influence, in advance, to pull off something like that?"

"Well we couldn't figure out how you pulled off what you did with the cams," he shrugs, narrowing his eyes at me again. "I didn't know what you were capable of."

"That wasn't me!" I slump down in the hot water. "I don't even—"

Knock, knock, knock.

"What the h—" Hawk whispers, whipping his head toward the sound.

I have a split second to respond. My heart leaps into my throat as I realize we're not playing our parts behind closed doors. My body begins moving before I really have a chance to think about it and I am gliding onto Hawk's lap with a huge splash just as the door to the suite begins to open. Hawk closes his arms around me at the same time and I let out a genuine shriek of surprise at the interruption. A woman's head comes from around the doorway, and I tuck my face against his neck with my hands on his shoulders.

Hide! Stella tucks herself into a cranny behind the nightstand that's next to the bed.

"Oh, I'm sorry." She casts her eyes to the floor. "I didn't think the room was—"

"What is your hacking problem?" Hawk explodes with deafening volume. The sheer rage in his tone makes my heartbeat stutter, and he's using that deeper, darker voice again. His hands grip my hips to keep me from moving, but I peek over his shoulder. "Did you even check to see if the room was being used?"

"I'm sorry." She looks terrified. "I-I didn't mean—"

"Where the hack is your boss?" he screams right over her. "I swear I'll have you hacking beaten for this, you stupid—" Hawk begins to move as if he is going to lunge at her from out of the tub, but before he's removed me from his lap, Serge's voice suddenly comes from behind the door.

"What is going on here?" Serge asks.

"Your stupid bitch barged in here after barely even knocking!" Hawk screams at him and his volume has me squeezing my eyes shut. "She's lucky I didn't snap her neck the second she walked in!"

"Calm yourself, my friend." Serge holds up his hands, placing his body between the terrified young woman and us. "I apologize for the mistake."

"You'd better! I travel multiple sectors for this shit?" To my surprise, Hawk shoves me away from him, but he uses the water to make it look like a more dramatic movement. "Get your ass up there!" he orders.

I realize he wants me to sit on the edge of the tub and I scramble up on it with shaking arms. I balance there, wrapping my arms around myself slightly. This bathing suit leaves very little to the imagination and my bruising stands out starkly against my pale skin and the bright red fabric. I'm sure I look awful. Serge's eyes are on me in an instant.

Hawk keeps screaming, pointing at the woman and turning his body toward them. He's careful to keep his lower half beneath the water line. "She had better pay for this!"

She what? Oh God! What is he doing?

"She will. I assure you." Serge bows and my stomach churns. I can't stop shaking as he quickly scrutinizes me, focusing in on my battered mid-section, before bringing his eyes back to Hawk. "Now, how can I make this right?"

"Why do your toys have a code to my room? I pay for privacy to do my business! How the hack am I supposed to know if they're going to barge in whenever the hack they want?"

"I can promise you," Serge says, still holding up his hands. "You will not be disturbed again. I don't know what happened with the code, but it will be corrected, I assure you. Let me make it up to you. Please. Your dinner and drinks for the night are on the house."

"And her?" Hawk points at the poor woman who shrinks with every scream.

"She will be punished for her mistake," Serge says with a severe nod. "She will know better in the future."

"Then get the hack out!" Hawk roars, turning around and dismissing him. Then he looks up at me. "And you get your ass back here and do your hacking job!"

I want to hit him. I want to scream at him. I do neither. I grit my teeth and crawl back onto his lap. He grabs the back of my head and brings my face down toward his neck as I glance up and see the door shutting. I want to rip myself off him the second they're gone, but Hawk holds me in place.

"Let go of me," I whisper, feeling tears threaten in my voice.

"Shh, shh, shhhh…" Hawk whispers in my ear. "I'm sorry, Gina. I know I scared you."

He lets me pull my head back to look him in the eye. I can feel the adrenaline burning through my system. I feel like a bundle of raw nerves all over again. Before thinking it through, I punch him in the chest. The knuckles of my last two fingers pop painfully as they hit and Hawk glances down at them with a frown. "You're an asshole," I whisper.

"No, Darius is an asshole." Hawk begins rubbing circles against my lower back with his fingertips. I realize he's trying to soothe me but it only makes me angrier.

"You made him promise to hurt her!" I screech in a whisper.

All I can see is the terrified young woman in her skimpy lingerie outfit, which I'm sure is a perverse uniform. I glance around at some of the torture-like devices in this room and I can't imagine what Serge is going to do to her. I'm furious, act or not, and soon

I'm embarrassed to feel an angry tear sneak out of my eye.

"Babe—"

"Don't call me that!" I hiss. "Why do you always call me that? You just—"

Hawk brings his fingertips up to press against my lips and I feel more tears spill from my eyes as I glare at him. "Gina, he's not really going to hurt her."

"How do you know that? You can't know that." I want to punch him again.

"He's the one who sent her in here." Hawk looks me straight in the eyes, raising both eyebrows. "Do you really believe he just happened to be that close by? He was trying to get a good look at you. I had to play his game."

"What are you talking about?"

"He was at the auction." Hawk slowly rests his arms back on top of the edge of the whirlpool behind him. "He was one of the people bidding on you."

The thought makes me sick and I glance back toward the door.

"When we were talking, I figured out that he's disturbed by how quickly the people that I purchase die off," Hawk sighs, closing his eyes for a moment. "He either suspects my real game—which is incredibly dangerous and a bad thing—or he wanted to check and see how you were holding up under my fist. He's seen your bruising now, though, so either way, he's probably convinced that you're surviving my beatings. It's good for my reputation, but I am sorry. I know it made you uncomfortable."

I realize that I am still sitting on his lap, so I scoot quickly back to the other side of the whirlpool. Hawk doesn't move to stop me. I glance down and watch the bubbles move through the water. They circle around and around, and I feel like other bubbles are tumbling their way through my racing heart.

"Ba—Gina." Hawk corrects himself quickly. "I'm really sorry. I'm not that guy, but I can't hesitate in those moments. You know that, right?" He shifts closer but doesn't touch me. He's trying to get me to make eye contact again, but I keep looking at the bubbles.

He was right. I don't like this Darius he's invented at all, but I may need to know more about him.

"Gina," Hawk says again, his tone pleading. "Please look at me. Come on. Don't let this stupid game mess everything up."

"Why don't Darius's slaves live very long?" I whisper instead, not taking my eyes from the water.

"According to everyone out there," Hawk says carefully, "he's a violent alcoholic. He beats them to death."

"Has …" the question feels stuck in my throat, "Serge ever seen a body?"

"Yes."

My eyes snap up to his face in horror and Stella squeaks from the other side of the room. He holds his hands up and out toward me. "Let me explain."

"Okay." I press my back into the plastic seat.

Hawk brings his body to loom over mine, making me feel small. I cringe away from him, but there's no room to move. For a terrible moment, I'm afraid he's going to try to kiss me, but he diverts his lips to the shell of my ear.

"There is a drug." He whispers so quietly that I struggle to hear him over the jets of the whirlpool. "Very hard to get, but it simulates death. I usually offer to dispose of a body myself so I can process them back into the Community somewhere else on the opposite side of the world. Sometimes they already have bruises. Sometimes they can end up with some after a few rougher self-defense lessons. It's always their choice." He pulls back just enough that he's looking right into my eyes. "Do you believe me?"

"Maybe … I don't know."

His eyes look sad for the briefest moment and then he scrutinizes my face. "You're looking flushed. You should probably take a break from the water." He reaches up and cautiously tucks a strand of hair behind my ear as I watch him without moving. "Do you need help?"

"No." I slide away from him, to the side. "I'm fine." I don't want him touching me. He backs up with a sigh and lets me go alone into the bedroom to think.

16

HAWK

I watch Gina retreat from me and want to strangle Serge for his timing. I've spoken with his staff many times. A couple of the people I've rescued through here emphasized that, for a slaver, he's one of the calmest hands they'd encountered. He prefers isolation and withholding needs for punishment, instead of brutality and torture. He doesn't punish them for these curiosity checks either—although, he's never pulled one on me before.

His business is based on the appeal of his product, so he hates anyone leaving marks on his staff. I've had to dance a fine line when playing my part. I've made Darius tight-lipped, impatient, and frighteningly calm when he's sober. I can only play him with a looser tongue and violent fist when I've been drinking, or pretending to be. I've only left marks on the ones I also left dead. Gina's bruises are the first he's seen on one of my living lovers. It should give him more to think about.

I climb out of the whirlpool and grab a towel to dry off while I try to figure out whether it's best to let Gina stew in her thoughts or try and divert them. She reacts well in the moment, but the aftermath is a bitch. If I can't keep her trust, she could end up bailing on me in a life or death situation.

I slip into some boxers and when I turn, she's laid down on the big bed. Worried that rib will come out again before it's healed, I grab a hand towel and roll it into a cylindrical shape. She's lying on her side. I sit down on the opposite side of the mattress, and she rolls farther away from me. "You want to take a nap until dinner?"

"That's fine."

"How's your rib?"

She glances back at me from the corner of her eye and then sighs deeply. "Sore."

"Here," I say, holding out the rolled towel. "You should lie on your back and keep this between your shoulders. It'll keep everything aligned and maybe keep it from trying to pop out again."

I slide the towel roll up against her spine and she rolls back toward me and onto it with a grimace. She's changed back into her t-shirt and cotton pants. I'm beginning to consider them her comfort clothes. I reach down and pull the blanket up to her chin.

"I'm fine," she says. "I'm not cold."

I wish I could just ask her to wear something better suited to the situation—like just her skin. Right now, I need to give her as much space as I can. "It's in case of extra eyes."

"Oh God." She pulls the blanket all the way up over her face.

I walk back over to the small wooden dresser and open the top drawer where Serge always keeps his in-house communications. Pulling out the flex, I sit back down on the bed to search. I scroll through the menus of dealers. Serge's place is one of the most popular markets worldwide and he works very hard to keep us coming back. He's got dealers at every level in his pocket.

Unfortunately, I now need something at an extremely high level. A couple of these names are familiar, but even more are new. That's never a good starting point. They could be anyone.

"What are you doing?" Gina's face is peeking back out from beneath the sheet.

"Looking for what we need."

"How does it work?" She rolls back slightly with eyes shining with curiosity and another wince. "Is there a menu of stuff?"

"Not really. You stay on that roll. I'll bring it to you."

She rolls back and I lie right up against her side so I can hold the flex up where she can see it. She tenses at my proximity, but apparently her curiosity is strong enough to override her fear. I'll have to remember that. She doesn't object as she reads the information.

"Who are all these people?" she asks.

"The dealers on site. See … here's me."

"What does palladium mean?" She points to the rating next to my name.

"It's a classification system for the level of tech we trade in. There's seven levels. Palladium means Darius typically deals in top of the line tech, but nothing experimental or with a strictly military focus."

"Would someone like me even be on this list?"

"As a dealer?" I chuckle. "If you were, you'd be down at a gold or silver level maybe."

"Gold isn't good?" She glances back up at my face.

"Nah." I pull up a menu with the classification ratings. There are no explanations listed for any of the levels—dealers have to figure that part out on their own. There are no photos of them either. It's just a simple list, from most advanced to least: tungsten, titanium, palladium, stainless, platinum, silver, and gold.

"How is anybody supposed to know what this stuff means?" Gina asks.

"If you don't, you're a newbie and likely a silver or gold. It's better not to ask. Most the dealers getting started were brought to the table by someone else, or they listen and learn before trying to fly—so to speak."

"I should probably know how this stuff works," she says, staring me down with her two-toned eyes.

"Probably," I agree. I'm not just going to spoon-feed you, Babe. "Where are your contacts?"

"They were hurting." Gina sighs and rolls her eyes. "Will you please explain it to me?"

"You know, I think that's the first time you've ever asked me for anything nicely."

"I'm very nice," she objects with a scowl. "Joe thinks so."

I cover my mouth to keep from laughing out loud. It's not a good idea to risk being overheard. "Joe looked like he was going to have a stroke when I wanted to say hi."

She rolls her eyes. "Are you going to tell me, or just keep laughing about how unkind I am?"

She reminds me of an armadillo lizard. They're these tiny creatures you can find out in the desert on the southern end of Solar continent. When threatened, they curl up into a ball not much bigger than the palm of your hand by biting their tails. They're covered in spiked armor and they basically try to look frightening enough to convince predators not to eat them. They're hacking adorable.

"Gina, why was Joe protecting you?"

She looks away and chews on her bottom lip again. "He's been a friend of the family since I was little. He used to live out in the Dregs."

"He was disconnected?" That would have been a long time ago.

"Yeah, years back." She shrugs. "We weren't really close then, but after my parents died I think he felt bad. He started … taking care of me, I guess."

Did he take care of loving her too? A twinge of jealousy tightens my chest. Man, that's none of my business. "Okay, okay." I chuckle. "Let's start from the ground up."

"Gold?" Gina asks, glancing back at the list.

"Yeah." I hand her the flex, so I don't have to hold it anymore and stretch out beside her. "Gold is reserved for scroungers. They deal some modern tech, but nothing above base level. They do most of their business with individuals out on the street, but from time to time they can be helpful in finding something much older, or even antique."

"Yeah." Gina nods. "I had an elite once who had an obsession with an old form of tech called a Blu-Ray. Any time I ever found one, they wanted the first chance to see it."

"What's that?" It sounds like a weapon.

"It was for playing vids a long time ago," Gina explains. "You used to have to use these circular pieces of plastic with data embedded on them to get it to work. Different plastic disks had different vids on them—lots of vids that have been erased from history by the Fellowship."

"Weird. Anyway, those are your gold dealers. Silver is the next level up. They may or may not have really old stuff, but they carry the basics—ghosters, jammers, pickers, Faraday shields, you name it."

"Okay. So just basic market people."

"Yeah. Stainless and platinum are both selling tech on the same level. The difference is the specialty they follow. Most the stuff they carry is around two to four generations old. Platinums focus on medical and wetware, but the stainless are strictly military applications."

"So are we looking for a platinum dealer?" She looks so hopeful, but I have to dash that hope.

"No way. What we're looking for is above my level, and I'm a palladium dealer like you saw. Titanium and palladium are twin ranks, like stainless and platinum. We sell top of the line shit, but nothing experimental. We don't sell stuff more than two generations old, unless it's by special request. Even then, we'll usually pass them off to someone more appropriate. My side of it focuses on medical and biological applications—everything new in wetware. I'm kind of surprised I never heard of the experiment Stella came from."

"So ... titanium dealers are basically really scary arms dealers?"

"Mostly, yeah. I run interference with some of them from time to time, but what I can do is limited without compromising my cover. But back to your question ... unfortunately, we need a tungsten dealer."

"What the heck do they deal?" Gina continues to chew on her bottom lip in a very distracting way.

"Absolute top of the line, and everything experimental they can get their hands on. Most of the names on this list are foreign to me because they're smart enough not to use the same name for long. In fact, the person we meet will not be the actual dealer, guaranteed. It'll be a rep. Someone disposable. Tungstens are actively hunted by the Community."

"So, we have to go find other people who are being hunted to help us? Isn't that asking for trouble?"

"There's no other way to get what we need." I shrug. "Whatever is in your head, we can't risk some random asshole reading it. Not unless you expect me to kill him. We've got to read it ourselves. If we found an older generation mind sweeper, which is crazy unlikely, it wouldn't have the decryption keys we need. We need someone to provide the most current keys available. Even I don't have access to those. Way above my clearance level."

"Well, crap." Gina throws an arm over her head and I dodge. "This all seems like a bad idea. How are we even supposed to find them?"

"We'll see who's at dinner."

17

GINA

I gaze into the giant bedroom mirror one more time—wishing I could add inches to the clothes Hawk picked out back at that stupid boutique. I'm not used to moving around in such a short skirt. The bikini top would look better if the bruising on my stomach wasn't so bad. I'll manage at dinner, but I wish I had a better idea of what to expect. I need to stay here and sleep, but there's no way I'm going to miss seeing how things work.

Hawk has been taking a nap for the last half an hour, and suddenly sits up. He rubs his hands over his face twice before climbing to his feet and moving. It's kind of amazing how easily and quickly he wakes up, but I guess my experience is a little off. I always wake up feeling like I've been in a fist fight.

"Is this what I'm supposed to wear to dinner?" I ask. He turns toward me and blinks with a somewhat owlish expression for a few awkward, silent moments. Eventually, I try again. "I'm not sure whether the jacket makes sense inside."

"Oh," he croaks through his rough, just-woken-up voice, shaking his head as if to clear it. "Right. Uh … yeah. Yeah, that works, but wear the jacket."

"Oh, thank God." I throw it around my shoulders. "How should I … act? I guess. I mean, do the women you usually—"

"Stop." He holds a hand up. "Don't over-think it. You're a terrible liar and I don't want you trying too hard. Just act exactly like you would if I were the guy I was pretending to be."

"I would hate you. I would be fighting you tooth and nail."

"Even if that button for your collar was still working?"

"Oh." I remember the crippling pain tearing through my neck and head as the cruel man pressed the button to put me in my place. "No. No, I wouldn't risk upsetting you. I'd bide my time, and look for a chance to escape. That was horrible."

"I wish you didn't know that, but I guess it helps." Walking to the closet, he tosses on one of the provided burgundy silk shirts.

It's a beautiful color against his tan skin. "I wanted to take that hacker's head off."

"I think you did." I can't help but smile slightly at the memory of the man holding his bloody nose in shock.

"When you were on the stage ..." Hawk turns toward me with a confused look. "What possessed you to stand there so defiantly?"

"I was terrified. I didn't want to look like easy prey. Was that bad?"

"It made you cost a lot hacking more. It helped, but could have made things worse."

"What do you mean?"

"It means that I had an excuse for wanting you over the others, and being willing to pay so much more. When Serge commented on it, I just fed him a line about liking your spirit. Most of those monsters are excited to see a spirit they can break."

Well ... That was certainly not what I intended.

"Since you've already shown your colors that way, though, I think it's safe to react the way that feels most instinctual," he says. "Just remember you're afraid of me, and don't really fight me on things. I need your help even if it doesn't make sense. I won't be able to explain shit out there. Darius wouldn't hesitate to use that button."

"Alright." I remember how he endangered the woman earlier and hate making such an open-ended promise.

Hawk gives me a slight smile in the mirror as he checks his clothes. He's paired the silk shirt with a pair of black slacks I could only imagine being designed for a dealer. They manage to look stylish and expensive while being covered in pockets and loop mounts for tech. He begins slipping dozens of small items into his pockets from his bag and his coat. A couple of them look like med injectors.

"Is that the crap you drugged me with? How many of those things do you have?"

"Those are some of my most important tools. Would you rather I run around just snapping necks, and bashing people's skulls in?"

"Of course not." I turn away when I realize I had assumed he defaulted to that.

"It's irrelevant now, though, because I used up my supply on the squids at the auction. I try to be prepared for what I can. These are antivenoms for the assassin." He heads for the door. "Now come on. I want to get out there early."

"What about Stella?"

He glances at her hanging in the closet. "What about her?"

"I want to take her with me."

"It's a bad idea. A bat will cause a meltdown at dinner if she's seen."

"She doesn't have to be in the same room I'm in. I was able to sense her pretty far away at the auction. She'll see things we don't."

"Alright, but we won't be able to do anything to defend her."

Thankfully, she's small and the ceilings of the rooms I've seen have been tall. I'll hide her in my coat until we reach an open space. Nodding, I slip her disk on behind my ear. She's antsy anyway and needs to hunt, so this will be good for her. Maybe she can find us a way out of here—in case I need it.

18

HAWK

Serge has us seated at his table in the private VIP dining rooms. There are two other restaurants built into this place on the first and thirty-eighth floors, but regular brothel customers use those options. These rooms are joined with only a small bar between them. Colorful oriental murals along the walls and thick cream-colored carpeting make them look exotic.

The four tables in each room are huge, round, and spaced widely apart. The entire center section of their circular tops spin, so food and merchandise can be moved around without having to pass items by hand. I wonder sometimes how much Serge had to pay for these carved wooden monstrosities, but part of the appeal of his market is the blatant excess. Dealers feel they can access major coin when they sit at these tables.

"How is the whiskey, my friend?" Serge asks from his high-backed chair, his elbows resting on the maroon, padded arms.

"Good." I nod and sip the amber liquid in my glass. I can feel it burn as it slides down my throat, and I worry for a moment about how much of this stuff I'm going to have to drink.

I normally find ways to dispose of what I can, but there's nothing nearby that's convenient. The scantily-clad waitress refills my glass immediately. I keep the glass in my hand this time and hold it dangling off my armrest to make it look like I'm drinking more than I actually am. "Who's coming?" I ask.

"Several ranks tonight," Serge says with a smile and a wave of his hand. "My dear, Darius. You work too much. Enjoy the food and the women. Relax."

Serge has Gina seated on a embroidered, maroon silk cushion at my feet, as he prefers for this setting. I have complete say over what she is served—although, all of the options are as extravagant as Serge's decor. When her food is delivered, they'll set it on a tray on the floor in front of her. I appreciate that more than ever tonight because I don't want the other dealers to get a good look at her.

My whiskey glass is slipped from my fingers, but I'm careful to keep surprise from showing on my face. Gina's not terribly visible, but I can feel the tension growing in my spine until I feel the glass slip back in place. When I toss it back again, I realize she drank some of the contents.

Oh, that's just fantastic …

"I have a business to run, Serge." I glance at the food that's being set in front of me as two new guests take their seats across the table.

"Ah, welcome," Serge says, gesturing for them to sit. "Take a seat, gentlemen. I trust that everything has been in order."

I recognize one of them immediately. Jordan Orwell is a titanium dealer with close ties to the squids. He's a strong man with an athletic build, a couple inches shorter than me with bronze skin, bleached hair, brown eyes, and an assortment of piercings and tattoos. He's one of their preferred arms dealers, and can be found in any sector at any given time. He's completely unpredictable unless you're more intimately acquainted with their plans and movements. Luckily, the only time I've met him before, I was Darius in a nearby sector.

He has the scent of a large cat about him. He could be a chimera, but I've never detected any other animal traits so it's unlikely. It's more likely that he works closely with a chimera with prominent animal DNA.

Jordan is an anarchist through and through. He hopes the squids succeed in tearing down the Global Fellowship, and fail in rebuilding anything in its place. If something is illegal, he has it or uses it. I've been told he drinks and smokes, but not to excess in either. As the waitress serves him something with vodka, cream and tons of garlic in it, he notes the slave at my feet and shoots me a look of disgust.

The second man is unfamiliar, and taking subtle cues from Jordan. He's much shorter—probably five-foot-six—and walks with a wooden cane but no limp. Where Jordan is lean like Serge, this guy is stocky with obvious strength in his bulk. His eyes and hair are an uninteresting brown against his pale, sun-reddened skin, but his gaze misses nothing as he surveys the table. Definitely an apprentice.

"Darius. Jordan. I assume you two are already familiar with one another," Serge says. "Could you introduce us to the gentleman you brought with you?"

"Connor Blackthorne." Jordan bumps his fist against the man's shoulder. "He's going to be handling some of my affairs."

Connor doesn't speak. He doesn't even blink.

"Yes," Serge says with a wicked smile. "I hear business has been very good for you lately. Our tentacled friends are much more aggressive in their efforts. Do you happen to know what it is they're looking for?"

"If only," Jordan says with a laugh. "I'd charge them a fortune for it."

"Wouldn't we all." Serge loves gossip and he's intensely curious about what the squids are after. He was trying to find out what I knew back at the auction. "I hear they're in such a tizzy that Gates himself is on the move."

Sir Issac Newton! Drustan Gates is a powerful player in the squid hierarchy. After his arrival on the scene nearly a dozen years ago, the squids became much more organized and their movements more premeditated and precise. He keeps an extremely low profile and rarely mobilizes with the men on the ground. The idea that Gina could have something inside her head that would mobilize him scares the shit out of me, almost as much as Cobra.

"Well, I wouldn't go placing bets," Jordan says. "He isn't moved easily."

"So I hear." Serge shrugs.

Food is brought out for Serge, Gina and me. Gina slips the glass from my fingers again during the distraction, and slips it back into my hand three quarters empty. I hope she's not a lightweight, or this could get messy fast.

Three more people join us at the table, and Serge actually stands to his feet for one of them. No question. This is our tungsten dealer. "It's wonderful to see you, Amar." Serge bows slightly. "Everyone, this is Amar Al-Mardini. He has some very exciting resources to show us tonight. I think there will be something to interest everyone."

"Good evening." Amar takes his seat as a drink is handed to him. He has dark eyes, dark hair, and brown skin. He's an average height with a slender build and well-tailored three-piece body armor suit. The cheery blue and purple orchid tucked in his breast pocket contrasts sharply with his bland expression as he glances down at the table.

The second man I know well. José Barridino is a platinum dealer who keeps most of the brothels and safe houses in this sector updated with the best medical tech they can afford. He's average height with tan skin, brown eyes, thinning hair and a trim mustache. I've dealt with him a lot, as he's one of the best routes for offloading my tech. I chose to be a palladium dealer because I prefer to dole out as much medicinal tech as possible. I don't personally care if squids or slavers need med pods, surgical bots, or medications. I would much rather deal in illegal methods of healing, then illegal methods of death.

"José," I nod.

"I didn't even know you were in sector, man," José says, barely acknowledging the waitress attempting to hand him a drink as he sits beside me. "It's good to see you. I've got customers that want upgrades ASAP. Can I see what you've got?"

I pull the rolled up flex out of a pocket on the side of my pants and hand it over. He sits back in his chair and begins reading it immediately. I hadn't planned on this. To keep from blowing my cover with José without alerting the CPG to where I am, I may have to contact folks I keep out of my official reports.

"José," Serge says with a laugh. "Order your food, for the love of science. The two of you are unbelievable. Take a moment to enjoy life."

"Yeah, yeah." José waves him off without even looking up from the list. "Just have one of your girls bring me what you're havin'."

Then, Gina catches his eye and he does a visible double-take. "Who's this pretty little thing?" he asks, leaning in toward her.

"Just something new from auction." I begin eating.

By far, the best aspect of this job is the food. Community meals and rations rarely offer red meat because they're not the best thing for your health. They sure taste good though. Serge's meals practically specialize in everything that is discouraged in a Community meal plan—red meat, saturated fat, sugar, alcohol. I glance down but I'm careful to look disinterested as I see Gina blinking at her plate in surprise. I wonder if she's ever had a steak before.

Unfortunately, José is much less disinterested in Gina than I'm pretending to be. I don't need him drawing excess attention to her from the men at the table. I toss back the remnants of what's in my whiskey glass as he reaches down and cups her chin with his hand—lifting it to look at her face. She yanks her chin back and leans away to hide her face behind her hair, but he's already seen it. There's no doubt in my mind he'll remember it too.

"Wowee." He smiles but his swallow of discomfort gives him away as he looks down at the bruising on her legs. "She sure is pretty. How much did she cost you?"

"Oh it was quite the sight." Serge laughs from across the table.

"That one has a steel spine. I bid on her myself, but of course Darius would not have it."

Shut up, Serge! I shoot him a glare. I don't need you telling them how much—

"Darius finally wagered one million coin to crush the spirit of his opposition." He laughs defiantly. "I had more product I still needed to buy, of course, so I let him walk away with the prize."

"Shit." José looks back down at her. "You should take care of an investment like that, man."

Gina is doing a great job of ignoring us as she eats. I give José my best do-not-hack-with-me look, and he turns away with an uneasy grimace. As the waitress sets down his food, he fidgets with his silverware. I've never seen José with a slave of his own, and although he's never challenged or criticized my habits, I can read him well enough to tell he's trying to figure out how to help her.

"What about you Adaline?" Serge says to the woman taking her seat on my right. "I don't think I've seen this one with you before."

Adaline's long, charcoal suit coat with paisley embroidery and fur-lined lapels highlight her ample bosom above her black leather corset. With her brown eyes, mocha skin, and black braids, she's a very attractive, larger woman. The three-inch-heeled boots beneath her maroon pants are the only thing bringing her to a height near most of us, and she wears an almost gaudy amount of tech jewelry. I don't know this woman, but rumor is that she inherited her business as a stainless dealer after her partner died.

"Oh I never bother with the auctions," she says, obviously pleased with his attention. "These days, they make it impossible to tell what you're getting, or what condition it's in. I always arrange direct purchases. It costs more, but I know I'm getting quality. I actually got this one in a package deal. Brother and sister. He's having a hard time adjusting, but his sister is doing very well. I'll have him broken in soon enough."

The man sitting on the cushion at her feet looks strong and remarkably healthy. He has extra slavers collars on his wrists, but there's no doubt in my mind that the sibling is the real weapon being used to keep him in line. People who are sick with OAS tend to be exploited. I pity the poor man.

"Can we cut the chit chat and get down to business?" Jordan scoffs with a disgusted expression. "Personally, I don't plan to own other human beings."

"Now, now, no need to criticize," Serge says with narrowed eyes. Why is Jordan pushing his luck? "We each have our own pleasures."

"Then why doesn't Darius give me a million coin and I'll give him something a lot more powerful and useful than a broken doll," Jordan glares at me with clear hatred. "You should really try blowing up Community shit. Better than sex."

"Actually, I find they can be about equal," Adaline says with a giggle.

I turn back to my plate, ignoring them both.

"Hey Darius," José says leaning over to talk to me quietly. "Do you think you could rent her to me for a night? I need a couple of these med pods you have listed, and I'd like to quality test them on her before I pass them along."

There it is … I hold back a sigh. Brave move for her José, but not this time.

"She's not for sale." I pin him with a glare.

"No, I don't mean permanent man," he says with wide eyes. "I mean … a million coin, holy shit. I just want one night, so—"

"No. No rent. No sale. Leave my property alone."

"Okay, okay," he pulls back with a sigh. "Sorry man. No hard feelings, yeah?"

I choose not to answer him. As I finish my meal, Amar begins lining up flexes around the turntable. Everyone waits for them to make their way completely around the circle, with a list placed at each person's position, before reaching out to survey the merchandise listed.

Amar is very quiet. We all know he's not the actual tungsten dealer, but the face currently playing the role for the puppeteer behind the strings. The list of goods is impressive, and Serge wasn't kidding about there being something for everyone. There are incredible weapons on this list that I've never seen before. Many of them are assault-style weapons that haven't just had the security features hacked or removed—they've never had them in the first place.

There is also an interesting variety of med and bio tech on Amar's list. A mobile poison and antidote experimentation lab, a surgical bot rigged for neurosurgery, and right at the end of the list is the latest generation of mind sweeper. The exact thing we're looking for. It feels too good to be true, and I set down the flex for a moment as my skin begins to crawl.

"Nothing you like?" Serge asks.

I don't answer him. I don't like the idea of walking into a trap, but if it isn't a trap I'd be stupid to let it pass. Even if it is one, maybe I can get my hands on the tech and still keep Gina out of sight. I flag my interest on both the surgical bot and the mind sweeper, and place the flex back onto the turntable.

Then I catch a whiff of a familiar scent and my senses come screaming to alertness. Cobra! I've known her all my life, and no matter how hard she's tried to mask her scent from me, she has never been able to manage it completely. Her internal chemistry isn't compatible with the scent blockers our unit has access to. I glance through the small crowd in the room, being careful not to move my head around much.

She's not visible among any of the staff. It's awfully public for her preferences, so I didn't expect her to confront us here. The venom she produces makes her task a much easier one. I rest my hand over the pocket that carries my med injectors with the anti-venom in it, to assure myself it hasn't been lifted while I've been distracted.

As soon as I learned she was being assigned to this case, I'd picked up my entire stock before pursuing Gina. If Gina is bitten, cut, or exposed in any way, I'll have to administer the anti-venom immediately. I've been exposed repeatedly over the course of my life, as we grew up in the officer's training school together, so I have more natural resistance to it, but not much.

I wonder for a moment how I'm going to draw Cobra out without letting Gina get too far from me. I toss back another glass of the whiskey, deciding to use inebriation as my excuse.

As the flexes are collected from around the table, Amar reviews them briefly, without reaction, and then sets them aside. He'll contact us later to make trade arrangements—goods are never delivered on site. It's Serge's strictest rule. I've done all I need to for now.

A few of the other folks around the table pass flexes back and forth, working out their various deals. José hands mine back to me. He wants the two med pods he mentioned, and the set of upgrades I've inherited for updating surgical bots with obstetric procedures that are no longer classified as experimental. I nod to him and tuck the list away in my pocket. I'll have to meet with him separately too.

Gina has finished her meal and is staring at the floor, still attempting to keep her face mostly out of view with her hair.

"Good food." I nod toward Serge, letting my eyes look tired and more relaxed. "Anything else?"

"That's what we have to offer for the night," Serge says with a wide smile. "If anyone would like to be invited to tomorrow's dinner, just let me know by midday. You're all welcome to our other services as usual."

"Good." Jordan stands up and walks away without a backward glance as Connor hurries after him.

I stand and Gina is quick to stand with me, but stays just behind my shoulder like a shadow. I let my movements flow slower and looser, grabbing her wrist and towing her behind me. I need to pinpoint Cobra's exact location, but she's blended her scent across the dining rooms well.

How the hack am I going to corner her here?

19

GINA

Come on back, Sweetheart. Fortunately, Stella was able to find a way out into open air to hunt, but there's no way I'm getting through the same space. I'm thrilled to get away from the flock of creeps we had dinner with though. I wish I knew whether we found what we need. I'll have to ask Hawk when we're back in the room.

An excellent buzz is working its way through my system and I feel better than I've felt in days. My brain blissfully doesn't care about the pain in my body anymore. I wonder if Hawk's had enough to affect him similarly. It's weird to see him play this part when he obviously disapproves of drinking. He honestly believes the crap the Community spouts. I tried to help, but still saw him toss back quite a few drinks. He's not acting too bad. He just has a slight unsteadiness to his gait, and is leaning on me a bit.

He leans in against the shell of my ear and whispers, "When we get to the room, don't walk ahead of me."

Huh? Okay …

With a hand on my hip, Hawk steers us over to the bar and Darius's gruff, angry voice demands another bottle of whiskey for his room. As soon as the bartender hands it over, we head back.

When we reach our door, Hawk pulls my back completely flush against his chest, his arm like an anchor around my waist. Come on, Stella, hurry back! The knob and lock click, but he only pushes the door an inch or two open and stands there. He breathes deeply and quietly through his nose a few times, and I wonder what the hell he's doing. Stella flutters in through the crack in the door just before he steps inside and shuts it behind us.

He doesn't drop his guard once we're inside, and that's when it registers that something is terribly wrong. He turns our bodies, still held together like one unit, toward the empty corner of the room by the door. As soon as he walks us into the corner, he loosens his grip around my waist and places a hand on my head—applying pressure to communicate that I need to crouch down.

Frightened of being caught in some kind of blast or firefight, I crouch down into the smallest ball I can manage; with my shoulders all the way down between my knees and my hands up over the back of my neck. Hawk pulls away and walks farther into the room.

It's hard to breathe. I focus on drawing breath in and out through my nose as quietly as possible. I can't stand not being able to see but Stella is here. She's uneasy again, but it appears to be Hawk himself that is making her that way. She's being flooded with my desperation to know if there's anyone else in the room.

As she alights under the light fixture on the ceiling, I can tell after a few seconds of her chirps that Hawk is the only person out in the open. It becomes easier to breathe.

He's looking inside the closet and bathroom. "It's okay," Hawk calls out quietly. "You can get up."

I spring to my feet and then lean against the wall, realizing I stood up a little too quickly. I sway slightly as my blood pressure struggles to adjust and my vision dims.

In an instant, Hawk's arm is back around my waist again and he begins talking quickly into my ear. "What's wrong?" he asks, and I can hear strain in his voice. "How are you feeling? Tell me what's going on."

"I'm fine," I mumble with a dismissive wave of my hand. "I shouldn't have stood up so fast."

"Did you drink too much?"

Well that probably didn't help … but this is a problem I always have. "No, I'm fine. Now what the hell is going on?"

"Cobra's here."

My relief instantly evaporates and my heart begins to race. Tingling spreads across my face as a faint ringing starts up in my ears. Every muscle in my body feels too tight. Stella reacts instantly, beginning to flap her wings with a screech as she's overwhelmed by my terror. She flies straight to the front of my jacket, trying to find a perch to cling to. It has a sleek design with no extra accents, though, so she flaps around in frustration. I pull it open, and her little feet grip onto the edge of my bikini top. She unfurls her wings completely as she hangs, and screeches at Hawk—blaming him for my discomfort.

Hawk gives her a blank stare for a moment, then smiles broadly. "You were using her to see."

"Of course I was. I could tell you were looking for someone."

That thought seems to sober him again and the smile falls from his face. "I'm gonna need you to keep her on for the rest of the night. And we need to get you changed quickly. I don't know how much time we have."

"Time for what?" How do you get ready for an assassin?

"Just come here." He grabs my wrist gently and tows me along behind him until we're on the opposite side of the bed from the door. Snatching up my bag along the way, he reaches into it to pull out my silk body armor and shoves it at me. Then he starts digging in my bag again. "Put that on. Hurry. I'm gonna grab mine too. I need as much of your skin covered as possible. Cobra uses venom."

Venom? I turn my back and start to change as he walks toward his own bag. He said venom again. Not poison. The distinction has my mind spinning. You can be poisoned by plants, chemical concoctions, or the toxins off of an animal's skin. Venom only comes from animals and insects that create the toxin to harm you through their bite or sting.

"Is she someone you've worked with before?"

"Sort of." He slips his shirt up over his head. "I know how she works." Looking at Hawk's size and obvious strength, I can't imagine that he's frightened of being overpowered by whoever this woman is. He's frightened of her getting the drop on us.

I slip into my body armor as quickly as I can. The lower half slips on like a pair of tights. It's completely enclosed all the way down to having individual spaces for my toes to fit into. As soon as I get it up under my skirt, I drop my skirt to the floor, and slide it the rest of the way up over the bottom of my rib cage.

Yanking the bikini top strap over my head, I let it hang. Then I tug the upper portion of the armor down. The body armor has built-in gloves that fold back to tuck into the sleeves beneath the wrist. I pull them out and slide them onto my hands. The fabric extends from the base of my skull all the way down to my hips— creating a double layer of protection around my abdomen.

My reflection in the big bedroom mirror captures my attention. Staring at myself for a moment, a chill washes down my spine. With only my body armor on, I look an awful lot like I did standing on that slaver's auction stage. I can practically feel the bare metal beneath my feet, and wrap my arms around myself.

"Why don't you wear these?" Hawk approaches from behind me in the mirror. When I turn, my white t-shirt and soft black pants are in his hands.

"But what if someone else comes in?"

"The only one coming through that door tonight is Cobra," he says with his mouth set in a grim line. "If someone else does, you're already wearing body armor. We'll have to talk our way out of it regardless."

"Should I not wear the body armor then? Is she really that dangerous?"

"Yes. Put them on. We may have to wait her out for a long time."

I take the clothes from him, and start slipping into the black cotton pants. "What if she doesn't come tonight?"

"I don't plan to leave this room again until she does. If I have to fake the world's worst hangover, I'll do it. I'm not gonna risk fighting her out there in front of everyone."

"Where did you see her?"

I kept my eyes and my face averted too much throughout the conversation at dinner. I suppose I should've been watching the crowd, but when she was inside I had Stella focused on the people at the table.

"I didn't," he says. "But I know she's here. Trust me on that."

"Fine." Why won't he tell me what he knows?

Hawk's changed into his own suit of body armor, but it's a lot more advanced than mine. The metals woven through the fabric are in much stronger and more defined patterns. My fingers are itching to touch it and inspect it in more detail, but it's on his body already. I ball my hands into fists instead. Hawk lets out a knowing chuckle as he watches me and it makes my cheeks burn.

"Now what?" I slip into my white cotton shirt.

"Now, we go to bed."

"You've got to be kidding."

"It's better to rest while we can." He shrugs. "She's likely to wait us out for a while. It's good you had some extra rest, but you sleep way too deeply. We can't afford for you to fall asleep tonight. Here, sniff this." He hands me a tiny spray bottle and I read the label. It's a fairly potent blend of stimulants.

"I've had quite a bit to drink." I'm a little nervous about blending depressants and stimulants in my system. I've been told it's a bad idea.

"Yeah, about that," he says with his expression growing more angry. "I appreciate you trying to help, Babe. But I thought we already went over this. I don't like you poisoning yourself. I've handled that situation many times before."

"Well excuse me for trying to be helpful. I wanted some anyway. Serge's booze tastes a hell of a lot better than mine, so deal with it."

"Well you're not drunk—which is good because they definitely would've noticed. Please remember that. I doubt there's enough alcohol in your system to be dangerous when combined with this stuff, but it's another reason I need to keep you awake. Just take a sniff and give it back."

"Fine." I spritz the stimulant cocktail in front of my face and breathe in deeply, handing him back the bottle.

I march back over to the bed and climb onto the side farthest from the door. Fear begins creeping back in, overriding my irritation. I roll over to watch the door and clutch my pillow tightly. Eventually, I convince Stella to flit over to hang from a towel in a ring on the wall over by the whirlpool.

Hawk shuffles around the room for the next few minutes until he crawls into bed beside me. When he does, he has me turn toward the wall and rolls right up against my back, fitting his body tightly against mine.

"What are you doing?" I whisper.

He folds his pillow so that his head is elevated slightly higher than mine and his face rests in the crook between my ear and shoulder. His shoulders envelop mine and he tucks the front of his legs up beneath the back of my thighs. "Shielding you from the door."

He pulls the sheet up over us, all the way to my chin. As he folds his arm in front of me, I realize he has a very large knife in his hand which he tucks beneath my pillow.

I dare to reach down and feel the fabric at his knee. It's a rough material—not his body armor. "What are you wearing?"

"My tactical gear," he whispers in my ear. "Now try to rest."

"Rest, but don't go to sleep? You realize that's not going to work for me, right?"

He's warm and solid against my back. It's like he's molded his body to fit perfectly over mine, and the thought makes butterflies flutter through my stomach. I've seen some of the shirkers at home sleep this way to try and stay warm, and I've wondered what it felt like. I haven't had meaningful physical contact since my parents died. I'm not sure this really counts, considering we're lying here waiting to see if an assassin will kill us, but it feels too good to deny. Strangely, the thought makes me overwhelmingly homesick.

"Gina, you're trembling."

"Well, yeah, you just gave me a stimulant." A traitorous tear slips out of my eye. "What did you expect to happen?"

"You're funny, you know that?" He chuckles in my ear, breathing deeply.

I smile slightly when I think of the look he must have on his face. He always smiles when he uses that tone. "Why am I so funny?"

"Most people get submissive when they're afraid. You get aggressive and prickly. It's pretty cute."

"I'm not cute." Being cute when I'm terrified can't be a good thing.

"See? Prickly as an armadillo lizard. Now what did you think of dinner?"

An armadillo lizard? I've never heard of such a thing. "The food was amazing."

"Have you ever had steak before?"

"When I was real little, my dad bought some once. It was nothing like that though. That was like … sinfully good. How much did it cost?"

"Serge was paying, remember?" He's quiet for a long moment. "Have you eaten any real food since you left your burrow?"

I know what he's asking, and it makes me squirm. He's talking about when I fed him my soup. "Someone donated a sandwich to me at the hyperloop station. I ate the whole thing in transit."

Hawk sighs. "I'm sorry. I should have been feeding us better."

"Don't be ridiculous. You shouldn't even be here."

He doesn't answer me and now I'm stuck with nothing to think about but my own accusation. He shouldn't be here, but he is. His bosses want me dead. I suppose he could be making up this whole Cobra thing just to scare me. I would feel really foolish if that turned out to be true. But if it's real, he seems to be going up against someone he knows.

"What will you do when she comes?"

"You can never predict stuff like that. Things happen too fast."

"What do you want to happen?"

"I want to talk to her. Tell her to go home and leave the job to me. Tell her there's a better way to solve it. She won't listen, though. She's always been stubborn and we've never gotten along very well."

She's not some other soldier he's heard of or read about. He's talking about someone he knows personally. He has a history with her and he's waiting for her to come in and try to kill me.

"Is there something I can do to make her listen?"

"Hack no. You stay as far out of the way as possible. You can't let her get close enough to touch you, or have a direct line of sight. She's got incredible aim with both pistols and throwing knives. Actually … you need a plan for if she takes me down."

"What?" I squeak. "No, I don't." I don't even want to think about trying to run from someone lethal enough to kill Hawk.

"Yes, you do. If I go down, don't you dare try to help me. Got it? If I'm down I'm dead."

"You're being ridiculous."

"Say it, Gina." He gives my shoulder a little shake.

"If you're down you're dead," I bite back.

"That's right. If I'm dead, you run straight for the door and for security. Serge will definitely help you, but you'll probably have to work for him. Jordan would help you too and so would José, though José's not a fighter. Serge and Jordan are formidable fighters and they always have weapons and people with them. Don't let her cut you and, for Einstein's sake, don't tell them you've got something in your head—whatever you do."

I don't like this plan at all. This is a terrible plan.

"Actually … do you have pockets in this thing?" He starts skimming his hands along my pant legs.

"My body armor has pockets at my wrists."

"Put this in it." He slips a small cylinder into my hand. "It's a med injector with anti-venom specifically to use if Cobra bites you, or cuts you with anything."

"Bites me!" I roll over to face him in a flurry of sheets. He doesn't meet my eyes or clarify. "Are you saying she's weaponized her teeth?"

"Just don't let her get that close." He swallows hard and asks again, "If I'm down, Gina, what am I?"

"You're dead," I whisper in horror as Stella screeches across the room.

20

GINA

She's not coming. She's going to wait until we leave this room. After lying here for a few hours, the thought brings a new wave of anxiety.

The odd combination of anti-pep-talk from Hawk, and the stimulants racing around in my system have ensured that I haven't fallen asleep. Hawk has been so still behind me that I would think he'd nodded off if he didn't keep rubbing my hip gently with his hand any time I'm completely still for long. I wonder how many times he's kept vigil like this before.

I've turned our predicament over in my mind a hundred times. He thinks I'm more vulnerable outside this room, but we can't stay in here forever. He has to meet with the tungsten dealer soon, or at least José. With Cobra's arrival, I'd completely forgotten to ask whether Amar had what we're looking for, but José definitely wanted something from Darius. They're not going to just go away without following up.

I don't even know what to expect if we find what we're looking for. Hawk thinks that somehow he'll know what to do if he can see what data I'm carrying around. But is that safe? Could it be something so dangerous that he would turn on me? I wouldn't be able to save myself. I want to believe he wouldn't turn if he knows it's not my fault, but what if it really is horribly dangerous to the Community he has fought to protect his whole life? Could I blame him? If he turns on me, I'm as good as dead.

Stella flutters in her perch and I think for a moment that I've unsettled her again, but she's watching the door. My body goes rigid as I close my eyes to see what she sees. The door is silently creeping open, an inch at a time, and for some reason no light is flooding in through the crack. I start tapping Hawk's leg with my finger frantically and he sets his hand over mine to still it.

Okay. He's awake. He knows.

Hawk silently moves my hand in his up to the knife beneath my pillow and wraps my fingers around the handle. He's moving painfully slowly and I can clearly see a slight figure slipping in through the crack in the door. I'm not sure how she hears Stella, but the figure snaps her head up and looks poised to throw something.

HIDE! I scream at Stella in my mind.

Stella slips into the towel and goes stone still, just as some kind of needle flies by her tiny body and clinks against the wall. Crap! Now I can't see!

One. Two. Three. Four. Five.

My heartbeat thunders in my ears. Quiet, quiet, quiet, I urge both Stella and myself.

Hawk's body tenses just before he moves. A feminine screech of frustration sounds from directly above us as Hawk spins. His hands hit my back, launching me onto the floor, and his feet push out in the opposite direction. I hear a grunt and a wheeze from the woman as I roll to my knees and try to see through the dark room with the knife clutched in my hand.

Suddenly, light floods the room. I blink against the visual onslaught, but catch my first good glimpse of the assassin. She's wearing a black short dress with long sleeves, a garter above one knee, and short black boots. She has fine, black hair in a spiky pixie cut. Her round, dove-gray eyes are narrowed above large, wide cheeks and full lips. She hisses, actually hisses, at Hawk, and I'm shocked to see a pair of fangs drop down and forward in her mouth like they would from a real viper.

A chimera! Why the hell didn't he tell me?

"Takisha, don't!" Hawk screams at her, standing with his body between us.

Cobra flicks several items from her fingers so fast that I can't track them with my eyes. Hawk knocks a couple from the air with his armored arm and one or two hit the wall behind me. Throwing stars. One grazed my abdomen and another rolled off my shoulder.

Hawk lunges for her, but she uses the doorknob to launch herself over him. I bolt for the whirlpool side of the room as fast as I can, as something else breezes through my hair just below my chin. In the mirror, I can see Hawk grab her foot as she's still moving across his shoulder and slam her into the ground. He drags her back and she claws at the carpet.

"Traitor!" Cobra screams, bringing a knife around toward his thigh.

Hawk catches her hand and holds back the blade, pinning her on her back with her other hand beneath his knee. I dive behind the whirlpool and peek out just enough to see.

"Hacking stop! Don't make me hurt you!" Hawk bellows. "Let me explain!"

"You think I care?" Cobra sneers. She brings up a knee and slams it into his back. I'm surprised it throws him off balance until I realize she's deployed some kind of small blade or puncture spike from the garter on her knee. She rolls out from under him, but he brings a fist down hard onto the floor and she's forced to roll back instead of closer to me.

Cobra leaps up to her feet and so does Hawk. They stand there for a moment, both coiled to move.

"You've finally decided to keep one of your little pets," Cobra says with a roll of her eyes. "I knew you would eventually."

"Takisha, please. You've been given bad orders. It's against regulation for them to order her death."

"Since when has regulation mattered to anyone but you, Hector?" Cobra laughs again and it's a mocking sound. "I'm not just here for her. I'm here for you. I was always going to be the one to kill you, baby boy."

"Don't make me kill you."

"As if you could!" Cobra feints a clawed hand toward his face. She spins beneath his defensive block instead, comes around him, and slams her heel down into the back of his calf, using it to launch herself onto the rim of the whirlpool. She throws two knives down toward me as she nearly clears the entire width of the water. One skips off my chest, as the other slices through my cotton shirt at my belly, and pins the fabric to the floor. I pull at it frantically.

Hawk catches her leg and brings her down hard on the side of the tub. The wind has been knocked out of her, but she claws at my legs as I rip my shirt away from the knife and I hear my pants shred beneath her fingers.

Holy God, she has blades on her fingers!

I kick her hard in the face as Hawk drags her backward into the water. I run back toward the bed and water sloshes everywhere as she flails beneath Hawk's hand under the water's surface. She kicks up, breaking back out, and slams a knife into his chest. He bellows and hurls her into the mirror on the far side of the room, which splinters but remains intact.

She groans, dragging herself up off the floor and Hawk holds the center of his torso where she struck. I can't tell if he's bleeding or not. With a sudden flick of her fingers, Hawk screams again and I see a tiny needle embedded in the side of his head just beneath the ear. He falls to his knees as she runs toward me.

My feet are frozen. If I'm down I'm dead … I'm supposed to run for the door, but I can't. She's going to be on me in two strides.

Then Stella's there, screeching and flapping in Cobra's face and Cobra jumps backward in surprise.

I'm moving. I jump onto the mattress and run across it, heading back in toward Hawk as pain from my rib tears through my back. I don't make it. Cobra recovers quickly and grabs my wrist, pressing her nails down painfully into my forearm. I scream and my knees buckle. I turn just in time to see her fangs fold down and her jaw extend open as she lunges toward my face.

Hawk's hand slams against her throat and hurls her back into the wall. Her head goes straight through the drywall. He pulls her back out of the hole and spins her in his grip into a choke hold.

"Please, stop," he whispers. His tone is nearly emotionless and the despair in his expression is utterly complete.

There's a puncture weapon sticking out of the underside of her boot heel, which must have deployed when she vaulted off of his calf, and she's driving it into the front of his leg again and again. She's clawing at his arms, and I let out an involuntary scream when her nails reach his face and claw bloody lines across his right cheek.

Snap.

I barely saw Hawk move, but Cobra's limbs fall limp. He just stands there holding onto her. He's not even blinking and I feel like I'm breathing loud enough for both of us from my spot on the floor. Then I see a single tear roll down his cheek and I'm moving toward him in an instant.

He stares at her lifeless body and slides down the wall onto the floor. I slowly pull her off his lap out onto the floor as he releases her in a daze. The flesh on his face is rapidly turning an angry red color around the edges of the lacerations. I pull the med injector he gave me out of my armor sleeve and stick it hard against the side of his jaw. He flinches slightly, with his eyes darting toward me, but then his gaze is drawn back to her again.

He cared about this woman. I'm not sure how he knew her, but it is evident by his level of shock. They'd called each other by what seemed like their given names.

Blood gushes forth from the puncture in his neck and the wound in his face, and for a moment I panic. Then I realize the wounds are expelling the venom. Something in the injector must cause that. I recall other places she struck him and start checking for more wounds.

There is a hole in the back of his pants leg, but not through the armor. I reach down and pull the body armor up over his head and he complies like a child. "Whiskey," he croaks. "Quick."

Right … angry drunk coming right up. With the amount of noise we just made, there is no doubt security will be here any moment. I bolt over to the mini bar, stumbling in my haste, and grab the bottle he'd ordered from the bar. I push it into his hands and he begins to chug straight from the bottle.

"Whoa!" I pull the bottle back away from his mouth as a little escapes onto his chest and he coughs violently. "Don't! We have to give them a coherent story."

All the lights in the room go dead and I squeak in surprise.

"She rigged the system before she came in. Clean escape route," Hawk mumbles in monotone. "Standard operating procedure."

"Okay." I sigh, trying to calm my rattled nerves.

Despite the sudden darkness, I can barely see him due to some kind of lighted strips along the ceiling. I reach around his back where I remember her striking him with her knee. My hand feels like it comes back clean. I check his chest, and my hand comes away clean again. I wish I could see better to be sure, but it will have to do. We have no time.

Hawk's eyes focus on me for a moment and then he gets a panicked look. He begins running his hands along my skin, slipping them under my armor at the waist to check for wounds as well.

"I'm okay. I'm okay." I push his hands away gently. "She didn't get through anywhere."

Hawk takes another alarming swig of the whiskey and I wrestle the bottle back down. Then I steal a tiny sip for myself.

"Come on, Darius." I remind him of his role and gently tap the non-wounded side of his face. "I need you to stay with me. They're going to be here any minute."

"Take your clothes off!"

Right … crap! I tear off my black pants and cotton shirt as quickly as I can, stumbling in my haste. When I get to the opposite side of the bed, I shove them under the mattress. Then I slip out of the body armor bottoms and look around for my skirt and bikini top. I groan in frustration as they're nowhere to be found. Tearing the body armor top off over my head, I'm thankful for the darkness.

"Thank the Law. She didn't cut you."

A shriek escapes when I turn to see Hawk staring directly at me from across the room. I want to be angry, but I heard tears in his voice. I pull the bed sheet off to wrap around my body, and I'm just shoving my body armor under the mattress as the door bursts open. I scream, pulling the sheet tighter.

"Stay the hack out!" Hawk bellows at the men piling in through the door.

"Stay back!" Serge barks in a tone I'm sure he never uses in front of guests. "Everyone back up. Darius, what in Tesla's name is going on in there?"

"Get in here, Serge," Hawk says.

Serge comes through the door with his hands raised to his shoulders, a flashlight in one of them. "I'm here to see if you are okay." Serge's eyes land on the dead woman at Hawk's feet and his face falls into a grimace. "How much whiskey have you had, my friend?"

"That's none of your hacking business." Hawk's tone is guttural and I realize he's rolling from shock into real anger. I can only hope that's good for us. "Why don't you tell me why your girl tried to kill me? You son of a bitch!"

"What in the Universe are you talking about, Darius? I sent no woman in here."

"She said …" I dare to speak from the sidelines and Serge turns the beam toward me as he struggles to see. "that you sent her as an apology."

"Shut up!" Hawk shouts at me, throwing a whiskey glass in my direction, which misses by a mile and shatters against the wall.

The lights come back on and I'm embarrassed to squeal again in surprise. I'm also surprised that Hawk is completely naked! Serge's eyes land on me clearly now, and I can see him putting together the false pieces of the web we're weaving. Cobra's body is developing a huge bruise on the right side of her face, which I realize is actually from my foot, and bruising on both of her ankles from Hawk's grip. Hawk is bleeding from his face onto his chest. You can tell we've had quite the battle.

"I swear to you, Darius," Serge says placing his hand over his heart, "on the success of my business here, I did no such thing. I asked if you would like extra company when you arrived, and you clearly declined. If I had sent her, I would have offered her myself. In person. Please, let me look at her."

"Fine," Hawk says, completely unconcerned that he's naked.

I curl in on myself and clutch the bed sheet tighter, letting my embarrassment show.

Serge motions to a couple of his staff, who leave the room quickly. Then he leans down and checks Cobra's pulse. Her eyes are fixed open and she's clearly lifeless. Serge narrows his eyes as he tears one of the partially-torn sleeves off her dress. His eyes open wide and he looks back toward Hawk. There are glittering silver scales running down the tops of her arms. "A chimera," he whispers.

"I noticed." Hawk takes another swig of his whiskey.

"Surely you can see she is not one of mine then," Serge says, emphasizing his point with his hands. "I do not employ these creatures, although some wish I would. I'm afraid you've made enemies within the Community, my friend."

"We all do eventually." Hawk shrugs.

Blessedly, two staff reappear with fluffy-looking robes. The slight woman walks over to me and holds it open so the fabric blocks the view of my body from the room. I thank her with my eyes, slipping into it and tying the belt around me securely. The larger man simply holds out the robe to Hawk, who grabs it out of his hands and puts it on in a couple of fluid motions.

Serge keeps poking at Cobra's body, investigating her differences. He pulls a scrawl out of his pocket and uses it to pull the fangs in her mouth down. Venom spurts out slightly as he does and he pulls his hand back with a grunt. "I think you were very lucky to get out with your life," Serge says, turning back to Hawk with a raised eyebrow. "It looks like it damaged your face."

"I carry antivenoms and antidotes with me at all times." Hawk makes his way to the bed and leans back against the headboard. "You'd be wise to do the same. I just hope what I've got works." He takes another swig of the whiskey and I am suddenly desperate to take it from him. It's going to hit him soon.

"Should you seek medical attention, my friend?" Serge asks.

"No. If I'm dead in the morning, just drop my body off for recycling."

"And what about your property?" he asks, turning his greedy eyes my direction.

"Give it to José. The woman too."

I glare at him, but can't put my heart into it.

"My dear," Serge asks, turning fully toward me, "were you injured during the scuffle?"

Scuffle? You call this a scuffle, you creep? I shake my head and back farther away from him, shaking from head to toe.

"Darius," Serge says in a pleading tone, turning from me to Hawk. "I seriously doubt your property got through this without damage. Please allow me to see if she needs medical attention. You've installed my equipment yourself."

"You damage her and I'll make you pay for it."

What? I don't want to go with Serge! Dammit! But if I appear clingy in any way, it will break my cover. "I'm fine." I back away again slightly, but my teeth chatter as I speak.

"I swear, I will not allow any additional damage to come to her," Serge says, stepping over Cobra's body and grabbing me by the upper arm. I let out a whimper of pain as he perfectly hits the old bruise right where everyone else does, and he loosens his hold on me instantly. "Please dear, let me get you the help you need."

"I need a body-seal bag." Hawk orders as he gets back up and leans over Cobra's corpse.

"You don't intend to dispose of it like the others?" Serge asks in a tight voice.

"No. A chimera is valuable on the streets. I'll sell her to an elite."

"Very well," Serge sighs. "I'll have my men see if José has one on hand. I can store it for you until you're ready to leave."

Sell her? How the hell are we going to carry her?

Serge tows me from the room by the wrist. I try to meet Hawk's eyes to beg him to let me stay, but he doesn't look up from Cobra's body. I slide off Stella's disk and flick it in the corner of the room on our way out.

Fear slams into my chest again like a sledge hammer as the door closes behind me.

PART 4

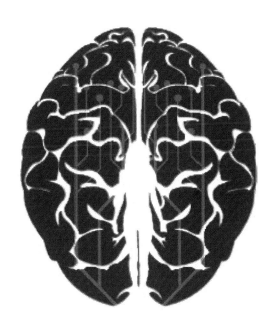

1

I'm sitting on an examination table in a small sterile-white room. Serge walked me in here, barked a couple of orders to the man and woman in the room, and then left just as quickly. The man appears close to my age, with dark hair, mocha skin and a thick beard shadow. He's dressed in nothing more than a pair of tight-fitting gold pants. The ebony-skinned woman is a little older and dressed in a feminine cat costume with a glittery collar.

"Oh, you poor thing." She hands me a steaming hot cup of tea. "I've heard stories about that monster of yours. I'm so sorry. I wish Serge had bought you instead of Darius."

"What is it?" I sniff the tea to see if I recognize anything.

"It's our own special healing brew," she says. "Designed to help us get over those over-eager hands and whatnot, as quick as we can. Drink up. You need it."

The dealer I recognize as José from dinner walks into the room completely disheveled. At dinner he'd been wearing standard traveling clothes for a dealer—tactical pants with numerous pockets and loops, a cotton shirt beneath a Faraday vest, hiking boots, and an assortment of tech jewelry. He'd been underdressed for Serge's setting. Now, he's in a completely unbuttoned silk shirt, straight from the closet, and a pair of awkwardly thin lounge pants. His hair is a mess, and it's obvious he's stumbled straight out of bed.

The woman who gave me the tea points to me and he blinks a couple of times before heading over to the exam table. Both staff duck out the door before I can ask them not to leave me with him.

"Hey, pretty lady." He looks me in the eye. "I'm sorry I couldn't introduce myself before. I'm José Barridino."

"I know." This is the guy that asked Hawk if he could rent me for the night, and I narrow my eyes at him.

"What's your name? I'm sure you've got one."

What was my name again? "Meredith."

"Okay Meredith," he says with a gentle smile. "I heard you've had a crazy night, but I think we all know it's been rough longer than that, so I'm going to check you out. Is that okay with you?"

Wow … He's actually treating me like a human being. Weird. "Why do you work with him?"

José averts his gaze with a grimace. "He has what I need." He closes his eyes and the long piece of equipment in the room begins to come to life and make noise. "If I'd been born in the Community I'd probably be an elite doctor, but I wasn't. I'm glad of that most of the time, but sometimes it's frustrating when I know I could help someone but don't have the tech I need.

"Darius … is a monster. I mean, there's no arguing that. But he's kind of a necessary evil in my life. He's not the only one, but he might be the only one that hasn't tried to cheat me yet. I'm surprised he's letting me look at you. It's a first."

Is that what he wanted to rent me for? What did he say … test out the med pods?

"You must be special," he says with a grimace.

"No. I think he just wants me out of the way. It was … it was pretty awful." I'm still trembling.

"I can only imagine." José shudders. "Chimeras are terrifying even when they're not trying to kill you. Serge said she was venomous, so we should check you for toxins."

"How?"

"I'd like to look at your injuries with the med pod they've installed here. Lucky for us, Serge insists on the best of everything."

He comes over and helps me to my feet, and then into the strange piece of equipment. He seems okay with me keeping my robe on and I'm thankful for that. After I lie down on the hospital bed inside, the sides rise up to form a tube with a pane of glass sliding over the top. I feel acutely claustrophobic and press against the glass.

"It's okay." His voice is coming through a speaker somewhere inside the machine. "Don't be frightened. It's going to be loud for a minute. I need you to lie as still as you can."

The machine begins popping and whirring, and lights dance over the surface of my body. I close my eyes and run songs through my head to keep down my anxiety. After all the events of the night, I probably have enough adrenaline in my system to break out of this tube by force. I open my eyes again when the noises stop. The glass slides back away, the sides lower, and I sit up on the edge of the bed. José is standing there with a glassy-eyed look and doesn't focus on me for several minutes.

"Wow," he finally says, rubbing the back of his neck. "Actually, you're doing pretty good, Sweetheart. It looks like you weren't bitten. No lacerations. We can check your blood for venom—"

"Please, don't. I don't think I can handle needles right now."

"Well, I suppose I see no entry point. You have quite a bit of bruising, but it all looks superficial. You've got a couple pretty nasty hematomas across your abdomen, but they look like they've been healing for a while now. A couple of bruises on your hips, back and forearm look like they're fresh. One of your ribs is pretty badly swollen, though, and you've got old connective tissue damage all over the place. Looks like you've suffered abuse before Darius."

It's a convenient excuse, so I don't answer.

He grabs a med injector and I shy back from him. "I don't want drugs."

"Meredith," he says gently. "This is just a mild clotting agent and a pain killer. It will help slow the bleeding so the bruises don't spread any farther, and make you feel better."

"He made me drink whiskey," I lie. And sniff a ton of stimulants. "And he made me inhale some kind of chem, for energy." I look down and let my voice trail off.

"Sorry about that," José's mouth pulls down in the corners. "It shouldn't interfere with this stuff. Not to a dangerous extent anyway. I told Serge I'd do what I can, so neither of us really have a choice in this. I promise, I won't do anything that'll hurt you."

I turn away as he sticks the med injector against my upper arm and flinch at the slight sting.

"So, how did you end up in this mess?"

"Didn't realize this was the cost of my hyperloop ticket."

"Yikes," he sighs, shaking his head. "Why did you need a ride so bad?"

"Uh …" I dredge back up the story I told Kisame, "Had a

dealer back home who wanted my company and wouldn't take no for an answer."

José looks sick. "That's just wrong, Sweetheart. I mean, Sir Issac Newton … you ended up with Darius."

"Yeah." I sigh. "Didn't exactly solve anything."

"Do you have anyone who should know?" He leans on the side of the med pod.

"No." I lie again.

"I travel pretty far these days," he whispers. "With a name, I could ask around. Maybe someone could buy you back?"

Should I ask him to look for Drustan? No. God, I couldn't live with someone like Cobra being sent after my brothers. Joe either. I shake my head. "Thanks, but I don't think that's an option."

"Meredith," José sighs, eyes darting back and forth across the empty room. "Look, I don't want to scare you, but you already know that Darius isn't the gentle type. I've heard of him sneaking out bodies before this one, and they weren't all assassins."

"Yet, you won't help me yourself. Will you?"

"I don't think we'd get far." He looks away, rubbing the back of his neck. "He's determined not to sell you. I don't have the coin to make it really worth it to him."

"He likes me." I shrug. "Lucky me. But he's going to get angry if we take too long. Is there anything else?"

"You look in relatively good shape, so I guess not." He gets that glassy-eyed look again. "Just … stay as safe as you can. I hear he's had quite a bit to drink."

"Maybe I'll get lucky, and he'll be passed out already." I give him a weak smile.

He turns away with a wince. "Maybe."

2

HAWK

I wish the whiskey would hit me faster. It's stupid to drink this much. I should care that my words and actions make sense, but I can't get the sickening snap of Takisha's neck out of my head. She wasn't a good person, and she and I have fought literally tooth and claw, but she was blood. Rob's words about kin echo in my mind. I wonder what he would think of me now.

I shouldn't feel guilty. She should have backed down. She should have found a way not to be the bloodthirsty monster we're always accused of being, but she took that identity and owned it. Death belonged to Cobra in a way nothing else ever did.

"The bag you requested." Serge comes back in the room with the body-seal bag.

Thank the Law José had one. At least now, I can preserve her until her body can be retrieved.

Taking the bag, I start prepping her for placement inside. I have to remove her clothes and all her weaponry. The bag has to make a complete internal seal to delay decomposition.

"It's strangely beautiful." Serge watches while I work. "Of course, the most beautiful creatures are always the most lethal."

I've known for years that Serge loathes chimeras. It was obvious by the simple fact that he'd never bought one as entertainment for his guests, and he banned servicing them long before the global ban was enacted a couple of years ago. If he had any idea I'm one, I'm not sure how he'd respond. It's best not to find out.

A sudden wave of nausea and dizziness hits me and I pause, steadying my hands on the ground.

"Are you alright?" Serge asks.

"Of course, I'm alright." I hate his false concern.

"Your prize may not be," he says softly.

"What?" My heart begins racing. Did she need anti-venom? I checked her over thoroughly and I didn't see any cuts. She'd used her own injector on me before I'd even come back to my senses. Just like the hacking soup!

"Depending on how bad her internal bleeding is, she could be a liability to you now."

Huh? "What internal bleeding?" I didn't see Cobra get a good strike in on her.

"It's hard to say, yet … but she was obviously wounded before this creature became your new problem. I could heal her here, through our own facilities, and you wouldn't be left with the frustration of taking care of them both. I assume this one is the more valuable of the two."

I realize he's trying to buy Gina from me again, and I'm suddenly irrationally pissed off. "You son of a bitch!" I burst to my feet, having to take an additional steadying step. Don't growl at him! By all that's lawful, I have to control my temper now more than ever.

"Darius." Serge backs up with raised hands and wide eyes. "I only mean to—"

"You mean to scam me out of a million GRIDcoin piece of property, you hack!" For the law's sake, I'm slurring. "You can't have her! I'll kill you first!" Where the hack did that come from? Bad choice of words, idiot.

Serge does not seem ruffled by my threat. He sighs as I watch his subtle change in stance. Ah yes, the martial arts master of the Golden Dragon. He probably thinks he can take me when I'm this drunk. Well ... maybe he can with his security force. Three wiry men that I recognize as Serge's bodyguards slip quietly in the door. I know better than to judge their power from their size.

"No, my friend. I'm trying to help you." Serge always plays the diplomat. "I'm not trying to buy her. Of course not."

Of course you are, you snake.

Serge motions to Cobra's body again. "I mean to help you with this new problem. Let me care for your prize until you get back. I'll feed her, heal her, and promise that no one will touch her in that time. I would expect payment for her care, but you could come collect her again as soon as you've handled this sale. What harm can come from that?"

"She stays with me." I struggle not to growl, beginning to see red. Serge is intent on weaseling her out of my grip. "End of discussion. Bring her back. Do it now!"

"I'll go collect her myself," Serge says with surprisingly visible frustration.

I get back down and finish zipping Cobra into the bag.

Serge pauses by the door, and tosses back over his shoulder a quick and angry, "Try not to kill her in the first month. It's such a waste."

3

—————

GINA

Serge returns and personally escorts me back to Hawk's room. "So, my dear … How are you enjoying my establishment?"

"The food is amazing. And the water's nice."

"How is your company?"

"Why would you even ask me that? I think we both know."

"I could offer to purchase you after he tires of you." He turns down another hallway.

"Meaning, you're not willing to pay full price for me."

"My dear," Serge laughs quietly. "I have never seen Darius this determined to have what he wants. I fear no price would be high enough. Not yet."

"I'm nothing special." I hope he can't hear the lie in my voice like Hawk can.

"On the contrary. Darius is motivated, so your skills must be impressive. Without all of this bruising marring up your skin, you're a thing of beauty."

"Thing." I sigh. "Interesting choice of words."

"My goodness, you're sharp." Serge laughs. "If you worked for me, I could make your life very comfortable. You'd have the finest silks for your frame and clients begging to spoil you. Many of our guests here are very wealthy."

"You offered another woman to Darius before we were even into a room."

Serge just dusts off the sleeves of his jacket.

"Wouldn't you just offer me to one Darius after another if I were here?" I shudder and rub my arms against a sudden chill.

"Well, I hope that time doesn't prove your decision foolish my dear," Serge says as he knocks on our door.

"It's not my decision anyway."

The door slides open and Hawk looks awful. I feel the blood drain from my face. His eyelids are half-closed and his cheeks are slightly rosy. He has a large bandage seal over the wound on his jaw and a smaller one on his neck. The smell of alcohol rolls off of him in a wave that is nearly palpable as he stands there in a simple pair of boxers.

"Best of luck," Serge says with narrowed eyes as he turns to leave.

"How is she?" Hawk shouts to Serge's back.

"My apologies." Serge turns back only briefly. "José has done what he can. Fortunately, she is not seriously injured. For now."

"Good," Hawk sneers, turning back into the room, expecting me to follow him.

I hear the door close behind me and watch him with cautious eyes. He crawls up onto the bed and plants his body face-down diagonally across it. His forehead is on his arm and the empty whiskey bottle is still gripped tightly in his other hand.

Good God … I approach him cautiously. He drank all of it?

"Ha-Darius," I correct myself. I have no idea if the cam and sound jammers are still active. "The bottle is empty. Why don't you let me have it?"

I gently grip the bottle and pull it from his fingers. He doesn't fight me and he doesn't even try to move. I sit down slowly next to him and lightly touch his back.

"Don't touch me!"

Yanking my hand back, I whisper, "I'm sorry."

I look at the floor where Cobra's body was and it seems terribly empty. All of the miscellaneous weaponry has been gathered up too. The hole in the drywall, the pockmarks from throwing knives, and the shattered mirror are the only evidence that anything transpired.

"How can I help?"

"You can't." His voice is something close to a growl—frightening.

"Okay."

I walk around and pull the remnants of my sleeping clothes out from under the mattress. The pants are shredded beyond use and I realize they probably all have venom on them. I wash my hands and walk over to the over-stuffed closet to check the options out. Most of it is embarrassing or terrifying. All the way in the back, however, there is a singular long, white, silk nightgown. It won't be very modest, but I can make it work.

I slip on a pair of the provided boxers under the nightgown and then head back into the bedroom. Hawk's big body is taking up the entire mattress and he clearly needs some space. Grabbing one of the pillows from beside him, I lie down on the floor and try to get some rest. Now that the adrenaline is wearing off, my legs are beginning to throb with nerve pain.

I'm in for a really bad night.

4

GINA

I've managed to doze off a few times beneath the subtle nerve pain running up and down my lower body. José must have included a pretty strong pain killer in the shot he gave me. Normally my fibromyalgia would be debilitating in a flare up provoked by such high stress. His pain killer has made the electric currents of shooting pains and throbbing more like background noise tonight.

Thump.

Something heavy lands beside me and rouses me fully from sleep. Hawk's familiar arms begin trying to gather me up, but his movements are clumsy. When he lifts me, he loses his balance and leans back until his upper body thumps against the bed.

"What are you doing?" I turn to steady myself against his chest.

"Get off the floor." His words are so garbled I can barely understand what he's saying. He reeks of alcohol as if his body is trying to force it straight out through his pores.

I remember his anger from the Emerald Suite. *I'm not gonna let you sleep on the hacking floor.* I only slept here because he was taking up the whole bed. He tries to lift me again, but he can't seem to make it work.

"Please," he whispers. The slight sob in his voice makes me desperate to see his face, and a droplet of something splashes against my cheek. "By all that is lawful, please not the floor."

"It's okay. Just let me get the light." I try to move, but he doesn't loosen his grip. "Come on, Darius."

"Don't call me that!" He tightens his grip instead of loosening it.

Oh great. I still don't know if the tech he uses to disable the cams and audio monitors is active or not. I turn my body so I can lean fully against him and press my lips right up against his ear. His big body trembles.

"Hawk," I whisper in what I hope is a soothing tone. "I know what your name is. I know that it's Hector too, but I'm trying to be careful. Do you know if the jammer you set up is still working?"

He bends his face down to nuzzle in my neck for a moment, breathing deeply. I can feel moisture from his cheek on my skin and realize that I can't even imagine Hawk in tears. I'm shaken by the loss of his calm and controlled exterior. Finally, he loosens his grip. "See if it's working," he whispers.

"How?"

"Three dots." He sighs. "Purple. Green. Blue."

I get up carefully and reach for the nightstand first. I tap my hand along the surface, until the light beside the bed activates. Thankful that I didn't hit the light for the whole room, I pad softly over to where I remember Hawk placing the jammer. It looks like it's still on with the three lights lit up on its surface. I walk back over to Hawk and kneel next to him on the floor. He has his face in his hands, with his elbows propped up on his knees.

"Looks like it's working." I touch his arm gently.

"Please. Don't sleep on the floor." He doesn't lift his face.

"Hawk, I wasn't trying to upset you. If you want me to sleep in the bed, that's fine. Look. I'll go." I grab the pillow and climb into the bed, hissing slightly against the awkward nerve pain that runs through my hips and down to my toes at the movement. I turn to face the wall, on the side farthest from the door, and close my eyes again. I ignore his awkward maneuvering back into the bed until he rolls up against my back and wraps his arm around my middle.

I let him get away with it when we were waiting for an assassin, but I'm not sure I should now. I'm about to object when he speaks softly in my ear. "Sorry. I thought you were her. Then, I thought you were dead."

Oh hell … That hadn't occurred to me. The last body he'd seen lying on the floor was Cobra's. The booze must be playing tricks on his mind.

I realize after a moment, with a slight twinge of guilt, that his guard may be down enough to get truthful answers. "Why did she call you Hector?" I turn to face him, but wind up looking at his collar bones as he wraps his arms more fully around me.

"That's the name my birth mother gave me." He leans down to rub his lips against my forehead. "Hector Warrenson. Cobra's name was Takisha Kinoshita."

"Why do you know her name?"

"We grew up together. I've always known her. Trained with her. I wanted her to like me, but she never did."

I remember the bizarre taunt she'd thrown at him during the fight. *I was always going to be the one to kill you, baby boy.* The thought makes me shudder.

Then I remember something else. Hawk's words back in my burrow as he begged me not to go alone. He'd said the Community would send someone else like him.

Like him? What did he mean, like him? He's made a big deal so far about not doing assassination jobs, but the person sent behind him was an assassin. One he apparently grew up with.

Where is a chimera like her even raised? There's no way it would be in the University. They teach the population to fear them. This makes no sense. "Hawk, where did you grow up?"

"Officers training school." He hugs me a little tighter.

"Where the shields go after University?"

"Yeah."

"Why?" Why would they start a two-year-old at OTC?

Hawk stays quiet and the answer hits me like a punch to the face. Cobra was a chimera—born as a blend of animal and human DNA. Hawk got defensive back in my burrow when I called him a super soldier. I was just referring to his obvious size and skills, but the original chimeras were born out of Old World super soldier programs run by various governments.

I try to keep the tremor from my hands as I skim my fingers along the skin on his chest. It might feel normal if I wasn't scrutinizing it. There's something unusually soft, almost glossy about the feel of it under the pads of my fingers. His skin was impossibly difficult to sew up when he was wounded, but he healed enough in a handful of days to hike across country with me.

When we were looking for the best entrance into the boutique from the roof, he'd only been pretending to look through the binoculars. I noticed him close his eyes just before he brought the binoculars fully against them. He's gone toe to toe with an assassin with obvious chimera DNA and came out the victor. Cobra had retractable fangs, and scales on the tops of her arms. I've seen Hawk completely naked, though, and I've never seen an obvious physical trait. Heat rushes into my cheeks again at the thought.

Hawk nuzzles his face lower and I'm so distracted by my thoughts that I don't realize his intentions until he kisses me. Part of my mind recognizes that his kiss is pleasant, and he tastes strongly of whiskey. His lips are soft and smooth like his skin and a quiver tightens my belly as he teases out my lower lip. The larger part of my mind is still hung up on the potential of Hawk being a chimera. In a moment of insane curiosity, I thread my fingers up through his hair and Hawk takes it as encouragement. He deepens his kiss and rolls his weight slightly over me.

Butterflies tumble through my stomach as my mind wages a war with itself. I don't get to kiss anyone very often—well, ever—and a rebellious little part of me that I've buried deep wants to take advantage of the forced intimacy of our situation. The more paranoid part of me is fixated on the texture of his hair. It's just as different as the texture of his skin. It's impossibly fine and shockingly smooth, much softer than any human hair I've ever felt before.

Hawk is also apparently an incredible kisser. I don't know if it's the whiskey, or his natural disposition, but his kisses are potent and powerful as he grows bolder and his tongue tangles with mine. I can feel the tension building in the muscles of his body as his mouth makes clear that it's sex he's after. One of his hands trails down my side as the other cups my cheek. Oh God, I can't do this! I push back hard against his chest and he pulls back.

"What's wrong?" He leans down to kiss my cheek gently.

"You're drunk," I choke out. Among a million other things. "I c-can't."

"You're so hacking beautiful," he whispers against the shell of my ear. "Let me love you, Baby."

"Please, don't. I won't sleep in the bed."

All of Hawk's muscles instantly tense. He slides his body down and tucks his face against my neck with a deep breath, resting back on his side with his arms still wrapped around me. "Sorry," he mumbles against my throat.

Taking a few deep breaths to calm my racing heart, I'm such a mix of emotions I'm nearly dizzy. The thought that he could be a chimera makes him almost as frightening as he was abducting me back in my burrow. Tingling spreads across my face again as I let it really sink in.

Despite that, Hawk is slowly but surely eroding the walls I've built between us and it unnerves me. I can't afford to trust him and I certainly can't let him have sex with me. He's breathtaking in his own way and gentle in a way you wouldn't believe when looking at his strength, but it doesn't matter how appealing the idea is. If we're incredibly lucky, we're going to get out of this mess and he's going to go back to his life and his job—two things that aren't compatible with any kind of real relationship. A relationship is something he would never even expect, and I would hate myself for not having.

"Sorry I'm not taking better care of you," he mumbles into my hair.

"What will you do?" I dare to ask. "If they will let me live, but want to take my memory?"

Hawk turns his face to bury it against the pillow.

"I need to know what you intend." I press harder, hoping to get an honest answer from the whiskey.

Hawk bunches his fingers in the bed sheet beside me into a fist a couple of times. He seems to squirm against his answer until I hear the sheet tear. "What do you want?" he asks.

"I don't want them to take anything from me. Losing your memory is just another way to die."

"I'm not going to let you die." He presses his face against my neck and wraps his arms tighter around me.

I let it go and try to sleep. It's already early morning and I don't know what will be expected of us today.

5

GINA

I awake sometime later to a soft chime from the door of our room. Hawk mumbles as I slide from the bed and grabs at the sheet. I'm startled as I throw my robe on, by what I see there beneath his hand. I recall hearing the sheet tear last night, but I expected a single uneven tear. There are four long, thin rips in the fabric resembling claw marks with faint traces of blood along their edges.

The next series of chimes draws me out of my thoughts and I rush over to answer the door before they wake Hawk. I'm about to open the door, when I realize just how stupid that is. Anyone could be on the other side.

I touch the panel beside it to engage a vid session. José's face appears and his eyebrows scrunch together before his face breaks into a wide smile. "Hey there," he says with a chuckle. "I was looking for the big guy. I wanted to catch him before he leaves."

"He's still asleep." I push the hair back from in front of my face, glancing back to assure myself that it's true.

"Yikes," José says with a grimace. "His hangover's gonna be full charge. How you feeling?"

"I'm fine." I shrug. I've slept long enough for the fibromyalgia to fade. I only feel as shitty as usual. "But I don't want to wake him."

"Yeah." José rubs the back of his neck. "Bad idea. Well, I won't be able to talk to you when I see you later, Sweetheart, so just know I wish you the best."

"Do you want me to tell him you stopped by?"

"No." José holds up his hands with wide eyes. "He'll see my messages when he wakes up. Don't tell him I spoke to you. I just wanted to make sure he wasn't already gone."

"Okay." I disconnect the vid.

I turn back around and debate going back to bed. Hawk doesn't appear to have moved, but I'll try the water one more time instead of crawling back in there with him. The memory of his warmth, his soft lips and strong hands has tingles running along my skin, making me more muddled up than last night. I rub at my arms to ward off the temptation.

Wandering over to the tiny wardrobe, I find that the red bathing suit Hawk retrieved yesterday really is the most modest one. Good grief. I don't think half of these even qualify and there's at least twice as many bottoms as there are tops. I sigh and retrieve the red one from where I tossed it in the bottom of the bathroom shower yesterday.

I slip into it, shuddering against the cold, wet sensation, and then trudge back out to the whirlpool. Looking at the water, a new worry assails me. Cobra got fully dunked in here with her venomous weapons and all. Hell, she probably sprayed some venom in here when she screamed. That's not even considering blood …

"I ran a cleaning program last night." I jump out of my skin as Hawk's hand circles around my waist. He chuckles in my ear with a, "Jeez, Babe, it's just me." He kisses my temple softly and my heart sinks for a moment as my skin tingles again.

Oh great, I wonder how much he remembers. Way to get yourself in a real mess. "I didn't hear you get up."

"It's not my fault your hearing is worse than mine." He walks around me and grabs another stupidly small men's bathing suit from the drawer. "The water's fine."

At least he goes into the bathroom to change. I slide into the water quickly, ignoring the shocking heat of the water as it engulfs me. How am I going to navigate this new complication to our relationship? I glance back at the big bed, feeling foolish for caving to my curiosity, when I notice that he's removed the bed sheet—

removed the evidence—perhaps hoping I wouldn't notice.

The tears in the fabric looked almost like claw marks, but I've seen Hawk's hands. He doesn't have claws. Of course, until last night he just seemed like a steroid-fueled soldier. I've excused away or ignored all the other signs I've seen. I can't afford to keep doing that!

He returns and sinks into the water beside me. Lifting me into his lap right away, he leans his face against the skin of my shoulder.

"Why did you take the sheet off the bed?" I decide to go on the offensive.

"They'll replace it when we go out to eat."

"Not because you didn't want me to see the claw marks?"

Hawk tenses.

"I might have assumed that they came from Cobra." I push myself off his lap. "If you hadn't tried to cover it up."

He lets me go and tosses his head back against the edge of the tub, rubbing his hands against his face. "Would you, really?"

"No." I settle into a chair on the opposite side of the tub. "I heard you tear the sheet and I already suspected before that."

"How long have you suspected?" He looks me in the eyes for the first time.

"The signs have been there from the beginning, but I didn't really put it together until we were … talking." Well, kissing really.

Hawk looks like I've struck him. He rolls over to turn his face toward the wall with his chin resting on his arm on the side of the tub. "Just do me a favor. Don't say it out loud."

"Okay." I sit there in silence for a minute or two, hoping that he'll explain more. He doesn't. "I don't understand. Why … why was there blood on the sheet?"

"Does it really matter?" His voice is low and rough.

"Yes. It does. If you do something shocking that scares the crap out of me, I'm likely to run from you even if I shouldn't."

"Do I frighten you now?" He asks without turning around.

"You've always frightened me. That's not new."

Hawk sighs and runs his fingers roughly through his hair. When he turns back around his face is set in hard, angry lines. It's like he's slipped back into Darius's skin. He holds up his hand and my eyes grow wide as razor-sharp claws curl their way out of his cuticles, at the base of his fingernails. I can't see blood, but I realize that they're pushing their way through his skin. They're not quite an inch long, and curved, but they could obviously do incredible damage.

I extend my hand toward his hesitantly and he raises an eyebrow. I try to keep my breathing even, but I'm terrified of startling him. He lets me take hold of his hand and look closer. I'd never noticed how much thicker his cuticles are, where the claws must have pushed their way through an unknown number of times. It looks as if the regular fingernail gets depressed beneath the claw as it's pushed out and past the fingertip. The hint of blood is only at the sides of each claw.

I touch the tip of a claw and it's sharp enough to prick my finger. His arm tenses as if he's going to pull away from me, but he doesn't. When I look into his eyes again, they're wide and curious, but his breathing is incredibly shallow. He retracts all of the claws and I watch them glide back beneath his skin as his fingernails slide back up in place. I wonder how his genetics pulled off such a thing. It must be an incredible advantage in a fight, but I don't remember him using them against Cobra. I bite my lip nervously and meet his eyes as I try to feel the claws within the flesh of his fingers.

"What are you doing?" he asks with a rush of breath, letting me explore.

"I can barely even feel them in there." I can't help the shy smile that escapes. "I don't think I ever would have noticed. You've checked me for injuries multiple times now, but your hands never felt any different."

"I can hide better than the others." His gaze burns through me.

"Why didn't you use them against her? Were hers claws too? I thought she had razor blades on her fingers."

"Claw implants," he says with a scowl. "She couldn't stand me having any advantage she didn't. She had those surgically connected to her venom ducts. It was stupid.

"And I did use mine. You couldn't see it because I was trying to grip her clothes. I couldn't leave evidence on her that would show what I was."

"That makes sense." I release his hand and retreat back to my seat. Drawing my knees up to my chest and wrapping my arms around them, I remember what he said about wanting her to like him. "Were you interested in her romantically?"

Hawk makes a sound of disgust in the back of his throat and stares at the water swirling in the tub. "She was my sister. Blood."

The bottom falls out of my stomach and it feels like the room tips on its side. I can hear his voice again, pleading with her not to make him kill her. A wave of nausea washes over me briefly as I remember the shock he slipped into.

"Oh, oh my God." I move toward him like I did when I saw the tear fall down his cheek last night. "Hawk, I didn't—"

He holds up a hand. "Don't pity me. If you just felt sorry for me last night, then you shouldn't have bothered."

He stands up and climbs out of the tub in a hurry. I don't know whether I want to bite something angry back at him, or ask him to come back so I can cry with him. Wrapping my arms around myself and sinking farther down in the water, I think about what it would feel like to kill Arthur or Drustan. Most Community siblings don't even know who each other are, much less grow up together, but Hawk and Cobra obviously did. They did because they were different, like I'm different. Thankfully, the water jets cover my trembling and absorb the tears I can't stop shedding.

6
HAWK

Well, that confirms it. It's impossible for me to screw this job up any worse than I already have. Man, my head hurts. Is there anything I didn't give this woman last night? I killed Cobra instead of letting her kill me—Universe knows this was her chance. I gave away the biggest secret, biggest shame of my life. Why? What if I'm wrong? What if she's been playing me this whole time? Hack! Even if she's not playing me, I've given up everything and she's scared of me—scared of the freak.

"Go pick something out of the closet to wear today," I say. I grab an outfit for me—a pair of the casual, black dealer slacks and a gunmetal gray silk shirt.

As soon as she comes over, I retreat into the bathroom to change. I can't stand looking in those beautiful eyes and seeing fear or disgust. I killed Cobra in front of her. I flinch as the image of Takisha's empty expression hits me again. No matter how much I drank last night, I couldn't drown it out.

"Will this work?" Gina steps away from the closet wearing a black leather corset, black mini shorts, and heels similar to the ones I picked out first yesterday, laced up her calves. She's so hacking beautiful it cuts like a knife.

She didn't want to say so, but I know she figured it out when she was touching me. Was it because of my skin? Did I feel gross? Her attempt at a smile is sabotaged by the redness in her eyes. Must suck to be stuck with someone so frightening. When I don't respond, her smile falters.

"Looks like something I'd pick," I say. "So, yeah. It'll be fine."

She fidgets with the jammers in her ears like she does every time she's nervous. I'm not even sure why she's wearing them—habit maybe. Why is she just standing there? I walk over to grab my boots and sit down on the edge of the bed to put them on.

"Do you have claws on your feet too?"

"Yeah."

She giggles, slapping a hand over her mouth instantly.

Hawking's ghost, Babe. I look up. "What's so funny?"

"Oh, come on," she pleads. "You have to admit. Deadly toes? It's funny."

Funny? "Yeah, well you're the only one I've ever met who thought so."

"Have other people figured it out before?"

"Just one." I finish slipping on my right boot. "But it didn't last long, so it didn't matter."

It's been a while since I thought about the kid. I hope he made it through the memory wipe okay. Either way, he's forgotten anything he knew, and he certainly didn't ask about my toes.

Sure, Gina's curious now. That overrides everything. As soon as her curiosity is sated, though, it'll be awful.

"You have better eyesight than a normal person, don't you?"

"Yeah, and a better sense of smell and hearing."

She's quiet just long enough to make me worry. "Is that why you're always sniffing my skin? Can you track smells? Do you have to remind yourself of it?"

"Uh …" I can't help but let a real smile slip now that she's caught me. "Yes, I can track. But no, once I've got it, it sticks. You just … smell really good." Am I blushing? Well, she certainly is. "Do you always ask this many questions?" I slip on the second boot and tighten the laces down with a mental command.

"Only when something's actually interesting. What happened to them? The person who found out before."

"They were reset the next day." Standing to my feet, I walk to the nightstand and start slipping tools into my pockets. "They didn't remember me at all after that."

"Is that why you answer my questions? Because you expect them to reset me?"

Hack! You just don't hold back, do you? Will we even get that chance? I'd take a memory wipe over seeing her dead every time, but I don't even know if that option will still be on the table. It has to be. Otherwise … "I don't know what I expect, Babe," I whisper. "I'm not even sure what the end of this thing looks like. I'm in unmapped territory right now."

"But Cobra acted like you'd done this before."

"Well, she was wrong." I turn to face her this time. She has to hear it from me. "Cobra thought it was stupid for me to check back in on the people I've helped, but there's nothing that says I can't. It's not the same with you because I'm not going to release you to a bunch of doctors who intend to kill you."

Universe, my head. Nausea roils through my gut and it feels like someone is stabbing me right between the eyes.

"Why don't we go to lunch, and get you some water for that hangover?"

"Sure." Closing my eyes, I check through my messages before we head out. It looks like José is worried I'm going to bail on him after last night, but we should have time to handle it before we leave. I send a quick message to my warehouse contact to prep what José's wanting. There's a message from Amar wanting to meet in the downstairs restaurant, so I arrange to meet them both. There's also an anonymous message.

INTERESTED IN YOUR SLAVE GIRL. WILLING TO PAY 4 MILLION COIN - UP FRONT. IF INTERESTED, REPLY FOR MEET.

"Hack!" I rub at the throbbing pain in my temples.

"What?" Gina asks.

"Someone here is offering four million coin for you."

"Four million!"

Stella shrieks and flies erratically around the room.

"Oh shh, Sweetheart—That's insane, isn't it?" Gina grabs Stella's disk and places it behind her ear, calming the tiny animal.

"Not if it's a squid. Or someone equally nasty."

"What should we do?"

"Get out of here as soon as we can."

Gina slips on her jacket. "But José wants to see you."

"We'll have to make it quick. Don't forget your collar."

She grimaces. "Oh, right."

7

HAWK

I sit down in the chair across from José in the crowded thirty-eighth floor restaurant. Diners throughout the massive room are crowded into wooden tables with interactive tops. Huge windows overlook the bustling district, with screens covering nearly every free inch of wall space—the programming on them a confusing mix of news and entertainment.

Closing my eyes, I pull up the menu and pick out something with a insane amount of calories for both of us. We're not going to have great food options after this.

"Hey man!" José's cheery voice is like a knife between the eyes. "Oh, sorry."

Gina stands next to me awkwardly for a moment. She's looking for another pillow on the floor to sit on, but I don't think they have those up here. Serge keeps them in his private dining rooms. Just as she moves to sit down on the black tile, I pull her into my lap instead.

Screw expectations.

José tosses a packet of something toward me. It's an ORS—a hangover cocktail. Pouring the packet into the small glass of water, I chug the mixture as fast as I can.

Gina then leans in to whisper in my ear. "You should let me go get you a pitcher of water." I don't know if she's making her voice low and sultry just to make me uncomfortable, or if she's actually trying to prevent being overheard. It works for both.

I nod as minimally as I can and shoo her with my hand. She walks over to the bar and I try to refocus on José.

"Looks like she managed to keep you alive last night after all." José leans back in his chair and laughs quietly. "Serge and I were taking bets."

"Who won?"

Gina returns with a pitcher of ice water, thank the Law, and sits back down. I pour myself another glass before she has a chance to. She needs to remember she doesn't like me. The thought sours my stomach as I remember her pulling away from me last night and this morning after figuring out what I am. No one likes a chimera, and only the sick and twisted love us willingly. Gina is neither and I've lost my chance. At least she's being more cooperative since last night.

"I did actually," José says with a smile. "Although, I'm surprised you had the right anti-venom on hand."

I pull back my bandage, so he can see the dead tissue around each of Cobra's claw marks. I checked it this morning and I know the tissue is well-blackened. Her venom is necrotic, so it always does a good amount of damage, even on someone as desensitized as me. It's neurotoxic properties are the real reason anti-venom will always be necessary. Or they were …

"Holy shit!" José leans forward to look closer.

Gina turns to look before I can stop her, shoving the side of her hand in her mouth and muffling a cry. She starts to pull away, but I keep a tight grip on her hip, yanking her back into place.

"Hey!" I hope I didn't move her rough enough to bruise. "You stay where I hackin' put you! It's not your hackin' face."

"Easy man." José turns those eyes full of pity on her again. "She's just scared."

Gina settles back on my lap and closes her eyes tightly. A tear slides down her cheek. I hope she's just being soft-hearted and isn't in pain. Shit! I hate not understanding her bruising issue better. I've never hated this role more than I do now. I re-adhere the bandage to my face. "Stay out of it."

"Sorry." José sighs, leaning back in his chair again. "We going to deal, or what?"

"You want my shit, man. What do you have to offer?"

José sets a flex down with his offers for each item. It's a good offer, but this time it's not enough. I need to offer more for the mind sweeper without drawing attention to my ghost accounts.

"I can get better offers." I shrug, and lift Gina off my lap to stand beside me.

"Whoa, hold up man," José says.

I stop to stare him down.

"You know I'm good for it," he says.

"I've got to get my face fixed. If you can't offer me better, someone else can."

"Wait." José jerks back the flex and adjusts numbers. When he gives it back, I'm surprised he's raised his offers significantly. He's offering three million coin more than the first time. He'll risk not turning a profit with numbers this high.

I raise an eyebrow. "You trying to pull something?"

"No man. I need that surgical bot. I've got a sector with three women expecting twins in the next six months."

"They need birth control." I drain another glass of water.

"They need a surgical bot." He'll do nearly anything to get his hands on it.

"Done." I lean back in my chair. "The usual arrangements."

"Thanks man." José lets out a relieved sigh. He'll deposit the coin into one of my ghost accounts and I'll send him the information and security codes for the warehouse locker I've stored the items in. Now that the goods have been prepped, automated warehouses mean less mouths to pay off.

"You treat her last night?" I nod toward Gina and regret it when pain hits me between the eyes again.

"Yeah …"

"Show me the scans."

"I didn't—"

I slam my knife, point down, into the table top. José and Gina jump at least three inches. Wooden tables really are the best for dramatic effect. The knife sticks up straight, slightly bent by the force. "Don't hack with me." I'm careful to keep the growl from my voice. "Show me."

"Okay, man." José swallows, quickly pulling out a separate flex.

He scrolls through menus blindingly fast and passes it over. I pull Gina to sit back down on my lap as I review the data, trying to glean what I can considering I've never actually studied medicine. José's personal notes are the most helpful. It looks like she was being honest about bruising easily, because there's no sign of deep tissue or organ damage. That, combined with the apparent age of many of the bruises, has made José suspicious about whether I was even the one who hurt her. It's not a safe suspicion, but I doubt he would share it with anyone else.

He also notes that she has an incredible amount of connective tissue damage of varying ages throughout her body. I have no idea what that could be from. Maybe from the explosion? Otherwise, she looks healthy.

"You show anyone else this?"

"No man."

"Serge?"

"I said no one!"

"Erase it from the pod?"

"Yeah, I transferred it."

With a couple swipes of my finger, I erase all the data from his flex. Then I toss it back. "No keeping data on my property."

Gina is quick to hurry off my lap as I stand and tow her along behind me. I pretend not to notice when she waves him a quick goodbye as a new wave of nausea hits.

8

It's amazing José puts up with Hawk in his Darius role. I have a hard time not being mad at him for being so mean, even when I realize he's faking the whole thing. José must really depend on what he supplies.

I have little time to reflect on it, however, as Hawk tows me immediately over to another table. I try not to look pleased as we finally meet with Amar, the tungsten dealer.

Amar is seated in a plush chair at a much nicer table. He's eating something that smells amazing and my stomach growls loudly enough that I watch Hawk hold back a smirk. Then I realize we were never delivered any food over at José's table.

Shoot! I'm starving. Stella agrees as she flits around the edges of the high ceiling, disappointed by the lack of tasty bugs.

"Good afternoon." Amar gives a polite nod as Darius takes his seat, then calls over a serving bot, which hurries back with a large pillow.

Great, and I had been hoping to see without Stella.

"I was not sure whether to expect you today." Amar's tone is casual, but he narrows curious eyes at Darius.

Man, word in this place spreads faster than in the Dregs.

"I'm hard to kill," Hawk says without any avoidance at all. He runs his fingers through my hair as I take a seat on the pillow. Is that an apology or a show of ownership? "And I have a business to run."

It's frustrating to be sitting down so low, because I can't see people's expressions. I realize quickly, though, that if I shift slightly closer to Hawk's chair, I can see Amar clearly reflected in the glass surface of the decorative interior windows around his table. Stella is determined to look for bugs, so I'm only getting glimpses of it as she carefully keeps out of sight.

"Ah yes." Amar smiles as the server bot delivers meals for all three of us—apparently moving tables doesn't confuse them. "You indicated that you were interested in two of my items."

The server sets Amar's and Darius's meals on the table and mine in front of me on the floor. I wonder whether Darius always orders the same meals for his property as he does for himself. If he does, it's a good thing, but it seems expensive.

The meal smells heavenly. It's some kind of thinly sliced meat that's been breaded and fried with vegetables, then coated in a rich, sweet-smelling sauce—much richer than anything I would have access to back home. The vegetables don't even look rehydrated. I start eating quickly, unsure of how much time we'll have before Hawk leaves the table again. I don't want to miss a bite.

"Can you deliver what you claim?" Hawk asks. "The tool is one thing. Codes are another."

"The codes will be updated again before the item is even transferred," Amar picks at a large bowl of something I can't see.

"How?"

"The data is being supplied by an elite. I'm curious what you need the device for. It's possible we could trade for information as well."

"Not possible." Hawk shakes his head without even looking up. "I'm working as third party for a buyer. Same as you."

"Interesting. I thought the squids had already purchased their own in recent days. Perhaps someone beat you to the prize?"

The squids bought a mind sweeper too? It makes sense. They must want to get the information from me as quickly as possible, so having the tool already on hand when they snatch me would be practical. I am so screwed! The four million coin offer was probably from them! Stella starts watching the room in earnest as adrenaline rushes through me, but I don't know if I would recognize a squid if I were looking right at them.

"Are you selling or not?" I glance up to see Hawk staring the man down. "If not, I'll find someone else. I don't care what they want it for."

"I mean no ill will Darius." Amar chuckles. "We're all very curious about what has triggered so much movement on so many fronts. I can't help but wonder if the attempt on your life wasn't specifically to prevent our exchange."

"Maybe." Hawk shrugs. "I didn't question the creature before killing it."

Creature … I shudder, looking down to eat more from my plate. It's painful to hear Hawk talk about his sister, and himself, in such terms. The people around him have no idea how abusive their basic conversations are. I would have had no idea, but I still wouldn't have ever referred to a chimera as a creature. They're just … really scary people.

Hawk runs his fingers through my hair again and I notice a server bot deliver him a small glass of whiskey. He sips from the glass more slowly this morning. "Extra security at the exchange?" he asks. "No risks of my shit ending up in the wrong hands?"

"Which wrong hands are you referring to?" Amar asks with a smirk.

"The ones that aren't paying. My buyer expects to get what they paid for."

"Of course," Amar says with a dismissive wave of his hand. "As long as your buyer can provide the funds that you claim, we will make the exchange in three days. I've sent you an encrypted message with the location and time."

"You'll be there?" Hawk asks.

"Yes, as well as the seller." Amar nods.

What?

"The seller?" Hawk sets his whiskey glass down with a clank. "Why? That's not how I do things."

"They assume you want to test the codes to confirm the quality of your product. They will be present with a test subject."

After a long pause, Darius agrees and continues to eat. We spend the next several moments in awkward silence as all three of us finish our meals. I make sure to finish with my own well before they finish with theirs, so Hawk is not tempted to delay for me.

As soon as he's finished, he tosses back the remainder of his whiskey and stands abruptly. "Three days." He walks away without looking back.

I stand and dizziness assails me, resting my hand on the table top while my vision dims and then comes back. Damn blood pressure! When it does, I hurry after Hawk who has just turned to glare back at me.

"Until then," Amar says quietly behind us.

9

GINA

There is an eerie stillness in this strange pocket of the world Hawk has brought us into. The normal sounds of autocabs, advertisements, and arguments faded into the background yesterday. Plant life is encroaching on more and more of our surroundings as we continue. I'm thankful to finally be back in my street clothes.

He's carrying Cobra's body over his shoulder. Getting out of Serge's place and out of the sector with it had been a ridiculous venture, but somehow he managed. I'd desperately wished that the cams couldn't see him either, because we were leaving such an obvious trail to follow.

He told me it was easier to navigate on foot without interference because he's moved a body like this before, and many of the witnesses along our route are accustomed to this occasional habit of his. It's an odd concept, but I don't dwell on it too much.

There are shiny green, very tall, reed-like trees growing up in bunches, and tons of green plants coat the ground like a blanket. My backpack has completely given up on wheels and deployed it's multi-toed feet to walk along behind us. I've only had to tip it back upright a couple of times, but Hawk looks like he wishes he could snatch it up off the ground.

Eventually, we reach an old abandoned building that even a shirker would hesitate to venture into. It's more rubble than structure anymore. I remain quiet as Hawk winds his way around the stones and twisted wire coated in some form of brilliant green moss.

Finally, he stops in front of a large moss-covered boulder and carefully lays Cobra's body down beside him. Then he reaches up and opens the boulder's face. A metallic whine comes from a hatch, and the boulder is not a boulder at all.

"What is that?" I ask, breaking our comfortable silence.

"It's an old storage tank," Hawk says without turning around. "I don't think it's been disturbed by anyone but me in a long time."

"You're just going to leave her in there? Will her body ever decompose if it stays in that bag?"

"I'll send word to have her picked up." Hawk glances at me over his shoulder. "The bag would eventually stop working, but I'd like to get her back to the CPG so they can recycle her properly."

Hawk lifts a large bag out of the hatch and sets it aside. He picks up her body and lowers it into the opening, lining her up to rest as flat as possible inside the rounded tank. His hand hovers over the zipper for a moment, as if he's considering opening it back up.

I step closer and rest my hand on his shoulder. "She won't look any better than she did before. She won't look like you remember."

"She didn't look like I remember when she was hurling knives at me either. She must have had more plastic surgery. She was never happy with how she looked, or what weapons she had."

"A lot of people aren't happy with the cards they were dealt at birth." I include myself in that bucket.

"I just wish ... never mind." Hawk slowly closes the hatch and sits down on the ground with his head in his hands. I want to thank him for saving me, but it feels wrong somehow. How can I thank someone for killing someone else, and wounding themselves in the process? I sit down beside him and search for words. Finally, I just take his hand. He looks down at my hand on his and then glances up at me with a raised eyebrow.

"I'm sorry," I finally whisper. "She was obviously very important to you."

"Was she?" he asks. "What was the name of that guy you left me with back at your burrow?"

"You mean Crazy Rob?"

"Yeah. He said something before he let me go, and I keep thinking about it. He said, you take care of kin. I've not really thought about it before, but she was one of the only blood relatives I have. I wanted her to like me so bad, but she hated my guts no matter what I did."

"Sometimes that's true in families."

"Well I wouldn't know anything about that." He runs his fingers roughly through his hair. "I still don't know why it matters so much, but I guess maybe what Rob said has some truth to it. I think I would have completely pushed her out of mind years ago if I didn't know she was blood."

"The Community lies when it says families don't matter." I glance toward the closed hatch.

"Well, I was born into a family like her." Hawk stands to his feet. "So, I'm better off without it."

"Families aren't just what we're born into. We can make them too. You'll never convince me that we're better off without them. That just leaves you alone for life, with nothing to show for it."

"Where is your family then?" He holds his hands out to the empty stillness around us, and I wrap my arms defensively around me. "Are they here? Are they coming to rescue you?"

"My parents are dead, or they would be. I haven't seen my brothers since Mom and Dad died, so that's not fair. If they knew I was in trouble, they would come."

"Sure," Hawk shrugs. "Instead you have me, and it's not because I'm family. It's because the Community assigned me to you, like they assigned my nurse to me. Everyone has a place they're suited to, and they fill a role that's needed."

"They assigned you to hunt me! Not to protect me. I don't think they assigned you very well at all. I just got lucky that you aren't who they want you to be."

"I don't want to argue about this." Hawk rubs the muscles at the base of his neck. "We need to keep moving."

"Where are we going exactly?"

"I'm going to meet Amar," he replies with a grimace, "and you're going to stay where I put you."

"I am not!" Like hell I'm going to let you leave me by myself! "Wherever you're going, I'm coming too!"

"Gina, you are the target, and the meet with Amar is a trap. An obvious one. I'm not just going to walk in there and hand you over."

"If it's a trap, then let's just move on. Why are you going at all?"

"I'm going because we need that mind sweeper, and I might be able to see which side is laying the trap."

"Who cares who's setting it? What if you don't come back?"

"Then do what you have to, to survive for as long as you can. For the Law's sake, change your name. Change your hair and eye color. Again. Often. Dig in deep, and stay buried."

"When are you leaving?"

"Tomorrow." He grabs the large bag he pulled from the tank and rises to his feet. "For now, we need to get you a lot farther out of reach. I don't want you anywhere near the exchange."

"I don't want to hide!" I stand up and start following him again. "I need to know what's going on too."

"It's not worth the risk. Just make sure you wait long enough for me to get back."

10

HAWK

"Let's power down here," I call back over my shoulder, pointing toward a doorway leading into a mostly demolished building. I've been here once before. There's an old concrete parking garage beneath it that is sheltered from the elements. I can smell rain coming, so we need to get out of the open as soon as possible.

The rain is a blessing, as it will wash away the scent trail we've been leaving behind us. I'm not sure how long we have before the CPG realizes Cobra is overdue reporting in. I wonder who they'll send next? I don't want to have to kill any more members of my team.

I open the heavy steel door, turning to see Gina following my direction without complaint. Her eyes are unfocused, and her movements are clumsy. She hasn't spoken in the last few hours, but being forced to go at a pace she can manage means we've only made it a few miles outside the district. "Gina?"

When her eyes snap up to my face, she looks startled. "What?"

I scrutinize her posture again and draw in her scent. As soon as she stands beside me, the smell of whiskey assaults my senses. I heard her drinking sporadically behind me, but had assumed she was drinking something helpful—like water.

"Are you drunk?"

"No," she says with a scowl, but her breath reeks of alcohol.

"Are you hacking stupid?" I clench my hands in frustration.

"No, I'm in pain!"

"Where?"

I look her over again. The bruising on her legs is beginning to fade to yellow around the edges, but her rib could be hurting again.

She darts around me, not meeting my eyes, and starts to head down the stairs behind the door.

"Answer me." I turn on a flashlight and aim the beam in front of her. "I need to know if you—"

"It's not—" Gina's foot slips on the edge of the second stair.

Lunging to grab her by the back of her pants, I pull her back against me and catch the railing in my grip—which comes part way out of the decaying concrete before it stops our descent. My ankle jams against the side of the stairs and I roar out a curse as Gina's body trembles against me.

"Stop!" I can't believe she's been self-medicating instead of telling me what was wrong for Universe knows how long! But Hawking's ghost, I need to calm down before I terrify her.

I lift her into my arms and her fists hit me in the chest as she shouts, "Put me down! I can walk!"

"Obviously not. Don't fight me, or you're really going to piss me off."

"Oh, like that's hard to do."

Keeping the flashlight aimed at the stairs, I make my way carefully down until we've reached the broken up asphalt floor. I don't trust her balance here any more than I did on the stairs, so I carry her toward the old vehicles that were abandoned here a century ago. They've survived remarkably well in the shelter of this building, while nature attempted to swallow up everything outside.

"We're sleeping here?" Gina asks.

"Yeah." I set her on her feet. "I've slept here before. It'll shelter us from the rain."

Dropping our bags at her feet, I roll the stiffness out of my shoulders and test my bruised ankle. It hurts, but it will still hold me. Then I head for the old cars to pull out the cushioning I cut out the last time I was here. I take out my knife, and cut more free from a second vehicle. The bed will need to be wider for both of us.

When I carry it back to drop beside her, she's got an RC halfway to her mouth. "Don't eat that." I snatch the flask from her instead as a priority.

"Hey! It's my food! And that's my whiskey!"

"First rule of long-trips, Babe. Eat the heaviest food first. I have some MREs in my bag. We'll use those."

"That's your food. I'm not going to—"

"Well, I'm carrying all of it, aren't I?" I begin arranging the stripped cushions into a crude mattress.

"You wouldn't be if you had a bag like mine." She shoves the RC back into her mechanical monster.

I've never met such an infuriating woman in my life, and the scent of the poison in her body makes my blood boil. "Why the hack didn't you tell me you were in pain?"

She looks away and doesn't answer me. She never answers me when I ask about the physical problems she has, and it sets off every alarm bell in my head. There is something wrong with her, but she's determined not to tell me what it is.

"Do you have the virus?" I finally ask with a sigh.

"What virus?"

The tightness in my chest eases, but only slightly. "The virus that's sweeping through the shirkers back in your sector. The one that's transmitted by love."

"Oh, that?" she says with a dismissive wave. "No."

"Are you sure? People are affected long before they know they have it. That's why it's spreading so bad." I don't know as much about it as I should. I've had special access to the preventative medications through my position, but Gina could have picked it up from anyone and been unaware.

"Trust me. It's not a problem," she says, "I'm tired and I'm hungry. Can I eat now please?"

"Yeah." I toss her an MRE and set one aside for myself. After eating at Serge's place, it's going to taste more terrible than normal, but we need to keep the RCs in reserve. I have no idea how long we're going to have to manage like this.

Pulling out my med injector and the two vials I need, I click the first vial into place.

Gina begins scurrying backward. "What is that?"

"It's a pain-killer. A lot better hacking solution than whiskey. I've got some antivirals here too … Just in case."

"I don't need them."

"Does everything have to be a fight with you?"

"The whiskey took the edge off," she says. "I swear. That's all I need. I don't have a virus, and I shouldn't take medicines I don't need."

"You could have picked it up from anyone, Babe. I've been on the antivirals for months. All operatives have. I think it's bullshit that they haven't given them out to the main population yet, but word on the street is that they're looking into a new inoculation."

"But only for Community members, right?" she scoffs.

"So I hear." I shrug. "Don't give me that look. It's not my decision. The point is, we shouldn't take the risk that you've been exposed. How long have you been bruising like this?"

"Forever." Her eyebrows scrunch together. "Hawk, I'm not sick. Why would you try to sleep with me if I was? Are you trying to catch it?"

"Don't be stupid. I just told you I'm already protected. I don't have to worry about it."

"Great," Gina laughs without humor. "You may be diseased, but you're hot enough to risk it. Gee thanks."

I refuse to take the bait. "Are you still in pain?"

The look in her eyes tells me she wants to lie. "Yes, but not bad enough to need meds. Trust me. We may need that, and I don't want to waste it now."

Good point, but I'm sure as hack not gonna give her the poison back. I put the med injector away, then tear into my own MRE and work to swallow down the lukewarm food blend.

As she eats her own, she begins to eye the mattress I've thrown together. "It looks like there's enough for two mattresses." There's fear buried in her tone and body language. I wonder if she'll ever trust me again, now that she knows what I am.

"It'll be warmer, and you'll be closer if someone catches us by surprise." The fact that I enjoy the feeling of her in my bed weighs heavily into the decision and honestly surprises me. I never let the women I sleep with stay in my bed. It's too much of a risk.

Gina caught on to the fact that I'm a chimera very fast—proof of why caution is necessary. But she's spent more time with me than anyone since I was a child. Anyone who isn't a chimera anyway.

"I'd be more comfortable in my own bed." She finally meets my eyes. "Please."

Shit. "Let me guess …" I stand up to rearrange the mattresses. "You're afraid of claws, right? Or is it my sense of smell that bothers you?"

She hesitates.

"You know what …" I hold a hand up when she finally starts to speak. "I don't think I want to know."

"You really can't handle it when a woman doesn't just fall into bed with you, can you?"

I grimace. It's one thing to decide to take the high road and walk away from something that isn't meant to be. It's been an entirely different monster to get to know her and realize that I really like her armadillo-lizard-like defenses and her courage. To have to look at her pretty figure, smell her delicious scent, and even hear her voice day in and day out—sleeping beside her is a consolation I crave more than I have a right to.

"Does it bruise your ego, Hawk? Do you expect every woman you meet to just give you everything you want because you're so unbelievably sexy?" She rolls her eyes and places the back of her hand against her forehead in a mocking gesture.

That does bruise my ego. I swallow down my retort and keep

my hands busy separating the mattresses.

"That's it, isn't it." She folds her arms across her chest. "You just—"

"Stop!" I turn back to her with my hands up in surrender. "You made your point. I'm sorry, okay? Hawking's ghost. Consider us separated."

I hear the rain start up heavily outside, and head back toward the stairs to retreat into the night for a few minutes. I'll come back in when I can stand to look her in the eyes again.

11

GINA

Hawk storms off and I want to hurl something at his back. Jackass!

I shouldn't have let him get away with sleeping in the same bed as me for so many nights. He obviously thinks he belongs there, and there is no way I'm going to let that slide day after day. Every day he gets more and more comfortable touching me and it gets harder and harder to remind myself that it's very stupid to let him. It's even more stupid to want it.

It had been so tempting to let it slide one more night. Why bother mentioning the single mattress when we're both so tired? It's true. It will be warmer … It'll also feel so much better having his arm draped over me with his strong frame pressed against my back.

God help me, I'm in so much trouble. What am I supposed to do here?

I'm flirting with romantic involvement with a shield! No. Scratch that. What Hawk wants has nothing to do with romance, and everything to do with sex. He's an indoctrinated Community member, through and through. Sex is just sex, and I'm convenient. Yes, he's made it clear that he finds me sexy. A lot of women are, I'm sure. He doesn't have any of them on hand. Just lucky old me.

I rub my hands against the pain in my legs now that Hawk isn't in the room. My fibromyalgia has come roaring back with a vengeance—severe enough to give me mobility issues. I'm lucky that Hawk interpreted my clumsiness and distraction as drunkenness instead of pain, but I don't want whatever cocktail he was trying to give me. I've got to get myself settled and still quickly, or this will keep me awake all night.

At least we stopped walking.

I finish the last of the MRE, thanking God that it's more filling and flavorful than the food tab. Then I pull one of the foil-like emergency blankets out of my bag and curl up on the mattress closer to the interior of the room. I could be wrong, but I suspect Hawk will want the one closest to the entrance. The already dim ambient light in the room has grown darker, and I realize the sound I'm hearing is heavy rain outside. Soon, the light will be gone entirely.

As I close my eyes, I coach myself to stay calm in the quiet dark. I shouldn't depend on Hawk's presence for comfort. Fortunately, the whiskey and the overwhelming fatigue eventually pull me under despite the electric-current-like pain running through my legs.

12

GINA

Ouch!

I startle awake when I feel a sharp pain in my forearm, but a heavy weight across my body keeps me from moving. I'm tired, sore, and instantly nauseous. Trying to remember where I am, I hear the barest whisper of Hawk's voice.

"Shhh …" His breath tickles the shell of my ear. "No quick movements."

Huh?

After a moment, I realize that despite clearly insisting on separate mattresses, Hawk's body is curled up behind mine all over again. Oh no you don't! If you—

I freeze when a scratching noise catches my attention from

somewhere in the room. I strain to hear it again, but the sound of the rain drowns everything out. It's pitch black, and my heart starts beating wildly. If this is some trick he's playing to scare me, it's working. "What is it?"

"A cat," Hawk mumbles low in my ear. "Big one."

A cat? How big? I've never had to deal with anything bigger than an angry alley cat. I've heard that there are still some mountain lions back home, but I've never actually seen one. I have no idea what to expect in North Continent. I slip on Stella's mind-link disk from my pocket, but she must be out hunting so far away that I can't sense her.

"I'm going to turn on a light." Hawk whispers.

I hear another shuffle, and this time it's much closer and louder. I scoot backward, pressing myself completely against him. I hear the click of the flashlight and a tiny red glow lights up in front of me as the light tries to escape the inside of his hand. He opens it agonizingly slowly, and the shuffling noises in front of us grow more constant as the room fills with light.

A pair of eyes reflect back at me and I gasp despite my best effort not to. Hawk quietly shushes me again and the eyes back up. A very large cat indeed. Much bigger than any dog I've ever seen in my life, and I've seen some big dogs. The cat's face is long and thin with large eyes and a strange blend of spots and stripes. It's underbelly is spotted white, which I have an excellent view of from my position on the floor. The cat looks curious and it begins to inch forward again.

"Do. Not. Freak," Hawk whispers.

Suddenly Hawk's chest rumbles against my back and he actually growls. I don't know whether to laugh or scream, but blessedly manage to do neither. I glance down to see Hawk's claws slipping out of his fingertips, and the cat backs up a couple of steps. Then the cat growls back and a tremor runs down my spine.

Oh … this is going to be fun.

Hawk growls louder, bordering on some kind of roar—which is super weird coming from a human being. He lifts his body slightly, shifting almost onto his knees over me with his weight on his clawed front hand. The cat snuffs loudly into the dirt and backs farther up.

The light dancing across the side of the large animal displays a confusing pattern as it begins to pace back and forth. It's coat is covered in spots, outlined in black, that are so large they make the cat almost look like an old patchwork quilt with spotted legs. It's not nearly as large as some of the extinct cat species, like cheetahs or tigers, but it's big enough to kill either of us easily.

"You don't want any of this." Hawk speaks to the animal in a voice bordering on the growl he was using.

The cat seems to agree. It pads off into a darker corner of the room and sits down to watch us with those eerily reflective eyes. I can't help but glance back up at Hawk's eyes, half expecting to see the same, but they're his natural, crystal, non-reflective blue. After a couple of very tense minutes, Hawk settles back down against my back, but keeps his clawed hand visible in the light in front of me.

"What now?" I ask.

"That's up to him."

"We're just supposed to sleep with him there?"

"I don't want to leave a blood trail if I don't have to. He's not going to tangle with a predator as big as he is. He's just getting out of the rain."

"Did you just ... call yourself a predator?" I smile in the darkness.

"All humans are technically predators," Hawk says in a flat tone.

"Hawk, I was teasing." Crap. I shouldn't make him more self-conscious than he already is. "The growling thing seems pretty handy."

Hawk shrugs behind me. "It's a pretty common trait in ... Well, intimidation factor, you know? I guess it was a priority in the early programs."

I remember his words back at the brothel. *Don't say it out loud.* "Why can't you say it?"

"I can. I just ... don't like to. I've spent most of my life being trained to hide it."

That I understand completely. Hawk and I are more alike than I thought. We've both had to hide from the world what we really are—all because of our genetics. Mine relate to weaknesses and his to strengths. I find myself once again overwhelmed with curiosity—which is helpful when trying not to sleep in a room with a large carnivore.

"Do you guys have disadvantages too?" I ask.

"Oh yeah."

The big animal yawns with a long, curly tongue.

"The biggest problem is the inability to blend in. Some of us wear contacts to hide different eyes. Cobra always had to wear sleeves—which didn't really help when she hissed at you. Wolf's got it bad. Nice guy with huge canine teeth and claws that don't retract. I hear I'm the best blend they've ever seen. All my traits are hidden, but I've got more tactical traits than almost anybody. I guess I got lucky—if I had to be what I am."

"How many of you are there?"

"More than most people think. Genetics are persistent once they take, I guess."

"Does it hurt?" I ask, touching his hand.

"The claws? Yeah, but I'm used to it. I don't use them much or they would eventually stop bleeding. The doc said if I sharpened them more they wouldn't itch so much, but that just … it's weird."

"Do you get along with any of the others?" I'm afraid of bringing Cobra to mind again, but I could very well encounter these people.

"Yeah, most of us get along fine. It's the weird common struggle we have I guess. We serve while the rest of the world gets to live their lives in comfort."

"But what is your life like?"

Hawk is quiet for a long time. "It's fine. I work. I help people."

"You pretend to be a monster, and the people you help don't even remember you." A deep sadness blooms in my heart at the thought.

"That's my role. Someone has to do it, and who better than me? It doesn't matter if they can't remember me. They're living better lives and they're not haunted by what came before—what they've seen, what they've been forced to do. I'm very good at scaring the shit out of people when I need to, and I've been lying since birth. It works."

It sounds completely miserable.

It's stupid to want him to acknowledge that it's miserable, though, even if it's true. I can see that alternate future now. Me, shuffling down the street after server duty—heading home. Hawk standing in the shadows—watching to see if my new life is going smoothly, disappearing before I even know he's there. I'm suddenly sure that was his original intention. "If they hadn't tried to kill me at the hospital, would you have come and checked on me too?"

The big cat licks its face, and shifts around to get more comfortable.

Hawk stays quiet for a long time. "Probably ... Definitely."

"Would you have introduced yourself?"

"I'm not supposed to."

"But would you have?"

"Yes," he says with a heavy sigh.

"If that ever happens, Hawk ..." I swallow around the lump in my throat. "I want to remember you."

"That's not the kind of thing they allow, Babe. I couldn't just give you back your memory once they took it. It's ... kind of a one-way deal. You wouldn't believe me anyway."

"I might if you showed me these." I pat his fingers gently. Surely, that would trigger some kind of memory.

"Yeah right," he replies with a bitter laugh. "You'd run away screaming and they'd have to reset you again."

"I didn't run away screaming the first time."

"No, but you didn't have much choice. Trust me. Everybody runs."

I roll over to face him and his expression morphs into mild surprise. Only when I realize he's not taking his eyes off the big cat, do I register that I've turned my back on it.

The discovery disturbs me. I shouldn't feel safer now, lying a couple dozen feet from a large carnivore, than I did when I went to sleep alone. But I do. This is ridiculous! "Do you do this to all the people that you abduct?"

"Defend them from leopards?" he chuckles. "Not usually. No."

"That's not what I meant."

"Babe, you lost me."

"This." I motion between us. "This safety thing. Do you do that on purpose? Make it so people can't feel safe without you?"

Hawk actually looks away from the cat for a moment and into my eyes, with his eyebrows scrunching together. "Safe?"

"Don't play dumb with me. I'm not buying it." He looks genuinely confused, but I'm frustrated by how easily I've shifted into this weird reality where I trust the man who literally kidnapped me from my own bedroom. "You … you super contain the environment. You get me everything I need. You put yourself between me and the current, unending death threats. You—"

"Babe …" he whispers, with his gaze back up. I hear more shuffling behind me. "You're making the big guy over there nervous."

I go very still and try to reign in my anxiety, dropping my gaze to stare at Hawk's t-shirt.

"For the record," Hawk says after a few moments, "taking care of you is my job. And yeah, I guess some people get that way … but most of them are scared shitless long before I get to them. I don't stay in contact with them this long either, so I guess I've never really thought about it."

"How long are you normally with them?"

"Two, three days tops. Then they don't remember me. They move on. So do I."

But the gentleness isn't his job. That's all Hawk. Yes, he's pushy. Yes, he's demanding and he gets angry with me. When it comes down to it, though, he's always giving me more space and more power than he really has to. The more paranoid part of me wants to say it's just another way to manipulate me, but maybe that's better than outright force. I don't know anymore.

"So where do you go home to?" I change topics before I give myself a headache. "Between jobs I mean."

"Nowhere."

"You don't have an assigned living space?"

"I can always sleep at one of the OTS barracks if I need to. But why bother? They're not even as nice as the cheap hotels and I wouldn't know anyone there. I just make more jobs for myself in the down times."

"They let you do that?"

"Sure."

"What kind of jobs do you make up?" Surely some of the tech deals fit in there.

"Mostly these." He smiles down at me briefly. "I occasionally get assignments for smuggling people out from under the slavers, but that's only when they have useful intel that we need. All the others I pick out on my own."

In the kinds of places he works in, he must meet hundreds of people being bought and sold like cattle. "How do you pick?"

"I aim for the weakest. The ones that aren't going to make it. It works with the whole scary predator persona anyway. There has to be a reasonable way for me to excuse it, though, which is sometimes a challenge."

"Women only?" I can't help but think of the first young man I was trapped in the cell with.

"No." Hawk shakes his head. "I'm not into guys personally, but I can fake it when I have to. I'm not gonna let some kid's gender decide whether or not I can help him. They're more likely to fight me, though, because they don't know that I'm not the huge, scary dude I'm acting like. My size scares them."

"What about the tech deals?"

"Most of those are authorized trades. I'm one of the easiest ways for the Community to offload their old equipment without taking a total loss on it. I prefer to deal medical tech because everyone needs it and it's better for everyone to have access to it. It's win-win, you know?"

"Like José and the surgical bot."

"Exactly," His smile lights up his whole face in the dim light.

The cat makes a big movement behind us and I stiffen with my nose against Hawk's chest. He lies eerily still for a moment, and I hear the soft padding of the cat's feet get farther and farther away.

"Were we boring him?" I whisper.

"Maybe." Hawk chuckles. "But he's probably going out to hunt now that the rain has stopped. They're nocturnal you know."

"Oh …"

I roll back over so that I'm no longer pressed up against Hawk's front, and he backs up to roll onto his own mattress again. I squeeze my eyes tightly shut as I realize I want him to hold me as I fall back asleep.

Stupid!

"Do you think he'll come back?" I ask.

"I doubt it." Hawk yawns. "But I'm a light sleeper so I'll notice if he does. Try to get some sleep. We've got a long walk tomorrow."

Sleep. Yeah. Right.

13

HAWK

I spend half an hour sorting the shit we need from our bags, tossing what we don't, and repacking a single pack to haul out of here. I can't believe she's still lugging around this robotic brick. It's noisy, leaves a trail a mile wide, and is ten times as heavy as it should be. I would've made her ditch it back at the brothel, but didn't want to leave any extra clues for whoever comes looking for us next.

Now I get to disturb my sleepy armadillo lizard, and see just how prickly she's going to be this morning. She looks adorable with her face smashed into her travel pillow and her hair mussed up. I lean down next to her, brushing a few strands of dyed hair out of her face and enjoying the smooth texture of her cheek beneath my palm. Drawing her scent deep into my lungs, I let it wrap around my senses like a caress.

She confused the shit out of me last night. One minute she was pushing me away with both hands, and the next she's all soft and inviting. I wish she would have stayed there. I don't understand why she was so mad about feeling safe.

There's something familiar about that …

Hawking's ghost!

I back away from her with my heart in my throat. *"Inability to feel safe or secure without the presence of the object of obsession."* It's one of the more severe symptoms of Obsessive Attachment Syndrome. OAS used to be prevalent in society back in the Old World. It was left undiagnosed and untreated, leading to mental and emotional distress and even violence in the population. It's the very reason the Community is so careful to prevent the development of long-term relationships and interdependence among citizens.

By all that is lawful, is Gina starting to develop an attachment to me? Is it my fault? Maybe she's right. Maybe it's something I'm doing … Hack! It's probably because we've been stuck together so long with everything so intense.

Okay, quick self-check.

Standing up, I close my eyes and bring up the list of other symptoms from my archive. *"Placing the needs and desires of the object of obsession above the Community of citizens and self."* Well … that's not really a fair comparison. Is it? It's pretty much my job. I guess the lines could get blurry if I can't find someone willing to help me correct her situation, but they probably didn't build the list of symptoms with these circumstances in mind.

"Residing with the object of obsession." We don't have much other option there, but that's temporary.

"Need to touch or hold the object of obsession in a way that is not exclusive to sexual intercourse." Sir Issac Newton, I was just doing that! Tightness builds in my chest as I realize she's not the only one with a problem.

"Worry or concern over the object of obsession's opinions and with pleasing them." I want her to know what I am without pulling away from me so bad that it aches in my gut.

"Emotional vulnerability." I sit down on the floor for a moment, feeling all the blood drain from my face. I've told this woman more truths about me than I could ever defend.

I never imagined something this serious could develop so fast. And in both of us? What the hack am I supposed to do about it? I put my head in my hands for a moment.

Stop freaking out and think!

What now? I can't change our living situation until she's safe. I can't take either of us to a doctor for treatment. Besides, the first part of treatment would be to separate us. I could try to avoid touching her any more or … wrapping myself up in that sexy scent all the time.

Hack! I grit my teeth against the instant frustration. I want to reject the idea automatically, but is that just the illness talking? It's unbelievably dangerous for a chimera to develop something like this. We can do so much more damage when violent than a human could.

I glance up at her sleeping face. She's depending on me to take care of her, and I haven't been paying attention. I've only been focused on the physical dangers. Once I get her stashed in the cave and head to the meet … maybe the separation will do us both some good.

But I'm no doctor. If we've already got symptoms, they say that handling things wrong could make everything worse. I'll try to see how we're both doing after the exchange. If we have any of the more severe symptoms, we'll have to wait to deal with it until a professional can step in.

Now I try to shake off the fear. I think about how to wake her up, and a grin forces its way through. Grabbing her portable mess kit, I drop it onto the asphalt with a deafening crash. Instead of jumping out of her skin and swearing at me, like any normal person would, Gina just groans and shifts around on her make-shift mattress.

"Gina, you need to wake up." I lean down to shake her shoulder. It's her own fault I have to touch her so much!

"Go away," she whines. "I don't wanna run away today."

The thought makes me laugh. Take the day off? If only. "Come on, Babe." I grab her gently under her arms and sit her upright. "We need to move. It's almost daylight."

"What?" she asks with an incredible pout to her face and her eyes still unopened. Her words are completely garbled. "Almost?"

"I know you're tired." I push her hair back from her face. "But we've got to hurry if I'm going to make it on time."

"One more hour," she pleads, trying to roll back away from me.

For the love of science! Maybe I can get her mad enough to

wake up. "Gina, I swear, if you go back to sleep, you can forget me staying on my mattress ever again." Yeah, right.

"Okay," she mumbles with a sigh. "Sleep."

What?

She rolls back toward me, grabs my arms, and pulls me off balance. I land in a heap, half-on and half-off of her mattress. She throws an arm and leg over me and squeezes like I'm some kind of big body pillow, burrowing her face against my chest.

Hawking's ghost! Well that didn't work. She's pressed up against me even warmer and softer than last night. A tremor of pleasure runs through me but I reject the temptation to kiss her senseless for it. She'd eventually freak over what I am. Thinking of it pisses me off all over again.

What did she say? She felt safe? I guess I need to make her feel unsafe because staying here any longer is plain stupid.

I wrestle my way out of her full body hug, completely frustrated that now I'm getting what I wanted. "Well I guess you can stay here," I say loudly, standing up and tossing the bag over my shoulder. "I've got to go. I had a better place in mind for you, but the leopard probably won't be back." I walk toward the exit, wondering how loudly I'll have to slam it to get her real attention.

"What?" I hear her struggling to sit up.

"I told you. I have to go. We need that—"

"You can't leave me here!" I turn back as she jumps up onto her feet. She looks like she's going to run after me, but then her eyes lose their focus and she starts to fall.

"Son of a bitch!" I rush back as her knees and hips strike the asphalt—barely getting an arm beneath her head before it hits. "Gina!" She's totally limp. Her eyes are unfocused, as if she's unconscious with her eyes still open. "Gina, what happened? What's wrong?"

After a moment she shakes her head and mumbles a very soft, "Sorry."

Thinking back, I've seen her do something like this a dozen times. She'll go from sitting or kneeling to standing, and all of a sudden she'll pause with a hand out to steady herself.

"Are you back with me now? Babe, what's happening? Is this

like a seizure or something?"

"No." She rolls away from me, up onto her hands and knees.

"You know, if you don't fess up pretty soon, you could get us both killed."

She transitions to a kneeling position and pauses again, breathing deeply. "It's not going to kill you."

"Oh yeah? What was it you said about me? Huh? If I do something to scare the shit out of you … Well you're scaring the shit out of me. I can't keep you safe if I don't know what's going on. You could have gotten a concussion!"

"I just stood up too fast." She stands to her feet and looks woozy again.

I grip her shoulder to steady her. "What does that mean?"

"It's my blood pressure." She yawns, holding a hand against her face like it hurts. "Okay? It just doesn't adjust well, so I faint a lot."

Blood pressure … bruising … what the hack? Then I remember something else weird that I've resisted asking. "Gina, why are there so many braces in your bag?" Her bag is full of them—a brace for just about every joint in the human body. Some I didn't even recognize. I'd brushed it off as too much prep, but she must need them.

Her eyes fly wide open for the first time. "You went through my bag again!"

"I can't keep carrying the amount of shit we have," I say. "I've got the essentials in just one now. No point in lugging a bunch of tech around when I have warehouses full of shit to trade. Your bag weighs a ton, even when it's empty, and it makes you stupid easy to track."

"What am I supposed to do if you don't come back?" She points to the duffel. "I can't carry that thing!"

"Just reduce the weight down until you can. Or lose it if you have to. You've got lots of pockets."

She looks stunned for a moment. "That's it. Forget the meet. You're not going." She walks back to her bag. "Just leave. Go home. Or go … to the barracks. Wherever it is that you go."

"And what the hack do you plan to do?"

"Head out on my own." She kneels down and starts shoving

the mess kit into the mechanical nightmare. "Like I should have done a long time ago."

"Oh yeah, because that worked out great."

"It doesn't matter."

"Why?" I kneel down beside her and grab her arm before I realize I've grabbed her bruise. She winces and shakes me off before I can let go.

"Because I'm not going to make it anyway!" She shoves a hand against her mouth and squeezes her eyes shut as tears spill down her cheeks. When she speaks again, there's a trace of a sob in her voice. "Just go. You're wasting your time."

Well shit. "Gina, I'm not gonna leave you."

"You should!"

"Why are you making such a big deal out of this?" She's making no hacking sense.

"Because you're going to leave me in the middle of the God-forsaken jungle, and walk. Knowingly. Into a trap," she bites back while obviously struggling not to cry. "Then I'll be alone. Without what I need to make it. You may as well just leave me here with the … the …"

"Leopard," I say because she's searching for the word with her hands.

"Whatever."

"Babe, we've made so much noise, he's long gone. You need to calm down. I know you're scared, but you need to trust me."

"I have been trusting you."

"No. You did what you had to, to survive. I get that. I'm not criticizing you. Trusting me is different. Trusting me is telling me what's wrong with you, so I know how to take care of you."

"Like you would have told me you were a chimera?"

I flinch at hearing the word from her lips and the level of disgust she obviously associates with it. It would've hurt less if she'd stabbed me.

"You know what …" I stand and gather up her things before she can, heading out the door with them. "Hack it. We don't have time to waste arguing. We'll stash your shit along the trail where you can find it if I don't come back, but now, we're moving."

14

GINA

I lie on my side, gritting my teeth against the pain running through me. When Hawk woke me up this morning, I was so miserable from exhaustion and fibromyalgia that I could barely tolerate it. I must have gotten only four hours of sleep because of that stupid cat! I managed to push through to make it to this cave, but toward the end, I was near collapsing. Hawk was concerned, but he didn't ask again. I'm slowly but surely facing the reality that I can't do this, as my tears drip onto the dirt.

If I could stay far enough ahead, take breaks for multiple days like I really need to recover, it might be possible. As it is, I'm never getting enough rest, and I'm not going to make it. Hawk is risking his life—trying to save me from drowning without knowing I have lead weights strapped to my feet.

I wish we hadn't gotten in yet another fight this morning. I can't handle the slightest bit of additional stress when I get this bad. I remember that about my mother. When she would get instantly and unreasonably angry or upset, we knew her pain was high without her telling us.

And even though we're not linked right now, I'm worried about Stella. I don't understand it, but her agitation seems to be increasing with my pain. I'm not sure how to protect her from it as we keep moving. Until I get a lot better, I'll have to use our mind-link sparingly, if at all. Thank the Lord, she can feed herself without my assistance, or she'd go hungry tonight.

The electrical nerve pain running up and down my legs is slicing, and by this point, I've almost completely lost the ability to use them. They are heavy and stiff, and with concentrated effort I can only manage to move them inches at a time. Every muscle in my body aches and the exhaustion is overwhelming. I'm desperate for something to help the pain, but Hawk hid my whiskey from me.

He probably thinks I'm an alcoholic or something—which is infuriating. It's my own fault for not explaining, but he has too many pieces of my puzzle already. If he were to include them in some report eventually, they wouldn't need my DNA to see what's wrong with me. They'd figure it out.

I wish I could be sure whether to trust him. He's had every chance to disappoint me but he hasn't done so—well, not since the whole abduction thing. I wonder if that's why he's helping me. Does he feel guilty that he turned me over to people who were going to kill me? If it's guilt, I shouldn't trust it.

We walked for at least four torturous hours this morning before he stashed me and Stella in this cave. I know where my abandoned supplies are and, if I can rest long enough and recover, I should be able to get back to my pack if I have to.

If Hawk never comes back. He told me to wait for him for two days. After that, I'm supposed to carefully make my way back to my things with only the essentials I have left in my pockets.

It gets hard to breathe every time I think of what he's trying to do. He's knowingly walking into a trap and hoping to outmaneuver them. But he doesn't even know who's setting it.

Once he'd been gone for at least an hour, I finally let the misery have me. I had a good long cry right here on the cave's dry dirt floor. Now I have a headache and can't stop the tears from coming. At least they have slowed.

I glance at my watch for the fifth time in the last hour. I wish I could just go back to sleep, but I hurt too bad. I wonder how long it will be like this before I'm incapable of holding my eyes open anymore. It's been several hours already.

Predator!

The sensation of being watched washes over me and Stella screeches from some dark corner. Glancing back outside, my breath stills in my lungs. The mouth of this tiny cave is narrow— only a few feet tall and a couple of feet wide. The brush outside hides the entrance very well, but it also makes it impossible to see very far. When I looked into the brush, I caught a glimpse of a pair of eyes. It was brief, but I definitely saw it.

Oh my God! Did the leopard follow us all the way here?

If it did, I'm screwed. I can barely move. I push myself up onto my arms and drag my lower body backward as far as I can. I find a fist-sized rock, and I hurl it toward the entrance with as much force as I can manage. It makes a dull thump when it lands and I hear a strange growl.

Jesus help me!

"Go away!" I scream at the animal, hoping to scare it off. "Get out of here!"

A face emerges from the brush and I gasp. Oh God. It's that face! The one I saw after I'd jacked in, growling at me with yellow eyes and menacing teeth. His upper canines are elongated well past his lower lip and his mouth is a broad scowl. He has short-cropped black hair and light, chestnut-brown skin with different shades across it in patches. As he raises up onto his knees, I can see he's wearing camouflage combat gear, with his skin only enhancing the effect.

It's all over. Another chimera assassin has found me.

I grab the enormous knife Hawk left beside me and hold it up defensively, but my hands are weak and shaking. I try to shuffle back away from him as far as I can, but my legs are next to useless with this much pain running through them. They're sluggish and stiff. Even if I could move them right, he's blocking my exit.

His reflective eyes bounce back the light from Hawk's small flashlight. They're yellow-green, and almost entirely filled with color instead of having a distinctive white area—deep set over extremely high cheekbones and a square jaw. He has a high, wide forehead and sharp, angular features. His empty hands have wicked-looking claws on them instead of fingernails, and his eyes narrow as we analyze each other.

Wait, I wonder … "Are you … Are you, Wolf?"

His eyes widen in obvious surprise, but he doesn't answer me.

"Hawk … he …" I struggle with what to say. "He s-said you were nice." Well, he said he was a great guy. I struggle to remember.

The man smiles and, despite the teeth, it transforms his entire face into something much less frightening. "He did, huh?" the man asks. "What else he tell you?"

"Is that who you really are?"

"Yeah, that's me. What gave me away?"

"He said it was harder for you to … blend in."

"Oh, I blend jus' fine," he laughs, and the sound is deep and rich. "I jus' don' blend in with people."

"How long have you been out there?"

"A while," he shrugs. "Once I caught Hawk's scent, it was pretty easy to follow back. He shouldn'a left you here."

My heart skips a beat. "Are you going to kill me?"

"Depends on you," Wolf says, with the smile falling from his face. "What's wrong with your legs?"

"I didn't tell Hawk," I say, dodging his question. "He doesn't know."

"O … kay …" Wolf chuckles. "What does that mean?"

"It means I don't want to say." I try to squish myself just a little smaller in the back of the cave. "They … they just hurt."

"Is that why you been cryin'?" He scrutinizes my face again.

"Yes."

"Well, if you come along real quiet," he says, crouching down and coming slightly farther into the cave, "I can maybe help you with that."

"Where are you taking me?"

"Funny thing. We're gonna go see Hawk. His old man suspected he would leave you behind. Wants to see what all the fuss is about."

"His … dad?" I try to imagine what Hawk's father would be like. "Who is he?"

"He's an elite. Not a nice guy, but few elites are."

"How did he know where we were?"

Wolf doesn't answer me, and he eyes the knife in my hand again. I drop my arm slowly, but keep the knife held tight. A pain spikes through my legs and I squeeze my eyes shut for a moment before I take a couple of deep breaths.

"That shit looks pretty bad," Wolf says. "An infection?"

"No." Embarrassingly, I whimper. "Hawk took my moonshine."

"Ah, yeah, he hates that shit," Wolf says with a roll of his eyes. "I think it's great."

"Do you have any?" I'd be stupid to take anything he offers, but I'm beyond caring.

"Sorry. Got painkillers though."

"Won't do me any good unless it's a nerve-deadener."

"No shit?" Wolf looks down at my legs again. "Ahhh ... that why they're not workin' right?"

Now it's my turn not to answer.

"Man." Wolf spits off in the corner of the room. "He's got his hands full with you."

"Do you rescue people too?" I feel brave enough to ask, closing my eyes briefly against another wave of pain.

"Nah." Wolf glances away and a strange sadness enters his eyes. "Nah, I just kill 'em. Rescuin' is kinda Hawk's niche. I can't get away with that shit."

"You could ... rescue me," I suggest with a forced smile. "I wouldn't mind."

"Not this time." He shakes his head and sighs. "But if you play nice, I won' have to kill you. That would be kinda nice."

There is no way to get away from him. Not now. "Do we have to walk?" I ask, glancing pointedly at my legs.

"Nope," he says with another grin. "I can carry you to the drone. Had one fly in and wait a ways back. Only way I can get you back to Hawk in time."

"How long will it take to get there?"

Wolf raises his eyebrows. "About an hour."

An hour ... the pain will be blinding in an hour, and will probably spread. High stress makes the pain worse the longer I'm exposed. The only way to slow it down or stop it is to sleep—long and deep. If I get on that drone, I'm going to panic. I can already feel the tension building in my stomach. If I'm going to die anyway ...

"Do you have something to make me sleep?"

"What?" Wolf looks at me like I've lost my mind.

"You know ... Hawk had a sedative he used when he kidnapped me. It would be nice to get a nap on the way there."

"Uh ... sure." Wolf laughs. "Anythin' else I can do for ya?"

"Yeah ..." How do I say this? "Just. If ... if they're going to wipe my memory, can you kill me instead? Please? But ... if they're going to kill me … I guess I'd like to not wake up first."

"Girl, you crazy." Wolf pulls out a med injector with a smile.

15

HAWK

Looking down over the meeting site, Amar has picked a good spot for a trap. The old warehouse would look safe to a newbie but the exits are bad or covered by two snipers on neighboring buildings. I've managed to elude detection so far, but I'm going to have to fight my way out if I go in.

I crawl backward on my belly until I reach the edge of the roof, and then pick my way down the series of ancient, rusting fire escapes to the ground.

Shit! I missed a cam. They already know I'm here.

I have the layout information I need; so, I walk boldly through the side door into a huge empty room. Amar is standing in the middle beneath the bright overhead lights. Someone's standing behind him in a hooded black suit coat. The two men jump in surprise as I enter.

Okay … so you weren't watching for me? It's so stupid I can hardly believe it. Maybe they took the cams down instead of using them?

Amar composes himself quickly. I resist the instinct to stiffen my spine when I realize I can't get a clear scent on the stranger behind him. If he's using a scent blocker, he knows what I am.

"Is this your seller?" I ask Amar, gesturing to the stranger.

"Indeed I am." The voice makes me snarl before thinking it through. "I'm glad I can still surprise you, son."

"What the hack are you doing here?" I start backing toward the door.

"Don't run." My biological father, Doctor Alexander Reginald Pennington the asshat, speaks with the typical knife in his tone. "I needed to talk with you, and this was the best way to make that happen. You wouldn't have come willingly."

"This has nothing to do with you."

Amar abruptly leaves the room as Alex motions to a mind sweeper in the far corner. It's not packed in crates. It's set up for use on the bare concrete floor, with a large chair and multiple viewing monitors.

I want to run, but I know this man better than that. There is no doubt in my mind that he's brought at least two chimeras with him. He's keeping them hidden from detection, but they're here. They're not going to let me leave easily.

"It has everything to do with me, you idiotic fool!" Alex spits back with a sneer. "You're risking everything. My life's work! For a silly little girl. Just what do you think you're going to do with her that you haven't already done?"

"They have no right to kill her. She had no control over the information that was put into her head."

"I see." His calculating look tells me he knows more than he's letting on.

Does he suspect I have OAS? Probably not. "You already know what's in her head. Don't you?"

"I don't, but that's irrelevant. I'm here to protect my investment."

Asshole. That's all I've ever been to him. An investment. Unlike other rational members of the Community, my father revels in the fact that I had the misfortune to be born a chimera. I'm amazed they let him breed again after Cobra. By the time I was born, he was already the head of the Chimera Research Unit at only 18 years old.

"Since we're here over the issue, however …" He waves his hand toward the back of the room. "Why don't we just take a look and see what she's carrying around for ourselves, shall we?"

A door in the back of the room creaks open and I feel a lead weight slide down the center of my chest as Wolf walks in with Gina. Her arms hang limp like a doll. He must have dosed her with something.

Son of a bitch!

If I had known my father would pull something like this, or that there would be another chimera on her heels this fast, I never would have left her alone. She's too easy to track.

"Wolf." I nod as he walks over with Gina's head resting on his chest. Wolf has been one of the closest people to me since we were kids, but I can't quite keep the snarl out of my voice when I ask, "What did you do to her?"

Wolf raises an eyebrow and looks back down at Gina's sleeping face briefly. Then he looks back into my eyes and cocks his head as if he's curious.

What is that about?

"For the law's sake, Wolf." Alex sighs from the sidelines. "Was she that much trouble?"

"She was in pain," Wolf replies directly to me, and I feel my shoulders tense in a flash of shame. "She wouldn't say why, but your crazy-ass woman asked me to put her to sleep. Said you took her booze man. Bad move."

My woman? Come on, Wolf. She's not my slave.

"Pain?" Alex mumbles, narrowing his eyes at them. "Interesting … what were her symptoms?"

Wolf looks back at me as if he's trying to ask my permission, but I'm just as curious. I shrug.

"Nerve pain," Wolf says. "She said regular meds are no good. Her legs weren't workin' too great either." He looks me pointedly in the eyes and I'm surprised to see accusation in them. "She couldn't have run from me if she tried. I'm not even sure she could have walked to the drone, so I didn't make her. Just put her to sleep like she asked."

Universe, the thought makes me nauseous.

"Nerve pain …" Before I realize what he's doing, Alex sticks her in the arm with a needle and Gina flinches.

"She doesn't want—" I move to stop him, but Mantis steps out of the shadows immediately on the opposite side of the large warehouse floor. Shit.

Alex takes the sample of Gina's blood and applies it to a small hand-held diagnostic unit. She starts to wake up as he walks over to a wheeled chair beside the mind sweeper to read through the information.

Mantis, or Kim Jing, has brown contacts to hide his strange

insect-like eyes. He's only about five foot six, but he's a nightmare in hand-to-hand combat. His nearly translucently pale skin contrasts dramatically with his short black hair, but has the ability to shift its color to camouflage into his surroundings. With Mantis and Wolf both here, it's obvious that Alex put together a team of the exact people I don't want to hurt.

"I don't wanna …" Gina whimpers with that familiar slur, pressing her face into Wolf's throat. "Five more minutes …"

Wolf stiffens even more than I do as his eyes dart back to me, but I just roll my eyes. "I don't think you want another dose of that stuff girl," he says.

Gina jerks awake so suddenly and violently, Wolf has to correct his footing to keep a hold on her. She looks up at his face and then wildly around the room.

"Gina," I say in a much calmer tone than I feel.

She makes eye contact immediately and then her face falls into a pout. "Sorry," she whispers with a slight blush to her cheeks.

You're apologizing for being caught by a chimera? You may as well apologize for breathing. "No, I'm sorry."

"Well, it's nice to finally meet you, Regina." Alex walks up with a wave of charm that makes me shudder. I'll never understand how he can transform his features from indifferent to caring with so little effort. "I hope you didn't let yourself get hurt before we picked you up for the meeting." His lower lip sticks out a bit too far.

"I'm fine." Gina blinks the sleep from her eyes. "Who are you?"

"My name is Doctor Alexander Cecil Reginald Pennington. I am this gentleman's father," he says with a chilling smile as he motions toward me. The confession makes me want to squirm. "More importantly, I am one of the heads of the Chimera Research Unit for the Community."

"So … you're here for Hawk?"

Alex raises an eyebrow at me because I've given her my standard alias. Mantis does too, but Wolf seems unsurprised. It's against regulation.

"Well, well." Alex stands back up and straightens the lapels of his expensive body armor suit. "It sounds like you're very well informed."

"Cobra said it," Gina hurries to say. "Well, actually she said his real name too, and she wasn't really talking to me. I'm guessing she wasn't supposed to?"

"Where is your sister?" Alex turns his full gaze on me for a moment, ignoring Gina's question.

"She's dead." I hold back all emotion or it will break me. I pull out the speed dial disk I pre-programmed with a map and toss it to Alex. "Her body is in the storage tank shown on this. Make sure she's recycled properly."

Wolf and Mantis look stunned.

"Dead!" Alex roars. "You couldn't disable her without killing her? Hawk, I expect more from you!"

"She gave me no choice!" I roar back, losing my grip on my anger. "Maybe she should have been taught to value life! Then she might've valued her own!"

"Is that what happened to your face?" Wolf asks.

I shrug.

"Such a waste!" Alex turns his back on us, slamming down his diagnostic unit and balling his fists. "You see why I am here now, don't you? The imbeciles that run the Community can't even see that they're throwing away their most valuable resources. If you don't stop this foolishness, they're going to eliminate you! I cannot accept that!" He breathes deeply, working his hands back open, then turns back with a scowl and looks down at his diagnostic unit. "An incredible waste. However, there's no use dwelling on it. Why don't we see what's wrong with Regina, shall we?"

I hate and envy how he can dismiss Takisha's death so easily. The shame is like an acid, eating through my guts.

"What are you doing?" Gina turns toward him in Wolf's arms. "Don't! Please!"

What does her health have to do with anything? He's reading her genetic code …

"I thought this was about what's in her head."

"Of course it is," Alex scoffs, "but you've obviously taken a keen interest in the woman, and I'd like to know what I'm dealing with."

"Oh, God." Tears stream down Gina's face. She twists and nearly escapes Wolf's grip on her, but she ends up standing awkwardly on legs that look like they're not going to hold her up very long. "Did you take a sample? Don't! Please! Don't put it on the GRID!" Wolf's grip around her abdomen is most of what's holding her upright.

"Wolf, don't," I say quietly. "She's bruised all to shit on her stomach man, please."

He slowly lets go, but Gina can't stand on her own. I move toward her, but Mantis takes another step forward—warning me without words. Wolf lets her slide awkwardly to the floor. She's completely focused on Alex.

She turns to me with eyes full of tears and a sob in her voice. "Stop him. Please!"

It kills me, but I can't get past these guys without risking hurting her in the fight. "Gina, what are you so afraid of?" My stomach is in knots.

"Why don't you tell him, my dear." Alex glances down at her, eyes narrowed with disdain. "Since you so obviously know your deficiency."

Deficiency? Gina reacts like he's slapped her with his words, and she crumples to the floor in a fetal position. "They'll put me in an institution."

Suddenly, it clicks, and I'm amazed it took me this long. The easy exhaustion. The unbelievable bruising without any deeper tissue damage. Her rib dislocation. Nothing about her health has made sense since I first picked her up at her burrow. I never even considered that it could be something genetic. I try to calm myself with the thought that if it's genetic, it may not be something Old World like cancer. "What's wrong with you?" I ask for what feels like the millionth time.

Gina lies there and cries with her head against her knees. The sound makes me crazy. Even now, she can't say it out loud.

I can understand that, but I hate it.

"She has a genetic connective tissue disorder," Alex says without emotion. "It's called Ehlers-Danlos Syndrome. It was once classified in various subtypes, but eventually became recognized as a spectrum disorder due to the large number of potentially affected genes. It's a very complex condition with wide disparity in how it presents in each individual. It means she's completely unsuitable for offspring."

"What?" Gina and I choke out simultaneously.

Wolf looks away from both of us for a moment, and Mantis looks like he would blush if he could.

"For breeding," Alex says with a sigh. "She's completely useless. You're wasting your time and you need to get rid of her before the Community has any more excuse to penalize you."

"I'm not trying to get her pregnant, you moron!"

16

GINA

I must be dreaming … I suddenly wonder if I am really still asleep on the drone as I wipe my tears on my shirt sleeve. But why the heck would I dream this up?

"Good," Dr. Pennington nods, steamrolling right ahead. "She's genetically inferior to even a basic human—much less someone with your specialized DNA." He's talking as if I'm not even here.

He's not quite as tall as Hawk, but it's hard to tell from the floor. He has paler skin, brown eyes, and deep brown curls kept short and styled. There is a dignified hint of gray in his short beard and at his temples. He carries himself like an Old World aristocrat, and he's undeniably handsome for a man of his age—although he seems a little young to be Hawk's father.

The resemblance is strong. If he's Hawk's father, he's obviously who Hawk's high cheekbones and long nose came from. Dr. Pennington has the same athletic build as Hawk, but it hasn't been maintained with the discipline of a soldier. As Community members, I'm surprised they even know each other.

"Can you imagine the set-back her genome would be in the progress of your own?" Dr. Pennington continues, pointing to me.

"I understand the attractive nature of her slightly superior intelligence, but for the law's sake, Hawk! If anyone had actually looked at this mess before she was born, they would have aborted her."

I feel smaller and smaller with every word that comes out of his mouth. My genes are a mess. My kids will be likely to inherit that mess … But my mother was the same way. Was it wrong for her to want me? Yeah, I'm in pain a lot, but I'm alive, and mostly I like being alive.

"Would you just shut up!" Hawk rails back at him. "You're insane! Why would you even be looking at that? I'm a chimera, Alex. In case you've forgotten, I couldn't take part in a reproduction permit if I tried!"

Holy crap! He said it out loud.

"You don't need a permit, Hector," Dr. Pennington—or I guess, Alex—scoffs. "I have all the authorization I need to partner each of you in pairings that will ensure the best genes are passed along to the next generation of our people."

Our people … I struggle to sit up through the nerve pain that traces around my limbs and hips at the movement, and take a closer look at Alex. He doesn't have any obvious physical traits, but then again, Hawk doesn't either. He obviously considers himself a chimera. I guess two of his children are.

"What are you talking about?" Hawk backs up a step.

"Do you actually think your genome is an accident?" Alex laughs, and it's an almost cruel sound—matching his expression perfectly. "Grow up, boy. I had to match my own superior genetics against hundreds of females to get a chance at the combination you present. I thought Takisha had been a success, but she had nowhere near your stealth. You can walk freely among the population, with no one the wiser."

"Are you saying …" Hawk growls, and I'm suddenly glad I already knew he could do that, "that you got my mother pregnant to make me like this on purpose?"

"Of course I did. Do you think you can accomplish such a sophisticated design in a lab? Useless! Breeding programs have been the only successful technique to improve chimera genetics from the beginning. They used labs to splice the genomes initially, but that's why the original chimeras were such general failures. You need the discrimination and determination of the human reproductive system in the mix."

"Are you listening to this?" Hawk turns back to Wolf.

"Don't look at me man," Wolf shrugs. "I just follow orders. Same as you. Well ... same as before."

"And what about you?" Hawk spins toward the guy with the pale, creepy skin.

Pale-guy doesn't answer. He stares at his shoes instead.

"Oh, Mantis is already in the program, son," Alex says with a smirk. "So far, the results look promising; although we'll have to see how the child does in its first few months of life."

"Look, I'm leaving." Hawk turns back toward me. "I can't take any more of this bullshit."

Wolf steps in front of me, and pale-skin-guy moves to his side when Hawk hesitates. They're not going to let him get to me.

Jesus, what should I do? I try to think of a way to get around them, but I'm too slow.

"Look, son," Alex starts again.

"Don't hacking call me that!"

"I get it. She's very pretty." Alex walks over, grabs my unbruised arm, and drags me to my feet. "I'd say you can keep her as a toy for your bed, but the entire world is downright obsessed with killing her."

You asshole! I glare at him but he can't be bothered to look me in the face.

"You're sick." Hawk swallows hard.

"Every true genius is eventually accused of such." Alex gets a glassy eyed look. "Aside from her intelligence scores, her genes are completely unsuitable. Why I'd bet her telomeres aren't even ..." His eyebrows knit together, his mouth turns down into a frown, and he lets go of me. I crumple to the floor and hiss when pain shoots through my wrist as I try to catch myself.

"Don't drop her!" Hawk is using full-blown Darius rage voice, with a little growling thrown in. "This entire discussion has nothing to do with why we're here!"

"Regina, who were your parents?" Alex mumbles to me without acknowledging Hawk's point, still reading something on his mental display.

What? Why?

Alex shakes his head and his eyes refocus on Hawk for a long moment. His eyes narrow as he glances between us. "You're right, son. Why don't we take a look at what's in her head, and find out for ourselves what everyone's so excited about?"

"Keep your hands off her." Hawk growls again.

"Hawk," Wolf whispers from beside him. "You need to see what's in her head, man. Don't let him mess with you. Just be cool."

Alex reaches down to grab my arm, pulls me to my feet, and drags me over to a large chair in the middle of several large monitors. Every step radiates agony. I grit my teeth against the awkward nerve pain in my lower body as I slide into the chair. He scrutinizes me like a bug, but he doesn't comment like I expect him to. He applies the silicone pad of a WSB to my cheek. "Is the pain fibromyalgia, or are you injured as well?" he asks as he gets a glassy-eyed look. "Hawk mentioned bruising, but that's to be expected with the fragility of your structure."

"All of it I guess. Is this connected to the GRID?" I grab the WSB to pull it from my cheek.

"Don't be stupid, girl," Alex sneers and jabs his hand painfully against my bruised abdomen. I let go with a squeak of pain, and Hawk growls again. "I'm not going to just throw up a flare with our location now, am I? Everything in this warehouse is isolated."

I'm not sure he's being honest, but it's comforting to believe we're off GRID.

"Watch the monitors, boys," Alex mumbles. "Let's see what Hawk's toy is hiding."

"I am not a toy!" God, this guy is a jerk!

I don't know how, but I can suddenly sense a program running. Data begins pouring through my mind like before, but this time I'm awake. Instinctually, I bring my hands up against the onslaught to defend myself. I don't want to drown beneath it again.

"What on Earth ..." Alex mumbles.

"What happened?" Hawk asks from his tense stance across the room.

Mantis and Wolf still stand between us, but their attention is drawn to the screens as well.

"I don't know." Alex says, manually pressing options on the station beside me. "I was ... I've been locked out."

"I thought you had the latest encryption codes," Hawk says.

"These are the latest encryption codes. This encryption is ... completely foreign. I've never seen one like it. It's not Community."

I find myself in the empty space I found among the data before and relax a little with relief. I can still see and hear everyone, but I feel oddly like I'm underwater, or in a clear glass bubble.

"What?" Wolf asks. "Then who put it there?"

Alex turns back to me with narrowed eyes. "It wasn't there a moment ago," he mumbles without taking his eyes off me. "Hawk ... when you came inside, did you follow standard procedure to avoid the cams?"

"Of course."

"Did you notice the extras I placed around ground level?" Alex raises an eyebrow, continuing to watch me with those frighteningly intense eyes.

"Not at first," Hawk says, glancing between us with a confused expression. "I thought it was stupid you weren't watching for me."

"Oh, we were watching." A creepy grin crosses Alex's expression. "But you weren't on them. In fact, we haven't been able to track you with a GRID cam since you entered the Golden Dragon."

"What? Me? Could you see her?"

"No, man," Wolf answers instead. "I found you back a ways by scent, but no cam footage. Swaine hasn't been able to find you. You were like a freakin' ghost."

"What the hack?" Hawk scratches his head.

"Who is Swaine?" I ask.

"What? Oh, he's the global security AI," Hawk says.

"Regina, dear," Alex addresses me, and his smile is suddenly charming again in a way that sends chills down my spine. He places a gentle hand against my forearm. "You want to know what information you're carrying, don't you?"

"Not really."

"Why not?"

"Because they already want to kill me for it. Knowing it might make it worse. I just ... I just want to disappear, and have everyone leave me alone."

"Interesting ..." Alex narrows his eyes again. "What about Hawk?"

"Hawk doesn't have to go with me." I ignore the glare Hawk shoots my direction. "I know he's getting in trouble. That's why you're here, right? For him? Not for me. He's just being stubborn. You can send him home, so they don't see him helping me. Just—"

"Shut up, Gina!" Hawk roars. "You are not leaving with this nutcase!"

"Regina," Alex says with an obviously forced calm, as he straightens the collar on his shirt, "unfortunately, you can see my boy is a stubborn one. It will help if we can see what we're dealing with. Perhaps if he can see that it's a lost cause, we can both convince him to do what's right, and leave you to your fate. Does that make sense to you?"

"Shut the hack up! I'm not leaving her!" Hawk looks angry enough to kill Alex. The longer he stays with me, the less likely it is that he will survive.

"If you can find out what the information is, do you think you could remove it?" I ask, still floating in my bubble with the data swirling around me.

"We may be able to write new data over it, but it depends on the size and scope of what we're dealing with. You were on an isolated server, and the data being processed on those is unpredictable. But we have to actually see it first. Why don't you close your eyes, and try to relax. Remember everything you can about your session."

"What the hack are you ..." Hawk's eyebrows are knit together above his falsely green eyes.

"Shut up, boy!" Alex shouts at him without turning around and I can almost see the viper in him from his backward glance.

I look at Hawk's confused eyes and clenched jaw, and realize we need to know what it is, whether I want to or not. I can't run from this. We can't plan a means of escape without understanding what everyone wants. That's what Hawk meant when he said he would know what to do once he found out what it is.

I close my eyes and try to remember what I can. I remember drowning in names and serial numbers before. Code names. Locations. I look at them through the window of my bubble.

Wait … Hawk! One of those names was Hawk! I can bring it to mind clearly now.

"Son of a bitch!" Wolf hollers and I jump.

Opening my eyes again, all of them have crowded up around my chair, and are staring at the screens.

"She's got our files man!" Wolf continues. "Who the hack was processin' our shit?"

"Hawking's hacking ghost …" Hawk whispers, and he looks pained as he stares at the screens. "This is all of us. It's everything."

Their files? The files on the chimera operatives?

"Not everything," Alex sighs, scrutinizing the data, "but enough to be very dangerous."

"Do you think this is why the squids want her so bad?" Hawk turns to speak to Alex calmly for the first time. The information seems to have sobered him.

"Unlikely," Alex says with a dismissive wave of his hand. "That server was locked down tight. No one, not even I, could have seen what was being processed. I suspect they took their cues from the Community's exaggerated response to her disappearance. They tipped their hand. Besides… there's a lot more here."

"More?" I ask.

Hawk glances down at me and brushes a lock of hair behind my ear. I'm surprised they've let him get so close. Then he glances back up at the screens and sets his hand down on my arm, rubbing small circles with his fingertips. "What is that?" he points to something I can't see.

"That …" Alex says. "That must be the real source of our problem."

"What is it?" I ask, feeling frustrated. "I want to see!"

All four men jump slightly.

"You did that, right?" the pale-skinned guy asks Alex. Alex glances back down at me with a raised eyebrow and that creepy grin. He doesn't answer. Then he spins a screen around in front of me with an almost delighted expression. I don't understand what I'm looking at. It's just a weird swirling ball of code.

"This, Regina," Alex says, ignoring his minions and Hawk again, "is the most impressive encryption system I've ever seen."

"Like the one that locked you out?"

"No, no," he says with bright, wide eyes. "That one was foreign, but this is something different. It definitely originated within the Community. It has their signature all over it, but it's much more sophisticated."

"Do you have codes for it?"

Alex laughs out loud. "Child. How do I explain this? If encryptions were measured like densities … whatever is housed in this brain of yours is equivalent to being wrapped in the core of the planet. It would take our most advanced engines multiple lifetimes to break through a code like this. Even if the squids got their hands on it, they'd never be able to read it. Their great-great-grandchildren might, but by then what harm could the information be? Of course, with it being protected this seriously … who knows?"

Oh God. We're going to die.

Hawk's fingers against my wrist have stopped moving. He's oddly still.

"Can you take it from me?"

"I don't think that's a good idea." Alex spins the monitor back away and gets that glassy-eyed look again. "It would take an incredible amount of code to overwrite it, and they will most likely kill you anyway. Ghosts of data are always left behind. There's no true way to cleanse a mind."

"What are you doing?" Hawk asks Alex.

"I'm copying it, obviously," Alex scoffs. "There's no use losing something this valuable when they finally kill her."

"I'm not going to let that happen." Hawk looks down at me with a serious expression.

"Oh, for the love of Darwin!" Alex laughs, jumping up and starting to pace. "Let's look at this realistically, son. There is no scenario where she escapes."

"You're a monster," Hawk growls back.

"No. I'm a realist." Alex sits back down in a chair across the room with a sigh. "I'm trying to keep you alive, despite your own stupidity and supposed moral compass—as if morals have any value in real life. I see three likely scenarios here, if you continue with this ludicrous self-imposed mission."

"I don't want to hear it," Hawk says dismissively.

Then with a startlingly fast movement, Hawk disconnects the cable from my cheek and pulls me up from the chair. The bubble pops and I'm in the room with them again—outside the data. He pulls my back flush against his chest, and the two chimeras hesitate as they look back to Alex for direction. It's incredibly weird to be the object of discussion and yet so obviously have no say, in any of their eyes, about what happens to me.

"Best case scenario," Alex continues. "You escape with her and manage to disappear. Good for you. Now what? Are you going to be her guardian for the rest of her life? You'd be throwing your life away, and all the comforts you have access to now."

My legs still feel awkward and numb, and one of my knees buckle despite my attempt to stand on my own. Hawk holds me securely against him with a single arm beneath my chest, just above my battered midsection.

"And yes," Alex steamrolls on, pointing at me. "She's emphasizing my point. She's too frail to keep up with the pace you need to set. And you'd better make sure she doesn't get pregnant, or at least put the child out of its misery. No matter what, you have to find more suitable breeding partners, and she's going to make that difficult."

This guy is insane ... He's standing there talking about murdering babies because of their genetics like he's talking about the weather.

"We're leaving." Hawk turns us around.

Wolf and pale-skin-guy move to stand in the way again.

"But the odds of that scenario playing out are incredibly

unlikely." Alex's voice gets sharper behind us. "If the squids catch up with you, what will you do? Will you kill her as duty demands, knowing how desperate the Fellowship is to keep this information from being discovered?"

Hawk doesn't answer him, and that frightens me more than any of Alex's words.

"I can pull some strings within their ranks, and ensure your life is spared," Alex sighs, "But you must cooperate. The same is true within Global Fellowship ranks. No one will question my authority, but you will have damaged your reputation and career beyond repair. You must swear to me, Hector. Son. That when you are caught, you will not resist. Run with the silly woman if you must, but give her up when she is beyond hope."

"Are you ever gonna stop hacking talking?" Hawk says without turning around.

"Regina," Alex calls to me instead. "You need to let him walk away. Tell him to leave you."

"Shut! Up!" Hawk turns around and roars with his claws bared on his outstretched hand.

Surprisingly, Alex does stop talking, but that creepy smile is back on his face again. He gestures toward the side door in the big room we're in, and Hawk picks me up and starts walking immediately. I watch them all from around Hawk's shoulder as we leave.

Wolf is suppressing a smile and I give him a shy wave of thanks. "Her stuff is in the drone outside," he calls.

Pale-skin-guy looks conflicted and then shouts, "Hawk! It's not just the data, man! You saw it!"

"Yeah," Hawk mumbles. "I saw it."

Saw what?

17

GINA

"Hawk, please," I whisper against the back of his neck. "I can't go any farther." It's a really stupid statement, considering I'm not even on my feet, but Hawk stops walking. I'm strapped to his back like some kind of amateur mountain climber. He pulled this harness out of the pocket on his cargo pants when we reached the entrance to the utility tunnels—like it was an average day on the job.

He said we can travel these tunnels across entire sectors in this region without ever being forced above ground. The main passages are a mix of concrete, cinder block, and brick, equipped with motion activated lighting and kept clear by maintenance bots. Even so, occasional leaks in the sewage ducts, vermin, and even a few inconspicuous shirker burrows give the place a foul smell and eerie ambient noise.

Hawk handed me his GRID glasses to wear and gave me a dose of painkiller. I'm watching to see if the cams down here pick either of us up, but so far we're both completely invisible. Alex wasn't lying. I'm sending Stella ahead as well—as much as she'll let me without getting distracted—to scout the area so we don't run into anyone who could remember us later.

"We need to find a place to sleep," he says.

"Down here?" I can't imagine how Hawk is dealing with the smell.

"It's the best option. If we're not visible on the cams yet, there's not much else to give us away."

"What about the alcove we passed a minute ago?"

"Where?" he asks, turning around.

"Back on the left. Or … well, now the right I guess."

Hawk backtracks through the tunnel until we reach the recess I remember passing. It's much smaller than I thought. It looks like it used to be the entrance of another tunnel that's been walled off after only a couple of feet.

"Do you need to lie flat?" Hawk asks.

"Not really. I'll manage."

"Will not lying flat hurt you?" He sounds irritated.

"No. I just said that."

"No, you said you'd manage. You manage to put up with a lot of shit."

I have no answer for that.

"Hold onto my neck tight," he says.

I grab hold with both arms and Hawk presses a release on the harness. Sliding down to the ground, I try my best to stand on my legs but they still feel rubbery. He slides me around in front of his body and gently helps me to sit on the floor.

Stella's winging her way back—flitting from one perch to another on all the wires and pipes running through here. It's muggy and gross, which she doesn't mind, but I hate. Before taking the mind-link disk off, I impress on her to go find something to eat. She needs a break from my distress, so I tuck the disk into my pocket.

Hawk drops the duffel bag and shoves it against the concrete side wall of the tiny alcove. Then he sits down and leans against it. I reach around him to pull out my travel pillow from one of the bag's pockets. It's no bigger than my thumb when deflated, and I spin the dial open quickly to let it self-inflate. Then I reach up to place it behind Hawk's head.

"Don't." He pushes the pillow away. "You need it."

"Where am I sleeping?" He is lying in the only space, and I don't think it's a good idea to sleep in the main tunnel. I had assumed I would be sleeping on top of him.

"Up here." He pats his chest and he can barely keep his eyes open. He's been carrying me for hours and I don't even understand where we're trying to go.

I crawl carefully up onto his chest. Balancing my hip against his, I tuck my shoulder beneath his arm—using his chest as a pillow. Then I reach up and not-so-subtly shove the pillow against the back of his neck again. He chuckles, but lifts his head and accepts the small comfort.

I want to talk about what we learned from Alex and his machine. I want to talk about a lot of the other weird things Alex said too. I'm not sure if it's caution or embarrassment, but Hawk's been completely silent since we left the warehouse. I'm sure he isn't up for conversation any more than I am now, though, so I close my eyes.

18

HAWK

I have no idea what time it is when I wake. That's the biggest down side to hiding in the tunnels. It's too easy to lose track of time without the reminder of the sun. Gina is curled up on my chest and I hate to move her, but I can't afford to let anyone catch up with us too easily. I'm not sure what to expect from Alex.

Breathing deep, I take in her scent. We've gotten pretty grimy over the last couple of days, but I never get tired of the way she smells. I pull up the clock in my field of vision.

Sir Issac Newton! We've been asleep for ten hours! "Babe, we've got to get up." I nudge her forehead with my nose as I work to sit up beneath her dead weight. "Gina. Wake up."

"Huh?" She nuzzles her face against my chest.

"I overslept." I sit her upright and she starts to blink the sleep from her eyes. "I'm sorry, but we've got to move. Right now."

She groans, but stands to her feet and then braces her hand against the wall for a moment like I've come to expect.

"Here, slip the harness back on." I try to hand it to her, but she pushes it away.

"I'm fine. I can walk now."

"Babe, we shouldn't—"

"Don't argue with me about my own body," she says. "I was a train wreck yesterday, but I've slept it off. You could easily end up having to carry me later, so there's no point in you doing it now."

"Alright." I shove the harness back into my pocket. "What about your braces?"

"Just give me a minute to put them on," she says with a dramatic, cat-like yawn. Mid-yawn, her jaw makes a resounding crack and she mumbles a soft, "Ouch."

It's unbelievable. She's hurt herself and she hasn't even taken a single step forward yet. I hold up a dose of painkiller with a raised brow and she makes a face and holds out her arm. It reminds me. "Now that I know what's wrong with you …" I inject the medicine. "Can you explain it to me, or do I have to keep getting pissed off every time you hurt yourself without telling me?"

"I guess. I'm screwed either way."

"Why were you hiding it if it was genetic? All they'd have to do is take your blood."

"The Community has funny rules about forfeiting your DNA, or demanding it to be destroyed. That's how I made it out of the hospital after the explosion."

"Right." I laugh ruefully. "Just like we have rules about not killing Community members without cause."

"Point taken." She starts trudging down the tunnel ahead of me. "What do you want to know?"

"Everything."

"That's much more complicated than you realize."

I grab up the duffel and glance back but Stella is nowhere in sight. "Where's your friend?"

"Oh crap." She digs through her pocket for the mind-link disk. After placing it behind her ear, she groans. "She's asleep. Or she was. Come on, Baby, come to Momma."

She coaxes the tiny creature with her voice for a minute or two. I am just about to declare it a lost cause when Stella flits over and clings to Gina's vest.

"Alright." We've taken much longer to get moving than we should have. "Let's go."

19

GINA

Oh my God, I swear this man is never going to run out of questions! He's worse than Drustan used to be!

Hawk has asked me about every aspect of my illness. We've gone over the blood pressure and heart rate issues that cause me to faint without warning. We've talked about the fact that I bruise easily, bleed easily, break bones easily, and often don't even know how I got hurt. We've talked about the dislocations—which ones I can remember ever having, and which ones most frequently. He's particularly disturbed by my fibromyalgia. That makes sense, since he saw me so debilitated recently. Heck, we've even talked about the Raynauds that makes me lose circulation in my fingers and toes prematurely—kind of like an allergic reaction to the cold.

I don't like that he keeps getting quieter and more thoughtful after each answer. His mouth has turned down into a disturbing frown. The last thing I need is for him to attempt to be some kind of human bubble-wrap. Although, he may finally be starting to realize what I already know.

"Hawk, I don't think I can do this."

"Do what?" He stops his endless march and turns around with a raised eyebrow. He looks frighteningly like Alex when he does that now.

"I can't keep running forever. I'm not like you. I'm just not built for the constant physical effort. I know you're doing everything you can, but I'm not getting enough time to heal."

"We slept for almost 10 hours this morning."

"Yeah, and that was great. I needed it bad. But you still don't get it. In my normal life, before the apocalypse hit, I sleep that much every day—not just when I'm really hurt. When I'm really hurt, I'll sleep for 12 to 16 hours."

"We can't afford to give them that much of a chance to catch up."

He starts to walk again, and I follow after him. "That's what I'm trying to tell you! I really appreciate you trying to help me, and I get that you somehow think I'm your responsibility. But I'm not. Your dad's right—"

"By all that is lawful," he growls without turning around. "Don't ever say that Alex is right about anything, and don't call him my dad. That man's a sociopath!"

"Yeah, I kinda got that vibe. But he seems to have a lot of

resources and influence. If he wasn't lying, and he can pull whatever strings he needs to so you can go back to your normal life, you should do that."

"I'm not having this conversation."

I stop walking. He continues on for about 10 feet before he stops and his shoulders slump with a heavy sigh. "Are we really gonna do this right now?"

"I'm sorry. I thought you weren't going to have this conversation."

Hawk turns around with a soft roar of frustration. Now that I know he can do that, it seems to slip free more often. He marches back toward me, but I stand my ground and straighten my spine. I refuse to be intimidated. Unfortunately, he grabs me around the waist, throws me over his shoulder, and starts walking again.

"You're being such a bully!" I thump my fists ineffectively against his back.

"If I have to bully you to keep you alive, then so be it. I've played that part before."

"Where are we going? Do you even have a plan?"

"Sure." He sighs. "Keep moving."

"That's your plan?"

"I'm working on it. You should have told me about your illness from the beginning! How the hack was I supposed to plan things to keep us safe, when I didn't even know what all the dangers were? I need time to figure out our next move, but we can't sit still while I do it, can we?" He's quiet for a moment. "I've always suspected you're smart, but for Alex to actually say it is pretty dramatic. His standards for everything are bogon high. So why don't you start using that big brain and help, instead of giving up and making everything more difficult."

"I don't want you to die," I admit in a small voice.

"I don't want to die either." He shrugs his shoulder up into my gut. "But I refuse to believe we can't both walk away from this."

He just doesn't get it! It's not like I want to die, but if I do my soul is safe. I have no fear of the afterlife. It's life, here and now, that scares the crap out of me. Hawk runs around and makes decisions like he's invincible, but he's not. He was raised without a knowledge of God. He has no idea that he's in ten times the amount of danger I will ever be!

20

HAWK

We found another alcove to bed down in for the night. This one is bigger. The heat down here is stifling, and I've developed a migraine from the smell.

Gina demanded that I put her back down after half a mile. She agreed to keep walking, but declared that she wasn't happy about it. Her defiant moments would be endearing if we weren't in such a desperate situation. I hope her silence means she's really putting that brain to work—instead of meaning she's given up.

We're on our last MRE. I offered it to her, but she insisted on splitting it. We supplemented it by splitting an RC.

"How long do we get this time?" she asks.

"I'll give us six hours, but you need to keep Stella on you. The disk I mean. If either one of us gets any warning bells, we'll have to move fast. Can you sleep that way?"

"Yeah, I've done it before." I don't see any tells that she's lying. She pulls out her travel pillow and inflates it. There's no way I'm going to let her give it to me again. We've shed everything but the essentials from our bag. Other than our jackets, or shedding our clothes, the pillow is the only option for bedding we have now.

"I think we should do what we did last night." She closes up the valve on the little bag of air.

"What do you mean?"

"I think I should use you as a pillow, and you use this."

"What happened to separate mattresses?"

"Obviously, we had more bedding then. We don't now. We're not getting enough rest as it is—so, we need to make what we have count. Stop looking at me like you're surprised. It's the smarter thing to do, isn't it?"

I bite my lip, stifling a chuckle and resisting the urge to say it always was. The night is definitely looking up. "Works for me." I lie down with my head on the funny air pocket and set my mental alarm.

Gina lies down on my right side; tucking her shoulder into the crook of my arm like before. Her head rests on my chest, her arm wraps around it, and she wraps her leg around my thigh.

Hawking's ghost. It suddenly feels like forever since I've loved a woman.

"Is this okay?" she asks.

It's fantastic. It sucks. "Yeah, you're good. Does the EDS make it harder for you to sleep when you travel?"

"It's hard to sleep at home," she says with a yawn, "but yeah. Not having a lot of pillows to work with makes it harder."

"What do you need extra pillows for?"

"It's kind of hard to explain." She gets quiet for a moment. "With my joints being as hypermobile as they are, my bones don't really like to stay in the right places. The shoulder I'm lying on tends to fold in toward my chest in an uncomfortable way, and my rib cage tries to fold in on itself, so I use pillows to prop them up. Having a pillow between my knees helps keep my hips from getting kinked into an awkward position too. Even with that, though, I know I toss and turn a lot because I'm uncomfortable. I'm sorry if that wakes you up."

It does wake me up, but I'd assumed it was stress making her restless. The thought of always being in pain, or uncomfortable, while you're sleeping is unsettling. "It doesn't sound like we can do anything about it. So, don't worry. I'm trained to function on very little sleep if I have to."

"Yeah, big guy, but even you can't do that forever."

True. I start walking myself through my mental shut-down routine.

"Hawk?" she asks in a whisper. "Do you believe in anything?"

What a weird-ass question. "Uh … I believe the ground is hard and I'm hungry."

"I mean, do you have any spiritual beliefs?"

The thought makes me laugh. "What, you mean like blood sacrifices and alters, and shit?"

"Well … I mean, I guess there are some religions that practice that stuff." She sighs. "But it wasn't that long ago that there were hundreds of world religions. Faith was a big part of daily life for most of the world."

"Says who?" I went to a training years ago on the subject. There are still some isolated pockets of indigenous peoples around the world who refuse to advance beyond the dark ages, and still practice spiritual rites and rituals. Some people with more extremist religious beliefs have joined the ranks of the squids over the years—intending to replace science with religion. I've met a few people in passing that referred to themselves as *people of faith*, but we never had a conversation on the subject. It's disorienting to think that Gina might be from one of those groups.

"How can you possibly live the life that you do and not know that the Global Fellowship rewrote most of history?" she asks.

"History is always a he-said, she-said game. The Fellowship fully acknowledges that. But I think you're making a bigger deal of it than it really is."

"You know, I passed most of those stupid little assessments because I know both versions of history." She's starting to get animated, occasionally thumping her fingers against my chest. "It was a lot harder to make sure I was giving the Fellowship answer, versus the truth."

"Give me one example—that's not religious."

"Interest rates and economics," she says with an adorable note of attitude.

"What about them?"

"Fellowship history says that interest rates have only ever been negative, because it makes sense that an institution would charge you a fee for having to hold onto your coin for you. However, for the entire history of the world before the last couple hundred years, interest rates were positive. The coin belonged to you.

"Banks would pay you a rate of interest to be able to have access to, and use, your coin while they were storing it. They made coin off investing it while it was in their possession without having to charge you anything."

She sounds remarkably convincing.

"The Fellowship has redesigned everything there is to know about interest rates," she continues, "and both micro- and macro-economics to suit their own needs. That doesn't make it true. It's just what they want the population to believe, so that they can set up the balance of power and coin how they see fit."

"I find that hard to believe."

"Would you find it hard to believe that they lied to you about me?"

Hack. There are a lot of things I didn't believe the Community would do, that they've already done to us. It's disturbing to think that I could be wrong about basic history. "You sound an awful lot like a squid talking like that."

She fidgets with the position of the pillow beneath my head. "I don't have to be one of them to believe many of the same things they do. That's like saying you sound like a squid because you believe the Earth is round."

"Alright. So what do you believe in then?"

"Have you ever seen this symbol before?" She sits up suddenly to hold something in front of my face. It's the necklace she wears. It's an elongated plus sign on a silver chain. I've seen the symbol around before and asked about it. I can't remember what the religion is called. It hadn't really mattered at the time. I think it had something to do with the worship of an old woodworker somebody considered a prophet thousands of years ago.

"I've seen it before, but I don't remember the details."

"The symbol is called a cross," she says. "It's a symbol of the Christian faith."

"How did you get into that?" I ask with a yawn.

"My father's family has been Christian for generations."

"You know, Babe ..." I roll toward her slightly. "We should sleep."

"But this is really important."

"Can you tell me tomorrow?"

"If we're still alive tomorrow," she huffs.

"I think our odds are good," I chuckle. "I've managed so far, haven't I?"

21

GINA

"So you're telling me that you believe in a god who created the entire universe, and this guy, Jesus, was some kind of human sacrifice for everyone ever born?" Hawk laughs as he walks.

"That's a very simplistic way of looking at it, but yes." I sigh. God, I'm screwing this up. A little help would be nice! ... How about a way out of this mess?

"You're way too smart to believe in something so far-fetched," he says.

"Maybe that should tell you it's not so far-fetched. Look Hawk, stop. Just stop for a minute."

Hawk turns back to me with an expression caught somewhere between frustration and amusement. "Okay, but you've only got five minutes." He sits down abruptly in the empty tunnel, leaning on our bag and taking a swig of water from his flask.

I sit beside him with my stomach in knots. The fibromyalgia roaring back is not helping me think, but we're out of painkillers.

Five minutes? "Just ... consider what the facts would be if what I believed was right." My knuckles pop as I wring my hands. "No matter what happens here, with this mess, we're both going to die eventually right?"

"Everybody dies."

I take a deep breath and meet his gaze. "Look me in the eyes, Hawk. I'm not afraid of dying. I'm afraid of being injured. I'm afraid of being locked in a cage. I'm afraid of other people having power over me. But dying? My parents are already dead. I believe that when I die, I get to see them again. They'll be there waiting for me."

"Don't you dare ..." His eyes narrow.

"I'm not giving up. I'm telling you that I don't believe death is the end. I believe my parents can see what's happening to me right now. But if I don't explain this right, and you don't understand before you're killed then ... then, you won't be there, and I can't

…" My throat is starting to cut my words off, and I brush a tear from my eye before it can escape. Crying is not going to help! Why is this so hard?

"Hey, hey …" Hawk whispers, and his warm hand slides against the side of my face. "We're going to be okay, Gina."

"You're not!"

"Why does it even matter whether I'm there or not?" Hawk asks with a confused smile. "Do you need a bodyguard after you're dead?"

"I owe you a mortal life." I try to reign my chaotic emotions back in. "I cannot possibly give that back to you, but I can help you find an eternal one—the only one that really matters."

"Shirker code?" he grumbles. "That's the best you've got?"

No. But what if he uses the truth against me? "God sacrificed his son because he loves us. The most important rule in my faith is to love others, and share his love with them."

Hawk's eyes shift instantly, drifting over me again as they have done so many times since we met. Then he shakes his head and closes his eyes. "I'm confused," he says. "I've wanted to love you since the first moment I saw you, and you've very explicitly told me you weren't interested. And I sure as hack don't understand how that has anything to do with your god."

"I don't mean sex." I sigh. "The Community hijacked that word to make it mean nothing more than physical attraction and sex. For centuries it meant a positive emotional bond between people. People that cared about helping each other—parents and their children, siblings, friends. It didn't have to involve sex or sexual feelings at all."

"What are you trying to say?" Hawk rubs a hand over his face.

"I'm saying I love you, Hawk." God help me. "You're a good man and I wish we could have met under different circumstances, but I … I care about you. I care about what happens to you, and when I die … I want you to be there."

"That's the OAS talking." Hawk grimaces.

"The … the what?" He already knows I care? "You think I have OAS?"

"I think we both do," he says. "I didn't think it was something that could onset so fast, but I realized it a couple days ago. You've got signs." He swallows hard. "And so do I. I'm sorry Babe, but there's no way I can get help for us right now."

"Whoa, whoa, whoa." He has OAS? Oh, God. He doesn't even know what he's saying! "What makes you think I have OAS?"

"It was the thing you said about feeling safe back with the leopard. And no, I definitely didn't cause this on purpose. It's too serious of a risk with someone like me."

"And you think you have it because …"

He starts to rub the back of his neck. "I … well I've got a lot of symptoms."

My heart starts to race.

"But like I said," he says. "There's no way to get us the right help right now so we just have to try to live with it."

Live with it? "Hawk, we're not sick."

"You can deny it if you want, but I know myself well enough to—"

"That's not what I meant." Oh Lord, don't blush. This is so awkward. "I don't believe that OAS is an illness. It's a beautiful thing that the Community pretends is unhealthy. Hawk, OAS is what I mean when I say I love you."

Hawk rubs at his eyes. "What?"

"Love, Hawk. Love is natural. It's meaningful. It's one of the most important aspects of life. Love is what makes a mother shield her child from danger, despite the danger to herself. Love is what made me feel special every time my parents went out of their way to spend time with me. It's what makes me want you to live a full and happy life, and to be there with me after I die."

Hawk leans his head back against the tunnel wall for several long moments, and his silence eats at me. "So what is it that you think I have to do?"

"You have to believe that God loves you and Jesus died for you, and invite him to be part of your life."

"Okay then, I believe it."

"No you don't." I stand to my feet again. "Lying to me doesn't count."

He catches my wrist in his hand and pulls me gently back

down. "Babe, you're asking a lot here. I want to help you with whatever this is, but you can't expect me to just change everything I've ever believed in an hour."

"I know, but I feel like I waited too long."

"We're going to make it. You haven't waited too long for anything."

Wait! I reach up and take off my necklace. Most people think that it's some kind of tech jewelry, but it's just a plain silver cross. It was a gift from my father, meant to be passed to my own child one day, but I'm sure he'd approve given the situation. "Will you wear this for me?"

"Isn't it important or something?" He eyes it like a spring trap.

"Yes." I reach up to connect the clasp behind his neck. It hangs low on me, but incredibly short on his broad neck. "If things get really bad. If … if it seems like we're not going to make it, just remember what I told you. Please? You don't have to do some crazy ritual to talk to God, you just speak your mind in your head. Ask him for help."

"Have you asked him for help yet?"

"Over and over again."

"And has he answered you?"

What an interesting question. I smile with my arms still around his neck. I should pull away, but I don't. "He sent me you."

He closes his eyes and takes a deep breath as a tremor runs through him, then he pulls me more fully against him. Oh shoot … Turning my head aside, he kisses me just beneath the jaw.

"So you say you love me." Hawk sighs. "But you won't make love to me."

"It's … complicated." It's so tempting it hurts. My skin feels more alive everywhere he touches me, and it takes all the willpower I have to resist the lure of his kiss. But he'd never understand what I want. "And you said we've only got five minutes, remember?"

"I could definitely change my mind." He chuckles, kissing my throat again.

I sit back, grab his hand and place it over the necklace. "What are you going to do if it gets really bad?"

"Ask your god for help." Hawk rolls his eyes. "If it makes you feel better, Babe, I swear.”

"Good." I stand and put some distance between us. "Now go on and impress me by getting us out of here.”

"You're right," he says, standing back to his feet with a stretch and a chuckle. "A bed would be much nicer than the tunnel floor anyway.”

Oh great …

22

_____

HAWK

Glancing up at the tunnel marker, we've passed into Region 220's Sector 21. Gina's nerve pain is getting worse, but she gets pissy with me if I try to talk about it. I absolutely hate her swallowing poison to try and cover up the symptoms, but it makes no difference now because she ran out yesterday. We're out of medicine too.

There's a small CPG base not far from here, and I've got at least one contact inside. I haven't seen her in a couple years, but I saved her ass once and we were lovers a few times. Which option is worse? Go above ground to get more alcohol and take the risk that someone has put the word out that information on us is worth coin, or see if my contact can supply a less poisonous alternative and risk the same?

Gina stumbles behind me, and I turn to see her holding a hand against the wall.

"What's wrong?"

"Uh … nothing." She keeps walking but she's favoring her left leg.

"How stupid do I look?"

"Just, don't worry about it." She shrugs. "We have to keep moving.”

I turn around and continue forward more slowly. "Did you take Stella's disk off?"

"Yeah."

So, she's trying not to let the bat suffer with her. Man, that's a bad sign. I need to find something to relieve her pain. I have no idea how bad this can get, but Wolf said she'd been unable to walk.

I can't leave her in these tunnels unless I find a safe space to tuck her into. Even then, risking the base will get me back to her faster than trying to find a dealer to trust on the street. I'm not familiar with this civilian sector. It's infuriating that I deal so much medical tech, and I don't have what we need now.

"Gina, I think there's a place nearby where we can get some help, but I don't think you're going to like it."

23
GINA

It takes a lot of mental energy to make sure my feet are doing what they're supposed to. The last thing I need is to fall on my face.

The pain is a sharp ache that always starts radiating from my joints. For some reason, mine focuses on my lower body first—my hips and knees, and eventually my ankles and feet. If it ever moves into my upper body I'm pretty much screwed, because there's nothing in the world that can stop the freight train at that point.

God I need a drink …

If I were at home, I'd shut myself in for the next day or two and wait out the misery until it passed. I'd drink myself to sleep if it got too bad. Out here without alcohol or medication, I'm as exposed as my nerves feel.

For the last hour, I've been singing in my head to keep my mind off the searing pain—which by now is cresting and dropping in waves about every three to four seconds. My legs are extremely sluggish too. Breathing deeply helps wash the intensity away some with the excess oxygen. Then an ache begins to bloom deep in my elbow, and a wave of panic hits me.

Oh God, no …

"Are you even listening to …" Hawk's angry tone cuts into my awareness, but it takes me too long to look up.

"I'm fine." I close my eyes for just a moment to ride the next
crest. "I'm just gonna … uh …" I try to sit down on the pipe we've
stopped beside, but my legs feel stiff and wooden. I slide off the
side and plop down onto the ground, sending a shock wave of pain
lancing through both of my legs. I cringe and pant before
reminding us both, "I'm okay. I'm fine."

"Son of a bitch." Hawk storms off down the tunnel.

I begin rubbing my hands up and down my legs vigorously. I'm
not sure why I do it. It doesn't really decrease the pain, but the
added sensory information confuses my mind and distracts me
from the intensity of my distress. I glance around as the panic
builds. I'm out of booze. I'm in the middle of a damn labyrinth.
The way the pain is increasing … I'm in for a full storm and I have
no means to dull it.

I try to slow my rapid breathing, but keep up the furious
movements against my legs. Don't panic. I've done this before.
Lots of times. There's nothing we can do anyway … just. Just
breathe.

I shriek as Hawk lifts me into his arms. I hadn't even noticed
he'd come back. "I'm fine." I groan.

"Yeah, you said that."

"Where …" I suck in a breath, "are you …?"

"I've found a place we can stash you in for shelter. You'll be
able to rest there."

Rest. Okay. Good.

I cringe through each shock-wave of pain that radiates down
my legs with every step he takes. After a moment, I realize I'm
digging my fingernails into his neck and shoulder. I move my
hands to instead claw into my own arms, locked more fully around
his neck.

"Here." He sets me down on a smooth concrete surface along
the far wall, in a room full of a huge mass of tanks, pipes, and dials.
"It's pretty tight in here, but if you can tuck your body back in
there you should be hidden from view."

"Okay." I suck my breath in between my teeth.

Looking over my shoulder, I can see what he means
immediately. There is a walkway no wider than a single person

between the pressure dials and the wall. The deeper I can crawl toward the back corner, the more the piping will block the view.

I can still move my legs, but I don't want to. The strange sensory storm running through them will just make me more panicky, and I don't want to do something really embarrassing like burst into tears—again. I reach back and drag myself farther in, only making tiny movements with my torturous lower limbs. The pain in my elbow begins spreading into my shoulder, as it blooms in the opposing shoulder at the same time.

"I'll be back in a second." Hawk walks off again.

Lying flat on my back, the pain is now beginning to bloom in the wrists and elbows of both my arms. I fantasize briefly about having both my arms and legs amputated—so, I never have to feel this pain again. But I can't run that way. Shit!

The hard floor is putting more pressure against my right side, so the storm in my system is strongest there, making me catalog each individual moment of torment more clearly.

God, I just need … what? What can I do?

I try bringing my knees up, but quickly put them back down when it affords me no relief. I begin breathing in through my nose, and pushing the breath out slowly through pursed lips. Stella comes in screeching and attaches herself to a perch above me.

In. Out. I can do this. In. Out.

Somewhere in the back of my mind, I'm aware that Hawk is back with our duffel, shoving it inside a small space under the pipes. Eternity passes, with me focused on my breathing and the unique pain radiating through every cell, before Hawk finally crawls into the walkway.

"What can I do to help you?" he asks.

A hysterical giggle bubbles up from my throat as traitorous tears finally leak from both eyes. "Nothing," I choke. "There is nothing."

Hawk doesn't seem satisfied with that answer. He grabs my waist, and drags me back beneath him. I let out a brief cry at the movement.

"I'm not an idiot, Gina," Hawk growls. He hovers above me with his hands and knees on either side of my body. "At first I thought you were just tired, but this isn't fatigue. You're in pain. How bad does this get?"

"Bad." I groan, and another tear leaks.

"Where is the pain?" he asks. "Is it your legs?"

"It's …" I grit my teeth, riding the next wave. "Everything. Everywhere."

"What?" Confusion colors his tone. "Tell me what it feels like. Is it moving? Is it changing? I might be able to find something to help."

How the hell do I explain this? I suck in another stuttering breath, and force it out. "It's like," I sniff, "like my body is in a press. With just … just enough pressure to … make me think my bones … might explode. You know? And like … there's a red hot … fire poker inside every … joint in my body. There's like … little electric currents … running up and down everywhere. Mostly … my arms and legs, though."

Hawk looks ashen, with wide eyes and a pained expression.

"Could you … cut them off maybe?" I attempt to joke, forcing a smile. "That might help." More tears leak from my eyes, despite my desperation to lighten the situation.

Hawk shuffles down my body on his hands and knees and places his hands gently against my calves. He simply hovers there for a moment. "The muscles here are spasming." Then he moves his hands up to my thighs.

"Yeah." I groan again. "They'll do that everywhere soon. It's … bad this time."

Hawk starts rubbing his strong hands up and down my legs, mimicking the movements I was making before. "Does this help?"

"It just … adds. More feeling, but not pain. It … distracts me."

Hawk keeps up the steady movement against my legs, and I clutch my forearms again and again to distract myself from the pain now firmly rooted in them as well. The pain is overwhelming, and I clench my teeth against the urge to wail like a dying creature. I hold my breath and then pant. Hold it again, and I can feel the darkness encroaching.

"Whoa, whoa." Hawk suddenly appears before my eyes and touches my face. "You've got to calm your breathing, or you're gonna pass out."

"I know." I pant again.

"Gina, even if you pass out, you're not gonna stay under."

"Don't care."

"Come on, Babe, I don't want to leave you like this," he pleads.

"Where are you going?" I've missed something important in my haze.

"I told you. There's a base nearby where I might be able to get my hands on some medicine." He sighs. "I'd give you a sedative, but I don't have any more. It will take me at least an hour to make the trip there and back."

He's right. I need something. Anything. There has to be another way to ... "Your bag. I need the bag." I shoved the stunner back in there when he wasn't looking, in case we needed it for camouflage again. I don't even know how it works, but being high right now sounds like a really good idea. "Please."

He shuffles back a moment and drags it up next to my head. He unzips it as I struggle to pull it to where I can see inside. Lying my head against the opening, I rest it in a convenient spot to hide my face. I start carelessly tossing items out onto the ground as I search.

Finally! As he scrambles to keep the discarded items from rolling away, I slide the skull-shaped emitter out of the remote and place it against my cheek. I press the first button I can find. The stunner sends a jolt of electricity racing through my face, as a strangely euphoric burn races through my brain for a fraction of a second. The shock of it sends me reeling back with a gasp.

"What are you doing?" Hawk turns back.

Can't let him stop me! With his hatred of alcohol, he'll definitely disapprove.

I jam my thumb down on the button again, feeling my eyes roll back at the severity of the current—my entire body going stiff. The current is so much stronger than I would have imagined. I would scream if my muscles weren't locked down completely.

"What the hack?" Hawk roars. "Let go of it!"

I'm consumed by the burning sensation searing from the inside of my skull and down to my toes. After a moment, the remote is ripped from my hand and the current stops.

A strange numbness begins to flood through my senses. The beautiful, awe inspiring numbness starts in my feet and spreads upwards—reversing the path of the terrible current.

"What have you done?" Hawk asks with a whisper, brushing my hair back from my face. "Oh, Baby, what have you done?"

The numbness spreads up my legs and through my abdomen. When it hits my torso, my heart stutters. It gets hard to breathe.

"No, no," Hawk says, slipping a hand over my heart beneath my shirt.

Then the numbness reaches my face and I don't care anymore. The pain is gone. I smile, as another tear leaks from my right eye.

"No, stay with me," Hawk barks. "Come on, Baby. Just—"

The numbness reaches my eyes, and I relax into the welcome darkness.

24

HAWK

I curl my body around Gina in the dark bedroom of the small hub, trembling from the potent mix of fear and rage. It had taken four minutes of CPR for her heart to restart after she used the stunner. I didn't even know she still had the hacking thing. When I opened it, I discovered all the limiters had been taken off. The dosage of current was lethal, unless the user was conditioned. Junkies develop a tolerance after long-term use and tend to jury-rig them.

A beep indicates that Rayne is coming in after her shift. I couldn't risk grabbing her before it was over, although I'd been desperate to. She's the only person in this sector that I know well enough to ask for help, so I broke into her hub carrying nothing but Gina.

I quickly stand and exit the bedroom, trying to look much less emotional than I feel.

The lights come on as Rayne walks in. She stops dead in her tracks as the door glides shut behind her. "Scott?"

"Rayne, I'm sorry, but I need your help." I force the words through my throat, but I'm not achieving Scott William's normally flat tone.

"By all that is lawful, you look terrible." She rushes over and runs her hand along the bandage seal over the stubble on my cheek. "What happened to your face? What's …" Through the open partition, she catches sight of Gina on her bed. "Who is that?"

"She's hurt." Man, I'm out of character, but unable to manage my normal calm. "I need your help."

Rayne's medical training kicks in and she steps away from me to check Gina's pulse. She pulls out a light and checks Gina's eyes, then touches the small burn mark on the apple of her cheek. "She's a junkie. Why didn't you just bring her to the base clinic?"

"I can't. But it stopped her heart, Rayne. I didn't know what else to do."

"Well, she's lucky then." She shrugs. "They don't always come back. Do you have the device?"

"Yeah," I pull it out of my pocket and hand it to her.

"Sweet Darwin," she says as she opens it. "This thing should be destroyed. There's nothing wrong with a little escape now and then, but if this is hers, she has a real problem. Have you thought about talking to her about retirement?"

I resist the urge to growl at the suggestion. There's nothing wrong with retirement. Hack, I've considered it myself more times than I can count.

But not for Gina. She wants to live—well, normally. She's full of life. I know she doesn't want to lose her memory, but memory resets are better options for someone to start fresh without dying. But … the memory reset wouldn't take away her pain. She'd end up knowing less about her illness than I do. I shake off the entire subject. "It's not hers. She was desperate. I don't even think she knew how to use it."

"Desperate for what?" Rayne asks, beginning a more thorough examination. "Good grief, Scott, this woman has been injured everywhere. What's happened to both of you?" She glances back at me with a hint of unease in her eyes, and I fight not to be offended. I know how it looks. I've used it to our advantage for days. Now it makes me look like a violent lover in the wrong setting. Hack! She may assume Gina's the one who clawed my face.

"She has a genetic condition, but I don't understand it."

"What kind of condition?"

"Ehlers-Dan … something," I shrug.

"How bizarre." Rayne looks Gina over again. "I didn't think there were any cases of EDS in our lifetime. It's considered Old World. Was she a shirker?"

"Don't know. When she used the stunner, she was in terrible pain, all over her body."

"I see." Rayne sighs, pinching the bridge of her nose. "It's comes from a problem with her nervous system. There are drugs that can help, but they're not always reliable."

"Could you get me some of those?"

"You must be joking. Scott, why didn't you just take her to the clinic?"

"You know I can't discuss my work." I let in a slightly darker tone.

I met Rayne Westhill when the squids attacked her deployment five years ago. She'd been wounded before I was dispatched to aid them and I saved her life. She's a good woman, and I've visited her on random nights when I was passing through sector. She's helped me once with a placement, but I've never had to ask this kind of favor before. I've always been able to go through my own channels.

"She's your work?" Rayne's tone is disbelieving.

"Yes. She is."

"How long is she going to be with you?" She clenches her jaw.

"Hard to say." I shrug. What's that about? "It would be good if the medicine could last me a while, just in case."

Rayne walks over and trails her hands over my chest. She's a tall strawberry blond, with full lips and bright green eyes. Strangely, I feel no response to her advance. She's a good lover, but I'm exhausted. Maybe it's the progression of the OAS.

"You've changed your hair." She runs her fingers through it.

Normally, Scott Williams is a blond, but I remembered to turn my contacts gray. "Yeah, I was trying something different for a while. What do you think?"

Gina gasps from behind us, and I spin to see her body tensing instantly as she's finally jerked back into consciousness. I'm beside her in a flash, taking her hand as she groans against the pain. I'd hoped it would have been eliminated by the high she fell into. She doesn't speak, but her teeth are clenched together hard.

"Can you help her?" I turn back to see Rayne's professional expression.

She walks over with a med injector and I check the label with a glance. Gina's body is rigid as tears leak from both of her eyes, but she doesn't make another sound.

"What's her name?" Rayne asks.

"Dianna."

"Dianna, I am going to give you something to make you sleep again," Rayne says as she injects the drug. It takes a minute or two for Gina to relax back into sleep. Rayne then sighs deeply and steps back a careful distance. "You saved my life, Scott. I'll get you the medicine she needs, but I can't get you more than a week's worth. What she'll need more than anything, is rest. Wherever you place her, the doctors there should be able to help. She needs the intensive care of an institution."

Institution. Gina had been crippled with fear by the very mention of it.

"Thank you," I whisper as she turns to leave. Even just knowing the name of the drug I need will help me acquire it later.

"Of course ... What are you going to do about your face?" she asks. "Do you want me to look at it?"

"No. The CPG will clean up the damage when I finish the job."

"Have it your way." Rayne turns back as she reaches the door. "Now, get her off my bed and put her on the couch. I have to sleep when I get back."

25

GINA

My body feels heavy and weak as I wake, but the pain is gone and the numbness that always sets in afterward has settled in its place. That's going to make walking more difficult.

There is a warm weight across my hips. When I finally manage to blink the sleep from my eyes, I realize I'm on a couch. Hawk's left arm is lying across me with his head in the crook of his elbow.

He's sound asleep and starting to look truly haggard. He's developing a hint of dark circles beneath his eyes. The dark hair on his jaw is caught somewhere between being stubble and becoming a true beard, not quite matching Darius's espresso extensions. I should probably check his bandage, and we both need a shower badly. I've never felt so gross in my life. Reaching up to thread my fingers into his incredibly soft hair, I'm no longer surprised when his eyes immediately snap open.

"Hi," I croak out through vocal chords still thick with sleep.

He sits up in a flash and looms above me, looking in my eyes the way a doctor would in an examination room. There is a wildness in his now-gray eyes and a jerky quality to his movements that is startling. He doesn't respond, but takes my pulse at my wrist.

"What are you doing?" I ask with a yawn.

He reaches down and presses against the bottoms of my feet. Where are my shoes?

"Can you feel that in both feet?" he asks.

"Yeah." They feel a little odd, but it's exactly what I expect from the after-effects of the fibromyalgia, and he looks too panicked to explain.

Where are we? The last thing I remember, we were in the tunnels. Now we're in some kind of cozy looking Community hub. It doesn't look like mine, but it's similar. I'm on a green suede couch and Hawk has been sitting on the floor leaned against it while he slept. Now he's on his knees, reaching up to touch both my hands.

"What about that?" he asks. "You feel that too?"

"Yeah, of course I do." I sigh. "What is going on?"

"You hacking tried to kill yourself!" he bellows and I jump so hard I almost hit his arm with my knee.

Hawk takes a deep breath and flexes his hands in and out of fists. They're shaking.

He stands up and walks away with his back to me, throwing his hands into his hair and keeping his arms up beside his head. An animalistic snarl rumbles from his chest. It should probably frighten me, but I'm confused. I give my head a shake to try and make sense of what he means.

The stunner ... I touch my cheek and realize there's a sore spot where the emitter was when I used it. What ... Oh God, what did I do? I don't remember ever having a flare up that bad before, but there really is no excuse.

My heart races as I wonder what happened. "Haw—"

"Shut up!" He turns back and stalks up to me. He throws a hand over my mouth as I scoot backward and press myself back into the couch. Then he leans in to whisper next to my ear. "By all that is lawful, my name is Scott Williams. Got it? Do not use anything else."

Scott Williams? He backs up to stare into my eyes and I nod my head. His eyes are narrowed in warning, but I realize there is moisture in them that wasn't there before and his body is still trembling. Something in my expression must give away the fact that I see it, because he lets go of me and leans back to rub his eyes against his shirt sleeve. I remember what it looks like when those tears escape his eyes—the death it took to provoke them before— and the bottom drops out of my stomach. He's about to push away from me again, but I burst forward and throw my arms around his neck.

"Dianna, let go." He's still shaking.

Okay, Scott and Dianna. I can remember that, but God help me, I must have terrified him.

"I'm so sorry, Scott," I whisper, bringing my lips up against his ear. I cling to him as tightly as I can, wishing I could turn back time.

He presses his face tight against my neck and shoulder, and wraps his arms around me in return. He pulls me off the couch and into his lap, rocking us back and forth, muscles flexing as he wrestles his emotions like an opponent he has to subdue. He's clinging to me with his iron grip, but the strength of it isn't bruising like I know it so easily could be. Even now he's trying to be careful.

"Scott," I dare. "What happened? I don't ... I don't really remember—"

"Hard to remember being dead," he growls out against my shoulder.

Oh God. How could I be so stupid? "I swear I wasn't trying to kill myself. I didn't think—"

"You know all the safeties were taken off?" he growls. "Your heart stopped for four hacking minutes!"

Jesus, forgive me. Tears flood my eyes.

Hawk's been trying so hard to take care of me. The image of him doing CPR on my body for that long in the heat and the stench of the tunnels makes it hard to breathe. I let the tears flood down my cheeks. I did this. I don't even know where we are, but I must have driven him back up here, above ground. Back into danger.

Alex is right. I'm going to get him killed.

"I'm so sorry," I whisper against his ear again, running my fingers through his hair in what I hope is a comforting motion. "I'm so, so sorry." There really isn't anything else I can say.

Hawk presses an open mouthed kiss against the crook between my neck and shoulder, and it surprises me into stillness. Then he presses another a little higher against the side of my neck, and another against my throat. I fight a tremor of pleasure. I know I need to stop him. I need to pull away, but my heart hurts and it feels so good.

"Let me love you, Baby. Please," he whispers against my throat. "Just this once."

Oh, this is such a bad idea. He continues his journey with his lips and tongue against my throat up to my jaw. He says love, but he just means sex. He trails his lips across my cheek.

Or does he? He thinks he has OAS ...

He leans in to capture my mouth, and I'm about to let him, when he suddenly pulls back with a vicious, whispered curse. He lifts me and dumps me back on the couch in one fluid motion as he stands to his feet and turns away. A beep sounds from across the small room, as a door I hadn't even noticed slides open.

"Mind if I use your shower?" Hawk says in an oddly flat voice as he walks away from me and the strange woman entering the room.

"Sure," the woman says after the door slides back closed.

I try to get my addled brain to take in the important details. That door slid open into the wall, which means this isn't a standard hub. It's probably either a medical facility or military. The woman is dressed in blue scrubs, so it might be medical.

She's a very pretty strawberry blond, and she narrows her eyes like she's sizing me up. "Mind if I join you?" she calls to Hawk, or Scott, without taking her eyes off me.

"Not this time. I'm gross," he calls back in that weird flat voice again. "Mind looking her over though? She just woke up. I'll be out quick."

The woman narrows her eyes and grinds her teeth. Oh wonderful. Did you seriously bring me to one of your girlfriends? Dammit! Then she opens her eyes again and attempts a sincere smile. "How are you feeling, Dianna? Are you still in pain?"

I realize I still have tears on my face and wipe them off with my hands as best as I can. "No."

26

HAWK

Stepping beneath the cold spray, I lean my forehead and arms against the metal wall of Rayne's tiny shower.

Hawking's hacking ghost! We are so hacked!

I'm so frustrated and angry that it's like sharing my skin with some kind of living, breathing fury. I hope Rayne stays out there with Gina to check her out, instead of trying to slip in here with me while my head is this messed up. She'd definitely decide my current state is an invitation.

And shouldn't I want that anyway?

The sick thing is, Rayne's attention wouldn't help. Gina's wrong. I can still hear her mocking me back in the underground garage, saying I just expect women to give me what I want. This isn't about my ego—although it's unbelievably painful she's so disgusted by what I am. It's about how desperately I want to make her feel alive.

She was giving up on me before she used the stunner. I saw it in her eyes, but I couldn't find the right words to bring her back from the ledge.

I can't stop the hacking shake in my hands. My eyes burn. I can still hear Stella's panicked screeching. I'd completely ignored her as she flapped in my face while I begged Gina to come back—to start her heart again. I slam a fist into the reflective shower wall and the metal dents slightly beneath the impact.

Oh fantastic.

What's wrong with me? I've never let a mark get under my skin like this before. I've lost one or two that were too weak to make it. I've even killed my fair share of people on assignment and learned not to dwell on it.

Gina dying made me crazy. Once her heart started again, I forced myself to function, but it wasn't until I heard her voice again that I felt the rage boil over. There's no question the OAS is advancing beyond my ability to control it. Hack! I don't even want to control it. I want to wrap her around me and tell the entire world to back off.

I left Stella, and all our gear, back in the tunnels. I don't think we can afford to go back for them. A new pain carves a hole in my chest because that's going to break Gina's heart.

I give myself a hard slap to the face and turn my face into the shower's spray. Gina doesn't need my emotions. She needs my action. I need to come up with a plan to move out of here fast.

We've already been here too long and I don't trust Rayne. She's been acting almost as weird as I have since I got here, and I know I'm not playing my part well. I need to get Gina hidden back somewhere safe, instead of hanging around right under their noses. Come on, Scott. Pull it together!

27

GINA

The woman steps into her bedroom after giving me a brief exam, and slides a textured glass partition shut between us. I breathe a sigh of relief. She introduced herself as Rayne, one of the doctors on the CPG base Hawk apparently brought us to. I had to fight to keep the shock from showing on my face.

I'm not very good at that, so I ducked my head and allowed myself to cry. I really hadn't intended to kill myself—or make our situation so much worse.

I also have no idea where Stella is. The absence of her staccato voice is an eerie silence in my mind. Hawk couldn't have gotten her to do anything without my help. I can only pray she'll find her way outside on her own, instead of dying wherever she's been stashed.

I glance at the door to the hub again. Hawk obviously has another identity here. It seems safe to assume that he can get around on his own without much suspicion.

Has Alex had time to contact officials in the Community yet, to convince them to spare Hawk if we get caught? Maybe not. The thought of him dying to protect me makes it hard to breathe. I need to try to get off this base on my own.

Standing shakily to my feet, I take an experimental step. My left leg drags a little bit behind me. Damn! I'll draw unnecessary attention if anyone sees me out there. I strain to listen to what might be behind the front door, wishing I had Hawk's superior hearing.

Glancing back at the bathroom, I jump with a gasp. He's standing there staring at me, in nothing but a pair of officer's pants. He glances between me and the door, as a muscle bulges at the side of his jaw. He mouths the word, "Sit," and points at the couch. I sigh, flopping backward onto it.

In a flash, he's moved soundlessly again to lean over me, now inches from my nose. He looks like he would be screaming if we were in private, but instead he burns me into the couch with a glare. I'm embarrassed at having been caught, so I glare right back.

His eyes snap up to Rayne's bedroom, and he stands up to pull a black t-shirt down over his head. I'm distracted for a moment by the scar in his side where he took the bullet for me not that long ago, and my irritation fizzles back into guilt.

Rayne slides the partition to her room back open. "She's going to be fine. There doesn't appear to be any damage to her heart—that my equipment can detect from its rhythm anyway. Her bruises and the burn on her face will heal in time, and I got the medication you asked for. Like I said, it will last you one week—at the most."

That's good to know. She hadn't given me more than an irritated 'You'll live' after the exam. I'm a little surprised Hawk has some kind of relationship with this woman because she doesn't seem terribly nice.

"Thanks, Rayne. I owe you one," Hawk says, walking over with an odd half-smile.

"Yes, you do. Will you be leaving in the morning?"

"We need to head out as soon as she's had a chance to shower," he says, nodding to me.

"Oh, come on," Rayne says, walking over to thread her arms up around his neck. "You haven't even gotten a good night's rest. Now that she's doing better, you should get real sleep. I'm sure I could help."

Oh fun. I wonder if she has ear plugs. Then again, if she distracts him, maybe I can sneak out and give him his life back. I ignore the twinge of jealousy in my gut.

"We've already inconvenienced you," he says in that weirdly dead voice.

"Nonsense," Rayne dismisses it with a wave. "Come on, please. Come to bed early with me. Dianna can come too, if you want."

Oh no, Dianna will not! I turn away from both of them. Gross.

"I think she'll be more comfortable on the couch," he says, and I close my eyes against the sound of a kiss. God, that hurts! "I'll see you in the morning, Dianna?"

"Yeah," I force out through my suddenly tight throat. I'm out of here the second they're distracted enough.

I hear the partition to the bedroom slide open and shut, and wish it had better sound proofing. I don't want to hear her blasted girly giggle, or the sound of the lips that were almost on mine less than an hour ago, or their stupid thumping and bumping around. It's like being stabbed in the chest. I know exactly how good he is at what he does and it makes me feel stupid.

I push myself up off the couch and force my legs to cooperate as I struggle to get to the door without making more noise than they are. I wish I could take the medicine she mentioned with me, but I don't know where it is.

Then his voice gets my attention. "Password." It's barely above a whisper, but it's in Darius's scary tone, not Scott's emotionless one.

Huh?

"Give me the hacking password."

Rayne whimpers in a way that has nothing to do with pleasure. I turn around and lean my back against the entrance to listen.

After a few moments, I hear a thump from the bedroom and then Hawk rips the partition back open, glances at the couch, and then locks eyes with me. "For the love of Tesla! You weren't even going to give me five minutes?" he whispers.

"What's going on?" I wish I could see Rayne from here, but all I can see is his big angry body gripping the doorway.

"Don't move. From that spot," he says. "I think we're in trouble."

Trouble?

He steps back into the bedroom and bends down to toss Rayne's limp body up onto the bed, then he throws the rose-colored sheet over her.

"Is she okay?" I ask.

"Yeah, I used her own tranq on her," he says. I can see him leaning over the glass surface of her desk beside the bed. He's scrolling through something. "Shit! We've got to move. Now!"

"What's wrong?"

"She ratted us out. They'll be here in minutes."

"Oh, God. Who?"

"Someone from off base. Looks like the medicine she requested was flagged. They must have gone back to your DNA sample after they lost you and learned what you would need."

There isn't enough time! They'll kill us both! "Leave me here!"

"Shut up, Gina." He growls as he races to me. "Get on my back."

"No!"

I try to pull away, but he grabs me and holds my face close to his with both hands.

"I will tranq you too, if I have to, Babe, but we're way the hack more likely to get caught if I don't have your help." He glares. "You choose."

There's no way I can overpower him or escape in my current condition. I nod and he tosses me up behind his back. I toss my arms over his big shoulders but can't get my legs to wrap around his waist. He hoists me up with an arm and slaps the control for the door.

Glancing into the hallway, it appears empty, so he takes off at a brisk but quiet pace. Seeing one of the hallway cams, I'm about to panic when I remember that they can't see us. I pray silently to myself as we duck down one hallway and then another. It's like trying to escape the hospital all over again. At least no one is shooting at us yet.

We find places to hide a couple of times as people pass by dressed in either scrubs or shield uniforms. After a few intersecting hallways, he ducks into a supply closet. He lifts a hatch in the floor and I muffle my shriek as he drops down into a dimly lit tunnel access with me still on his back. He reaches up just long enough to bring the hatch back down and takes off. At least we're out of the CPG buildings.

Thank you, Jesus!

"Where are we going?"

"We've got to put as much distance between us and the base as we can," he calls back over his shoulder.

I lie my head down against the side of his neck and pray that we made it out in time.

28

HAWK

Thank the Law I got a nap in before Gina woke up.

I'm powering down the tunnels as fast as I can without making an insane amount of noise. I took a different route out of the base than I did going in, but they'll check the routes in all directions. Operatives use these access points all the time, so less questions get asked when we're moving from place to place. They would have had the whole base locked down above ground too quick for us to get out any other way.

"Is Rayne going to be okay?" Gina mumbles next to my ear.

"Yeah, they'll head to her unit first." I hate to hear the real question in her voice.

I didn't hurt her. I hated scaring the shit out of her, but I needed her password to get into her chat logs. I'd heard the chime for her com system go off while I was getting out of the shower, and when I'd headed out to confront her, I'd caught Gina trying to sneak out. I'd been so pissed, I nearly delayed checking it out.

"How did you know?" she asks.

"Rayne didn't want you there. She was helping because she owed me. Then all of a sudden she wants to cozy up and include you? Bullshit. She was delaying us. Once I got into her chat logs, I could see the whole thing. I can't believe you were going to sneak out on me!"

"I wasn't going to stick around and listen to you two."

"I mean before that," I growl. "When I—" I stop dead in my tracks. There's another chimera here. I can smell him even above the stench of the tunnel. Shit. Smells like a reptile.

"Slide down, Babe," I whisper.

Gina doesn't argue for once. She slips her feet back down to the ground and I wrap an arm back to keep her behind me. Stepping back, I press her into the recess for a ladder in the tunnel wall.

"You didn't bother to mask your scent, newbie," I call out into the tunnel.

"Not a newbie," a rough, male voice barks from the tunnel ahead of us. "Just no time."

This is bad. I don't recognize the scent or the voice, which means I've got no clue what kind of skill I'm up against. We're completely exposed here and I've got nothing but a couple of tranqs on me.

Are we far enough through the tunnels to be in the civilian streets? Whoever this guy is, he hasn't shown himself yet. I take a calculated risk, turning toward Gina to tuck her against my body and whisper into her ear as quietly as I possibly can. "Climb the ladder, Babe. Now. I'll be right behind you." Hopefully it's not a complete lie. "Whatever you do, don't scream."

Gina shakes her head no, but we don't have a choice. I step back just enough to spin her around, place a quick kiss on the back of her head, and then grab her waist and lift her as high up the ladder as I can. Just as one of her feet makes contact with a rung, he slams into my side like an angry bull.

Shit!

Impacting the tunnel wall, I don't hear more than a muffled squeak from Gina. Good girl. Don't bring more of them running.

I break the guy's hold and land a kick in his gut that knocks him back into the opposite wall. Then I step back in front of the ladder.

Why didn't he just shoot me? Has Alex already made his calls? If he told them where we were, I'll kill him.

"Give her up, Hawk," the operative sneers. "I don't know you man, but you're way out of line with this shit. She's not worth it."

Then everything I thought I was serving all my life is a lie. She's innocent and inconvenient, beautiful and kind. They don't have a right to kill her and he doesn't deserve a hacking answer.

Through the dim light, I can finally tell he has bright yellow eyes and green scales across his neck, cheekbones, and forehead.

"You think so, huh?" I whisper so low that only someone with my hearing can make it out.

He tilts his head, but doesn't reply. I hope she can get that access cover off without catching his attention.

"Come on, man …" he starts again.

I lunge for him, pulling back when he takes a swipe at me with a combat knife. When he tries again, I get a hold of his wrist and turn it back on him. We wrestle against the tunnel wall, struggling for control of the blade before he deploys an additional blade from the toe of his boot. I bring the top of my knee up hard into the tendon beneath his knee cap, and he lets out a curse just before I pin his boot beneath my own.

The strength in his arms is incredible, but I let my claws free and they dig into the flesh of his wrist and arm. He shouts with a terrible screeching noise that hurts my ear drums, but two can play at that game. I let out a deafening roar of my own. He tries to pull back as my claws tear deeper into the flesh of his arms and he drops the blade.

I don't want to kill him, but I've got to get Gina away from here! I sink my claws higher up into his arms as I use the pain to turn him. As soon as I'm behind him, I have the advantage. I sink my claws into his throat.

"Stop! Or she dies!" a nasal voice shouts from above us.

I pause with my claws part way in and glance up the ladder. The chimera gurgles for air without struggling further. I can feel his blood draining down my hands, as my own blood drains from my face at the sight of the gun pointed at Gina's head. She managed to make it to the top of the tall ladder, but someone was waiting for her.

"Release him!" the voice orders again. "We're going to bring her up here, and you're going to follow, or we'll kill her right here and now!"

"Don't hurt her!" I snarl.

"Come up here, you stupid woman," the man sneers.

More hands reach down and grab Gina by the shoulders. It's all I can do to hold back a roar of fury as they haul her beyond where I can see.

"Move forward," I growl in the operative's ear, without releasing my claws from his flesh. As soon as I do, he's dead.

He walks forward, one laboring step at a time, and then I order him to climb with me. His pain must be terrible as I manage the climb with only one arm, while my other uses him as an anchor point, but eventually we make it to the top.

As my head clears the grating, I can see an entire team of soldiers surrounding Gina. Half of them have their weapons trained on me, and the other on her as I struggle my way out of the hole with the wounded man. "What are your orders?" I ask the group.

"You're both to be taken into custody," the soldier bellows while holding Gina by her hair with his fist.

I'm scared shitless—like I've never been scared in my life. My skin feels cold and numb, and my heart's trying to burst from my chest. We've come up into a broad street, but they've cleared the civilians out of it already. Even then, there is no way to get to her before they kill her. There are too many of them. My chest hurts as I stare at the tear that escapes silently down her cheek.

"Don't fight them, Babe." I hope they're telling the truth. Even if they are, we're not going to make it out of this alive. "You hear me?"

She nods as another tear escapes. I drop the wounded chimera.

Four men are on me in an instant and I let them throw me to the ground. I put my hands behind my head as they take their vengeance with blows to my head and gut. It's infuriating to feel their knees on my shoulders when it would be so easy to throw them off.

"Stop it!" Gina screams. "Stop! Leave him alone!"

"Don't you dare fight them, Gina!" My guts twist at the thought of the weapon still trained on her. "Don't move!"

A broken sob leaves her throat as I take another decent kick to the ribs. I've been through beatings way worse than this, but she doesn't know that. Even if she did, she's too soft-hearted.

"Enough!" the nasal voiced man roars. "Pick him up."

I let them lift me by the shoulders and stand to my feet as they place my wrists into zip cuffs in front of me.

You've got to be kidding, right? These guys are idiots. With a well aimed claw, I can be out of these cuffs in seconds. They're obviously used to handling civilians.

The other chimera has finally succumbed to his blood loss so there's no one to warn them. I'll have to wait, though, until I have an opportunity where there isn't a gun pointed at her. If it ever comes.

In the distance, I hear the sound of a helo-drone.

29

GINA

As a helo-drone sits down in the deserted street, my knees are shaking so hard I can barely stand and the shields start pushing me toward it. My feet drag awkwardly as I struggle to cover the distance on my own. Climbing the ladder had been nearly impossible. I don't want to take my eyes off of Hawk, but he nods toward it and I'm forced to turn and look at where we're going.

The large, black drone has energy weapons mounted to the ceiling inside. When the shield at my shoulder shoves me roughly inside, the interior guns move to point at me. "Was she really worth all this trouble?" he sneers.

Hawk doesn't answer him—his expression carefully blank. I wipe my tears with my hands, as Hawk is brought up to climb inside beside me. We're shoved into a large cage in the center.

"I hope they retire you for this, you big brute," the shield says.

I'm lunging for the man before I know it. "Would you just shut up! You—"

"Gina!" Hawk barks, and I freeze as the guns shift restlessly above me. "Don't look at them. Look at me." I turn back to him, and his face wears a gentle smile that I know must be a strain. "They don't matter, Babe. They don't make the decisions, right? They just follow orders."

He's right, I remind myself as the cage and drone doors are shut and locked behind us. Maybe Alex was able to talk to someone.

Hawk leans against the cage's back wall, and I watch the ground drift farther and farther away as the drone lifts off. After a few moments, the glass turns black. My body starts to tremble again.

Even if Alex did call someone, I'm going to die. I wish I had thought of something to leave with Crazy Rob back home. I should have left a message for Drustan or Arthur. If they come looking for me someday, Rob will tell them that I ran. He won't know it's already too late.

I should have found a way to escape from Hawk before we were caught. Should I have taken José or Serge up on their offers back at the Golden Dragon?

I glance back at Hawk and his expression has me confused and more than a little frightened. He's usually analyzing the situation, and you can see him calculating the options in his eyes. Now his eyes are blank—hollow like they were when he held Cobra's body after he'd been forced to kill her. "What are you thinking?" I place my hand on the side of his face until he raises his eyes to mine. "Hawk, please. I'm scared."

Pain flashes in his eyes and he leans toward me until he's only a breath away. I know what he wants, and in this moment, I want it too. When I touch my lips to his, heat rushes through me. Every cell in my body feels more alive, chased by heartache that causes tears to slip from my eyes again. Hawk would never tell me we were beyond hope. He would never want me to give up, but we both know I'm not going to make it out of this.

He pulls away to get his arms around me, with his zip cuffs behind my back. Then he pulls me tight against his chest and deepens our kiss. As his hands cradle the back of my head, I try to memorize the feel of him. I'm so thankful I don't have to march to my death alone. He's done everything he knew how to give me a chance. He bargained, and pushed, and fought until there were no options left. It's more than I could have ever asked for.

Hawk pulls back and gives me a rueful smile before kissing the tear tracks on my right cheek. "I'm thinking I wish I knew you better."

"Me too," I admit. "Thank you for giving me more time."

"I need you to be brave for me, Gina."

"I will." I pray that Alex was able to contact the people he talked about, and bargain for his son's life. If I don't fight them, if I don't provoke Hawk into defending me, then he may still be able to be taken back to Alex. With that hope, I can be brave. "I promise."

Hawk stays quiet and watches me with a sad smile, occasionally sipping from my lips or brushing his nose against mine, until the drone sets down. After the door slides open, a shield pulls me from the cage by my arm, and I'm surprised the bruise is healed enough that it no longer hurts. It's almost ridiculous enough to make me laugh.

We've landed in some kind of gigantic hanger, which the drone entered through a double door high above us in the ceiling. After I'm out, Hawk stands and exits with shields on either side of him— guns still daring him to move wrong. Despite his hands being bound in zip cuffs, they're obviously frightened by his very presence. His eyes never leave me, but I'm forced to turn away to see where I'm walking as we're led down long hallways of metal and concrete.

After we leave the main hanger, we pass intersection after intersection, and door after door, until we finally arrive in a small room full of medical equipment. I hesitate at the sight, but a shield drags me forward. There are surgical bots, complicated medical scanners, and a large vertical medical table to the right. The guard walks me over and spins me so my back presses up against the table's cold steel. "What's going on?" Hawk barks from the doorway as he's escorted inside too. "Who's in charge here?"

"I am, boy," a gruff voice says from somewhere behind me. A man walks into view in a high-ranking shield uniform. I've never seen someone wearing one in person, although I've seen an outfit for sale before. He has gray hair and wrinkles etched deeply into his dark face.

"Sir," Hawk says with a nod, as the shield beside me begins strapping me onto the table. "I was originally assigned to—"

"I know who you are," the man sneers. "Hector Everette Warrenson, or Hawk. Chimera first class. Decorated Civil Peace Guard officer. Field agent for the last thirteen years, and a gigantic hacking pain in my ass!"

"Sir, I request permission for the classified information on why my assignment is not being reset through standard procedure," Hawk insists with the muscles straining in his jaw.

"You may as well tell him," a young woman in a blue lab coat walks into view beside the old shield. "He should know the kind of peril he nearly caused."

"Young man," the old shield sighs, "you could have caused the eventual collapse of the entire global system through your little stunt."

I feel oddly numb hearing the accusation—almost like an audience member instead of the subject of discussion. I can't even imagine what information I could have that would be that damaging.

"What are you talking about? The files in her head are—"

"It's not about the blasted information in her head!" the old shield roars. "She is the threat! She is the greatest weakness to the GRID we've ever seen!"

I'm what?

"You've been carrying around an atom bomb under your shoulder! The second the squids or anyone else got a hold of her, they'd unleash a mess on this globe like nobody's ever seen before! If Dr. Pennington wasn't a very influential man, you'd be dead already, you snot-nosed brat!"

I am an anomaly! Something in my GRID inoculation went wrong, but what does he think I can do?

"Good night, my dear," the young woman is suddenly in my face as she connects a WSB cable to my sinus cavity.

30

GINA

My consciousness is pulled into the chaos I experienced during my first and only GRID session. I'm drowning in data as it pours through my mind, and my mind follows it though thousands of paths at once. I want to scream but I can't surface. I can't find my way out!

Where is Hawk? Oh God. Help me!

An artificial rhythm is controlling my breathing and I fight back against it until it is more comfortable—like I did the first time I jacked in.

My heart races in my chest as terror overwhelms me. Where is Hawk? I can't see! I'm going to die and I can't see!

A path clears through the sea of data, and I realize I can see. It's confusing at first—like I'm standing outside of my body. I'm surrounded by data swirling in all directions. Pulling at me. Confusing me.

Leave me alone!

The data disappears and I'm right there in the room. I can see my entire body standing beside Hawk, but I can also see my body strapped to the table across the room. Hawk is watching my body. He's saying something, but I can't read his lips.

Dammit I need to hear him!

"—understand," Hawk's voice breaks through all around me. "What do you mean she did it?"

She being me? I glance back at my body. I walk right up and pass my hand through my own face, but I can't touch anything. No one else seems to see me. How is this even possible?

"Look," the young woman says, pointing to the monitors next to me. "Her breathing patterns. You can see them change here. She did that in her first session too, but we don't know how she's doing it. We need to scan her brain to see the anomaly fully. Then we need to do a full slide tissue dissection to understand how it works."

"Are you suggesting that she is actually changing the programming from inside the GRID?" Hawk says with a roll of his eyes. "That's not hacking possible."

"Lots of things are possible." The young woman activates the scanning device next to my body. "They're just very rare. It's important to capture as much data about them as we can, to try and prevent weapons like this from getting loose in the population."

I can change the GRID? My body begins to shake on the table as adrenaline rushes through me and an alarm starts going off next to my table.

"What's happening?" the old shield barks.

"I don't know." The young woman tightens down some straps. "Her heart is racing."

I try to feel my way through my strange new form of sight, and realize I can separate out my view from multiple angles. I spin in a circle, and can see the tiny black lenses attached to surfaces throughout the room. It's like I can feel each individual one tickling my senses from somewhere within the sea of data flowing through me.

The cams! I'm looking through the cams!

"You're going to kill her!" Hawk roars without moving.

"Of course we're going to kill her." The old shield laughs. "You don't think we're going to do a live dissection do you?"

How am I hearing them? I follow the sensation of their voices and spin around until I face a small GRID kiosk in the corner of the room. There is a tiny dictation microphone built into the screen there.

"No, this is a real problem," the young woman shouts and I turn my attention back to her. "We can't map the bioelectric portion of the anomaly after she dies. We could lose the data! I'm going to sedate her further."

The arm of one of the surgical bots comes around with a med injector on the end. They're going to drug me! Then, with a strange clarity, I realize I can feel the arm too. It's swimming out there somewhere. I can feel it close to me, but I can't seem to affect it. The arm comes closer and closer to my skin.

Stop!

The arm falls dead beside my body.

"What happened?" the old shield roars, walking over to the surgical bot and trying to wrestle the med injector out of the arm.

Stop! I can't feel the old man anywhere in the data.

"I've lost the whole bot," the young woman says in an exasperated tone. "I've been locked out of it."

"You see this?" the old shield yells at Hawk. "You see what kind of damage a weapon like this can do?"

"Help him!" the young woman barks at one of the two guards behind Hawk and he moves to assist.

"She's not a weapon," Hawk growls, and I spin with a silent gasp to see that he's unlocked the zip cuffs on his wrists. "I am."

No!

I stand there, helplessly screaming as Hawk bursts into motion. The guard behind him shouts and fires his weapon just as Hawk strikes him beneath the arm. The energy bolt bursts forth from the pistol, but hits high on the wall above my body, missing Hawk entirely.

The guns! I try to find them, but there are so many. I don't know which is which. I can feel a long list of serial numbers swirling around me, and I begin squashing them all like venomous spiders.

Hawk grabs the startled shield by the back of the neck, and blood sprays everywhere as his claws sink beneath the man's skin. Hawk hurls him against the other guard, and the two of them land in a heap on the floor at the old shield's feet.

Squish, squish, squish. Come on! This isn't happening fast enough! I try to follow the serial numbers to where they start, and I see a huge gate of some kind. I slam my consciousness against the gate and the numbers stop coming out. They disappear.

Hawk leaps over to the old shield, and grips his throat—ripping it out as he tosses him to the floor. The sight makes me nauseous as one of the shields on the floor begins crawling away through the huge pool of blood. His hands slip and he collapses flat to the ground just as Hawk brings a boot around to collide with his face. His head snaps back, then he lays limp on the floor.

A loud whirring starts up all around me and I turn to see a pane of glass sliding down in front of my body. I search for it, and start swimming through more of the data. Eventually, I can feel a steady stream of new data coming in and forming strange pictures. I snatch one from the air and pull it up in front of me. It's a picture of my brain. A slice right through the upper portion.

Oh no you don't!

The young woman who started up the machine has fled the room. I do what I did with the pistol spiders. I follow the stream to it's beginning and crash into the source. The noise stops, and so does the flow of pictures.

The shield Hawk catapulted across the room by his neck is lying still on the floor beside the one that took the boot to the head. I can't get a good angle to see, but he's lying in a huge pool of blood. With the three shields down, Hawk runs across the room and begins shredding the restraining straps off my table with his claws.

What are you doing? I shout, but he can't hear me.

"Come on, Baby," he mumbles. "We've gotta go. Wake up for me now."

He's reaching for the cable on my face when something sharp embeds itself in the front of his left shoulder, high on his chest. It knocks him backward, and he lets out a cry of pain as my body drops to the floor. My silent scream is trapped within the cams.

A knife! The blade looks like a small throwing knife, but Hawk leaves it in place as he turns toward the shields piling through the door.

Hawk! Hide! My body is lying in a useless heap at his feet.

Hawk stands up, and places his body between mine and the new soldiers. No! Don't! Soldier after soldier tries to fire their weapons, but look down at them in confusion when they refuse to respond. As some of them react by throwing knives, Hawk grabs a small medical tray and uses it to block incoming blades. Within moments, they all rush him.

Hawk tears through them, one after another. Blood sprays across every surface in the room as he claws at necks, faces, legs, and anything else that comes within reach. They do their own share of damage to his arms and legs with any blade that can make contact. I would hold my breath if I could—bones snap, men scream, and sickening thumps of flesh against flesh fill the room.

Oh God, how can I help? There must be something! I try to find something in the data that will help, but it's just a turbulent swirl.

Hawk takes down more than a dozen men, and a body lands on me. It's getting harder to breathe.

Then they overpower him. Two have his arms as a third sweeps in and slashes a blade along his abdomen, and a fourth cracks him over the head with the butt of a large rifle that can't be fired.

Oh. God! Hawk slumps to the ground and doesn't move.

I scream inside my head, and it's like an endless, voiceless cry. From outside of my body, I crouch over his, but I can't lift him. I can't touch him. Grief washes through me—drowning out everything else. The machinery all over the room begins flashing and sparking. The data around me begins corrupting.

"What in the name of Tesla is going on?" a new man in blue scrubs screams as he barrels into the room. "By all that's lawful!" He slips in the blood on the floor and almost falls as he races over to my body. He rips the cable off my face and suddenly I can't see. I feel heavy. I begin to feel tingling on my face, and voices fade in from around me slowly. They're shouting.

"Get him out of here!" someone yells.

I manage to get my eyes open and stare at Hawk's face where he's fallen right beside me. I can't see the rest of him. His eyes are closed, and I hear an echo of his voice whisper through my memory.

If I'm down, I'm dead.

I hear boots thumping all around us. You were supposed to live! No! My mind rages against what I see.

I wrench my hand out from under my body and the two bodies that have fallen over me. I manage to touch the blood-splattered skin of his sweet face. It's still warm and smooth, but soon it will be cold.

"What do we do with the bodies?" A man with a shaky voice asks from above us.

"Take the soldiers to the morgue," another man, maybe the man who took my cable off, answers from behind me. "I've still got to scan the woman once we sedate her. Hawking's ghost, it's a mess in here. Put the chimera in a body-seal bag. They'll want to do a full autopsy on him for research purposes. Find out what the hack went wrong."

Autopsy! White-hot rage burns through me.

Leave him alone! I want my cable back! I want my GRID connection! I'll squash you like a bug, you monster!

Suddenly, I can feel the data around me again. I close my eyes. I don't know how, but I follow my instinct through the new access point into the heart of it. I begin snatching up the cams and microphone, bursting forth into the room and out of my body again.

There are four shields and a man in blue scrubs in the room. Two other shields are carrying a downed comrade out across the threshold. Three shields look like they're about to pick up Hawk's body, and no one seems to have even noticed I'm awake.

Leave him alone!

I turn toward the door and realize I know how to close it. I trigger the door and men begin shouting as it slowly starts to drop. I concentrate on the lock-down.

"What's happening?" one shouts.

"It's her!"

"No, it can't be her!" the man in scrubs shouts. "I disconnected her!"

Two men roll beneath the heavy, steel door and out of the room—just before it descends and locks. The two shields on the inside begin frantically trying to override the door's programming from the panel, but I flood the panel with conflicting instructions and short it out.

The doctor moves to grab my body, and another wave of rage burns through me as I see every object in the room more clearly than ever before. I take control of the surgical bot that held the med injector and start up the internal arm with a small circular blade. The doctor turns toward the sound as I bring the blade down into the side of his neck. He screams, and backs up trying to hold pressure over the gaping wound.

"What the hack?" One of the shields by the door shouts as he turns back.

I sense a large surgical unit on the ceiling above us. It has dozens of tentacle-like, cable arms with various tools attached to each one, which can extend all the way down for use on a flat table.

As the two shields rush toward us, I bring the weapons down on them. The first man blocks the scalpel coming toward his face, but is caught by the bone saw that enters his back. He screams and falls across Hawk's back, then starts to drag himself back toward the door. The second man picks up a small surgical stand, and swings it wildly at the arms—twisting their way toward him like metal serpents.

The arms on the surgical bot falter as a searing pain tears its way through the side of my skull. Pressure is beginning to build behind my eyes.

Then one of the arms strikes him hard across the chest, knocking him off balance. He trips in the tangle of limbs, and falls—slamming his temple on the sharp edge of the mobile surgical bot's foot.

I pause in the center of the room for a moment and my rage is all consuming in the silence. The man in scrubs has stopped moving. He's no longer holding pressure on his neck. None of the shields on the floor are moving. People are trying to break through the door from the outside, but I'm alone for now.

I open my real eyes again to see Hawk's face. I shrug the bodies off my back and struggle my way out from under them. I crawl over and shove the other bodies off Hawk, pulling his head and shoulders into my lap. A small throwing knife still protrudes from high on his chest. He did what he's always done—put his body as a shield in front of mine.

There's a tremor in my hands as I touch the side of his face and gently kiss his unmoving lips. They can't respond.

He'll never respond again.

A scream tears its way out of my chest and up my throat. I clutch him to my chest and rock; screaming and screaming until the pressure in my head makes me believe it will explode.

I never got to ask him what it was like where he grew up. I never ... told him how sorry I was that he'd killed his own sister to save me. I couldn't make him leave me. I couldn't make him run. I didn't know how, and now it's too late!

They're going to treat him like a sick science experiment!

I've never felt so angry in all my life, and I'm overwhelmed by the need to know what they planned. I close my eyes and find the data around me again. I've never been on the main GRID before now—just an isolated server. There should be files somewhere. The data hits me like a tidal wave, and I struggle to orient myself. There's no rhyme or reason to anything.

I need to find the information on the chimera programs.

I bump into a wall of some kind. Angered, I bump against it again. The wall gives way, and I begin swimming through file after file of chimera data. Profiles. Names and code names. Ages. Health records. It seems familiar.

Cobra! I pull her file up in front of me. She was several years older than I was. Her date of death is listed as unknown, but her status is listed as pending. Pending?

I bump into another wall, slamming against it again and again. When the wall gives way, I slam into another one. The more the system tries to keep me out, the angrier I become. I force my way through at least four more walls, until I encounter data I don't want.

Cobra's autopsy records. Harvest records. Experimentation logs. Not just her. Many, many others. Old chimera women bought up off the streets. Young chimera children, and babies that were retired before birth. Terminal experiments and experimental drugs. Vid logs and photographs.

Another sharp pain tears its way through my skull, and jars me back from the data. My whole body is shaking and I can't stop screaming. They're monsters! The Community doctors are monsters!

I can't allow this secret to die with me. My gut roils with rage. I want to bury them with it. I want the whole world to see what I see, but at the edge of my senses, I notice a section of tech far away from me that's suddenly gone dark.

Come get me you bastards!

I reach out with my mind to capture the glass panel in front of me. Finding the vid feed of the closest cam in the room, I scoot enough to face it directly. I zoom in and my face looks odd. Other than the blood splattered across it, there is blood seeping through the tissue in my right eye. I wipe my nose on my shirt sleeve and project my image on the screen in front of me. "Hello," I choke out through my raw vocal chords, and realize I will have to shout to be heard well through the mic on the other side of the room.

Then I close my eyes and start capturing every piece of smart glass I can find in the sea of data. Tens. Hundreds. Thousands. The pressure in my head builds and it's nearly unbearable, but I keep reaching—farther and farther out. I project myself as a vid onto every screen I can find.

Bang!

I jump as a loud thump sounds on the heavy door, followed by the sound of gunfire. I lose access to another section of tech at the edge of the building.

Reorienting my thoughts, I refocus on the connections to the glass surfaces and start up the vid of my face again. "You people think you live in this perfect Community!" I shout at anyone who may be watching. "You think everyone is treated fairly and your leaders play by the rules! You're idiots if you think they don't break their own laws!"

In the place of my face, I begin pouring data from the chimera files across the screens. Vid logs of children strapped into experiments. Horrific photos of autopsies. Four-year-olds in training at the Officer's Training School.

"You throw away anyone who your doctors view as imperfect!" I scream. "You use them! You abuse them! They die, so you can go home and sleep in comfort! I did nothing wrong, but they're going to kill me anyway!" I can't keep my voice from edging into a sob instead of the rage I feel.

Bang, bang, bang!

More thumping on the door.

Another section falls—coming closer.

"Look at it!" I scream, clutching Hawk's body tighter to my chest. "Because, by God, you have to live with it! Your perfect system is built on the bodies of innocent people! When you cooperate with them, you're helping them murder us!"

BOOM!

A blast blows a hole beside the door, knocks me onto my side, and jars me out of my vid. I close my eyes, sitting back up to bury my face in Hawk's bloodied shoulder as I struggle to maintain my hold on the screens. I switch back to flooding the feed with the data from the chimera files.

Losing connection with another section, very close, I let go of everything but the tech in the room with me. I move the surgical bot closest to the door toward the opening in the wall, everything sharp on it engaged and swinging. The other mobile bot can't get past the bodies littering the floor, but I bring down the cable arms of the one on the ceiling to defend myself.

"Stay away from us!" I scream around Hawk's shoulder, as people swarm through the hole in the wall. My cam view is growing fuzzy.

"Stop!" Someone screams from beyond the bots, waving blurry arms at me. "We're here to help you!"

"Liar!" I lash out with the mobile bot, clutching my hand against the dagger-like pain on the side of my head as he dives out of the way. "Get away or I'll kill you!"

"For God's sake, just disconnect her!" Someone I can't see shouts.

"She doesn't have a cable on her, man!" A woman screams, rolling out of the way of the bot's blades as she fails to approach from the side. "Where the hell is Rob?"

I lose access to the outside of the room and begin to sob. "I'm so sorry," I choke out in Hawk's ear. "You died for nothing, and it's my fault. It's my fault!"

In an instant, the whole room goes pitch black and I lose access to everything around me.

"Stay away from me!" Nausea and dizziness roll over me in waves. There's so much pain in my head, I'm going to puke.

"Get back!" someone roars from the doorway. The voice is familiar. "I said get the hell back! All of you!"

I remove a hand from Hawk's body long enough to pat down a body behind me. I manage to wrestle a knife out of some kind of holster as a light blinds me.

"Go away!" I sob, clutching Hawk's body. I try to scoot backward. He's too heavy, and there are other stupid bodies on him.

"Gina!" the familiar voice says. "Little Girl. I need you to put the knife down, Honey."

Rob? No way.

I try to put pressure against the pain in my head using the handle of the knife. "Who's there?"

"It's me, Gina," he says, and the beam of light turns until his face is lit up.

Crazy Rob is standing there in the middle of the room. His

clothes look new, but I'd know his face anywhere. Am I hallucinating?

"Hey, I'm here to get you out, Sweetheart," he says, turning the light back on me and edging toward me cautiously. "Who's that you've got there?"

I glance down at the harsh shadows cast over Hawk's lifeless face and more gut-wrenching sobs escape me.

"Tell me what's going on, Little Girl," he says, edging closer.

"They killed him," I sob. "It's my fault. I didn't know what to do. He … tried to stop them and I—"

A wave of pain slices through my ears as they begin ringing, and I turn away from him and retch. Rob's hands hold back my hair. When I turn back toward him, I struggle to see his face.

"Get him up." Rob is mumbling to someone beside us. "Come on. Get him off her."

"Please," I whisper, beginning to lose the feeling in my face. "Please bury him. Don't let them cut him up in pieces." I clutch the front of Hawk's shirt in my fists as someone lifts his body off my lap. I don't have the strength to hold on.

"Good God, what's going on with your eye, Gina?" Rob whispers, staring at my face.

He's not listening! "Promise me!" I scream at him, but then I start retching again and I can't get my breath back.

"Goddammit, get a medic in here!" Rob shouts. "I promise, Gina. Breathe, Little Girl. Breathe!"

I want to, but I can't.

Sorry, Rob.

Just keep your promise.

PART 5

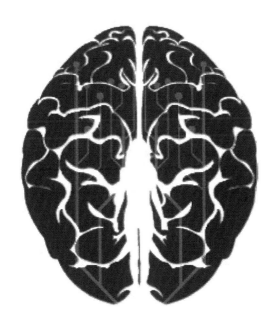

1

HAWK

Beep. Beep. Beep.

The monotonous tone is pulling me from an unnaturally deep sleep. I've been drugged, and I struggle to pull myself out from under the sedation. My head feels like it's in a vice and the wound on my face aches again.

Where am I? I can't remember where I was when I fell asleep. Did I fall asleep?

No. I got hit over the head. We were …

Gina!

I try to sit up, but something is restraining my wrists. A slicing pain tears through my abdomen, and I remember someone trying to gut me before I was hit. I breathe deeply to stop the room from fading to black. I'm scared shitless that I'm going to look down and see my own intestines, but when I manage to get my eyes open all I can see is a white bed sheet. With a panicked glance around the room, I realize I am in a hospital.

But where's Gina?

Beep-beep-beep-beep-beep.

The heart monitor has picked up speed and is announcing my fear. Dizziness washes over me when I can't shake the image of Gina strapped to the table.

Suddenly, the door bursts open and a heavily pregnant woman in light blue scrubs comes in with a surprised expression. She has dark skin, blue-black wavy hair, and bright brown eyes. "He's awake!" she shouts into the hallway. "Go get him! Quick!"

Him who? Oh Einstein, it's probably Alex! I'd rather die than see him right now.

I start pulling against the zip cuffs and let out an involuntary groan of pain as my abdomen protests again. A new tearing pain high in my right pec stabs me, and I vaguely remember a knife appearing there.

"Hey, hey," she says, coming closer with her hands raised.

"Calm down. Don't do that or you'll hurt yourself. You've only been out of surgery a few hours."

"Surgery?" My voice is gravelly, sounding more like an animal than a man.

"Yes. You were hurt badly," she says, taking a cautious step closer. "I was afraid for a while there, that I wasn't going to be able to get you put back together. Your intestines are going to take a long time to heal. You're lucky the cut didn't go very deep and only made a few small perforations, but it's already a miracle you didn't die from blood loss … or that small perforation in your lung. So, why don't we take it easy."

"Where is Gina?" I test the zip cuffs for weak points but they've got them turned around so I can't get a claw in.

"She's dead," a male voice barks in a deep tone from the doorway. "Get away from him, doctor."

Dead.

I stop struggling as the blood drains from my face. My ears start to ring and my hands shake. The doctor says something to me, but I can't understand her over the noise.

I close my eyes and see Gina, cut and dyed locks curling around the side of her face, as she slept beside me in the tunnels beneath the city. I remember the curiosity in her eyes as she tried to feel my claws through the pads of my fingers—her smile as she laughed about deadly toes back at the Golden Dragon.

I can't breathe. I clench my teeth together against the pain in my chest. I remember kissing her on the drone as she thanked me for more time.

I didn't save her, but I didn't die.

My pain claws its way out of my throat in a roar that could shake the walls. The pregnant doctor jumps back from me and bumps into the chest of a man I don't recognize. They both throw their hands over their ears as my roar morphs into a scream of denial.

A new wave of dizziness and nausea wash over me and I fall back limply against the bed with a groan.

Gina. Baby, I'm so sorry. I failed. I groan into the bed sheet, but I can't stop it from morphing again into another roar and another scream. Cobra died for nothing too. They're both gone. For no hacking reason! I sound like the most horrific, tortured blend of man and animal. I feel exposed, but I can't control it.

I want whoever these people are to leave! I want to be alone. I need to turn away from them, but I'm chained to the hacking bed. The thought reminds me of being strapped down to the bed in Gina's room in the Dregs, and I can't suppress a sob.

"I'm … I'm sorry," the man's voice says from beside me and it's uncomfortably close. He must have walked all the way around the bed.

"Get away from me," I manage to whisper.

"I'm afraid we need to talk," he says, pulling at his collar, "and we need to do it now. We're going to have to move soon."

Move? I open my eyes and struggle to see him through the tears. He's average sized for a man—around six feet. He has blue eyes and excessively curly, short, red hair over equally red stubble along his jaw. His expression is difficult to read.

"Who the hack are you?" I spit through a throat that now aches.

"I'm the man who saved your life." He folds his arms over his chest. "But you'd probably know me as Drustan Gates."

Drustan Gates … I settle back against the mattress, shaking my head to try to clear it. I immediately regret it when pain sears through my head behind my eyes.

I've been captured by one of the more powerful members of the squid hierarchy and I don't even know how it happened. It should be more important to me than Gina's death, but it feels strangely like just another stroke of bad luck.

"What do you want?" I fix my eyes on the far wall instead of meeting his stare, teeth grinding. I don't have the strength I need for a battle of wills or wits right now.

"I want you to tell me everything about the girl," he says. "Why you ran with her. Where you've been. What she could do, and who else knew about it."

"Tough shit," I chuckle darkly. "Go ahead and kill me."

"We don't have time for this," he says, gripping the bed rail. "Were you working with someone else?"

I close my eyes again. This is going to suck. They'll torture me for information. Maybe I can provoke them into killing me first, but at the moment I'm not up for it.

"I want to see her." The words are out of my mouth before I have a chance to think it through.

"Why?"

I don't know. Part of me is terrified of seeing her body. I've seen lots of bodies before and it's always awful.

I want to say goodbye. I barely knew her, but my chest aches at the realization that I knew her better than I've known anyone outside my unit. She knew me in a way even they never have. She found what I am undesirable, but she never treated me like less than human. I'll never know if I could have convinced her, if I'd just had more time.

"I … I just … need to see her."

"She's not in any kind of condition to be seen," he says.

The doctor from the compound said something about dissecting the anomaly. I growl with fury as my hands ball into fists. "What did they do to her?"

"You expect me to give you information when you won't give me any? Give me a reason why I should."

The thought of a doctor cutting Gina up makes me crazy. The metal cuffs connecting my wrists to the hospital bed rails may be sturdy, but the railing connections on these newer beds are weak enough. I slam my body against the railing with all the strength I possess—ignoring the blinding pain from more places than I can count—and snap the railing clean off the bedside.

The doctor screams from the foot of the bed as I lunge for Drustan. He steps back with a shocked expression, but I get a good hold on the front of his throat—careful to keep my claws sheathed for now. He can't talk if he doesn't have vocal chords anymore.

"What the hack did they do to her?" I roar. My abdomen feels like it's tearing and I feel blood trickle down my front. The heart monitor flat-lines as wires detach from my chest. Drustan is starting to turn purple. "Did they dissect her? Is that it? Did you? Tell me you son of a bitch, or I'm going to—"

I roar again as something sharp is jammed into the back of my shoulder. I toss Drustan backward, grip the bed railing still attached to my arm, and turn to slam it into my attacker. When I spin, the pregnant doctor is standing behind me with the med injector. I pause with the railing held high. She's well within striking distance.

"You idiot!" How could she take such a risk in her condition? "I could have hit you!"

Drustan's arm is around my throat. The drugs crash through my system as two men pile through the doorway with guns.

"Shoot him!" Drustan shouts behind my head.

Yeah! "Shoot me!" I choke out from beneath Drustan's arm. I feint a swing at him with the bed rail. "Shoot me!"

"For the love of God, don't shoot!" the doctor screams, shoving one of their guns toward the floor and waving her hands. "You'll hurt them!"

I want to bring the bed rail up again, to really strike him and force their hands, but the drugs are making my arms too heavy. Shit! I'm stupidly weak.

"Look! I've sedated him!" the blasted woman shouts again. "Get my nurses! He's losing too much blood!"

"Doctor the patient is crashing!" another female voice screams from farther away.

The lights in the room flicker. Drustan drops me back heavily against the mattress with a shout of frustration.

Hack! They're going to keep me alive! "Kill me, asshole," I order Drustan with a slur.

"You're not getting off that easy," he scowls down at me.

I can't hold my eyes open anymore.

"Get me some bandages!" the doctor shouts again. Pain tears through my abdomen as she shoves against the wound on my stomach. "Get these leads reconnected! We have to focus on him! Hurry!"

For the love of Science ... please, just let me die.

2

HAWK

The room is dark when I open my eyes again, and the smell is different—more sterile than before. Man, how long have I been out? I must have been moved. There is a sliver of light coming from the doorway, and people are bustling around outside. I'm in a new bed too.

This time they've strapped my entire body down with wide woven straps against my chest, over my arms and wrists, and down my legs. I can't move more than an inch in any direction. I can still lift my head just enough to glance down. My bed sheet is gone and I'm amazed by the sheer number of bandages that are covering me.

Not dead.

I drop my head back down against the mattress. They either don't know about my claws, or they don't think they're a danger if I can't move. That might be true if I was trying to harm them.

Gina is dead.

My heartbeat trips on the monitor, and I hold back a growl as I realize I can't grieve without someone coming to observe me.

What now? If Gina is dead, I have no one left to protect. The only people that still need me are my unit. The chimeras need my silence. The Community does too. My only responsibility is to either escape or die.

I close my eyes again as someone enters the room smelling of sickly-sweet women's perfume. They poke at my IVs and the machinery in the room for a moment and then leave again just as quickly.

Community first. Self second. It's the rule I've been taught since I was young.

I'm a captive of the squids. They'll want intel, and they'll probably only heal me enough to interrogate me. Or, they'll use drugs to make me talk. The information in my brain is highly classified, but can only be read if I'm still alive. The only way I can help the Community now—not the assholes who killed Gina …

but the people living their lives within it—is to die.

I curl my claws carefully out from within my fingers. It's not going to hurt much more to die now. I'm already in more pain than I want to remember. They must have me on some pretty potent painkillers since I don't feel much from my body when I don't move. My real pain is something else entirely.

I told Gina to trust me, and she did. I've never been such a failure. I should have fought harder, should have found another way out. I should have kept them from hurting her and taking her apart like one of Alex's deranged experiments. The feeling of tears running down my face catches me by surprise.

This must be what the severe stages of OAS are like. They weren't kidding about the potential for violence. I don't even know how many people I killed trying to save her, and I wince when I realize I would do it again. I tried to die for her too.

If I bend both my wrists as far as I can, my claws can just barely reach them. I wince as my claws catch the skin. I work to tear as much flesh away as I can manage without making a sound, biting down on my lip until I taste blood. Fighting to keep my heart rate steady, it falters once or twice. Hopefully they'll ignore it, since they just came and checked me. In a few seconds, I can feel the blood beginning to pool beneath my hands. That should be enough.

I wonder what Gina would think.

She can't think anything because she's gone.

What was the odd thing she said to me back in the tunnels? She believes people's souls never die—that they can still see and hear us after they're bodies do. The idea hurts. She's probably mad if she can see me, but that wouldn't be too unusual. I smile, wishing I could see her mad at me again.

She said she believed in her god—someone big out there who actually cares. Well, if he's real, he either doesn't, or he hacked it up anyway by saving the wrong person.

Yet, it feels right that she can still hear or see me somehow. It would be nice not to die alone.

"Miss you, Babe," I whisper into the darkness as I feel my body growing weaker. "I'm really sorry. If your God is real … give him shit for me. I hope you found your parents."

3

HAWK

I'm in cloud and I can hear her voice. Are we dead? The air is heavy and the heat is intense.

Oh, yeah. I remember. I carried her into the steam room. Thank the law the Emerald Suite was available. I had no hacking idea how badly she needed it. Her bruises are terrible.

My blood boils to think of what must of happened to her at the auction house. I'll make sure Kisame pays, when I'm done with this job.

But, she's here with me now ... safe and warm and sweet. The steam will do her good. "Try to breathe into the bottom of your lungs."

I sit and listen to her steady breathing as it gets deeper and she starts to relax, drawing in her intoxicating scent. For a while, I allow the weight of our situation to fall off me and revel in the moment. She doesn't mind me close to her in the steam. Maybe not seeing me helps ... She doesn't like chimeras.

The way I catch her looking at me sometimes when she doesn't think I see, I wonder if she might even enjoy being close here in the private intimacy of the steam. Will you ever let me touch you, my prickly armadillo lizard? I won't hurt you, I promise.

"They didn't hurt me."

Don't be embarrassed, Babe. You don't have to lie. It's too obvious. "Then why are you so badly hurt?"

"I bruise easily ... Trust me. If I could fix it, I would've done it by now."

"I'll try to be more careful."

More careful. I shouldn't have risked the CPG base, but I was sick with fear she might still die. This OAS makes me crazy—angry, and fearful ... and euphoric. I know I shouldn't, but I kind of like it.

4

HAWK

Beep. Beep. Beep.

What is that noise? Son of a bitch! Reality crashes in on me as I start to wake—Gina is dead.

No, no! She's right next to me with all her warmth and sweetness ... and fragility. I fight to go back to the steam room, but I can't get there. It's not real.

How the hack am I not dead yet?

I try to come out from under the drugs fighting, but my body isn't as willing as my mind.

"Hawk?" Hearing my name from a woman's voice makes my heart stutter on the monitor, but my mind too quickly reminds me that it's not the voice I want to hear. "Can you open your eyes for me?"

I open them and blink against the harshness of the light in the room. The walls are yellow against a white suspended ceiling. After a moment, I realize the face looking down at me is the pregnant doctor from before. She looks like she's been crying.

"Oh, thank God," she says with a huge sigh as the corners of her mouth turn down. She starts patting my chest awkwardly and there's something metal beneath her hand. "You're going to be okay. It's going to be alright."

Who is this woman? Why does she look so relieved? And how the hack docs she know my name?

Oh shit! They hooked me up to a mind sweeper in my sleep. I can't assume that any information stored in my brain is safe.

I've failed again! I test out my claws for a moment, but there's something binding the ends of my fingers. I can't force my claws through whatever it is.

"I'm so sorry I didn't get this back to you sooner," she says, patting the metal on my chest again. "Please forgive me. Your necklace had been set aside to clean after surgery."

My what? Not my necklace—Gina's. The tiny silver cross that

held my promise to ask for help. Shit. What did she say the guy's name was? If you're up there asshole then … take care of her. Get her to her parents. I don't need help from someone who wouldn't save her.

I'm so sorry, Baby.

"Why …" The lady doctor throws a hand over her mouth and for a second she looks like she's struggling to compose herself. "Why would you do this?" She rests a hand on my wrist gently, but I can't look down to see it. "You have no idea how hard it has been to keep you alive. If you didn't heal as fast as you do, it would have been impossible."

"Guess they should have made it easier for us to kill ourselves when we need to then." I close my eyes, dismissing her. I never imagined I would need a poison pill.

"You don't need to, Hawk," she says. A terrible screech fills the room as she drags something across the floor and sits beside me. "Please talk to me."

"I hate to break it to you, Doc," I say, winded just by speaking, "but we're not on the same side."

"I think we are." She narrows her eyes. "But you haven't been awake long enough to figure that out. I need you to live. More than you could possibly understand."

"Why?"

She looks conflicted for a moment. "I'm not allowed to tell you."

"See?" I roll my eyes and close them again.

"Would you tell me about her?" My heart lurches in my chest. "About Gina?"

My eyes fly open, as I intend to burn her with my fury, but her gaze is fixed away from me. Her eyes are unfocused. I remain silent.

"Was she your lover?"

No! I want to scream it at her, escape her. And yes. I wanted to share that with Gina more than I've wanted anything in years. The longer I was with her, the stronger the desire became. I wanted to give her pleasure and ease her pain. It had been strangely peaceful to see her face over and over again when I opened my eyes. My mind had given her an odd kind of permanence in such a short period.

I had no idea something so wrong could feel so amazing.

I wanted her to desire me too, more than anything, but she didn't. I can't blame her. She was stranded with me by circumstance and dependent on me without choice. She was continually confronted with my inhuman traits, and it must have frightened her. What she wanted from me was safety, and I failed her in that.

I drink in the memory of when she let me kiss her on the drone. It was so small a thing, but I wanted it so bad. I can't imagine how frightened she must have been. Afraid of dying. Afraid of me.

A tear escapes from the corner of my left eye. It shocks me back into the present, and I'm horrified that I'm letting this doctor mess with my head. Does she know I have OAS? She must. Is she trying to help me, or using it to hurt me?

She notices the tear immediately and I'm so strapped down I don't even have the means to wipe it away. She reaches for my face and I growl at her. She yanks her hand back with a gasp.

"Is this how it's going to be then? Emotional torture, instead of physical?"

Her brown eyes open wide and her jaw drops. "No! That's not what I want at all. I'm just trying to understand … your relationship. She … she kissed you goodbye."

"How do you know that?" Why would the squids be watching the drone cams?

"I've seen the vid from inside the compound. I know what happened inside. I know you tried to save her. It was very brave. Did you know we were coming?"

"What?" I shake my head to clear it, but only succeed in sending a blinding pain shooting behind my eyes. When I breathe deeply to push down the pain, a scent catches my attention and I can't breathe at all. I'd know that beautiful scent anywhere.

Gina's scent can't be mimicked, and even if it could, would they even think to try?

My emotions are too invested. Maybe the OAS is getting worse and I'm hallucinating. Maybe the doctor was handling some of Gina's clothes … but after that mess her clothes would have been covered in multiple people's blood. It couldn't be from handling a corpse, because she would reek of death.

"What do you mean she kissed me goodbye?"

"After you were concussed," the doctor says, seeming to choose her words carefully, "there was a period of time where Gina was awake and alone in the room. Everyone else was dead. She probably thought you were dead too and she was visibly very upset. She pulled you into her lap and she kissed you. She held you for a long time. It made me wonder if you were … lovers."

Gina was awake after they took me down? Nausea washes over me with a wave of horror. "Oh, I'm gonna be sick." Why didn't she run? What the hack was she thinking?

I press my head back against the mattress and breathe deeply through my nose to try and force the bile back down my throat. The scent is there again, stronger than before, and my eyes fly back open. The doctor is holding up a sickness bag by my face and the scent of Gina is all over the sleeve of her scrubs. She's touched Gina, and it was recent.

Gina's alive!

Hawking's hacking ghost! Gina's still alive! My heart feels like it's going to burst, and I struggle to keep a smile from breaking out on my face. And she's here! Somewhere …

I need more information and I need it fast.

"We weren't lovers." I grimace, turning my face away from the bag. "But she would have been upset anyway if she thought I was dead. I kissed her on the transport because she was frightened. It's probably like you said. She was saying goodbye."

"I think she cared for you," she says with a sigh and another pat against my sore wrist. "I don't think she would like you trying to sabotage my efforts to save you."

"Gina cared about anyone who didn't actively hurt her. She was too quick to put herself last. If what you say is true, why didn't she run?"

"She couldn't," she says with a shake of her head. "She was trapped."

"Then how the hack was everyone else dead? Multiple people took me down."

"I can't ..." she sits back in her chair, "tell you that either."

Of course not. I resist the urge to roll my eyes or growl. "Can you at least tell me how she died? Did you retrieve her body?"

The doctor won't look me in the eyes and it's all the confirmation I need that Gina isn't dead at all. Thank science.

"I'm authorized to tell you that she died from an inoculation complication," she says. "She was an anomaly, and when her talents were activated ... she suffered multiple severe bleeds in her brain. The bleeds damaged portions of the brain that induce strong emotion, sometimes rage, and it seemed to drive her to use it even more. Eventually she collapsed."

"Are you saying she could actually do what they claimed?" No way.

"I have no idea what they said she could do," she evades.

Fine. There are more important things for now. "What does your organization plan to do with me?"

"For now, I'd like to see you make a full recovery," the doctor says with a sad smile. "You've lost a lot of blood—multiple times—but you make it much faster than a normal person. Are you going to fight me on it?"

"Gina's gone. The only thing I can still protect is information. I can't do that if you succeed."

"Information isn't what we want!"

"Yeah? Then how do you know my name?"

"They already knew that before they even got to the facility," she says, looking away. "I can't tell you how."

"And you seriously believe they're not going to torture me for information?"

The doctor looks uncomfortable. "I believe the woman I saw in that vid would be very upset with you if she found out you had lived, and then chose to die anyway."

No question. I've got to heal up fast.

5

***

HAWK

I don't think these people appreciate the enormous amount of information that can be gathered by the simple act of lying still and listening while no one thinks you're paying attention. In the first two days, I picked up the names of the guards on rotation outside my door: Hackenmeuller; Cappellini; Jacobson; Hook, whose first name is Andre; Basra, who is called "Sweets" half the time; and a young man who goes exclusively by Rainbow. They're on two-man, eight-hour shifts which change out at 2:00 am, 10:00 am, and 6:00 pm.

They don't understand that I can hear them, even with the door closed. When they leave it open, they may as well be inviting me into all the gossip—not only in their own circle, but at the nurses station out in the hallway. It's not like I've had anything else to do.

The most surprising revelation in the last two weeks is that Drustan Gates is the father of the child my doctor is carrying. I'm not sure what the social dynamic is because the squids live very differently. I got the impression, though, that they're long-term lovers.

The most important information I've gathered has been about Gina. She's not only alive but in this hospital. They're keeping her in the room next to mine. They're practically offering me direct access. The shop-talk among the nurses indicates that they're keeping her in a medically-induced coma.

Drustan comes down to personally check on her condition daily. It's probably the anomaly he's after, but I'm not sure what he's going to do with it if it's true that it injures her. He doesn't speak when he is with her, so he must be getting his information on her from the doctor when they're away.

I need to get Gina to safety, but I have no way of knowing how much she's been able to heal since we were captured at the facility. The doctor said that she was conscious after everyone else was dead. I hope that was true. I'll have to wing it and hope she's ready, or get her more help after I get her out of here.

I didn't heal as fast as I expected, but I would have been able to run a week ago. I've played it off that I'm weaker than I am, so they continue to be lax in their security measures.

The doctor was concerned my intestines wouldn't heal properly without having me get up and move around. For more than a week now, the nurses have been taking time to release me from the full-body restraints and walk me through an exercise routine within the confines of this room—with four armed guards on hand. They never let me out of the claw guards which cap the end of each finger in steel, and connect along the tops of my fingers to a clasp around my wrists. The clasps are impossible to open without fingernails or claws. The nurses have also been letting me make trips to the bathroom, thank the law.

I've had about all I can take of this cheery yellow room with easy-clean furniture and wild flowers hand-painted around the windows. Now's my chance to make my move. Drustan finished his daily check an hour ago, and the doctor took her lunch with him. The guards outside, Rainbow and Cappellini, are both the smallest of the bunch. Bad move. I hit the button at my bedside to page the nurse.

It takes a few minutes for the thin, young brunette with caramel skin to show up. I wish it didn't have to be her. She's terribly nice and always very chatty. All the staff here know what I am, but she doesn't shy away like most of the others. Her name is Cassidy, and I'm about to change her mind.

As she walks briskly in the room, with her hair in a messy bun atop her head, she smiles like I expect. "What's up, Hawk?" she asks, walking right up to my bedside.

I listen carefully and the guards outside don't even pause their conversation about GRID surveillance to pay attention to us.

"Gotta pee." I make an effort to make my face look tired.

"Well we can take care of that easily enough." She begins unfastening my restraints. She and I have done this routine many times over the last week: first the straps from my legs, then from my arms, and finally from around my torso.

I make an exaggerated effort to sit up and take a play from

Gina's handbook to pause as if adjusting.

"How are you feeling?" she asks. "Do you need help?"

Perfect. "Yeah."

She tucks her shoulder beneath my arm and helps me stand. Then I lean on her heavily as we make our way toward the bathroom, and she drags the IV pole along with her other arm. I haven't been hooked up to an IV in a week, but they keep me tethered to the monitor for vitals at all times.

Cassidy keeps a set of scissors in the outside pocket of her pink scrubs and I fake a stumble to pick her pocket.

"Whoa there." She laughs. "Not too much farther."

"Sorry."

She pushes the door to the bathroom open and we continue inside. I reach back with my foot to push the door shut behind us. As she looks up into the mirror in surprise, I morph my face into Darius Volkov. Her eyes go wide, but I pull her back against my chest and slam my hand over her mouth before she has a chance to let out a scream.

Then I bring the scissors, opened up like a blade, against the soft flesh of her throat. "I'll cut your throat if you scream." I lie in Darius's voice as I meet her terrified eyes again in the mirror.

The poor woman is shaking. She tries to shake her head no, but I hold her still.

"Unfasten the guards on my hands."

She obeys but she's taking too long. The guards will know the door is not supposed to be closed if they bother to pay attention.

"Hurry up!" I give her a careful shake.

A tear slips from her eye as she scrambles to unfasten them with her nails, and she lets out a muffled sob that makes me wish I could apologize. I can't though. Gina's counting on me.

The first claw guard pops open and I can hear the voice of one of the guards coming through the hospital room door as she begins working on the second. "Cassidy?" It sounds like the young woman, Cappellini. "Rainbow, man, get in here."

I spin to face the door, using Cassidy's body like a shield and a threat at the same time. I still have the scissors against her throat.

The guard pushes the door open suddenly with her

electroshock weapon already raised high, and the second claw guard pops open. "Put her down!" she shouts. "Now!"

"Holy shit!" Rainbow comes up behind Cappellini. He reaches for the radio on his shoulder.

I shove Cassidy at Cappellini hard, and the guard tries to dodge, but in the confined space she's unable to get a shot off without hitting the woman. I close the scissors and hurl them at Rainbow in one fluid movement. They lodge into the back of his hand, and he pulls it back away from the radio with a scream. I pivot to the side, snatching Cappellini's wrist and twisting it just as she gets a shot off. The weapon's prongs lodge in her uniform, and I let go before the voltage hits. Cappellini convulses and hits the ground hard.

Rainbow's recovered from his shock and is about to run for the door. I lunge and the leads for the monitor of my vitals rip off as I get an arm around his throat. He puts up a good fight, but it only takes a minute or two to choke him out.

Why isn't Cassidy screaming?

I turn around, just in time to see her trying to shove a med injector into my back. I catch her wrist and twist, trying not to break it. She screams as I get my other hand over her mouth. Tears run down her face and she tries to claw at my hand. I glance at the med injector label and it's a sedative. Not as strong as the one I normally use, but it will knock her out for at least two hours. I shove it into the side of her neck and inject it into her system.

"I'm not going to kill you Cassidy," I whisper into her ear as the poor girl sobs and struggles beneath my hand. "You're too nice for that." Her struggles get weaker and weaker, and after a few moments she succumbs to the drug. I realize my abdomen still hurts somewhat as I pick her up and set her down in the armchair beside my bed.

I glance into the hallway, but the struggle hasn't drawn any additional attention. It's completely vacant.

I pick Cappellini up and check her pulse. Thankfully, the current didn't wipe out her heart's natural rhythm. I lie her in my bed and strap her down under the restraints. Then I use a bed sheet to tie a gag around her mouth for when she rouses.

She has a real gun on her. Thank the law she didn't use it—

although that makes no sense. So, I take it with me. I also take a few more med injectors from the drawer Cassidy grabbed hers out of. Nice of her to leave it open.

I grab Rainbow by the back of his armored vest, shove my items in his pockets, and toss him over my shoulder. The scissors came out of his hand during the struggle, so I grab a small towel from the bedside to wrap around it and keep the blood from leaving a trail to follow. Then I sprint down the hall with him into Gina's room.

6

HAWK

The sight of Gina freezes me in my tracks.

Oh Universe, Baby.

She's lying in an open med pod, connected to dozens of tubes and wires. She may be using every single life-support system the thing has. Her hair has been shaved and her skin that is visible is bruised in new ways. I struggle to breathe.

I can't afford to be in shock right now. There isn't time.

I shake it off and push the door shut. The design of the room is identical to mine except that there's a comfortable looking chair and a vase of fresh-cut flowers beside her. I drag a small metal chair into the far corner of the room and set Rainbow down on it, leaning him into the corner.

I rip a strip off my hospital gown and tie it as a gag around his mouth. Using the zip cuffs from his belt, I bind his hands to the cabinet handle above him. The blood soaking through the towel should make anyone that comes through the door hesitate.

I could take his pants, but the guy is scrawny enough that I'd never get them on. I take his vest instead, ripping off my hospital gown, and loosening the straps as far as they go to get the thing over my torso. At least they let me start wearing underwear a few days ago. Then I take my supplies, and more of his, out of his pockets, and set the guns and sedative injectors down on Gina's bed within easy reach.

The alarms on Gina's med pod start going off.

"No, no, no, no, no!" I try to override the failure. "What the hack?" I scramble to get the monitor to display what's going on. Her brain activity is spiking, her vitals are dropping, and for some inexplicable reason the breathing apparatus has shut down.

An alarm is sounding in the room and the hall.

"Shit!" This is going to bring everyone running. So much for slipping out quietly. I should prepare for them, but I need to focus on trying to override whatever the hack is happening to the machine keeping her alive.

"Don't go in there!" Drustan's angry voice bellows from the hallway.

The door bursts open a second later. To my surprise, it's the pregnant doctor, and she's wheeling my stupid IV pole along with her. "What are you doing!"

"Trying to stop your hacking machine from killing her!" I roar back.

"Put these on! Quickly!" she runs straight for me, but stops when I raise one of the pistols up as a bluff.

"I said get out of there!" Drustan barrels through the door and rips the doctor behind his body, placing himself between her and the barrel of my gun.

"What the hack is happening to her?" I shout.

"You have to put the leads back on!" He shoots a panicked look toward Gina.

"Hack you! Don't come near me!" I point the gun at his face.

Drustan closes his eyes and there is a tremor in his hands. He pushes the doctor behind the wall of the tiny bathroom beside him and out of the line of fire. Then he drops to his knees and shoves the IV pole toward me. He raises his hands in surrender. "Please," he says in a broken voice I can barely hear above the wail of the alarms. "Don't let her die like this. Please. Reconnect your leads."

What he's saying makes no sense, but I can't imagine what he would gain by bluffing. I keep the pistol raised with one hand, and connect the lead for the heart monitor to my chest. Then I connect the one for my breathing. Drustan's eyes have fear in them, but they are fixed on Gina. I'm fumbling with the tiny blood pressure band around my arm when Gina's breathing apparatus starts back up. "What the hack is happening? What are you doing to her? Holding her hacking hostage?" I shout as I finally get the band reconnected. It immediately begins the process of taking my blood pressure.

"You almost killed her, you Goddamned monster!" He stands back to his feet with his fists tensing, and I train the pistol on his chest. "Do you have any idea what you could have done?"

A dozen soldiers begin piling through the door behind him, and I raise the second pistol to point at Rainbow.

"Stay back!" Drustan shouts to his men as they fill the doorway with weapons raised.

"I said, what the hack is happening? Why is your equipment trying to kill her?" I roar in frustration.

"Gentlemen!" the doctor screams from inside the tiny bathroom, drawing both of our attention.

"Don't you dare step one foot out here!" Drustan says.

"If you don't tell him the truth, you're going to get Gina killed," she says loud enough for both of us to hear.

"What's the truth?" I ask her, keeping my eyes on Drustan and my weapons steady.

Drustan grinds his back teeth together, then draws a sharp breath. "She's in our system somehow. Her mind. It's in the damn computers. Ever since we connected you to the monitors, she's been watching you. Don't ask me how. It makes no bloody sense. When you crash, she crashes. Every time we've nearly lost you, the machines keeping her alive have gone haywire."

"I told you I need you alive!" the doctor says.

"What you're saying is impossible." I glance back at the machine which is now functioning normally again as her vitals are beginning to recover.

"Gina can do a large number of impossible things," Drustan says.

"They said …" I force the words out, trying to keep my hands from shaking at the overwhelming sense that I'm betraying my duty by talking about it. "They said she was an anomaly. That she could be used as a weapon. Against the GRID."

Drustan nods, but I don't understand the sadness in his eyes. "She's the greatest weapon against it we've ever seen."

"Why are you keeping her in a coma?" A weapon like that would be deployed, unless they felt she'd turn against them.

"Drustan, please let me show him," the doctor pleads. "I need to see if she's bleeding again!"

"Don't come out of there!" he shouts.

"I know my way around a med pod," I say. "What am I looking for?"

"Bring up the brain imaging," she says. "Look for anything that indicates new blood."

Blood? The doctor said Gina died from bleeds in the brain after activating the anomaly ... I drop the pistol I have pointed at Rainbow and hurry to pull up the latest imaging. Then I order the machine to do a new scan.

When the images start to appear, my heartbeat trips and I sit down heavily on the side of Gina's bed. Weakness forces me to lower the gun, but I keep it aimed at Drustan. "By all that is lawful ..."

There is hemorrhaging everywhere. Most of it is focused within the center area of her brain, but the swelling has caused her brain tissue to shift. The pressure on it must be incredible.

"I know it looks bad, Hawk," the doctor says in a calm voice. "But she's alive. Just remember that, okay? She's alive and she's still fighting."

"Unless I die?" A sharp pain slices through the center of my chest.

Drustan visibly tenses and looks away from me, grinding his back teeth again.

What is his deal?

"Yes," the doctor says. "Then generally all hell breaks loose."

My eyes threaten to fill with tears. I can't let them see my OAS or they'll use it against us. I look back at the scans again. They don't look any different than they were an hour ago. "No new blood."

"Oh thank God." I hear her slide down the wall between us. "She can't handle another surgery yet."

I look back up at Gina's shaved head. There are incisions along its surface. "How many has she had?"

"Two so far," the doctor sighs. "It's a gamble every time, but the pressure was too high. We've been keeping her in the coma to try and give her brain time to heal, but we're honestly not sure if she'll ever wake up."

They just want to use her as a weapon. "Oh, I'm sure that will be such a loss for you," I growl, glaring back at Drustan. "You're prize, unable to be the weapon you want."

"You don't have any idea what you're talking about!" he explodes. "If you hadn't interfered, none of this would have happened!"

"What is that supposed to mean?"

"At the hospital!" He tenses his fists again. "You kept my men from getting to her, you stupid animal! Then you jumped my men at the auction!"

"She doesn't want to be part of your game! She hates the squids! She just wants to be left alone!"

"She's my sister, Goddammit!" He looks as shocked as I feel.

"Finally," the doctor whispers from the tiny bathroom.

That's impossible. I glance back toward Gina and then scrutinize him. There's a slight resemblance between them, but it's minor. Then again, the resemblance between Cobra and I wasn't strong either …

Gina needs me. I can't let their mind games make me forget that. "So what?" I shrug, lifting the pistol again. "Blood means nothing."

"Maybe to a Community dog it doesn't."

"Drustan!" the doctor scolds him.

"What will you do with her if she wakes up and doesn't want to play your game?" I ask. "Will you let her leave?"

"With you?" He laughs without humor. "Not a chance."

"Then we have a serious problem." I stand back up and point Rainbow's gun against his temple, keeping the other trained on Drustan.

"What the hell are you doing!" Drustan holds up a hand to keep the men behind him from moving.

"You need me alive," I say. "I'm here to protect her. From you. Whether you like it or not, we're stuck like this until she wakes up, and I'm not leaving her side. I don't want to hurt anyone else, but don't think for a moment that you can contain me without paying a price."

"So what do we do now?"

"Now, we negotiate my surrender."

ACKNOWLEDGMENTS

My deepest thanks to all the people who came together to help me bring the world and characters of *The Infinitus Saga* to life. **Thank you all for believing in me.**

To my editor, Joy Anne Vaughn, and editing assistant Bethany Rozanne Grothe, for your endless hours wrestling with me over everything from plots holes and story sequence, to eye color and repeated words. Also, to our families, who gave up days and weeks with us, offered support with munchkins, and helped keep us fed. This book could not have realized its full potential without your selfless contributions.

To my amazing cover designer, Brandon Moore. Thank you for once again creating such a perfectly beautiful design.

A huge thank you to my stellar beta readers: Nikki, Alicia, Ryan, Alisen and Mike.

Thank you to my amazing cheerleaders and all of you who encouraged me along the way. To my loving husband and avid reader, Clayton Allison, thank you for the years listening to the details of my story before a word was ever even written, and for helping me unsnarl the plot whenever I fell into another hole. To my amazing dad, Robert Vaughn, thank you for your enthusiasm and tireless support and for making my whirlwind coast-to-coast book tour one of the best trips of my life. To my fellow writers LoLo Paige, Wendy Brooker, Nikki Hyson and Sharon Aubrey, thank you for your words of encouragement, doses of hope, and your own awesome stories and victories.

A humble thanks to the members and leadership of the Alaska Writers Guild. I was honored to receive a 2018 Lin Halterman Memorial Grant, which went to support the publication of this book. I have learned so much through provided resources, and networked with amazing writers from across Alaska and the country. Thank you all for your hard work and dedication.

Lastly, a huge thank you to all of my amazing readers. I always love hearing what you think.

Stay tuned for Book 2 of *The Infinitus Saga*, CHIMERA RISING! For book release updates, sign up for my newsletter at www.InfinitusSaga.com.

CHIMERA RISING

For three months the world has held its breath with no word of the Red Queen after her bombshell broadcast exposed the horrific Community exploitation and maltreatment of chimeras—human-animal hybrids born of the reemergence of Old World genetic experimentation. Word of their unexpected champion's message spread like wildfire through the GRID and galvanized chimeras worldwide to unite against Global Fellowship control. Loyal chimeras spurn the Red Queen's message and fight, in the name of their fallen comrade-in-arms, to safeguard their Community from the anarchy unleashed by her mind. As the Global Fellowship deploys scorched-earth tactics to eliminate her, an uneasy alliance forms between the traditional freedom fighters and the very Community operatives and assassins they have fought for so long.

Hector 'Hawk' Warrenson, former covert chimera operative, waits at the bedside of the woman he failed to protect. The Global Fellowship wants her dead. The rebels want to control her. He wants her free and safe. But is he already too late? As Hawk fears his deterioration into Obsessive Attachment Syndrome, he's determined to find a way to protect her—no matter the cost.

Did you miss The Global Fellowship?

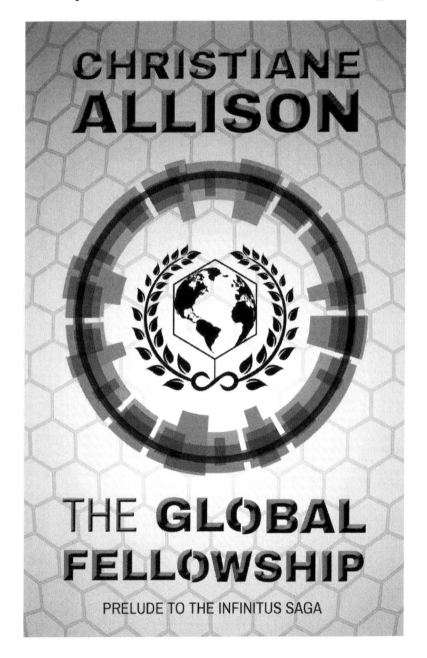

CHRISTIANE ALLISON

THE **GLOBAL** FELLOWSHIP

PRELUDE TO THE INFINITUS SAGA

HE HAS NO CHOICE.
SOMETIMES, DOING WHAT'S RIGHT
MEANS RUNNING AWAY.

Earth was once in chaos, divided between hundreds of warring nations. Now, united in peace and maintained through a worldwide computer system known as the GRID, the Global Fellowship provides all citizens free access to food, housing, education, and medical care. In return, citizens allow the GRID to use their brains as temporary servers. Those who don't contribute are *the disconnected*, shirkers who live destitute and on the edge of starvation in a world where GRIDcoin is beyond their reach.

After his parents' sudden death, Arthur Mallorey, a severely-disabled teenager living in the largest shirker camp in Central Continent, knows he has to find a way for him and his sister to survive. Battling pain and exhaustion, he looks for salvation in the very heart of the Community he was raised to fear.

"The Global Fellowship introduces an intricate dystopian world full of conflict and hope."—*Online Reader*

LEAVE A REVIEW

Dear reader,

Did you enjoy <u>Infinitus</u>? Sign up for my newsletter at www.AllisonPublishing.com to stay informed about the release of Chimera Rising, other new releases, author signings, and exciting news. You can even find my personal playlist for <u>Infinitus</u> when you visit:

www.AllisonPublishing.com/books#/infinitus

While you're there, please leave a quick review for this book. The more honest reviews I have, the more readers will see my book and know if it's one they'd like to read. Here's an easy link:

http://smarturl.it/rev_Infinitus

Thank you for helping me out!

ABOUT THE AUTHOR

Photo © 2018 Liz Shine

Christiane Joy Allison is a multi-award-winning author, activist, and public speaker. She lives with her sprawling, loving family in the beautiful state of Alaska. Living with Ehlers-Danlos Syndrome (hEDS), she understands the struggle of disability.

In 2018, Christiane was the proud recipient of both a Rasmuson Foundation Individual Artist Project Award and an Alaska Writers Guild Lin Halterman Memorial Grant. Her first children's picture book won five honorable mentions in the 2018 Purple Dragonfly Book Awards. She's making her debut in dystopian science-fiction with this series. You can connect with her at:

www.AllisonPublishing.com
www.Facebook.com/ChristianeJoyAllison
Twitter.com/CJAllison7
www.Instagram.com/ChristianeJoyAllison
Amazon.com/author/ChristianeJoyAllison

Made in the USA
Columbia, SC
08 October 2022

69059621R00274